HIGHLANDER UNDONE

Also by Connie Brockway

HIGHLANDER
UNDONE

CONNIE
BROCKWAY

Montlake
Romance

Text copyright © 2015 Connie Brockway

Published by Montlake Romance, Seattle

www.apub.com

Amazon, the Amazon logo, and Montlake Romance are trademarks of Amazon.com, Inc., or its affiliates.

ISBN-13: 9781503945487
ISBN-10: 1503945480

Cover design by Mumtaz Mustafa
Illustrated by Dana Ashton France

Printed in the United States of America

For Cavan with love from the Na'n

PROLOGUE

North Africa, 1886

He had seen dying men before. He was a soldier.

He'd listened to whispered pleas, held cold hands, watched eyes dim, and stayed with them. Captain John Francis Cameron of Her Majesty's Cormack Highlanders had always kept faith with his men.

But the man he held now wasn't one of his men. He was one of the Sikh officers, a man who had either saved Jack's life by accident or, for some unfathomable reason, chosen to trade his life for Jack's. Whichever it was didn't matter. Though his men yelled for him to head for the safety of the *zariba*—the improvised stockade eighty yards away—Jack wasn't going to leave him to die alone.

So he sat down cross-legged on the hot white sand and cradled the man's head on his lap, shading the man's face, keeping him company while the blood drained from the massive mortar wound in his side.

After five years of Foreign Service, Jack no longer knew why his men were bleeding to death beneath this blazing African sky. He no longer knew what the point was, or what the prize. But even though his tenure here had stripped him of a whole universe of illusions, he still understood the price he owed this man and sought to repay it as best he could.

The Sikh, as remote and alien as the landscape they occupied, stared past him. Jack didn't know what words to murmur, what comfort he could give a man whose culture was so incomprehensible to him. He felt bitterly inadequate, an emotion that had grown all too familiar of late.

"Why?" the man suddenly whispered in Hindi. Though his voice was a harsh rattle, his tone was no more than curious, a rhetorical query expecting no reply.

Carefully, Jack wiped away the bright red foam from the man's beard. Jack looked away, up and over the littered battlefield.

Most of the Dervish attackers had withdrawn, slipping back across the heat-shimmered sand dunes. In their wake, the dead and wounded lay sprawled like the carelessly abandoned dolls of a spoiled child. Dozens of them.

Jack's regiment had been returning to the zariba when, without warning, they had been attacked, his men horribly outnumbered by over a thousand Dervishes. It would have been even more of a massacre had not the Sikh regiment, one of the mercenary companies stationed inside the fort, poured from the gates, racing to their aid.

The fighting had been hand to hand, brutal. A bayonet had scraped across Jack's ribs. A saber had slashed the back of his left thigh. Still, he had managed to remain upright, emptying his rifle a half dozen times into the screaming swarm.

And then, as the tide of the battle turned, Jack's overheated rifle had jammed. He had been wrenching savagely at the bolt when something careened into him, knocking him to his knees. He regained his feet only to stumble over the Sikh officer who lay bleeding on the sand behind him and realized at once the mortar that should have lodged in his own back had found the Sikh's chest instead.

A few unintelligible words rasped from the Sikh's mouth, shaking Jack from his preoccupation. He looked down. The Sikh was still watching him.

"I won't leave," Jack said in Hindi. "Rest."

"You speak my tongue," the man said.

"A bit."

"An Englishman speaking Hindi." The Sikh paused, siphoning air into his lungs. "It is an oddity."

"I was always good at mimicry," Jack said, aware of how inconsequential the words were but needing to say something, anything. "Quiet, now. Rest."

"Soon, I shall rest . . . in paradise."

Jack brushed away a fly from near the man's eye. The Sikh did not appear to notice either the fly or Jack's gesture, but simply stared up at him.

"I'm sorry," Jack murmured, uncertain of where the apology came from or why he voiced it. It seemed supremely fatuous.

A series of sharp reports sent puffs of sand exploding a dozen feet away. Jack ignored them. It was only the indiscriminate fire of retreating men discharging their rifles.

"Sorry? I believe you are. Another oddity." A cough rattled in the man's chest before he continued in a breathless whisper. "Most of you officers pretend knowledge you do not have, playing the part of all-knowing father and forcing others to the role of children."

Jack had no reply. He'd always been uncomfortable with the condescending attitudes many of his fellow officers adopted toward their native commands.

"You," the Sikh panted, "you do not belong here. You do not . . . understand this country. You never will. Not in a thousand lifetimes."

Not in a million, thought Jack. Another cough shuddered through the Sikh and more red foam dribbled from his lips.

"Save your strength."

The man smiled, a gentle smile of rebuke. "For what, Captain? It is most important you listen." He tried to lift his head from Jack's lap and failed. "Tell your superiors. They will hear you. This land is not yours to fight for."

"I'm not fighting for land."

Scorn surfaced beneath the expression of patient endurance on the Sikh's dark face. "Why, then?"

"Slavery. A man, any man, deserves to be free. Her Majesty has sent us here to put an end to the slave trade."

The Sikh was very weak now. The whites of his eyes were turning a matte ivory. Beneath his swarthy complexion an ashen hue bloomed rapidly. "Do you really . . . believe this, Captain?"

Did he? Five years ago—his fervor still fueled by idealism—he had believed it. But, five years ago, he had never seen a native "mutineer" blown to pieces after being tied to the barrel of a cannon, or his own commander "punish" an African city by burning it to the ground.

Three Dervishes broke from cover near the walls of the zariba. They dashed across the open sand, heading out beyond the range of the guns. Jack watched them with little interest, detached, emotionless. The cut in his side chafed painfully against the coarse lining of his jacket. The sun blistered the back of his neck, the salt of his sweat stinging the burnt skin. He'd lost his sun helmet.

"Do you?" insisted the dying man as though it was essential he have Jack's answer.

Why does he care? Jack thought tiredly. "Yes."

"Captain." Faint now, a hiss of air—or was it life?—escaped his barely moving lips. "There are many . . . who profit in the human trade. If you seek to end slavery, look at your own people."

Jack stared, shocked. He couldn't be understanding the man correctly. "What do you mean?"

The Sikh's eyelids drifted shut.

"What do you mean?"

The Sikh opened his eyes. His words were faint but clear. "There is an English officer of the Black Dragoons . . . very proud. But for money . . . pride . . . can be bartered, honor betrayed . . ."

"What do you mean?"

"He has been . . . able to accommodate . . . the slavers. Because of his position . . . He delayed orders. Khartoum."

General Gordon's rescue at Khartoum the preceding year had been one day too late. One day. The man's intimation that the delay had been orchestrated shook Jack to the core, every fiber of his being recoiling from such an accusation. He shook his head. "You're mistaken."

Anger briefly animated the Sihk's features as his fingers tightened on Jack's sleeve. "I have seen proof . . . I was his batman. He boasted. He showed . . ." He broke off abruptly and a whistling gasp sounded from his lips.

"Who?"

The Sikh stared mutely, his gaze fixing into a stare, his fingers loosening.

"Who?"

He barely managed to shake his head. The faintest of sounds issued from his unmoving lips, "Roy . . . al Dragoons." Jack leaned forward. The man's eyes were lifeless.

He was dead.

Delayed orders? Jack thought numbly.

He eased the Sikh's head off his lap and rose to his knees. The one thing Jack valued of his years in Africa was a steadfast faith in the integrity of his men and fellow officers.

English officers trafficking in slavery? Sacrificing soldiers' lives for profit? *His* men's lives? The idea was unutterably foul. And only an accusation, he reminded himself.

But one he would not put to rest until he had discovered the truth.

Using his rifle as a prop, Jack struggled to his feet. If there was proof, as this man claimed, he would find it. By God, he would.

He stumbled toward the zariba, face fierce with determination.

A shout from the top of the wall reached Jack's ears an instant before the shrapnel hit him and the brilliant African sun shattered in the sky as darkness embraced him.

West Sussex County, 1887

R ed satin bed hangings.

They gleamed like a thick cherry cordial in the morning light. Jack reached out from his seat beside the bed and fingered the luxurious fabric. It slipped over his skin like heated oil.

The drapery reminded him of the rich tapestry-lined walls of a sultan's palace he'd once visited—a concubine's room redolent with the scent of jasmine and orange blossoms. For his first few weeks at the dowager's cottage at Gate Hall, he'd believed that was where he was. It had been a pleasant madness, those delirium-induced dreams, certain exotic memories fanned to life by these sumptuous surroundings.

And heavy doses of morphine.

His slowly returning faculties had taught him a less agreeable reality. There wouldn't be any dusky, sloe-eyed beauty appearing at the foot of his bed. Instead, there would be a wooden-faced, middle-aged butler with an improbable penchant for scented hair pomade: the ubiquitous Wheatcroft, Jack's factotum-cum-nursemaid-cum-valet. Aside from the small tweenie—Wheatcroft's niece—who arrived with Jack's food and took care of cleaning the room, he saw no one.

He didn't need to. Wheatcroft, with his upper class intonations and his unflappable demeanor, was the quintessential family retainer. His presence alone had made the obvious inescapable: somehow Jack had been transported from the Sudan to England without one clear memory of the entire trip.

It had been five months since the Dervish's shrapnel had exploded into his left shoulder; four months, Wheatcroft had informed him, since he'd arrived here. He released the satin drapery. His legs were stiff from inactivity; his eyes were bloodshot from reading—the only occupation open to him in this weak condition; and the lace-edged bedsheets Wheatcroft had so carefully tucked about him were twined around his legs. The fine sheen of sweat he always seemed to wear made the linen cling to his skin.

Irritably, he pushed himself upright. In response, a drill of pure agony speared his shoulder, reminding him with savage acuity that he wasn't yet healed. Stifling a gasp, he stared blindly out the bedroom window, trying to control the pain.

The soft, green-filtered light of the West Sussex countryside touched his face through the open window. Slowly, the pain ebbed and he relaxed. Amazing how a simple thing like daylight could be so dissimilar in different parts of the world. This mild illumination was nothing like the mind-dazzling brilliance of the sun reflected off bleached African sand . . . white sand.

White sand. A hot, pale sky. A blood-spattered tunic, words spoken in Hindi, damning words . . .

Jack closed his eyes. Frustration, waiting impatiently in the background, bloomed anew. How much longer before he was well enough to act? Before he could begin his search for the truth about the suspected traitor who'd forfeited his men's lives for profit?

He opened his eyes, his gaze falling on the desk situated on the other side of the bed. Neat stacks of correspondence sat atop the mahogany surface, each one answering queries that, with Wheatcroft's aid, he'd sent out to various bureaucrats, functionaries, department heads, and fellow officers over the last two months. Collectively the answers had revealed a pattern of direct commands subverted and orders delayed and unaccountably misdirected that had resulted in the North African slavers eluding capture.

There was no other conclusion to be made other than the Sikh had been right: there was a traitor amongst the Black Dragoons officers. But who? What was the proof he'd seen? And did it still exist?

He stared at the damning missives. He'd learned everything he could through correspondence. He would have to investigate it himself from here on out.

But how? Any hint that a captain of the Highlanders was asking questions about the Royal Dragoon officers posted to the Sudan would send his unknown enemy to ground. Frustration tightened Jack's jaw. There must be some other way and he would find it. He owed a debt to the men who had died as a result of this bastard's greed and he would pay it or die trying.

The doors leading to the terrace beneath his third-story window squeaked open, and the unintelligible murmur of polite voices drifted up to him from below, drawing Jack's attention. They were the voices of two artists, Theodore Phyfe and Gerald Norton; and Phyfe's widowed sister, Adelaide Hoodless. Jack's uncle's wife—a lady Jack had yet to meet, as she was not in residence—had invited them to make use of the dowager house terrace to paint the landscape. Sometimes the two men came alone; often it was the brother and sister, and occasionally, as today, all three.

Jack cursed, caught anew in a moral dilemma. It was too late to shut the windows without revealing himself and yet he did not like being in the role of unwilling audience. He did not want them to see him. If they did, they would inevitably ask Wheatcroft about him and, in being told about his convalescence, realize that he'd been here for weeks and therefore, by virtue of his bedridden state, an inadvertent eavesdropper on their conversations. It would make them all—especially her—unendurably self-conscious.

Some of the siblings' conversations had been intensely private, not meant for a stranger's ear. When he'd gained enough strength and had heard them before they appeared on the terrace, he had, of course, shut the windows to provide them privacy. Nonetheless, in those weeks before he had been able to rise from the bed, when they'd appeared suddenly and without Wheatcroft's prior knowledge, he'd heard . . . much.

"Ah! Sublime! How can one single vista be more lovely with each passing day?" a reedy, affected male voice enthused. Gerald Norton.

"Lady Merritt did claim the dowager house's back terrace held the best view in all of West Sussex and I must admit, she spoke true." It was the deeper, languid voice of Theodore Phyfe.

"To be sure, but is it worth so much of your time?" Jack's attention sharpened. The soft, deep contralto tones were hers. Addie's. "You've been painting the same scene in a dozen incarnations over a half dozen weeks."

"Is every light the same in every hour? Every season? No. Shame on you, Addie Phyfe. And you, the daughter of a renowned artist."

"It is Addie *Hoodless*, Ted."

"More the shame," her brother drawled.

"Wishing does not make a fact of a thing." Her voice was gentle but firm. "And I know our father as well as you and he *never* painted the same scene twice."

"True. He had a capricious muse. It made him restless."

"Or quickly bored."

"Perhaps . . . unfixed."

"Like a shooting star?" she suggested.

"Brilliant and ephemeral," he tacitly agreed.

"But you are made of steadier stuff."

"Just so."

She laughed at this, a rare sound that caught at Jack's heart. He had learned much about Addie, his unsuspected presence making him privy to things she would have only said to a brother.

But it had been her voice that had first called him back from blood-splattered sands in drug-induced nightmares. When he'd regained consciousness, her voice had given him something to focus on besides his unsound body, a body that stubbornly refused to heal and strengthen, a body that blazed with internal fire for days on end. And later, after he'd begun the slow, fitful journey toward recovery, her voice had given him respite from the knowledge that somewhere there might be an officer who had grown as bloated as a leech on the deaths of soldiers. His soldiers.

He'd never known a woman as intimately as he knew Addie.

She liked Brahms and felt guilty for finding Wagner boring. She indulged a sweet tooth and disliked liqueurs. She preferred seascapes to landscapes and brambleberries to strawberries.

But anyone in her immediate circle might know the same. Jack's knowledge went far deeper.

He knew that she turned her face to the sun like an apostate awaiting a benediction, for her brother was always telling her to mind her complexion. She was constantly asking her companions if they'd seen the flash of a certain bird in the shrubbery and thus he knew her gaze was often fixed beyond her companions. She was spontaneous in her appreciation of any number of subjects, from politics to art, from the ladybug that she lured to her fingertip to Burton's search for the source of the Nile.

And he knew that she'd married a man who'd beaten her and when her brother intervened, her husband had run him down with his carriage, shattering his leg.

"I shouldn't be twitting Addie if I were you, Ted," Norton said. "She might refuse to act as your hostess this Season, y'know, and then where'd you be without a proper lady to chaperone all the little debs who'll be flocking to your studio to have their portraits painted?"

"Hardly flocks, old fellow. I already have accepted as many commissions as I can possibly honor and only a very few are debutantes."

"And pray whom are these willing prisoners to your art?" a new, female voice demanded in querying tones.

"My dear lady!" Norton exclaimed. "We did not know you were in residence. Why didn't Wheatcroft inform us when we arrived?"

"Because he did not know to expect me," his uncle's wife, Lady Harmonia Merritt née Gate, replied. "I have only just arrived this moment back in England and, being told that my dear friends were down here at the cottage, came at once."

"What a delightful surprise," Addie said, and Jack could hear the smile in her voice.

"Addie, my dear, how pleased I am to see you are looking so much improved in health since the last time I saw you." Her voice lowered. "You . . . no longer pine?"

She could not mean that Addie pined for Hoodless? But then Lady Merritt, unless she was far more intimate with Addie than anything he'd heard suggested, would not know. Just as he was not meant to know.

One of the men made a rough sound, as though in protest. Ted, no doubt. Addie answered quickly before he could speak. "I am well, thank you."

"And you, Ted, what is this about having commissions? You had best not think to bury yourself in the studio. As your patroness this Season, I have already planned a number of gatherings and fêtes at which I shall introduce you to those people you must know, and by whom you must be known, in order to achieve artistic prominence."

"I am, as always, humbled by your generosity and will be honored to oblige."

This gracious acceptance of what, to Jack's mind, was nothing less than a direct order did little to placate the lady. "And do you think you should have accepted so many commissions without conferring with me? I must say I am worried. I should hate to see you waste your time and talent on painting some mushroom's self-satisfied visage, to have it displayed above his dining table wall where only his shopkeeper friends will admire it."

It appeared his uncle's wife was a snob.

"Not at all. I have been commissioned to do a series of portraits of the officers who served so nobly in the relief effort of Khartoum. The Black Dragoons."

And with Ted's words an idea bloomed in Jack's imagination.

2

"I feel obliged to say it once more: I have reservations about this. Distinct reservations." The trio was still on the terrace apprising Lady Merritt of their plans for the Season while Jack made his own plans.

"Pray, do not needlessly concern yourself, dear lady," Gerald Norton said soothingly. "We shall all, my poor self included, make every effort to see that dear Addie's reputation remains as clean and pure and spotless as mortal man can make it."

"Are you sure you haven't confused my reputation with an advertisement for nappy detergent, Gerald?" Addie asked.

Jack smiled. Lady Merritt made a startled, and not altogether pleased, sound. He heard the scrape of wrought-iron chair legs against stone and Addie murmured "thank you."

"Forgive me." Addie's voice was officially contrite. "But you all concern yourselves far too much with my reputation. I am not some green debutante. I am a widow."

This brokered a disdainful *harrumph* from Lady Merritt. "And that is precisely why your reputation needs guarding, Addie," she said. "The decision to come out of mourning before the full year has gone by cannot be made lightly. You must remember, not only was he your husband, he was a war hero, and war heroes must have their due."

"Believe me, Lady Merritt, I have already amply paid any dues Society would extract."

"Oh, my dear! Of course you have! But people might talk."

"Let them talk." Ted spoke, his tone languid and smooth, but an underlying steel set it apart from Norton's more affected intonations.

"Ah, the voice of an affectionate brother. Or was that an opportunistic brother?" Addie cut in, sounding equal parts amused and relieved.

"I am wounded, Addie. Heartsick, in fact."

"As if you had a heart," scoffed Addie. "If I had promised my efforts to Gerald, I'm sure Ted would be agreeing with you, Lady Merritt. Now, don't worry about me, please. Ted, for all his failings, likes to think of himself as a doting brother."

"And if he is to become society's premier portraitist, he will need someone to lend him a respectable cachet. As the only one in my reprehensible family who aspires to respectability, the task falls to me."

Jack could imagine her smiling, indulging the impish streak he supposed others would find hard to warrant she owned, as she hid it so well. Like now, as she set about so innocently, and consciously, stirring things up. For the thousandth time, he wondered what Addie looked like. He'd only had a glimpse of her from above, a peek of dark hair and the sort of figure that pervaded a man's lustier dreams.

" . . . and I shall make a perfectly irreproachable doyen. When society madams trot their daughters over to Teddy's studio for a sitting, I shall teeter on the edge of a straight-backed chair and glower. The mamas will love it! They'll regard me as a dragon of morality, standing twixt their beloved pink-cheeked daughters and the dissolute—though immensely talented—Theodore Graham Phyfe."

"Well, thank you for the 'immensely talented,' anyway," Addie's brother drawled. "But really, Addie, my tastes run to something a bit more—"

"Teddy!" Gerald Norton broke in, openly scandalized. "How ever shall we convince Lady Merritt of our good intentions when you can't even be trusted to behave yourself in her home?"

"Oh, Gerald, he only says those things because he thinks it lends him a rakish air. Quite calculated about it, too."

"You know me too well. However shall I contrive to be mysterious?"

"Enough. Enough," said Lady Merritt sharply, the conversation having gotten away from her. "I can quite see that you've decided to set Addie up as your hostess with or without my blessings."

"As my sponsor—and my dear friend—I shall of course give the utmost attention to your concerns," Ted said, "but Addie's mourning is soon over anywise. What possible difference could a few weeks more or less mean?"

"I can see that I am outnumbered. Besides, I can hardly dictate Addie's life to her."

Not that you haven't already taken a damned good shot at it, thought Jack.

"You will do whatever you wish to. It is in your artistic nature not to be tied by the bonds of a common code. We will discuss it no further," Lady Merritt pronounced dramatically. "Now then, I have arranged to take tea in the portrait gallery.

"Ted, you may take Gerald up to Gate Hall and browse the gallery. Addie and I will be along directly. I've added a new Whistler to my collection and"—chairs squeaked and heels clicked across the terrace in unseemly haste.

"You can release my hand now, Lady Merritt," Jack heard Addie say, her tone gently amused. "I promise I won't bolt. Why did you send those two scuttling away?"

Lady Merritt mumbled something.

"Please." Addie's voice warmed with honest affection. "We have known each other far too long for you to ever be 'too familiar.' My family's land has marched along Gate Hall property for over a hundred years."

"I am not really worried about how society might view your attenuated mourning, m'dear."

"I didn't think you were."

"I just hate to see you immerse yourself so thoroughly in your brother's circle."

Addie must have raised a questioning brow, or given some other indication of surprise, for Lady Merritt hastened on. "Not that they aren't all perfectly charming, delightful people. You know I have always been an ardent patron of the arts. Indeed, in encouraging my son Evan's friendships with young artists, I have . . ." Lady Merritt's voice dropped to something resembling a growl, ". . . weathered considerable marital discord."

"So you have confided in me," Addie said shyly. "That is why I am finding it so surprising that you would object to Ted's friends."

"Only on your behalf, dear."

"My behalf?"

"It's different for you, Addie. Evan is a boy. He plans to pursue a future in aesthetic endeavors . . . if his father ever returns from America with him." The flint returned to her voice. "But you are still a young woman with a future to consider.

"You should think of remarrying and I doubt whether you will find a likely candidate amongst the fribbles, would-bes, and panderers that dog the careers of truly inspired artists like your brother."

"I like fribbles." She was trying for valiant humor and failing.

"Oh, Addie." Lady Merritt sighed, misreading her intention. "How can one believe that, after having known your dear, departed husband? It is hard to imagine a more masculine, dynamic being than Lieutenant Charles Hoodless."

Long minutes passed and Addie didn't reply. Jack imagined her, head bowed, lost in a past she would not share, unable to respond to the woman's monumental misconception of her husband, her marriage.

"I should think you might like to reestablish ties with your husband's old friends," Lady Merritt finally said in a soft voice. "These artists? Very nice, very gentle. But such a drastic contrast to Charles! I fear you seek their company because you have decided never to wed again. And you know that if you never leave the artistic community you will never have to risk your heart again."

"You are very perceptive," Addie said in a closed, strained voice.

"You must be brave, Addie. You must carry on. You are still young. There is much of life ahead of you and I would hate to think of you living it alone."

Addie did not respond.

"Perhaps amongst Charles's fellow officers you might find a sympathetic suitor, someone as virile and forceful and handsome as your Charles."

"Please . . ." Addie's voice was no more than a whisper, raw with emotion.

"I know, m'dear. I know. But he died a hero's death. And now, in honor of his memory, you must go on." Lady Merritt clucked consolingly.

Damned fool woman!

"Please," Lady Merritt continued. "Allow me to arrange a small dinner this Season. Your mourning will officially be over then and an informal party of twenty or thirty will not be unseemly. I will invite some of the local army chaps, Lieutenant Wilkins or Lance

Corporal Hartopp. And wasn't Major Paul Sherville a particular friend of Charles's?"

"Yes," Addie broke in roughly. "Yes. Please. Lady Merritt. Do not."

"Do not what?"

"I have no desire to meet again my husband's friends. Ever. It is . . . too painful. The memories they would awake too unendurable. I knew those men. They dined at my table and they were . . . too much like Charles. It would be excruciating."

"But surely—"

"I want nothing to do with Her Majesty's officers. Ever." Addie's tone steadied and grew ardent. "Excuse my bluntness, but you must understand, no one will ever take Charles's place. I will not allow it."

Jack became aware of his own labored breathing, an odd constriction in his throat.

"My dear!"

"I'm sorry, Lady Merritt. I . . . I have forgotten I am bespoke elsewhere within the hour. Please, we . . . I must leave."

"Of course. I understand," Lady Merritt said, her voice rife with sympathy. "I do."

So did Jack. Addie had painted all soldiers with the same brush as her husband, assuming that his brutality was endemic to a soldier's nature.

He would have to abandon the nascent plan he'd formed. There was no way Addie Hoodless would accept Captain Jack Cameron into her brother's studio or help him uncover the bastard responsible for the deaths of so many good men. His jaw tightened with frustration. He couldn't abandon the plan. It was the only one he had and the debt he owed those dead soldiers would not be gainsaid.

But how could he convince Addie? She loathed soldiers and a soldier was all Jack had ever been . . .

His eyes narrowed with inspiration.

Until now.

3

I can't ask you to help me in this deception, Wheatcroft. When it comes out, and it will come out eventually, it may well mean your position." He owed his life to Wheatcroft. It had been the butler who had tended him, changed his bandages, and nursed him from the very brink of death. "In fact, this may already mean your position. How ever did you manage to keep my presence here from Lady Merritt?"

They were in the second-floor bedchamber of the dowager's cottage, the same room where he had spent the last six months. Now, one day after Lady Merritt's arrival, those few belongings that had returned with him from the Sudan were packed again.

Wheatcroft nodded unhappily, his loyalties clearly divided.

"Gate Hall is one of the largest country houses in West Sussex, sir, employing a full staff of forty-eight in the house and twenty-six on the grounds. But when Her Ladyship is not in residence, we make do with a much smaller staff and the dowager's cottage is left untended. No one knew you were here except the cook, my wife, and Therese, the maid, who is my niece. They had been asked from the start to be mute as to your presence."

"I see. So my great-uncle Cuthbert had ensconced me here without either the knowledge or the consent of his wife?"

Wheatcroft remained impassive. "Lord and Lady Merritt often neglect to discuss their respective plans."

Jack snorted. "But it is her house, is it not?" The tone that had earned Jack the unquestioning obedience of an entire regiment underscored the query. Its effect was not lost on Wheatcroft.

The butler took a deep breath.

"Lord Merritt was informed of your condition just prior to leaving on an extended tour of America with Lord Evan. He'd already shut up the London apartments and Lady Merritt was occupying the family's townhouse.

"At the time, Lady Merritt was extremely angry with Lord Merritt's decision to—how did he put it?—'flush out the noxious influence Her Ladyship's damned pantywaists had been exerting on Lord Evan.' His words, sir, not mine."

"Understood. Go on."

"Had Lord Merritt asked Her Ladyship, she almost certainly would have refused to, er, entertain any of his relatives at her family's country seat."

"Entertain?" Jack echoed blankly. He'd have chosen a different word for what he'd spent the last months doing.

Wheatcroft plowed ahead. "If you are asking my opinion—"

"I am."

"Lord Merritt possibly concluded it would be the most politic course to have you brought to the country, rather than to the townhouse, thereby avoiding an unnecessary discussion with Lady Merritt." He paused. "And, really, there was nowhere else to send you."

"But my great-uncle must have realized that at the end of the Season his wife would eventually appear and we were bound to meet?"

"Not necessarily, sir." The butler did not say more. He didn't have to. The fixed way he stared beyond Jack was more than an adequate amplification of his thoughts.

"I see," Jack said. "It appears I have scotched things a bit by recovering rather than succumbing."

Wheatcroft swallowed audibly, clearly nonplussed. "The surgeons in Alexandria held out little hope for your recovery. When your shoulder became septic, they informed Lord Merritt as your only living relative."

"And a distant one at that. I haven't seen him since I was a lad."

Wheatcroft kindly ignored this interruption. "When informed of the gravity of your condition, His Lordship would hear of nothing but having you brought to England. He did not want you to . . . er, expire on foreign soil. He said that the old earl, your great-grandfather, would haunt him if he didn't do his duty by you."

"I see. I'm sorry I didn't oblige you by dying. Where were you planning on burying me body, laddie? In the kitchen garden?"

"Sir." Wheatcroft's expression was long-suffering.

"I'm twitting you, man. Thank God for my uncle's machinations. It might, just might, allow me the opportunity to ferret out the traitor, Wheatcroft. Where is Lady Merritt now?"

"Up at the house, sir. Soon to enjoy her afternoon tea."

Jack nodded, still pondering whether or not the plan he had devised could possibly work. That some man had made a fortune on the slave trade the British army had been sent to eradicate made a mockery of not only Jack's entire career but also the deaths of every man who had expired in that endeavor.

He had to discover what officer had returned from the Sudan richer than when they'd arrived. He needed to know who had been where, during the relevant times.

And he considered the best place to do so would be at Phyfe's studio. A man, bored with long hours posing, might be lured into a casual exchange that would help pass the time. With a few well-chosen, seemingly innocuous questions, Jack could learn valuable information. But it was a shot in the dark and he knew it.

"I'm not sure I should not simply come clean and take my chances elsewhere," he muttered more to himself than the butler.

"If I might be so bold, sir," Wheatcroft said. "Do you think the impersonation you intend might help you discover the blackguard that sold out his men for profit?"

The Black Dragoons was a closed brotherhood. They would not permit anyone outside their ranks to have a drink with them, let alone make him privy to their secrets. But an inconsequential fribble, no more noteworthy than a piece of furniture, loitering about the edges of some artist's atelier, might overhear some slip, some aside, that pointed to a traitor.

Right now, he had no direction at all. Nothing. The thought infuriated and depressed him.

"It is my best hope, slim though it be. But I hate involving you in the deception."

"I am already involved, sir, and I assure you I understand what oughtn't be done and what *needs* be done. I nursed you for all those months that you were not in your right mind.

"In your delirium, you oft cried out against this traitor, searching for him in your nightmares. When you woke, I wrote the letters requesting the information you sought. I admit, I expected once you were well you would have notified Whitehall, but you haven't. I can only assume you have your reasons." This last was said questioningly.

"Whitehall?" Jack said. "Do you have any notion of how incestuous the military machine is, Wheatcroft? Were I to contact the 'proper authorities' with such an accusation, it would be common knowledge within hours." The hopelessness of his position replayed itself in his mind for a thousandth time. "The traitor would be put on guard, allowing him to destroy any and all connections he had with his ugly little venture. And Whitehall might well do nothing at that. What proof do I have except the gasped last words of a dead, nameless native? No. There will be no help there."

Wheatcroft nodded. "I expected something of the sort. Which is why I mean to assist you in whatever way I can in your endeavor."

"I appreciate the offer, Wheatcroft." Jack sighed. "But I balk at embroiling you further in what may prove a fruitless venture."

"Sir." Wheatcroft faced him, raw emotion battling to be expressed on his stoic countenance. "Some bastard may be having his portrait painted using money he earned by betraying his men! You said how he had delayed orders, altered deployments . . . he is responsible for soldiers' deaths. Soldiers who trusted him, may he rot in hell!"

The butler turned away, obviously trying to regain mastery of himself. He forcibly thrust an errant bloom back into a vase. "Maybe you can uncover the bastard at Mr. Phyfe's studio," he said thickly. "Maybe you can find him amongst those there. Expose him, revile him . . . perhaps you can see him hung."

"Who was he, Wheatcroft? A son?" Jack asked quietly.

Wheatcroft looked out of the window, silent a moment before speaking. "My sister Peggy's boy. Therese's brother and my only nephew. A brave soldier, sir."

"When?"

"'82. In the Sudan. He was with the forces sent to rescue Gordon. Perhaps his life was lost because of some misdirected missive. All so some wretched slavers might have time to escape!

"It sickens me, sir. Whoever he is, he has taken advantage of his position, grown bloated on the corpses of boys like my—!" He spun around, his voice breaking on the last.

Jack nodded. Wheatcroft's grief magnified his need to take action, demanding justice. He had no choice; any opportunity, no matter how remote, had to be taken. "I see."

He dragged his hand through his unruly hair, delaying the actual commitment though his decision was already made.

"How can I hope to pass as an artist? I have no skill."

Wheatcroft gave a little snort of amusement, startling Jack. "That should not pose a problem, sir, skill not currently being a requisite to term oneself an artist. And one quite expects to find a number of visitors in the more famous artists' lofts, both fellow artists discussing the work and the subjects' friends keeping him, or her, company."

Wheatcroft scowled at a bowl of copper-colored chrysanthemums. With a sniff, he started rearranging the brilliant flowers. "It's a good plan, sir. There will not only be senior officers at the atelier. Any of the junior staff that can manage the wherewithal to afford it will be lounging about Mr. Phyfe's London studio hoping he'll paint them. Mr. Phyfe's man has often described the scene for us in the servants' hall."

"Why is that?"

Wheatcroft sniffed. "Mr. Phyfe, so goes the *on dit*, knows how to produce a manly figure from scant material."

"You know far more about this than I, Wheatcroft. What, in your estimation, will prove my greatest challenge, then?"

Without hesitation, Wheatcroft answered. "Mrs. Hoodless."

"Why is that? You think her so perceptive she will immediately see through me?"

"No. It's not . . . It's more a matter . . ." Wheatcroft shook his head. "I . . . I do not know how to say this without overstepping . . . It is only my impression, through observations, and it is . . ."

"Out with it, man."

Wheatcroft swallowed. "Mr. Phyfe is very protective of his sister. Very concerned that she suffers no needless discomfort."

"Yes."

"In order for him to grant you unlimited access to his studio, he must see that Mrs. Hoodless is comfortable in your company."

"And this will pose a problem?"

Wheatcroft clearly struggled for his next words.

"Please, Wheatcroft."

"Mrs. Hoodless is uncomfortable with men in general, but more so with men with forceful character, men who are physically imposing. To put it bluntly, manly. And a gentleman need not be . . . domineering to invoke her withdrawal. Our vicar, a forthright, robust, and good man, has her retiring into frozen silence."

Of course. Given her history, it only made sense. He hated the idea of pretending friendship and encouraging intimacy for disguised reasons. She did not deserve such treatment. But his men had not deserved to die, either.

He would make sure to keep as distant from her as possible, to be nothing more than an unremarkable presence hovering in the background so that when the charade ended, she might think him foul, but she would not take it personally.

"Then I will adopt a persona that is mild, even benign," he murmured.

"And the more . . . androgynous, the better."

"I shall contrive to be nothing more than an old auntie."

"Excellent, sir." Wheatcroft nodded approvingly. "When do we begin?"

"We start now," Jack said, his tone cold and implacable, the tone of command. "I have prepared a list of officers who were in the Sudan at the same time as the Sikh's regiment. There are only nine. As all the Black Dragoons have been recalled from North Africa to their London station, our man will be there. Somewhere."

"What shall I do, sir?"

"After I've narrowed down the field further, you can use your connections with the serving halls. You will undoubtedly know someone, somewhere, who serves or has served in some capacity with these men." In its own way, London's servant population was as close-knit as any regimental unit.

"Would there be anything else, sir?"

"Yes, Wheatcroft," Jack said. "Find me some clothes worthy of an androgynous artist."

"I believe Lord Evan's wardrobe might hold just the thing. Lady Merritt bought them for him and his father left them behind."

4

Darling, I am so glad to see you," Lady Merritt said, pouring out a cup of black tea for Addie. "After you left, I felt so guilty. I hadn't realized how painful Charles's loss still was for you. And I'm usually so sensitive to others' feelings."

Addie lowered her eyes. She hadn't meant to offend her ladyship. But Lady Merritt's kindly meant and absolutely horrific proposal had stunned her, making her realize anew that, with her reappearance in society, it was inevitable that she would encounter some of Charles's old military friends.

It had taken weeks for Ted to finally convince her that he truly needed her to act as his hostess for this most important Season. It had taken days longer for her to gather her resolve and agree. She had left here yesterday desperate to renege on her promise to him.

But she would not be a coward. Not now. Not ever again.

"Of course," Lady Merritt continued, her voice rising in one of her dramatic pronouncements, "I, of all people, should realize how someone with your sensitive, sublime spirit cannot be ruled by the calendar.

"And if you choose to divert yourself with your brother's artistic triumphs—and triumphs I assure you they shall be—you have my blessing and my endorsement. No one will dare reproach you!"

"Thank you," murmured Addie.

"Now, I have something to give you. It's nothing, just a little . . . Well, let me get it for you. I don't trust Therese to recognize, er, find it." Lady Merritt rose and sailed out of the room, turning at the last minute to scowl at Addie. "Please, m'dear. I know I inadvertently made you sad on your last visit. Someday, you will forget this pain. The past will release you." And she was gone.

Forget? Addie thought, frightened by the bubble of laughter the suggestion inspired. Forget Charles! Impossible.

She had spent nearly a year struggling to do just that, each day trying to obliterate him from her thoughts, trying to distance herself from each brutal memory. But every time some well-meaning sympathizer mentioned his name, he lived again.

If it were not for Charles's parents, she could retire from society, burn these hypocritical mourning rags, and forbid his name from ever being mentioned in her presence again. But she could not hurt his parents, not now, not when, after a lifetime of heartache, they finally believed their only son had ended his life as a changed man.

Yes, she owed the Hoodlesses this year of hypocrisy. They'd tried so hard to persuade her not to marry Charles. For her sake alone they'd swallowed what pride Charles had left them and revealed what type of creature he was.

How excruciating that must have been for them. They had been specific, relating in detail their son's vile acts, the years they had spent covering up, making excuses, paying off blackmailers, until finally finding a milieu in which men of Charles's breed could hide: the military.

Life in the military had fit Charles like a glove, the men there made from the same raw mold as he, savages with Eton accents, beasts wearing badges of honor. Bullying, intimidating, hurting. It only surprised her that her husband had died a mere lieutenant. With his proficiency in violence, he should have died a general.

At eighteen, when she'd first met him, she hadn't seen beyond the dashing surface to the thing beneath. She'd been swept off her feet. Charles had seemed so romantically arrogant, confident, and strong. And, idiot that she'd been, she saw now that she'd been as much enamored of the crimson coat as the muscular back it had stretched across.

She'd been secretly thrilled by the dangerous flash of fire in his black eyes when his opinions were questioned, his savagely growled response to a minion's incompetence. Charles Hoodless was a man who knew what he wanted and how to get it. It had been electrifying to realize that he wanted her.

She'd been such a fool!

Her subsequent marriage had amounted to nothing less than five years of emotional carnage. But the Hoodlesses *had* tried to do right by her and now she would do right by them, just as she had ever since realizing the sort of monster she'd married.

She had never, not once, said a word against her husband. She had borne the consequences of her decision alone, in private. Except for that one and only time, after a particularly horrible bout, when Ted had appeared unannounced and seen . . . She hadn't been able to stop him from confronting Charles.

She cringed back from the memory of Ted standing in front of the carriage, of Charles laughing as he whipped the horses, driving the carriage straight at him, the screech of wheels, Ted's cry of pain, the sight of her brother, unconscious, his leg bent back at an impossible angle . . . She was responsible for that, too.

It is the past. I have to move beyond it. Charles is dead.

"He's dead." She took a deep breath. He no longer had the power to hurt her and she would never bequeath that power to anyone else. She was older and infinitely wiser. She was going to free herself of Charles's influence. She forced her hands to uncurl at her sides.

"Here it is, m'dear."

Lady Merritt reappeared, trailed by a little maid carrying a large box. Addie waited politely as Lady Merritt flipped open the lid and lifted a garnet-hued swath of soft-looking cloth from the tissue-lined interior.

It appeared to be a gown of some sort. A gown without sleeve puffs, collar, or an inset waist. There was no visible bustle or fichu, in fact, no visible shape at all.

"It's from Mr. Arthur Liberty's establishment," Lady Merritt said.

"A Liberty gown?" Given her recent thoughts the name was ironically appealing.

"Yes. The Aesthetics are all wearing them this Season. I found this at his shop and immediately thought of you, Addie. I'm sure it will fit." She looked the straight tube of fabric over dispassionately and said with sudden frankness, "I think it would fit just about anyone."

Addie smiled. Lady Merritt might be dictatorial and pretentious but she had a generous heart and sometimes, when she forgot she was an arbiter of the arts, she was even charmingly candid.

"Won't you try it on?"

"Do I look so awful?"

"Oh, no, no!" Lady Merritt said, though, Addie noticed, without much conviction. "It's just that soon it won't be necessary for you to wear that interesting shade of gray—puce, did you call it?—and as your dear brother's hostess, it would behoove you to be a fashion leader amongst the artistic community."

"I thought the idea was for me to appear dowager-like, a bastion of established propriety."

"Indulge me, Addie. Try it on. Therese will show you where."

Lady Merritt dropped the dress back into the box, and Therese led Addie to a small anteroom where the maid silently helped her peel off her crepe mourning gown and began unlacing her corset.

"It is worn without a corset?" Addie asked, a bit scandalized.

"That's right, ma'am. 'Tisn't. Lady Merritt was most specific. And no petticoats neither, ma'am," the maid said as she untied Addie's waistband and dropped the fulsome underskirts to the ground. Addie stepped over them and into the circle of subtly textured cloth Therese held out.

The material slipped up and over her pantalets and chemise. It flowed against her, clinging to her unbound curves. It was an odd sensation. She peered into the full-length mirror.

This was interesting, she thought. Rather like wearing one's night apparel to lunch. Somehow for all its vague shape it conspired to be a bit . . . well, fast. Even though the neckline was high and the only ornament was a simple black braid, the way the soft fabric lay against her breast and hugged her hips made it seem provocative.

Addie looked at Therese. "No foundations at all?"

"None, ma'am."

"Well, at least it is comfortable," she said and headed back to the terrace.

Hearing her approach, Lady Merritt, who'd been pulling brown leaves from the bouquet of roses on the table beside her, straightened, saying, "See? You're already changed. Such a gown would be much more efficient than having to have one's maid tug and pull and . . ." Lady Merritt's eyes grew round as her gaze found Addie. "Oh . . . my . . . word."

A discreet cough sounded from beyond the French doors.

"What is it, Wheatcroft?" Lady Merritt murmured, still staring at Addie.

"There is a gentleman to see you, Lady Merritt."

"A gentleman? I'm not expecting any gentleman. Unless . . . Oh, heavens! It must be Mr. Morris's artisan. William told me he might send one of his protégés from Scotland to me for the Season. But he said 'might'! There were no firm arrangements. But to have him show up now!"

"Madame, I believe you may be laboring under a mis—"

"Whatever are we going to do?" Lady Merritt cut Wheatcroft off, casting her gaze around fretfully, as though looking for a potted palm large enough to hide Addie behind.

She suddenly gave a stomp of one large foot and thrust her jaw out. "Oh, what of it?" she exclaimed. "It isn't as if he would have no experience with Mr. Liberty's designs. He is, after all, an artist. Let him in."

"He isn't—"

"One mustn't pay mere lip service to one's convictions," Lady Merritt lectured Addie. "I *said*, show him in, Wheatcroft. Now be quick about it."

Addie felt a twinge of guilt in her amusement at the predicament her hostess found herself in. Her ladyship was obviously embarrassed over Addie's attire.

Addie wasn't. She was far too familiar with artists and their ilk to expect to be paid more than cursory attention. Her family's household had been perpetually filled with models, blowzy creatures who lounged about the withdrawing rooms in sheer silk kimonos during the breaks between sittings. Even in their *dishabille,* they had excited no more attention from her father and brothers than a bowl of fruit. A sack of a gown like this would hardly bring a flutter to an artist's dispassionate eye.

She waited, unable to keep her lips from twitching as Lady Merritt's expression grew more forbidding with each passing moment. Lady Merritt responded to anything that caused her discomfort with a chill demeanor. She was nearly glacial now.

A low voice—cultured, brushed with the faintest of Scots burr—came from the drawing room and a second later Wheatcroft reappeared again, stepping aside as he murmured a name.

A man, his eyes fixed carefully on the ground before him, paused in the threshold. He was dressed much in the style of Gerry Norton and very thin, his leanness accentuated by the tight fit of his trousers and the jutting cheekbones. Beneath a velvet jacket he wore an ivory cambric shirt, its lace cuffs falling over his wrists, the soft, oversized collar turned over a hastily knotted red paisley cravat. Hesitantly, he stepped out onto the terrace and into the sunlight.

He was extraordinary.

He seemed fashioned of light, so pale and lithe and elegantly was he formed. Though his above-average height and the breadth of his shoulders suggested a medium bone structure, there was a sparse, finely drawn quality about him, a lean delicacy unusual in a man.

His classic beauty was heightened by long hair, brushed back from his forehead, a rich, tawny color turning into gleaming gold curls at the ends. The effect was dramatic. He lifted his head, and Addie decided that light hadn't fashioned him. Fire had.

His face was sculptural, the fine, underlying bones dramatically visible. The hollows beneath his high cheekbones were scored with deep lines, the skin fitting taut, too taut, across his face, defining the shallow indentation of his temples. It looked as though all the spare flesh on him had been burnt away, leaving an unholy, tragic beauty.

Slowly, he raised his gaze, almost as though he were afraid. Addie heard the breath catch in her throat.

He had beautiful eyes, clear azure beneath a thick fringe of short sepia-colored lashes.

He stared back at her and she was helpless to do anything other than gaze back, transfixed by his eyes, dimly aware of the dark-winged brows arching dramatically over them, the tiny lines—of laughter?—radiating from the corners.

The thick drumbeat of her heart climbed to her throat.

Suddenly, improbably, his wide mouth curved into a smile and she found herself smiling back.

"You know each other?" Lady Merritt asked, clearly bewildered. "Well, of course, the artistic community is not so large that—"

"No," Addie heard herself say in an odd, faint voice as fear raced in to supplant that extraordinary sensation of familiarity, of . . . of elation. Such instantaneous rapport, such a strong, nearly primal attraction frightened her. The last time she'd felt it she had ended up making a terrible mistake.

"I'm afraid I've never had the pleasure," the man said, his gaze slowly releasing hers as he turned toward Lady Merritt.

He reached out his hand. It shook, a slight but definite tremor.

Addie's eyes narrowed. Other signs leapt out at her: his rapid breathing, the fine sheen of sweat on his forehead, the way his gaze kept falling to the ground when he walked . . . he was nervous. Exceedingly so. His every move proclaimed it, even to the flush mounting his pale cheeks.

The affinity Addie had instantly felt toward him returned full-bloomed, and this time without caution riding herd. She understood now that odd affinity; it was one of kindred spirits. Addie knew what it was to be tense with apprehension.

And he was an artist!

Many of her father's and brothers' colleagues were introverts who tried to hide their insecurities beneath a front of bravado. Some had even given up potentially lucrative careers rather than placing themselves under the abrasive scrutiny of society. To them, putting themselves forward was akin to torture.

Addie studied Lady Merritt, who was just allowing her knuckles to be lifted to his lips. Her nose was inching higher by the moment.

Obviously, she was still embarrassed by Addie's dress and trying to hide it beneath a disdainful facade. Small wonder the man was growing paler by the second.

He took a step back, losing his balance. In a trice, Addie was beside him, catching his arm and steadying him.

For all his angelic good looks, the gentleman obviously needed a champion.

Well, now he had her.

5

Steady on, laddie, Jack repeated silently. He'd understood that he'd been attracted to the young widow before he'd ever seen her and so had expected to be enchanted. He had not expected this devastating torrent of sensual awareness. He strove to keep his attention fixed on Lady Merritt, a big woman of some forty years dressed in a satin turban. Her countenance matched her voice, blunt and mulish. She was making stiff introductory sounds but try though he might, Jack couldn't focus on her words.

All he could think of was Addie.

Before he had even really looked at her, before he had catalogued the form and features that summed up the woman named "Adelaide Hoodless," there had been that one, intense moment of affinity. Her smile in that blinding instance had been filled with a deep, ineffable recognition. A recognition that had transcended the physical.

But then he had looked at her. And immediately realized that the attraction he'd assumed would take place hadn't taken into account that Addie could ever look like this.

His whole notion about a sympathetic *tendre* was shattered, blasted in a second, blown like ashes in brisk wind, having no substance in reality. Because his reckoning hadn't taken into account "sex."

Addie Hoodless epitomized the word.

If only, he thought, forcing himself to stare at the lorgnette swinging from Lady Merritt's bulwark-like chest, Addie had been a standard type of English lady, a handsome widow, or just a pretty girl. But she wasn't.

She looked like a gypsy's randiest dream, her strikingly pale face framed by clouds of hair so deep a titian red as to appear mahogany. Her features were too decisive to be termed fine, too bold to be called pretty, with lush, full lips, strong, wide cheekbones, and long, exotic, heavy-lidded eyes the color of wild honey. Knowledge lurked in those amber eyes, knowledge and wariness and unawakened sensuality.

Lord, thought Jack, frowning in a frustrated attempt to concentrate on Lady Merritt's words. He was all but breaking out in a cold sweat, unable to drag his attention away from Addie who, having leapt to his side when he stumbled, was even now supporting his arm with her own, her breast pushed lightly against him.

If only she'd back away, give him room to breathe, maybe he could recall the gentle infatuation he had harbored for these many weeks. As it was, it was all he could do to keep his face carefully averted as the scent of her drifted up, causing his nostrils to flare greedily.

She smelled sun-kissed, as sweet as the honey color of her eyes. And that hair! Silky coils, glazed with plum-colored highlights by a late afternoon sun, bound in a loose, fragrant chignon.

During the months of his recovery he'd occasionally wondered about Addie's physical appearance. From the casual remarks he'd

overheard, he'd assumed that she was handsome. Handsome . . .
not devastating.

And why the hell was she decked out in that, that *garment*?
The lustrous, dense cloth eased intimately across her breasts, relating their fullness with each tiny movement. It shaped the saucy
curve of her buttocks like a lover's hand. It defined her long legs
so clearly Jack had to avert his eyes or be caught with the images
in his mind betrayed by the tight fit of Evan's narrow breeches.

He swallowed, ignoring her as she slowly withdrew her hand.
If she turned, standing close to him as she was, she'd rub against
him once more. He clenched his teeth and noticed Lady Merritt
staring at him with icy expectation.

"So, he sent you to me to be taken care of, did he?"

Jack frowned. Did she know about his convalescence here after
all? Now not only did he risk looking like a satyr, but a stupid satyr
as well.

"Shipped you here to me. Without informing me beforehand.
Don't deny it." The downward angle of her brows bespoke her
impatience.

Well, at least he would not have to deceive her. Or Lady Merritt.

"Yes, ma'am. I am afraid so."

"Well? What do you do?"

He frowned. "*Do*, my ladyship?"

"I don't have a portfolio on you, young man. No one has told
me the least thing about you. I only know you have arrived at my
door and that you are from Scotland."

He stared at her in confusion. Portfolio?

"Lady Merritt," Addie broke in, "obviously your guest is tired
from his journey. Shouldn't you order a small repast for him before
you continue your inquiries?"

Lady Merritt blinked, obviously startled. As was Jack. In all the months he'd listened to her, he'd never heard her use anything approaching the scolding tone she'd just employed.

"Of course. Certainly," Lady Merritt muttered before adding, in a ruffled undertone, "but I think it poor of Morris to send me a Scot who hasn't even the rudiments of conversation."

Jack felt his spine straighten with the implication that he was an uncouth Scot. His mother had been all but disowned by her grandfather, Lord Merritt, Earl of Luce, when she'd eloped with his father, a Scottish officer. Jack had seen his maternal great-grandfather only once, at his mother's funeral. The man had looked him up and down and with perverse satisfaction pronounced him a savage little cub.

Upon succeeding to the title, Jack's great-uncle Cuthbert, Lady Merritt's erstwhile husband, had been a bit kinder. But even Cuthbert's rare letters had made clear he viewed Highlanders as being something just shy of barbarians, just as they also made clear that he secretly delighted in his Scottish relations' supposed savagery.

Well, Jack was tired, shaking with this damnable palsy, and in no mood to be grateful for scant grace and grudging obligation.

"Lady Merritt, I may be nothing more than 'the Scots lad shipped you,' but I am also John Francis Cameron, grandson of the Earl of Luce, your husband's great-nephew."

Lady Merritt froze in the act of ringing the bell for Wheatcroft. "Excuse me, young man?"

"My mother was Beatrice Catherine Cameron, née Merritt."

Lady Merritt's hand dropped. The bell fell against the table and rolled to the edge. "Damn, you say," she breathed.

Jack, already regretting his arrogant tones, shook his head in negation. "No, ma'am."

What the hell did it matter to him what Lady Merritt thought? She was studying him intently and Jack had a sudden, awful premonition that any minute now she would recognize her son's clothes and demand their return.

"*You* are the Scottish lad?"

"Yes." How many times did he have to agree? What did she want, a burr?

Out of the corner of his eye he caught Addie's grin. Not smile. *Grin*. It was utterly charming. Behind her, Wheatcroft had slipped silently onto the terrace.

Lady Merritt's eyes flashed with some unholy emotion and she clapped her big hands together.

"And you are Cuthbert's relation?"

"Yes. Of course."

"*You* are the brawny, cudgel-wielding, kilt-wearing Scotsman?" She looked unaccountably pleased. The stiff, imperial manner she had used on their initial meeting softened. She stepped closer, smiling coyly at Jack and tapping him lightly on the hand with her lorgnette.

"Excuse my unfortunate outburst," she said. "But if you only knew the harangues I have been subject to on your account . . ."

In answer to Jack's expression of astonishment, she hurried on, her eyes aglitter. "Cuthbert is constantly holding your branch of the family up as an example to us of what a 'real man' should be. Your father was a soldier, was he not?"

"Yes."

"Poor, dear Evan and I were quite made to believe your family ate raw meat, wore animal hides, and bathed—on a seasonal schedule only—in icy lochs."

In fact, Jack had on more than one occasion dove into a lake soon after ice-out.

"Indeed, you have been Cuthbert's ultimate threat," Lady Merritt continued. "He often swore that if dear Evan pursued an aesthetic discipline he'd send him to Scotland." She shuddered. "Where your family would make a 'man' out of him."

"There is no family. I am the last of the line."

"No? Oh." The news didn't appear to awake any sympathy, only a vague interest. "I'm afraid I haven't kept track of, ah, your family as perhaps I should have. But I will now. Especially now that I have discovered you are an artist."

The thread of the conversation was well beyond him. Though she had after all appeared to know he'd been sent by her husband to convalesce, she also apparently assumed he was an artist. Why?

"Surely you can perhaps understand my elation upon discovering you are not the uncouth barbarian I have been led to believe, but rather an elegant artist." Here Lady Merritt cast a speaking glance over Jack's velvet jacket and silk cravat. "Hardly the typical Scots. They are so aggressively . . . masculine." She said the word with excessive distaste.

"Indeed, he is not," Addie interjected forcefully.

He tried in vain to keep from feeling affronted that Addie had so quickly relegated him to the ranks of—what had she called them?—fribbles.

"I only wanted to introduce myself, ma'am, and now that I have, I will remove at once to the nearest inn."

Instantly Lady Merritt laid a restraining hand on his arm. "You'll do nothing of the kind. I won't hear of it. You'll stay here at Gate Hall with me. I insist! After all, you are my husband's only living relative."

Her lips twitched with unsuppressed glee. "And once the Season starts, I insist you stay with me at my Berkeley Square address and allow me to sponsor you. That's why Mr. Morris summonsed you from his Scottish workshop and sent you to me in the first place, isn't it?"

Mr. William Morris. He'd overheard Norton and Phyfe discussing him on the terrace. Things began to make sense. Lady Merritt had mistaken him for an artist she'd been half expecting, a man sent from the workshops of the liberal Scottish craftsman

William Morris. That he was also her husband's relative only made his appearance at her home more likely to her mind. His thoughts raced.

He'd planned to pose as a dilettante, not as an actual artist.

"He expects me to introduce you to the right sorts of people as well as the local artistic community. And dear Mrs. Hoodless's brother is quite the premier member of the exclusive little stable I've gathered, isn't he, Addie?"

"I am sure Teddy would agree," Addie said with a wry smile. Jack turned and his eyesight blurred with the sudden motion. Spending so many minutes upright after being abed so long had taxed his much-depleted strength. He could feel a fine sheen of perspiration start on his forehead.

"Really, Addie," Lady Merritt was saying, "I realize it is hard to appreciate genius in one's own family, but you do not give your brother enough credit."

"Why should I, when he is always there ahead of me, taking it?"

Caught off guard by her unexpected sauciness, Jack burst out laughing. She smiled a bit sheepishly at him. "My brother has many sterling qualities, Mr. Cameron. Modesty is not one of them."

"I often find modesty a convenient virtue. It pretends to hide what it wants others to discover," Jack said.

The effort of the descent from his third-floor chambers along with having spent so many minutes on his feet was taking its toll on him. He reached into his jacket pocket, silently blessing Wheatcroft for his foresight as he withdrew a brilliant cerise square of silk and dabbed his forehead, trying to make the gesture appear an affectation rather than a need. He didn't want Addie's pity. Though he could use it.

"And in 'hiding,' puts up a signpost directing one's attention?" Addie asked.

"Precisely, ma'am."

"I shall henceforth consider my brother's boastful declarations a moral victory. False modesty being the worse offense."

Lady Merritt had stood uncharacteristically silent during their exchange, her gaze flitting with avid interest between them. "You will stay, then, won't you, Jack? I may call you Jack, mightn't I?" Jack noticed she didn't offer him the use of her Christian name in trade. "At least stay until Cuthbert arrives back in England with our son."

Wheatcroft, who'd played silent sentinel to the entire proceeding, cleared his throat. "In which room would milady care to have the young gentleman's luggage sent?"

"The northeast corner, the one with the view of the river. As soon as you're settled we shall begin planning your introduction."

Jack turned sharply and to his utter mortification found he needed to brace a hand on the back of one of the wrought-iron terrace chairs in order to steady himself. He'd be damned if he'd allow himself to clutch the cursed chair with both hands.

"Perhaps," Addie said, "that is, I would be pleased to help in my own small way."

"What a munificent notion!" Lady Merritt piped. "Mrs. Hoodless enjoys a splendid reputation amongst the *ton*. She has aristocratic connections, you know. Her husband was a war hero and her mother a Sommerset of the Sommerset Comptons. Once you have her endorsement—along with my own, of course—your reputation will be made!"

Addie colored, not the fresh pink stain of a flustered belle, but a wave of deep rose flooding her gold-glazed cheeks. "Lady Merritt overstates my influence. But whatever aid I might render, I shall gladly extend."

It would be completely unscrupulous to allow her to do so. His plan had been to fade into the background of her brother's studio, to be an innocuous and unremarked presence there, not to be the recipient of her championship or inveigle himself into her life and use it to spy on her brother's clients. The very idea was offensive. And impossible to refuse.

It was a better opportunity to uncover clues as to the traitor's identity than he'd anticipated. She was bound to converse with the officers having their portraits painted. He could become part of those conversations. Steer them.

Men had died. He owed them his every effort, no matter if it cost him his honor, his soul, his heart.

"Thank you, Mrs. Hoodless."

6

"Please, won't you be seated, Mr. Cameron?" Addie asked, trying to comfort the obviously uncomfortable gentleman. Though there had been occasional flashes of wit from him, he was clearly not accustomed to putting himself forward amongst strangers. She read the tension underlying his urbane demeanor in the paling of his face, the trembling of his hand.

Lady Merritt and Wheatcroft had left them alone on the terrace as Lady Merritt went off to attend some domestic matter.

In reply, Jack—as Addie found herself thinking of him—relaxed his grip on the back of the chair. His gaze skittered nervously over her, but he smiled politely enough before dropping heavily into the settee across from her, his long legs sprawled, reminding her of Ted, who adopted just such an insouciant attitude when most uneasy.

"I'm certain Lady Merritt will rejoin us soon."

Jack merely nodded and she subsided into silence, content to study him as he, in turn, stared out the window. A soft smile of pleasure suddenly curved his firm mouth.

"Do you enjoy horticulture, Mr. Cameron?" she asked, eager for a topic of conversation that would put him at ease.

"Yes," he said, turning toward her. "My mother was an avid, if frustrated, gardener. As all gardeners in the Highlands are," he added wryly.

"Your mother?"

"She died when I was a lad."

"I'm sorry."

His smile was gentle with memory. "I have inherited her appreciation for gardens if not her determination to wrest one from Highland rock."

"Determination is perhaps overrated," Addie said softly, her thoughts spiraling uncontrollably toward Charles's grim resolve to bend everything and everyone to his will. "Those gardeners who accept nature rather than confine her to a plan often produce more interesting results than their more restrictive counterparts."

She looked up and found herself being watched. His gaze was compelling, direct, and something more intense. She had the sudden feeling that he knew exactly what she meant, that he'd somehow divined the history behind her simple opinion and that it angered him. It was unnerving.

It was also unsettling. Addie had too much experience with anger. Involuntarily, she shrank back in her seat. Immediately, the brilliance bled from Jack's blue gaze, leaving it once more placid.

"I am in agreement with you, ma'am," he said in his charmingly accented voice. "Unfortunately, my opinion is not based on any aesthetic considerations."

"On what do you form your opinion, then?" Addie asked curiously.

"Pure, unmitigated sloth. Grappling with vines and topiaries and hedges is such a Herculean endeavor." He fanned himself theatrically with that riotously colored kerchief. "Much better to let nature run amok and then accept praise for one's *avant-garde* approach."

She laughed at his folly and won a spontaneous grin from him. He looked so harmless lounging there, his hand flapping the puff of silk, his eyelids drooping, that Addie began to doubt whether she had, indeed, seen fire in his gaze.

Jack tucked the silk back into the breast pocket of his atrociously ill-fitting jacket. Poor lamb, thought Addie, having pretensions toward fashionable elegance without the wherewithal to pursue it. He was absolutely gorgeous—there was simply no other word for him. But his clothing . . . ! Once more he seemed to read her mind, for he gave her a wry, self-deprecating smile.

Impulsively, Addie rose and went to join him on the settee. "You must beware, you know."

"Beware?"

"You are going to be used quite ruthlessly."

"I am?"

Addie nodded sagely. "You, I suspect, are to be the opening salvo in a campaign that has been forming for over a decade."

"Indeed?"

Addie frowned at yet another cursory reply. The man's verbal abilities seemed to have been cut off the moment she'd moved to sit beside him—Addie's eyes widened. Why, she flustered him!

As far as Addie could remember she had never flustered anyone in her entire adult life. It was a heady sensation, somehow empowering, and deep within her an impish remnant of the young vixen she'd once been urged her to test her newly suspected power. She forced the mischievous impulse away.

Instead, she laid a reassuring hand on Jack's sleeve. The muscles beneath the cloth, surprisingly hard and unyielding, flinched beneath her fingertips. He shifted uncomfortably on the seat, crossing his legs and rearranging the hem of his long velvet jacket over his lap.

"You were saying, Mrs. Hoodless?"

"Ah, yes. The War. Lord and Lady Merritt have had an ongoing battle for years, their son Evan being the contested ground, if you'll excuse my use of the military metaphor."

"Not at all. My family has military connections going back for generations. My father was an officer."

She frowned. More and more she found things they had in common. She could just about guess how a family of bloodletters would respond to finding an artist in their ranks. Particularly an artist without a mother to shield him.

"But please continue, Mrs. Hoodless," he said. "I'm all atwitter to discover how such a poor specimen as myself might be used as artillery in a domestic war. Does Lady Merritt mean to hurl me from her townhouse roof upon her unsuspecting spouse?"

He blinked so innocently that once more Addie laughed. "No. I fear your part is much more enigmatic. You are to be sprung on the unsuspecting Cuthbert the first time he opens his mouth to pontificate on 'pursuits fitting a real man.' You are not at all what he has assumed—unless you toss cabers and dispatch wolves with your bare hands. Lord Merritt has depicted you as a tree-hurling, hairy-legged behemoth—"

Abruptly, her hands flew to cover her face, her cheeks burning with embarrassment. Legged? Had she actually said "leg" to a complete stranger? Good Lord! He must think her a veritable romp.

She peeped at Jack from between her fingers. He was smiling, pleasure lighting his elegant features. He was made for smiles, the tiny lines radiating in a sunburst of amusement from the corners of his brilliant eyes, twin dimples scoring his lean cheeks.

Without a trace of self-consciousness, he leaned forward and gently dragged her hand down. His touch was oddly galvanizing, awakening a firestorm of conflicting sensations: fear, longing, curiosity. "I won't tell."

"Tell what?" Addie asked, pulling her hands from his. His eyes narrowed in perplexity as her fingers fluttered nervously in her lap. She couldn't help it.

"I've heard the word before," he stage-whispered, ignoring her discomfiture. "At least twice."

He was teasing her, she realized. No one ever teased her anymore—except for Ted who, as her brother, saw it as more or less his obligation. The impulse to respond in kind would not be gainsaid.

"'Heard' the word, indeed." She sniffed haughtily. "I suppose you account yourself very raffish because of it."

He nodded complacently.

"But have you actually ever said it?"

He leaned forward. On any other man his expression would be wolfish. But she considered his leer far too self-conscious to be taken seriously. "Leg."

She recoiled in mock indignation.

He leaned closer still. "Leg."

She feigned a gasp but her attention was elsewhere. This close, she could see the soft thicket of his lashes, the smooth, clean texture of his skin, and was teased by a wild impulse to touch him. Madness.

"Leg!" he pronounced with delicious deliberation.

She fanned her face frantically with her hand. "Desist, sir, I beg you! I cannot withstand such an assault on my sensibilities. You artists are a reprobate lot!"

The wicked grin froze on his handsome face. He scowled as though considering some momentous decision and, lifting his head, took a deep breath.

"I am not an artist," he said. His tone made his words a confession. He held her gaze with a deep, level one of his own.

"I know," she said.

"You do?"

"Yes." She nodded then, breaching the distance between them, and gently captured his right hand. She turned it over and, with her forefinger, gently traced the ridges and scars that marred the tensile, sculpted beauty of his fingers and palm. "Paintbrushes don't leave cuts, and a palette doesn't raise calluses such as these. You have a workman's hands, Mr. Cameron." He stared at their joined hands, his large one quiescent in her much smaller one, but didn't say a word.

"Mr. Morris has spent years trying to achieve for the craftsman's work the same degree of esteem garnered by an academy artist's piece. What do you work in? Stone? Wood?"

She studied the broad slash of a white scar on his hand. A thick coil of her hair, loosened when she had donned the "Liberty" gown, had worked free of the chignon and fell across his hand. Hesitantly, delicately, he rubbed the strands between his fingertips.

She turned her head in order to repeat her question and caught on his face an unguarded expression of hopelessness. Immediately, he let her hair slide free of his fingers, as though worried that he'd overstepped the bounds of propriety.

He had, of course. But his gesture had seemed so guileless she could not have taken offense. His look of concern was all out of proportion to his simple breach of decorum.

"I know this is unconscionably presumptuous of me, but given your awareness of my other all-too-obvious social liabilities," she said with a small smile, "perhaps you won't be too shocked at what I am about to say."

He inclined his head.

"It might appear that my offer of social support was said casually, a whim. I assure you, I do not act on whims anymore."

She had his attention now. "I feel a certain sympathy toward your untried position—not only amongst the *ton*, but amongst your fellow artisans. I would not be averse to easing your way where I could."

"You are too kind, ma'am," he said uncomfortably.

She scowled in frustration. Each year social etiquette grew more punishingly rigid. It was nigh impossible to say what one actually meant anymore, to distinguish courtesy from intent in "polite" conversation.

Addie had had enough of masks. She would say what she meant, society's rules be damned.

"Let me be frank. I can help you. You look to need friends. Particularly as Mr. Morris might not be in London this Season. It is one of his latest affectations, to disregard society's calendar. Without his support, you might flounder."

She felt herself flush beneath his careful scrutiny. For an instant Addie wondered if she might have misjudged the man but then realized that she was prepared to take the chance. And that alone felt good. It had been a long time since Addie had taken any chances . . . let alone a chance on a man.

"We are being frank, Mrs. Hoodless?" he asked.

"Yes."

"What do you get out of this arrangement?"

Well! That was frank, indeed! She started to bite at her nail but, executing her new determination, she forced herself to calmly face him. He looked quite ill at ease . . .

Dear God, did he think she was ensconcing him as her . . . her . . . *cicisbeo*? If she weren't so adept at control, she would burst into hysterical laughter. At least in this she could ease his mind by telling him the simple truth.

"I will, I hope, gain a friend, Mr. Cameron. It has been years since I was in London for a Season. I confess to being somewhat apprehensive and, worse yet, suspect that my brother's pleas for my support have less to do with any real need on his part than with his concern for my . . . reclusive state. But were I to feel I could actually help someone, perhaps the discomfort I anticipate might not seem so overwhelming."

"You want a project? A diversion?" Lord, he was frank!

"Yes. I suppose you might see it like that," she murmured. Such bluntness made her suggestion sound unpleasant.

He was silent a moment, considering her words. "And what if I should make a poor project?"

"As I am not familiar with your work, I have no expectations. And having no expectations, you cannot disappoint me." She could not help the bitterness in her tone. But it was a milder bitterness than she was accustomed to feeling.

"I doubt I am worthy of so munificent an offer." She would have suspected sarcasm, but the words, so oddly emphasized, so overstated, held not the slightest trace of insincerity.

"I will be as direct as you, Mr. Cameron." She took a deep breath before plunging on. "I believe I may need you, as much as I suspect you may need me."

"Then Mrs. Hoodless," he said in an odd voice, "I am yours."

7

Lady Merritt sailed into the room, followed closely by Wheatcroft and a tall, loose-limbed man dressed entirely in silk maroon, from knee breeches to frock coat to the elaborate bow obscuring his lantern jaw.

He saw Addie and, without a glance in Jack's direction, hurried to her side. "Addie! My dear, dear lady."

The phrasing was unmistakably Gerald Norton's.

"Do hurry up, Teddy," Lady Merritt said as a second man strolled onto the terrace, the tap of his silver-tipped walking stick timing his unhurried progress across the flagstones.

There was no need for anyone to tell Jack that this was Addie's brother. The resemblance was remarkable. The same curling auburn hair, the same straight dark brows, and clear, pale skin. But while on Addie the exotic features and singular coloring produced a vivid and flagrantly female countenance, the very same characteristics made this man, some five years Addie's senior, almost too handsome, like a statue come to life, the quality heightened by a singular lack of expression on his smooth face.

"Mr. Phyfe, Mr. Norton? Mr. John Cameron." Having finally herded the gentlemen onto the terrace, Lady Merritt was apparently determined to do her spot as hostess. "Mr. Cameron, Mr. Gerald Norton and Mr. Theodore Phyfe."

Norton thrust out his lower lip, eyeing Jack suspiciously.

"Mr. Cameron is one of Mr. Morris's Glasgow lads," Lady Merritt said.

"Morris, eh?" This bit of information somewhat allayed Norton's initial hostility. His lip shrunk to a normal size and he stuck out his hand. "One of the Aesthetics then. Good lot. Not a craftsman myself, struggle with the sable. Impressionism."

"Impressions" of what? Jack wondered, shaking the man's outsized paw.

"What medium do you work in, Mr. Cameron?" Ted asked politely.

The only medium Jack knew was old Peg MacGilly, a table-rapper who enjoyed a certain notoriety in the Highlands, but before he could try to frame an answer, Wheatcroft's voice cut across the room. "Should I have your woodworking tools sent on to London or would you prefer them to remain here with you, Mr. Cameron?"

Every eye in the room turned in shock. Wheatcroft had interrupted a conversation and, judging by the open-mouthed expression of wonderment on Lady Merritt's face, Jack was willing to bet Wheatcroft had never before committed so grave a transgression.

"Did you say something, Wheatcroft?" Lady Merritt intoned incredulously.

"Ah-hm." Wheatcroft cleared his throat. "Pardon me, milady, Mrs. Hoodless, sirs, but there are several crates of woodworking tools that have just been delivered that are awaiting Mr. Cameron's attention."

"Woodworking tools?" Addie left Norton and came to Jack's side. She smelled of cloves and exotic flowers.

A man could forget his native language looking into her brilliant topaz eyes. He found himself nodding unthinkingly. Without a doubt he'd have nodded to anything she said just to keep her face tilted toward his, alive with interest and approval—

"Are you moving permanently to London? Away from Mr. Morris's commune . . . er, guild . . . whatever he calls his community?" Lady Merritt's query broke the spell.

Jack fought his impatience with the intrusion by doing what he had always done when confronted with imperious authority vested by breeding rather than capability: he stood at attention.

"No, indeed, ma'am," he managed politely before turning to Wheatcroft. "You may have my things sent on to London, Wheatcroft."

"You haul your tools about with you wherever you go?" Ted asked laconically, lowering himself into a chair. Jack shot him a quick glance. There was nothing laconic about Ted's sharp scrutiny, however he masked it.

Jack had known a pasha with a very similar manner. The man had yawned while, with ruthless precision, ferreting out the conspirators in his kingdom. Jack did not know whether Ted might be his enemy, but he instinctively knew he was not a friend.

Becoming aware of his military stance, Jack made himself relax. He plucked an apple from the bowl of fruit on the table and bounced it in his hand. "Chap can't let his talents atrophy, can he?" he asked vaguely of Ted, who returned his smile with one that did not quite reach his eyes.

"Oh, heavens, my dear boy! You won't have time to set up a studio, er, atelier, er . . . guild." Lady Merritt *tch*ed. "Drat the man! Mr. Morris sent you here without any idea of what to expect, didn't he?"

"Well, not specifically—"

"I am to introduce you, Jack. Nothing more. Next year you can have a show. You can't just suddenly arrive in London and hold an exhibition! It would never do. Never! Even were I to invite all of my friends and dear Mrs. Hoodless all of hers, without proper—and prior—introduction, it would be doomed. Doomed!" She threw up her hands as if to demonstrate just how doomed such a program would be.

"'Mrs. Hoodless'?" Ted asked, his gaze flickering toward his sister.

"Yes." Addie rounded on her brother. "I will be helping Mr. Cameron establish himself in society."

"Interesting," Ted murmured. "But what of your obligations to me? Where will you find the time for Mr. Cameron?"

For some reason, Jack did not quite believe the peevish tone. He was sure they masked an altogether different interrogation. Ted was studying Addie closely. There was more here than a spoiled man who did not want to share his sister's attention.

"I have a sitting with Miss Zephrina Drouhin in less than a month," Ted continued. "And after that the Black Dragoons will be invading my studio."

"Black Dragoons?" Addie echoed. Her lips parted, a single anguished moment, before she gave her head an angry little shake.

"Yes." Gerald Norton beamed. "Those military chappies are quite inundating Ted with petitions to paint them now that Whitehall has commissioned their senior officers' portraits. These army types seem to travel as a herd."

"Well," Addie said, "I daresay I can pour Miss Drouhin tea, but I doubt very much whether a Black Dragoon needs my company to ensure his reputation. More than likely the presence of a lady would only make him self-conscious."

"Too true," Ted said. "Self-conscious enough that he might actually hold his pose."

"Ted."

"You promised."

She drew a deep breath. "Yes. I did."

"Yes, yes, yes," Lady Merritt muttered impatiently. "Addie promised. Now, I have news." She patted Jack's arm fondly. He had to keep his mouth from dropping open. "Not only is Jack Mr. Morris's protégé, he is also Cuthbert's great-nephew." She fairly twinkled with malicious pleasure. "Cuthbert's Scottish great-nephew!" She laughed, unable to contain the bubble of delight.

"Really?" Ted asked, fixing a puzzled frown on Jack.

"Yes," Addie said, returning to Jack's side. With her back to the rest of the party she caught his eye and gave him an encouraging smile.

"Deuced fortunate for you, old chap," Gerald said, scowling. He clearly couldn't decide whether or not he ought to give up his protective posture and welcome his hostess's relation into the artistic "fold" or treat Jack as potentially usurping his place in the affections of a very generous patron.

During his convalescence, Jack had judged Norton an amicable fellow. His next action proved it. With a sudden sigh of capitulation, he clapped Jack on the shoulder. Unfortunately, the well-meant blow landed squarely on his wound, causing Jack to catch back a hiss of pain.

"Indeed! How fortuitous. One might even say convenient," Ted said blandly.

"Oh, Ted. Leave off, do!" Addie said. "You are cursed with a suspicious nature."

"Suspicious?" Lady Merritt said. "There's no reason to be suspicious of Jack. Lord Merritt's estate is entailed, there is no possible way Jack could ever inherit the title, and certainly his chosen profession isn't going to ingratiate him with his uncle. Why on earth would anyone want to impersonate Cuthbert's Scottish great-nephew?" Apparently Lady Merritt had put some thought to the question herself.

"Why, Ted, why indeed?" Gerald asked, shooting Ted a disgusted look. Having decided to befriend Jack, he did so wholeheartedly.

"Yes, why, Ted?" Addie demanded. Even Wheatcroft appeared to arch a brow disapprovingly.

From his place amongst the semicircle of his unexpected champions, Jack smiled innocently at Addie's brother. Ted shrugged. "I can't think of a single reason."

With a sniff, Lady Merritt beckoned Wheatcroft forward as Addie, having won her brother's capitulation, offered Norton a cup of tea. For a second, Jack faced Ted without witnesses.

The smile never left Ted's face as he softly added a single word for Jack's ears alone. "Yet."

8

"Tell me, Cameron, what do you think of Whistler's *Nocturne?*" Ted asked without lifting his gaze from the white-clad croquet players determinedly swatting balls on the dark green expanse of the Merritt lawn.

Autumn had the countryside firmly in her bittersweet embrace. The sky overhead was the paling blue of late October. The air was crisp and sweet.

From his place beside Jack, Gerald Norton popped a chocolate-cloaked strawberry between his lips and mumbled around the mouthful of fruit, "Indeed, tell us, Cameron. What do you think of it?"

Masking his unease, Jack, reclining in a hammock set between two ancient beech trees, swatted idly at a honeybee that had wandered from Lady Merritt's nearby herbaceous border, looking for a last bit of pollen.

In the two weeks since he'd begun his masquerade, Ted alone remained suspicious. He was constantly, if subtly, quizzing him. Thus far, Jack had managed to duck those subjects with which he was unfamiliar, or answer in such an exaggerated and affected manner that the weak substance of his remarks was obscured.

Now he bought time, searching his memory for some reference Wheatcroft might have mentioned regarding a nocturne. He hadn't realized he'd need to know something of music as well as art. But clearly from Gerald's expectant expression, it was assumed he would.

"Very . . . pretty," Jack allowed cautiously.

"Agreed," Gerald said, "but his use of—"

"Yes, yes," Ted cut in. "But what element do you find the 'prettiest'?" His gaze was challenging.

Jack returned his regard placidly and tossed up a strawberry with his good hand, catching it expertly in his mouth before answering. "La!" he said. "Why, the strings, of course!"

Gerald stared at him a second before abruptly bursting out in a loud guffaw. "Did you hear that, Ted?" he asked. "The strings, the man says! One would think he was serious. Good show, Cameron!"

Jack nodded complacently, having no idea what had garnered him the accolade.

"You are a wag, Jack, there is no doubt of it," Gerald said. "Strings, indeed! You've turned the orchestral title of the painting subject into a *bon mot*."

"Thank you, Gerry. It is so nice to have one's wit appreciated." Damn. *Nocturne* was a painting.

"I take it, then, that you do not approve of Whistler's smears of yellow and cobalt?" Ted asked, looking a bit irritably toward Gerry.

"Not entirely," Jack said carefully. Ted was the one person he needed to befriend. Yet, despite his obvious distrust, Ted seemed more than willing to accept his company. In fact, he'd gone so far as to insist that Jack be included in all of Lady Merritt's plans for his upcoming shows, fêtes, and introductions. Jack was at a loss to explain why.

His thoughts were interrupted by Lady Merritt's arrival. Dressed in swaths of drab blue fabric, girdled with bright yellow chains and wearing some sort of turban device atop her head, she looked like an odd hybrid between medieval abbess and penny opera singer.

"This is late, even for Addie," she complained as she approached. "I am growing concerned. If Ted were with her, I'd not mind—but Ted came earlier. Without his sister." She shot Ted an accusing glare.

He shrugged. "I told her that if she were more than a quarter hour delayed she would be arriving alone."

"I can't support such a lack of civility," Lady Merritt said sternly.

"Quite right," Ted replied equitably, deliberately misunderstanding. "For all that I'm quite fond of her, one mustn't encourage such impoliteness, even in one's sister."

"Oh, Ted, behave. Go and fetch her," Lady Merritt said, abandoning her disapproving stare.

"I really must decline, Lady Merritt. I have declared, on principle, that I would not be late for one more social engagement on my sister's account. On principle, I must adhere to my resolve."

Lady Merritt, obviously miffed by Ted's lofty and—Jack suspected—contrived refusal, tapped her foot impatiently.

"I'm sure she's all right," Ted said.

"Well, I'm not!"

"Allow me to go and fetch dear Addie," Gerald offered gallantly.

"No, no, and no," Lady Merritt said, stamping her foot in emphasis. "The Dowager Blumforth has specifically requested you partner her in the next round of croquet. She is the most tiresomely insistent woman." Ted and Gerald exchanged an amused glance.

Her gaze turned on Jack. "You will have to go and fetch her, Jack."

"But Lady Merritt," he said. "Would that be seemly? I am, after all, not a relative or even a friend of long standing." He did not want to go to Addie, to find her, to be afforded the pleasure and pain of her rare company. He had no rights there and he had spent too many hours with her already, hours of disturbing plea-sure riddled with guilt. Hours of deception when he only learned even more about her, his knowledge keeping pace with the under-standing that the very masquerade that gave him access to her, once it came out, would put her forever beyond his reach.

She would never accept his deception as necessary. Never forgive his using her brother . . . and her, no matter how good the reason.

He had tried to stay clear of her but circumstance and Addie's own unaccountable determination to champion him threw them together. In the past two weeks he'd added a visual vocabulary to the things he'd learned about her without ever laying eyes on her: the way one corner of her lip crooked when she was trying to suppress her amusement; the soft inhalation that accompanied her sponta-neous appreciation of a novel she was reading; above all the telltale deadening of her expression whenever her husband was mentioned.

"I really do not think it would be seemly for Mrs. Hoodless to be alone, unchaperoned, with an unmarried man."

"Oh, Jack." Lady Merritt tittered in real amusement. "I don't think anyone could take exception to you driving her here."

He had apparently managed beyond his wildest expectations in his depiction of a fop. No one, least of all Lady Merritt, considered him capable of compromising a lady . . . or anything else for that matter. Even Gerald was trying to hide a smile behind his hand.

"Yes," Ted prompted. "If I am unconcerned, I doubt anyone else would raise objections. Run along, Jack."

There was nothing he could do but acquiesce, eagerness and pain his tandem companions as he made his way to the stables.

———◆———

How can I always be so late? Addie asked herself as she clucked to the mare.

She had thought she'd given herself plenty of time to get ready for Lady Merritt's picnic. But ever since Jack Cameron had arrived she had found herself spending more and more time at her toilette, choosing and discarding gowns, having the maid arrange and rearrange her hair, fussing with her few pieces of jewelry.

And then, when she'd finally gone downstairs, having decided she simply wasn't going to look any better no matter how many more gowns she tried on, it had been to discover that she'd given the footman—who occasionally acted as her driver—the day off.

In a rare, confident mood, she'd told the groom to hitch the rig and announced her attention of driving herself. It had proved a happy decision. As a girl she had often handled the carriage reins, letting her horse fly over the countryside lanes and roads. Now the air's clean, sharp tang revived dim memories of other freshening winds, winds of nearly forgotten autumns. Exhilarating autumns.

With a sound of pleasure, she urged the little mare to a faster pace, uncertain whether the breezes or the thought of seeing Jack Cameron brought the color to her cheeks.

She had just crested a small rise when she saw a rider. For a moment fear made a lump in her throat. Then, nearly as quickly as it had surprised her by appearing, her fear surprised her again by vanishing.

After all, what was there to fear? A casual rider chance met on a glorious autumn day. What was the danger in that? Her lack of trepidation delighted her and she laughed out loud. It was only when he drew closer that she recognized him and her heart leapt in response.

Jack.

He was seated on a mild-looking roan hack, looking for all the world born to the saddle. It was only when he kicked the horse forward that she noticed how awkwardly he held the reins.

"Mrs. Hoodless," he hailed her. "I am come to rescue you."

"Rescue me?" She tilted her head. He was so handsome, so lean and splendid, he put her in mind of a greyhound, quivering with nerves and barely contained power.

Power? she wondered uneasily, backing away from the estimation. Powerful men were dangerous. Besides, he looked barely able to rein in his horse. She relaxed.

"Yes, dear lady. From your toilette." His lazy, casual gaze traveled over her lilac-edged, pearl-gray gown.

She laughed. "As you can see, you are too late to play the savior. I have long since escaped the clutches of my dressing table."

"But not before it has exerted its influence. Might I say, you look very charming."

She dimpled. "Thank you. Now, Jack, why are you really here?"

"Lady Merritt was concerned for your safety."

Addie felt herself blush. "Am I so late?"

Jack nodded. "You've missed lunch. Or will have by the time we return. Norton was gobbling the dessert with unprecedented speed when I left. By the time we return, he may well have eaten his way through the centerpiece's wax fruit."

Addie laughed again but then grew sober. "Is Lady Merritt very unhappy with me?"

Jack waved his hand dismissively, squinting in feigned contempt. "She'll survive. Frankly, I think she's more upset about not having won a single game of croquet. As I was her partner, I believe sending me off to look for you served a dual purpose. Now she can find a more worthy teammate."

"She sent you?" Addie could not keep the disappointment from her voice. Jack noticed and at once dropped his teasing manner, studying her with gentle eyes.

It was one of the things she most liked about him. For all his foolish wit and insouciance, there was little that escaped his attention. He always managed to say just the right thing to make people feel good about themselves. He was so perceptive, so innately kind, traits that were rare in most men.

"She sent me, aye. But her request only sanctioned my own desire."

He'd spoken lightly enough, but there was something in his gaze . . . Sadness? Why would wanting to be with her make Jack sad?

"Shall I drive?" he asked. "Or do you prefer to continue?"

In answer, she slid over on the narrow bench. Jack dismounted and tied his horse to the back of the rig and then climbed up next to her. He moved with smoothly oiled economy.

She pulled her skirts away and he took the seat, his thigh pressed intimately along hers. Her heart thudded dully and she was aware, even through heavy skirts, of the length of his leg and its hardness.

"I feel obliged to warn you, you are undoubtedly vastly better at it than I." He took the reins from her and clucked at the mare, starting her forward in a leisurely gait. Addie glanced over at Jack. His jaw was set and a small frown scored his high forehead. He was concentrating fiercely on his driving.

They rode for a while in silence, only the birdsong from the hedgerows and the rustle of papery leaves beneath the carriage wheels accompanying the clip-clop of the horses' hooves.

"You must be looking forward to London after so long an absence," Jack finally said.

"I enjoy the atelier," she returned, skirting the question.

"Have you ever acted as your brother's hostess before?"

"Oh, yes. Brother, father, uncle . . ." She trailed off.

He raised a questioning brow.

"My family is rife with artists. My father, you know."

He shot her a questioning glance and she studied him in interest. Perhaps she was overly proud of her parent, but she was surprised he didn't seem familiar with her father's work. He was quite a well-known artist.

But then, she decided, Jack was the sort of considerate gentleman who would pretend ignorance just to offer his companion a topic for polite conversation. So, she obliged.

"My father was a member of the Pre-Raphaelites for a time. Before he turned to the Nabis."

"Ah. And your uncle?"

"Another *avant-garde*." She grinned. "Yes. I'm afraid the lot of them are bohemians. Along with myself, my mother is the sole practitioner of conventionality in our family, and she is not, I am afraid, very good at it. Which is why the hostess duties fell to me. Mother was always too . . . distracted."

"You are conventional?" His tone bespoke skepticism.

"Relatively speaking," she allowed laughingly. "Even when I was a child, Mother claimed I was always trying to bring order to our household. But it was like trying to bring order to a typhoon. People coming and going, showing up unannounced in the middle of the night and staying for weeks or months."

"People? What sort of people?"

"Oh, every sort. Models and travelers, artisans and historians. They gravitated toward our house like iron to a magnet."

"You enjoyed it?" It was not a question.

"More than I realized," she replied softly. "I am afraid that like many young people I had scant appreciation for what I had and longed after that which I did not."

"Which was?"

The flippant response she had been about to give faltered on her lips as she thought back to her girlhood aspirations. "Order, consistency, stability. A family that did all the normal things. You know. Tea with the vicar, servants one did not have to hush, decorous conversation"—she smiled—"decorous dinners."

"You did not have these things?"

"Lord, no! Father hates the vicar. He keeps trying to have my father excommunicated."

"Your father is an atheist?"

"No. The vicar just doesn't like him. He created a stained glass for the church's nave. Judgment Day."

"That hardly sounds like a reason for animosity."

"It does when the vicar's face is plainly depicted next to Christ's index finger," Addie said and felt the corner of her mouth twitch. "His *left* index finger."

"Good Lord!" Jack broke out.

"Exactly."

"What of the family dinners?"

Addie shook her head. "They were more feeding time than dinners, always *en buffet*. Mother never knew how many would be sitting down, you see. Dinner parties were invariably forums for debate, people thumping their fists on the table, chattering, shouting."

"And the servants?"

"Oh, we had them all right. But more often than not, they'd be called to join in to whatever debate was going on."

He burst out laughing.

"What of your family?" she asked, pleased she'd amused him.

He shrugged. "The usual in Highland fare, I suppose. Hurl a few trees about to work up an appetite, chase down a rabbit for dinner, scratch at the odd flea and call it a night."

Now it was her turn to laugh, though she realized he did not want to talk about his family. "I suspect you are embellishing a bit."

"A bit." His blue eyes found hers. True to her suspicions, he turned the conversation from himself. "You've told me what you wanted as a child. What do you want now?"

She smiled. "Now? The freedom I had in my youth, that sense of anticipation, of possibilities always unfolding. I used to wake each day and resent the fact that I did not know what it would bring—or perhaps I should say whom." She paused a second. "What fools the young are."

"I should think those things still possible."

She shrugged. "No. I'm older now. Wiser."

"Ah, yes. Decrepit," he said solemnly. She smiled. "But surely—"

She interrupted him, suddenly aware of how self-pitying she must sound. "Besides, I would not really want the helter-skelter life I led as a girl. I suppose what I would really like to find is . . . balance."

He cast her a troubled glance. "After the death of your husband, why didn't you return to live with your parents?"

The abrupt question caught her so off guard that she answered him without hesitating, honestly. "I could not go back. The girl they raised no longer exists and to masquerade as her would be too painful. Both for them and me."

And besides, they didn't know. She'd never told them about Charles. He'd threatened to hurt her brothers if she did. Badly.

Only Ted had guessed and it had led to his crippling. And now, with Charles's death, there was no reason to hurt them with the knowledge of what she'd . . . endured.

Her answer seemed to bother him. The clear blue of his eyes clouded over. He made a sound of frustration and turned in his seat, inadvertently jerking the reins.

It startled the mare and she sidled anxiously in her traces just as a pheasant burst from the hedgerow, cackling as it flew directly across her nose. Before Jack could react, the mare reared, pulling the reins from his ineffectual grip. He cursed and grabbed for the reins. Too late; the terrified mare already had the bit between her teeth.

Behind the carriage, Jack's gelding neighed shrilly, dashing to the side of the rig, his trumpet of fear spurring the mare further. She plunged forward, spewing dust and pebbles from beneath her hooves.

Frantically, Jack flung an arm around Addie and pulled her to his side as, one-handed, he hauled ineffectually at the reins, unable to fight the mare back under control. She thundered forward toward a sharp turn in the road, her neck extended, ears flat on her outstretched head. The rig rocked and shook as it hit rut and stone, jolting them with each bone-jarring impact.

They were going to overturn.

Desperately, Addie seized the reins from Jack's grasp, twining the leather straps around her fists and, setting her heels against the floorboard, stood up, pulling fiercely at the bit to drag the mare's mouth down. She kicked frantically at the brakes, Jack holding tight to her.

"Pull!" he shouted in her ear.

She closed her eyes as he reached around her and grabbed the reins, adding his strength to hers. The mare bucked, fighting the bit, but slowly, inexorably, the pain in the mare's mouth overcame her fear. She skittered to a stop, lathered and quivering. Behind them the gelding bucked unhappily a few times before quieting.

The air escaped Addie's lungs in a whoosh of relief. She sank down, light-headed, her pulse racing. Around her ribs, Jack's arm tightened convulsively. He'd been as frightened as she. She looked around at him.

He was pale, so pale as to appear white, and his eyes glittered fiercely as he stared at her. Silently, with trembling fingers, he reached up and touched her cheek. Then, his breathing rough, he gently tucked a strand of hair behind her ear.

"It's all right," she reassured him.

"No, it's not. You might have been hurt . . . killed. I couldn't hold her. I couldn't—I am not the man—damn!"

Angrily, he thrust his left hand out for her inspection and condemnation. The long, artistic fingers shook uncontrollably. Impulsively, she caught them in her own. The shivers in his warm hand translated themselves into some stronger emotion in her heart.

She laid her cheek against the back of his hand. He didn't have to be a hero for her. He had tried. That was all that mattered.

"My God, Addie." His voice was a hoarse rasp.

"It's over. No one was hurt."

"If only because of you, your bravery, your strength." There was no prick of hurt male pride in his tone, only admiration.

Wonderingly, she studied him. She had saved them. She—timid, cowed Addie Hoodless—had met a crisis without fear.

"You're an exceptional woman, Addie Hoodless," he said. "Most women would have screamed that mare into mortal flight."

She smiled, uncertain how to respond to his strange and heady admiration. It felt suddenly too intimate, this fragile thing between them too rare to examine now with danger so recently escaped.

"Well," she said, "I wasn't about to let that handsome lace jabot of yours be soiled."

He stared at her, clearly confused. She slowly relinquished his hand and touched the fine lace on his chest. The casual contact sent a thrill of awareness through her.

He followed her impish gaze to the ruffles spouting from his pristine white shirt. And then, like an actor assuming a role, a mask slipped over his features, hiding his nature behind an instant caricature. She thought she understood. He'd learned to deliberately exaggerate his affectations as a defiant answer to what would have certainly been his family's military expectations, and now it was second nature whenever his manliness was brought into question.

She only wished she could tell him that, in her experience, manliness was a coded word for brutality.

He fussed with the jabot, plucking at the tatted edges, scowling heavily at the snowy white folds. "Thank God for your devotion to fashion, ma'am," he drawled. "I am quite fond of this jabot."

"It is so special?" she asked, uncertain how to call back the man who hid behind this posturing.

"Oh, yes. 'Tis a family keepsake, passed from son to son to son down countless generations."

"Really?"

"Well . . . " He sniffed and without ceremony withdrew his arm from around her waist. Instantly, she regretted the loss of its warm strength.

"Well?"

"Perhaps there was some paltry daughter who got her greedy little paws on it at some point in its history," he said severely.

"I see." She chuckled and he matched her smile, apparently gratified his silliness had met with success.

Having won her laugh, he snapped the reins sharply on the mare's rump. They passed the rest of the ride in companionable banter, but Addie could not help feeling that something lovely, something precious, had been shunted aside and replaced with nonsense.

9

"We will leave for London in a fortnight," said Lady Merritt. She speared a piece of exquisitely prepared turbot and squinted at it. "Needs more cream. Remind me to speak to Cook."

In his chair across from Lady Merritt, Jack offered thanks the servants had not yet lit the tapers. The cavernous dining room, steeped in shadows, masked an annoyance that had grown with each day. Though weeks of practice under Wheatcroft's critical tutelage had honed his thespian skills, it still took conscious effort to eradicate fifteen years of precise military bearing.

A month of playing indolent jackanapes for Lady Merritt's amusement was about as much as he could contrive. His strength was rapidly returning, and this forced inactivity was driving him to distraction. But going to London without Lady Merritt had proved impossible. She insisted he stay and unless he wanted to make an enemy of her—and making an enemy of Ted's sponsor meant he would be excluded entrée to Ted's atelier—it was necessary he oblige.

"A fortnight? So long?" Jack said. "I thought you wanted to be firmly entrenched in your townhouse by Christmas. That is the unofficial start of the Season, is it not?"

It had been over a week since Addie and her brother had left for London. A week since she'd secured his promise to visit them as soon as he arrived in London; a week since she'd teased him about his overlong hair and modishly pale complexion. He missed her; it didn't matter that he had no right to do so.

"Ted seemed quite adamant that they arrive in London prior to the New Year," he said carefully.

"I understand. Eager to get the bit between your teeth, are you, Jack?" Lady Merritt popped another bit of fish into her mouth. "But dear Teddy has portraits to complete before the Royal Academy opens its show in May. You are fortunate in that you have no tiresome old despots attempting to regulate your genius."

He was still astonished by the fact that in all the time he'd spent with her, Lady Merritt had yet to request so much as a glimpse of a sketchbook. Not that he had one, but, in anticipation of that eventuality, he had manufactured a rather nice tale about its whereabouts. "It's just that I am loath to keep the world ignorant of me any longer than necessary. 'Twouldn't be Christian."

Lady Merritt snorted in amusement. "You are a fool, Jack Cameron," she said fondly. "And far more a pagan than a Christian."

The sooner he could get to London and Ted's studio, the sooner he might learn something about the men he suspected of treachery. And the sooner he would walk out of Addie's life.

The thought speared through him, agonizing with its inevitability. Each day he had spent in her company had made it clear that in any other guise he'd never have been allowed through her front door. Addie greeted every reference to the military with a nearly physical withdrawal. Any mention of officers or regiments chased the animation from her face.

For weeks Jack had taken advantage of Addie's perception of him as some sort of gelding.

While he'd not denied himself her company, he had been careful never to be alone with her again. Not after that eternal and torturous carriage ride.

It had proven that with her he could not trust himself. She awakened in him ungovernable desires, made him yearn after things he could not have, and would not allow himself to want.

Well, now Addie was in London. As were her brother and the officers he painted. And Jack was stuck here, acting the court jester for Lady Merritt.

"Aren't you, Jack?" Lady Merritt's self-congratulatory tone broke into his thoughts.

"Aren't I what?"

"A pagan."

"Naughty Lady Merritt," he purred. "You've divined my secret. I am Bacchus's creature!"

"Give over, Jack. How you do pose!" Lady Merritt chortled. "Bacchus, indeed. You rarely even indulge in a second glass of wine."

Jack sighed dramatically. "As long as I contrive to amuse, I suppose I am not completely wasted here." For a second he wondered if he'd pushed too far. Lady Merritt was not one to allow her largesse to be undervalued. She shot him a sharply assessing look.

"You feel you are wasting time? Languishing here?" she asked in chill tones.

"Languishing?" He paused as though considering the word. "No. Luxuriating, yes. 'Tisn't safe to indulge so heavily in fine wine, opulent surroundings, and superb conversation with one's charming hostess. Only see how I have been seduced into spending weeks of enervating bliss?"

Lady Merritt's eyes widened. *Now*, thought Jack, *a subtle jig of the lure*. "Art," he continued mournfully, "is a harsh mistress, dear lady, and a jealous one. She deserts those who do not regularly worship at her shrine. My art demands a price which I have too long neglected to pay."

She'd not only taken the bait, she was gill-hooked. Her mouth formed a plump little circle of delight. "If you should want a place in which to practice your craft, I can prepare a room for you!" she gushed in such open apology that Jack's much-abused conscience rebelled.

He squelched the insurrection.

"Dear Patroness," he said, sadly. "If only it were that simple. But no. You must remember the reason why I have ventured from my own poor corner of Scotland: to brave your thronging towers, your milling hordes"—Lord he would soon be penning penny-dreadfuls at this rate—"your rife and rampant London! I need the inspiration of her teeming streets, her opulence and her squalor, her vice and virtue. My art, being no longer content with pastoral beauty and nature's tranquility, demands a new stimulus. It demands . . . London!"

There were no two ways about it: he was getting damned good at this. Lady Merritt sat pressed against the back seat of her dining chair, her hand flattening her brocade-upholstered bosom, her eyes aglow. For a moment she just stared at him before breathing in a throaty sigh, "We'll leave tomorrow."

Addie sank back on her heels. Her paint-stained smock pooled around her as she eyed the wall panel before her. With a sound of satisfaction, she once more rose to her knees and dipped an ostrich fern into a tray filled with gilt paint, then pressed it onto the aubergine silk panel.

Slowly, she peeled the long frond back. A perfect impression of the leaf interlocked with the golden silhouette of a fern above it, trailing a graceful latticework from ground to ceiling. There! She'd transformed the second-story boudoir into her own private withdrawing room.

It had been a long time since anything had been well and truly hers. She would never have guessed that this house could ever feel welcoming. And yet, it did. For the first time since her marriage, she was able to please herself.

The thought gave rise to an impulse, one she would have never heeded a year ago. But she could be impulsive now. She could afford to be.

With a feeling of delicious abandonment, she slid her shoes off and peeled back her stockings from her calves, hiking her skirts so that her bare legs and feet lay exposed in the bright square of warm sunlight on the floor. Closing her eyes, she lay on her back, wiggling her toes.

She was rather surprised she was still capable of impetuousness. Indeed, she'd viewed the slow reawakening of her boldness with no little mistrust. After all, had she not been impetuous, she might have heeded the Hoodlesses' loving warnings and never eloped with Charles.

It is Jack Cameron's fault, she decided, but could not find a frown for that conclusion.

Each day spent with the handsome, nonsensical, yet oddly vulnerable Scotsman had fanned to life a tiny ember of self-confidence. It was not altogether comfortable. Like finding out that a favorite gown you'd thought lost years before had merely been put into a cedar chest. You long to try it on, and yet you are afraid if you do it will look ridiculous. Or worse, it will no longer fit.

Oddly enough, Jack's very vulnerability encouraged her own self-assurance. The manner in which he masked his self-doubt with such a provocative and blatant caricature stirred an inclination to nonconformity in her.

She suspected that she alone refused to accept Jack as the effete, overcontrived fribble he presented to the world. His conversation certainly never hinted at any weaknesses—oh, dear Lord, no! The thought made Addie smile. Jack was all arrogant disdain and witty repartee. Mr. Wilde himself would be hard-pressed to keep up with Jack's drawled *bons mots*!

But then, just as she was upbraiding herself for romanticizing him, she would see it: a keen, thoughtful intelligence, a perceptive remark that belied his pose of absolute self-involvement, an unexpected gentleness in dealing with another's frailties.

And then, too, even more rarely, but just as undeniably, she would surprise on his fallen-angel's face a fleeting, hunted expression: a mixture of dismay, uncertainty, and awful longing.

She did not understand what authored that haunted look, but more and more often lately, she found herself wondering how she would feel if she was able to be the object of it.

When had she begun to anticipate his presence? When had his reaction to her—his physical tentativeness, his avoidance of her gaze, the tension of his body when she approached—begun to challenge her?

A sudden crash overhead disrupted her thoughts. Probably the workmen breaking through the rafters for the new skylight in Ted's new atelier. Initially, he'd been hesitant to accept her offer to turn the top floor into a studio. But it only made sense that he should.

She was refurbishing the house anyway and the large upstairs ballroom, if drafty, had high ceilings and banks of expensive glass windows. Perfect for an artist's use.

Also, the house was located close to the artists' quarter but still was well within the boundaries of respectable addresses. Doting mothers of this Season's debutantes would have no misgivings about trudging their bedecked and beribboned daughters here to have their portraits painted.

But most importantly, she hadn't wanted to be alone here, with only Charles's ghost for company.

A few days after they'd eloped, Charles had discovered that she was not the heiress he'd imagined. He'd demanded she give him control over what money she did have. She'd refused. He had been furious. Within minutes, her amazement at his transformation had become terror as he'd made her understand what her future held.

It had been a very physical lesson. The only thing for which she had to be thankful was that his abuse had never taken a sexual form. He had, after those first few nights of marriage, left her alone.

She'd been in the process of leaving him when he'd discovered her plans.

At first he was remorseful, but that had quickly disappeared when it became clear his contrition was not going to change her mind. So, he'd beaten her again and then told her point-blank that if she ever left him, he would seek his revenge on her siblings. She would, he swore, never humiliate him.

Fear for her family had kept her from fleeing, and over the next five years she had learned to an acute degree just what humiliation meant. Her only insurrection had been a covert one. When her grandfather had left her a small fortune, she had not revealed it to Charles. She had vowed to herself that he would not spend one cent of her inheritance.

It was only after the vicar had mentioned how accident-prone she'd become and suggested that she see a doctor for her "instability" that Charles realized how close he came to being revealed as a monster. His pride would not stand for that, either. He'd become mockingly cautious of her physical well-being thereafter. He found other targets for his rage. The tweenie and the boot boy appeared with bruises. Favored pets disappeared. Her mare went lame and had to be destroyed.

When he finally grew tired of her, he shipped her off north.

In some ways that had been even worse. He came unannounced, like a nightmare, upbraiding her and terrorizing her before disappearing as suddenly as he'd come. He'd known full well that anticipation could torture.

She was nearing desperation when he'd been killed.

Small wonder she did not wholly welcome the resurrection of the carefree, impulsive girl she'd been or thank Jack Cameron for reviving her.

"Odalisque."

As if in answer to her thoughts, she heard him speak. His voice—husky, unique—made the word an endearment. She didn't open her eyes, but thought back over the past few minutes.

Slowly, she slit her eyes open, looking at him from beneath the thick brush of her lashes. Jack stood in the doorway, unaware he was being observed. For a brief instant, his pose was uncontrived. He held himself taller, his shoulders squared, his body poised with supple grace. His face was taut, his expression defined by some inner extremity.

Then, he realized he was being watched. His shoulders slouched, his eyelids drooped, and the beautiful mouth twisted into a moue.

"I should have guessed you were awake and alert. Harem women are notorious for their intrigues," he drawled, leaning back against the doorjamb and crossing his arms over his chest.

She opened her eyes. For some reason unknown even to herself, she did not scoot upright as she ought, but instead stayed lying as she was. "How would you know what harem women are known for?"

"I was quite a pet of the seraglio." Though his tone was light, his gaze kept moving away from the sight of her as though he found it . . . unsettling. Did she unsettle Jack Cameron? The idea was electrifying.

"Have you been using mineral spirits in your toilet, m'dear? What an interesting concept. Declare your aesthetic tendencies with an aroma. All the professional beauties will be clamoring for an *eau de palette.*"

"With very little further effort you might yet achieve offensiveness," she said, robbing the words of censure with a fond smile. "I was stenciling leaves on the wall. And what 'seraglio' would that be?"

"My second cousin's. Did I not mention he was a pasha?"

"I thought you were Scottish."

"Oh, we quite keep our less conventional connections buried deep in the old skeleton closet."

Addie laughed and pushed herself to a sitting position.

"No," Jack said abruptly, coming across the room. "Please. Stay there. You look like an elegant little cat waiting to be stroked."

"And are you going to stroke me?" She didn't know what made her say the words. He stopped short.

She thought she heard the sharp hiss of his indrawn breath. She'd shocked him. She shouldn't have teased him like that . . .

"I'm sorry," she said. But she didn't feel sorry. She felt something exciting stir her blood.

He looked down at her. "No more than I," he whispered.

10

Despite having arrived in London just that morning, Jack had already found an excuse to be with Addie, and now here she lay at his feet, luxuriating in the light, her slender, naked calves glazed golden, her narrow feet bare, asking if he was going to stroke her.

God.

A taunting gleam appeared in the pooling darkness of her eyes and then was gone. She bit her lower lip. Her gaze sidled away.

He nearly swore. He wanted back the wanton who'd betrayed herself an instant before. He stood tightly strung as a bow, quivering with longing and desire that he couldn't act on. Not now. Yet, he could not deny himself the opportunity to steal just a few more precious seconds beneath her guard.

He reached down, offering her his hand. She accepted it easily. Her fingers felt strong yet delicate, like a swift's fine-boned wing. He pulled her up and she rose as gracefully as a ballet dancer. Slowly, he released her hand. It slipped from his grasp with something like reluctance. She did not move.

He was so close he could see where the overstarched lace on her collar had chafed her neck.

Wariness and curiosity warred in her gaze as he leaned forward, dragging the sun-sweetened scent of her skin through his nostrils. He didn't touch her but she must have felt his breath stirring the tendrils of hair at her temples, the banked heat of his gaze sliding over her lips.

He fully expected her to withdraw as he bent nearer, but she didn't. With the slightest twist of his head, he could kiss her. He was that close. A matter of inches. A sigh. No more.

Her lips parted. He could just make out the bottom of her front teeth, pearly white behind the rosy curve of her upper lip. See the darker hue of her tongue. He shifted, bringing himself nearer still, the advance of a hunter, an oblique predatory approach.

The lace covering her bosom shivered in response to some interior agitation. Her breath grew staggered, a tiny pant. Of what? Alarm? Anticipation?

Closer still.

Where could this lead? he wondered angrily. His body was reacting in defiance of his mind. Yet still, he found himself committing to memory the fine texture of her skin, the faint remembrance of summer's freckles across the bridge of her nose, a tiny crescent-shaped scar on her upper lip.

He opened his mouth to taste her very breath and closed his eyes, angling his head a hand's span from her neck. A wave of physical desire welled up, drowning his senses. It was an intimacy she hadn't offered and yet from which he hadn't withdrawn. It was not nearly enough and he had only to move that final space to touch her mouth with his, but to risk further . . .

He stopped. She stared up at him and he could read her alarm in the pulse beating at the base of her throat, see her confusion in the agitation stirring the lace covering her bodice.

She shifted but, rather than distancing them, the small movement brought her closer. Color crept into her pale cheeks. Her chin angled higher. Her gaze met his.

He wasn't going to steal the kiss she bravely offered.

He had already stolen the unpalatable facts of her marriage to Charles Hoodless without her consent, eavesdropping, but since then had discerned much worse through what he'd observed: the fleeting expression of fear and the unconscious manner with which she rubbed her arms whenever her husband's name was mentioned, as though soothing a bruise.

Small wonder Addie feared a certain type of man.

It made Jack profoundly grateful for Hoodless's death. Because he had the overpowering conviction that if Hoodless were still alive, he would have killed him.

But now, apparently, Addie had embarked on a course of eradicating her apprehension. And what better man, thought Jack, to practice being fearless with than him, the most harmless and negligible of males?

The thought was sadly amusing. He almost wished he could resent her experimentation. But he could not. Having already compromised his integrity by using her in order to serve the debt he owed his men, he found "masculine pride" easily abandoned.

Lord, he admitted ruefully, he would have offered his body, his heart, and his soul to any of her uses. And still he wanted more. But he had at least a shred of decency left. He wasn't going to use his disguise to purloin her kisses . . . Or was that pride speaking?

She was regarding him with puzzlement, a touch of hurt in her amber eyes as she fell back a step and, just that quickly, the moment had passed, and she was turning from him. She wandered away from his side, her hand idly grazing the tops of her paint pots and brushes, lost deep in thought. He watched her move away, torn between regret and relief.

"Jack?" she finally said, her voice tentative.

"Yes?"

"Is there . . . is there anything . . . singular about me?"

Singular? "Everything." His intensity caught her off guard.

She looked up sharply at that, catching her lower lip between her teeth. "Irregular?"

"Why do you ask?" he asked.

"No reason."

"Come. When one makes such inquiries there is generally a reason. You aren't applying for a position as headmistress at some girls' school, are you? Because they shall never hire you. Never."

His teasing revived her sense of humor, albeit in a tremulous form. "Because my behavior is so singular?"

"Behavior? Pish. You have perfect manners. Considering your upbringing."

"Thank you . . . I think."

He waved away her gratitude. "No, Addie. It is your appearance that is singular. Your coloring. Your . . . form." Damn it, he could feel his body clenching again.

"I see." She spoke too quietly.

He tried a different tack, one that would not lead to declaration and admissions. One a fribble would take. "You are quite too singular looking to be entrusted with the likes of girl-pups. They might try emulating your style. I do not think London is prepared for a Season of debutantes wearing that atrocious color of gray. No, no. You'll have to seek other means of satisfying your creditors, should the need arise." He paused and tapped his forehead as if with sudden inspiration. "I know! Have Ted hire out as a housepainter."

"Oh, Jack." Addie laughed. "I'm quite solvent. It's that . . . well . . . I have not consciously put myself forth, but Mr. Lafayette has approached me."

Jack's urbane manner slipped. "Really?" he said. "And who, pray tell, is Mr. Lafayette?"

"I made his acquaintance last week. He is a friend of Gerald's. A photographer. He has a studio off of Prince Street."

Jack didn't say a word. Addie shifted on her feet, blushing profusely. He waited. Only the tiny tick of muscle in his jaw betrayed the effort his silence cost him. What did this man mean to Addie? What did she mean "approached"? All his protective and, sadly, possessive, instincts thundered to life.

"He is a very good photographer." She sounded defensive.

"Doubtless," Jack murmured, tugging on his shirt cuffs and trying not to betray his fervent need to know why this man had the power to make Addie blush. "But what has that to do with you?"

"Other people have had it done. Perfectly respectable people. Jennie Churchhill and Miss Churchhill. There is nothing about his request that is, in and of itself, unsavory." She fidgeted. "Is there?"

Jack left off fussing with his cuffs and frowned. "Forgive my obtuseness, but I haven't the least idea what we are discussing. Have what done? And what request?"

"Mr. Lafayette asked me to pose for a studio portrait. He sells them. To the general population."

Jack could not help his feeling of relief. "I see. And how does Mr. Lafayette's request tie in with your singularity?"

"I am at a loss to explain why he felt free to approach me. Do I . . . do I appear the sort of person who would welcome public attention?"

Good Lord, she sounded guilty! Had Hoodless berated her for some imaginary immodesty? Had her intelligence and exuberance threatened him so much he'd bullied her into questioning her natural vivacity? Damn the man to hell.

"Is there something about me that would excite uninvited comment?" She held her breath.

Jack turned away from her so that she could not see his involuntary snarl. He faced the panels, pretending to be studying them while he collected himself.

"Jack?" Her hand brushed his coat sleeve. He hated her beggarly tone. He cast about for the right tone, the right touch.

"Of course. You are gorgeous, my dear."

Her breath caught and he turned back to see her eyes widened with surprised pleasure.

"You needn't look like a cat with cream, vain creature," he said, plastering a fatuous smile on his face. "You are undoubtedly a pretty wench, Addie, but you can't accept any of the glory for those physical attractions you possess.

"Even I, in all good conscience, must ascribe some credit to my parents for their hand in producing the masterpiece you see standing before you. If you are singular, you must blame your parents."

But though his words had pleased her, they persuaded her.

"Give over, Addie," he said in a far gentler voice. "Any qualities the proletariat chooses to ascribe to you just because you are a rather artful eyeful is their concern, not yours."

He brushed a nonexistent piece of lint from his shoulder. "If they want to think of you as Bathsheba or Saint Agnes there is little you can do to alter their perceptions. And frankly, while I do not know about you, dear lady, I would rather not take any credit for the fevered imaginings of the lower classes."

She finally laughed at that. "Jack, no one could possibly be as much of a snob as you pretend to be."

"No?"

"No," she avowed. "But your point is well taken. I cannot worry about other people's opinion of me, but need only concern myself with what I know to be true about myself. Thank you."

"Is that what I said?" Jack lifted his eyebrows. "Rather ponderous prattle so soon after lunch. I shall have to contrive some sort of penance for being so tiresome. Perhaps I'll forgo my nap. No, no. I'll only disappoint my dinner companions by appearing unrested . . . hm."

"Oh, do stop," Addie pleaded, giggling, "and tell me straight off, ought I to sit for Mr. Lafayette?"

"Become one of the so-called professional beauties?"

"I'm not comfortable with that term."

Jack shrugged. "What does Ted say?"

"Well—"

"Ted thinks that if his little sister agrees to sit for anyone, it should be Ted."

Jack and Addie swung to find Ted standing in the doorway behind them. There was no way to tell how long he had been there. He was leaning slightly on his silver-tipped cane, his eyes sliding lazily from Jack to Addie and back again.

"Cameron." Nodding a greeting in Jack's direction, Ted moved in his deliberate pace into the room.

"Where have you been, Ted?"

"Oh, hither and yon. Actually I was with a French émigré. He was telling me all about Mr. Seurat's Société des Artistes Indépendants. I believe it has some ties with your own enclave, Cameron."

"Really," Jack replied indifferently. He had as much as he could do to keep hundreds of English artists straight. He knew nothing about the French.

"Tell me, are Mr. Morris's anarchists holding a Christmas party this year?" Ted's tone was utterly bland.

"Anarchists?" Jack repeated, uncertain of whether Ted was twitting him.

"Come now," Ted said. "I thought that as one of Mr. Morris's protégés you would have a near-religious dedication to social reform. Isn't it mandatory amongst your little brotherhood?"

Bloody hell, Jack thought, Wheatcroft had never mentioned

that Morris and his ilk were revolutionaries! Wonderful—a career soldier involved with a pack of bloody socialists.

"I have only one master and that is my art," he pronounced.

"Very nice," Ted murmured. "Been reading the *Le Décadent*, have we?"

"Excuse me?"

"Really, my dear chap, if you are to be successful as an . . . artisan, you must learn the cant. *Le Décadent* is a review periodical. The symbolists' forum."

"I wasn't aware you fancied yourself a symbolist." His attempt to turn the conversation worked. Ted's singularly uncommunicative face became even more shuttered.

"Oh, I'm not. I am well and truly society's creature. My fellow artists quite shun me as the *beau monde*'s pet. I paint pretty portraits. Nothing more."

"Self-important snobs!" Addie burst out. "Pack animals, the lot of them! They have more rules and regulations than the governments they seek to overthrow!"

"Thank you for your championship, Addie, however unnecessary. I assure you I do not feel the loss of my peers' company any more than they feel mine. Although I would dearly love to watch Degas work . . . and this new fellow, Rousseau. Someday I must cross the Channel." His eyes narrowed on some envisioned work for a second before his attention returned to Jack. "But you, Cameron. You must be knee-deep in all the intrigues of *avant-garde* aesthetics—moral, social, and artistic."

"As I have said, I have only one muse."

"The muse of woodworking? I hadn't any idea there was such a creature. Who would that be?" There was no mistaking the malicious gleam in his eyes.

"Ted," Addie said. "Leave off teasing Jack."

"Ah! Feeling frightfully protective today, are we, Addie?" Now, undeniably, there was sharp interest in Ted's gaze. "How refreshing," he continued, smiling at his sister, a fond smile that made Jack almost forgive the thousand little rapier needles he'd endured from Ted's tongue. Ted turned back to Jack. "What are you doing here, Cameron?"

"I am here in the capacity of courier. I have come to hand-deliver an invitation to Addie."

"I'd have thought Lady Merritt paid her footmen rather handsomely to fulfill that duty, Jack."

"But Ted, you know I would seize any opportunity to bask in your sister's divine presence." He held Ted's gaze steadily a second before bowing deeply in Addie's direction.

"Really? Well, be careful you don't get sunburn . . . the woman seems to be positively glowing today."

Addie swatted her brother on the arm and then, as if the impulsive act startled her, her eyes widened. "Stop roasting poor Jack, Ted. What do you want?"

"I need you."

Addie lifted her brows questioningly. "What? Tea and cakes? Your pillow hasn't been adequately fluffed?"

"Children, children," Jack scolded.

Ted shifted his weight back and forth on his feet, the simple movement in this incredibly self-contained man conveying a wealth of unease.

"Ted?" Addie asked, suddenly alert.

"Miss Zephrina Drouhin has sent a note. She decided she must see the progress I've made on her portrait. She will be arriving shortly, sans mama, with her usual entourage."

"What entourage?" Jack asked.

"A military one. Miss Drouhin positively exults in the company of Her Majesty's armed forces."

"I see." Addie had gone still. "When?"

Ted pulled a watch from his trouser pocket and glanced at it. "Damn! Within the quarter hour. I am sorry, Ad. She is a presumptuous, spoiled, and willful girl but I cannot yet afford to send her to the devil where she belongs." He sounded positively heated. His jaw had tensed and his entire posture bespoke anger.

Jack was impressed. He'd never seen such an overt display of emotion from Ted.

"It's all right, Ted," Addie said, but Jack noted the forced lightness of her tone.

"I can't have her risk her reputation," Ted said. "Unfortunately your housekeeper has taken another day off and I can't come up with an acceptable chaperone on such short notice."

"It's all right, Ted. Really. This is exactly why you wanted me as your hostess and though I have avoided Miss Drouhin and her friends for the past week, this was inevitable. Indeed, I quite look forward to meeting her. No one could be as awful as you make her out to be."

"Don't be too sure."

"Your Miss Drouhin is not a model then, but a lady?" Jack asked.

"Yes. A young lady."

"Pretty?"

"Fair enough if you like teeny, bright-eyed little pusses with unusually strident dispositions."

"Rich?"

"Very."

"American," Addie offered.

Jack widened his eyes in feigned interest. "I've never met an American *lady*. I admit I didn't know they existed. Mind if I tag along?"

"Oh, yes. Please do," Addie said eagerly.

"Ted?"

"If Addie will have you, I have no objections. But we'd best go now," Ted said and, turning, disappeared into the dark hall.

11

"Nice picture, Phyfe. Like the colors. Pretty."

Young Corporal James Veitch clasped his hands behind his back and rocked on his heels, lip out, brows down, studying a sketch Ted had abandoned against the wall. He reminded Addie of a bulldog: short, stout, and muscular. "Not that I would have such a thing in my house. Not manly enough, what?" His frown deepened. "I say, Phyfe. Do you think you could rig up some sort of sling and have me horse hoisted up here for me portrait?"

Addie, caught off guard by this absurdity, cast a covert glance in his direction. He was a typical example of one of Her Majesty's military officers: self-important and overbearing.

"I doubt it, Corporal," Ted said.

Veitch made a disgruntled sound and resumed his wandering about the studio. "Where the devil—'scuse me, ma'am"—he nodded curtly in Addie's direction—"are the lads and Miss Drouhin? Thought the boys said she was to arrive by two o'clock. It's past three o'clock."

"We all must suffer Beauty's whim," Jack said, giving a refined sniff from where he stood idly swinging his monocle. "Though I must admit, I can't see myself inconveniencing myself for some American girl."

"I'm sure of that," replied Veitch, his gaze traveling disparagingly over Jack's attire: his cobalt blue velvet jacket and buff-colored trousers, the hems turned up at the end, the soft stockette tied in a drooping bow beneath the soft collar of his shirt. In comparison, Veitch, some inches shorter, looked positively scrubbed, from his ruddy cheeks to his pomaded and curling ginger hair to the heavy, carefully trimmed mustache quivering above his thick lips.

"I mean, what's the point? She has so many suitors already, or so I've been told. Why suffer the indignity of losing oneself in the crowd?"

"Apparently, er, sir," Veitch said, "you understand little. It adds to one's consequence to be seen squiring Miss Drouhin about. Tremendously. All the officers vie for her attention. It is the thing to do."

Addie, her nerves fading as her amusement increased, fixed Jack with a disapproving stare. He was being appallingly mischievous at the corporal's expense, baiting the poor, oblivious man like that . . . *Poor man?* When had she last thought of anyone in a red coat as "poor"?

Jack's gaze widened innocently, nearly making her laugh.

Veitch peeked under a cover and Ted sighed loudly. "Please, Corporal. Some of them are still wet."

Guiltily, Veitch fell back and then, in a manner with which Addie was all too familiar, his discomfiture transformed into anger.

"Well, sir. If you expect to paint my picture, you'll just have to find some way to accommodate me . . . and me horse!"

Good heavens, he wasn't still going on about his horse?

"Confound it," he continued. "Managed to get me horse all the way from Bristol to Arabi. Don't see why you can't get old Charger up here." The huff of indignation at the end of the pronouncement rippled his mustache.

"You were in Arabi?" Jack had gone quite still.

"Yes," Veitch said shortly. "There was the small matter of a war going on. But perhaps you hadn't heard, being otherwise occupied with your paints!"

"Jack isn't a painter," Ted said.

"Well, whatever bloody—'scuse me again, ma'am—however way he wastes his time." He glowered at Jack, who contrived to look confused rather than insulted. Finding no joy there, Veitch looked around and caught sight of Addie.

Immediately, she wished she'd kept her gaze discreetly lowered. The last thing she wanted was to attract a soldier's attention. Any kind of attention. She fixed her gaze on her lap, but too late. Veitch stomped toward her.

"Don't see how I can have my portrait done without Charger. At least, not a proper military portrait. Don't you agree, ma'am?"

Addie glanced up. The corporal loomed above her, feet spread wide, barrel chest swollen, fists set on his hips. He stared down on her, willing her compliance. He would not leave her alone until she yielded. He would stand there for hours just staring at her with that horrible curl to his lips, knowing eventually she must forfeit. Her heart would race and her skin would grow damp and her vision—she swallowed hard, her hands clenched together on her lap.

"Well, ma'am?" His voice boomed down from above her bowed head.

Numbly, she felt herself nod in acquiescence.

"See?" exclaimed Veitch. Having won, he turned and stomped back toward Ted. "Even your sister agrees, Phyfe!"

"Yes," she heard Ted say in an odd voice. "I see."

"Man learns to trust his horse," he told her confidingly, happy now that he'd won. "His life often depends on his steed's courage, heart. Indeed, a man's fate is in his horse's . . . his horse's—"

"—hands?" Jack whispered in her ear. She hadn't noticed his

approach. She'd been too caught up in Veitch's aggression. Her shoulders, held so tightly they'd begun to hurt, relaxed. "I lay you odds, here and now, he will say 'hands.'"

"Do continue, Corporal," Jack said more loudly as he stepped from behind her chair, polishing the nails of one hand on a brilliant silk kerchief.

The corporal looked him over contemptuously.

"A man's fate is in his horse's hands, sir."

Jack turned his head slowly and met her eye. The unholy glee in them teased her own sense of humor back from hiding.

"Any campaigner would say the same," Corporal Veitch went on. "Not that you'd know much about that."

"About campaigns?" Jack asked. "I beg to differ, sir, but I have been most arduously involved in the campaign to free women from the oppression of the bustle. In fact, we are having a meeting on Saturday night. Men Against Bustles. If you would care to subscribe—"

"Good God!" exploded Veitch.

"Indeed! My sentiments exactly! All those contraptions enslaving our sisters and mothers and—"

"Are you mocking those of us who have fought to liberate real slaves?" sputtered Veitch and, without waiting for an answer, went on. "I have had the honor of serving with men who were willing to lay down their lives to free these black pagans from the chains that bind them. Real chains. Not some . . . some . . . fashion thingy!" He puffed out his chest. "Real men, sir! Men sworn to the service of bringing order to chaos and morality to heathen ignorance.

"We keep the world a decent place. And in our ceaseless efforts there are only a few things a man can depend on. God, the Queen, his fellow officers, and his horse. An officer needs a good mount," he finished triumphantly.

There was a moment of stunned silence during which Addie tried valiantly to keep her lips still though they quivered with the effort. And then, quite clearly, Jack said, "Hell, I know I'm always on the lookout for a good mount."

It took a few seconds for Veitch to comprehend Jack's outrageous innuendo and when he did, he turned a magnificent scarlet. In a trice, he closed the distance between Jack and himself, grabbing Jack's orchid-colored lapel and hauling him toward his outthrust face. Or rather, he tried to haul him. Jack was apparently a good deal heavier than he looked.

So, Veitch tried shaking him; Jack didn't shake.

Almost casually, Jack wrapped his fingers around Veitch's wrist. The corporal's face expressed a mixture of incredulity and discomfort, but he was not about to be shown up by a mere artist. He was a soldier, after all.

He raised his free hand, curling his fingers into a fist—

"Corporal!" Without thinking, Addie bolted to her feet and thrust herself between the two men and, splaying her hand flat against Veitch's chest, pushed him away. "I do not know what has precipitated your current behavior," she lied. "But please, sir! Unhand Mr. Cameron."

Utterly flustered by her intervention, Veitch dropped his hold of Jack's lapel. Slowly, Jack released the corporal's wrist.

"How charmin' of you to be concerned for my safety, Addie," Jack drawled, his burning blue gaze fixed on Veitch's face.

"Stop it, Jack," she said tightly. The slender artisan didn't have any idea how close he had come to getting hurt. Had he ever even felt a hand raised to him in anger? Did he know the physical pain of having been beaten? The guilt of having it happen? She didn't think so and, by the Lord, she didn't ever want him to know.

It had all happened so quickly that Ted was still on the other side of the room, his lame leg making speed impossible. He was watching her intently, his worry and frustration evident by the dull flush rising in his cheeks.

Veitch stepped back and Addie snatched her hand away from him as if burned.

"Beg pardon, ma'am." He bowed. "This person made a certain suggestive remark. That he did so in the presence of a lady merely compounds the offense. But I would not offend you by giving him his due here. I will seek a more suitable place and time for that."

"I am sure you misunderstood Mr. Cameron's statement." Her words, though soft, were nonetheless clear and firm, even though she was shivering as she said them.

"I'm not," Ted said. "Sure you misunderstood Jack, that is."

"You are not helping, Ted," Addie ground out angrily.

"Really, old man," Jack said to Veitch in his most officious tone. "I was only trying to join into the *esprit de corps*. You know, all us fellows with all our mounts."

"Worse and worse," muttered Ted, shaking his head sadly.

Veitch lurched a step in Jack's direction and Addie slipped between them again, her back against Jack's chest.

"Mr. Cameron is a guest in my home, Corporal," she said. "You are my brother's potential customer. I would urge both of you to remember your respective positions."

Veitch's lips flattened with distaste at her boldness. She didn't care.

"Bravo," Jack whispered, his breath warm in her ear.

Without another word, Veitch turned on his heels and stalked from the room.

"Well, there goes a customer," Ted said.

———— ◆ ————

Not one day into London and already he was punching holes in his masquerade. Once again his emotions were running riot, ruling his actions. The damnable part of it was that, given the same choices, he didn't know if he'd do any differently.

He'd been unfazed by that preening ass Veitch's contempt but when the great huffing bore had taken a stance looming over Addie and thundering in her ear, his disinterest had evaporated. Her face had paled and her gaze had raced, like a trapped thing, about the room.

He shouldn't have interfered. Veitch was a member of the Black Dragoons. While he was low enough in rank to have scant dealings with troop deployment and strategy planning sessions, he might have known something. Some snippet of conversation, some story, which he might have been induced to relate in order to feed his vanity.

Jack shook his head at his folly. Addie's shoulders were still pressed against his chest, her form marking him as clearly as a firebrand. He wanted to surround her with his arms and pull her tighter against him. It was an effort just to keep his hands by his side.

She had stood up for him. She had spent nearly an hour staring at her hands and mumbling words at her lap, but when she had thought he was in danger, she hadn't hesitated to interfere. His heart beat thickly in an inextricable rhythm of guilt and pleasure.

"I'm sorry, Ted." She stepped away from Jack and his hand lifted without conscious volition, as if to plead for her return. He let it drop at once. Of course.

"Makes no difference. Besides, I really can't have a horse stomping around up here, leaving road apples on the carpet and eating the wax fruit."

Addie dimpled. "But, Ted, you always promised me a pet."

"Sorry. Can't have it. Charger stays in the stables. Along with his master, I'll warrant. We'll just have to be content with Jackie here." He turned an innocent smile on Jack.

"Jackie is, of course, honored to oblige," Jack replied placidly.

Finding no joy to be had teasing Jack, Ted sighed. "Where the deuce my real client is, I would dearly love to know."

"Why, we're here, Mr. Phyfe," an amused voice announced.

Miss Zephrina Drouhin knew how to make an entrance, Jack would grant her that. Tiny, laughing, absolutely self-confident, the golden, green-eyed beauty entered the studio with the regal certitude of a newly named princess. She twirled about, motioning the small coterie of guardsmen huddling in the doorway with a finger.

Jack froze, scanning the faces of Miss Drouhin's red-coated attendants. Some of these men might well be on his list: John Hopper, Miles Neyron, Paul Sherville, William Lobb. They alone had had the opportunity and authority to "arrange" for troops' delays, arrivals, and deployment.

"Do come in, gentlemen," Miss Drouhin was saying, "I am not sure Mr. Phyfe has adequate seating but perhaps his artistic eye can arrange you in a seemly fashion about his studio. What say you, Mr. Phyfe, can you find uses for my friends?"

Ted watched her blandly, but Jack could have sworn there was a small sneer to his lips as he inclined his head in her direction and bowed.

"I would very much like to tell your friends where to go," he said smoothly. Miss Drouhin frowned, apparently not sure what to make of his words. He went on, "How kind of you to appear at my poor abode. Finally."

Zephrina smiled and dropped her mantle to the floor. One of her soldiers leapt forward to retrieve it and draped it over his arm. She took no notice, her bright gaze on Ted. "Not angry with me, are you, Mr. Phyfe? I was under the impression that the princely sum your portraits command might go far toward compensating for a few minor inconveniences."

"My inconveniences are, of course, included in the price. My sister's, however, are not."

"Your sister?" With an expression of childlike inquisitiveness, Miss Drouhin twirled about, her gaze lighting with interest on first Jack and then Addie.

Jack glanced over to gauge Addie's reaction to the American girl. She wasn't looking at Zephrina at all. Her face was pale, and her eyes were black and wide with fear as she stared at the doorway and the man who stood in it.

12

She'd known she would see him again. It was inevitable. But nothing could have prepared her for the wave of loathing and fear that rooted her to the ground, leaving her slack-jawed and trembling. Paul Sherville had been the sole member of Charles's odious companions to not only have known about Charles's treatment of her but to have sanctioned it, sniggering at impromptu spectacles of her humiliation. How many times had he goaded Charles to "take his wife in hand"?

Black-haired and handsome, barrel-chested and hirsute, he strode forward and captured her unresisting hand. He raised it to his mouth and pressed cold, damp lips to her knuckles.

She recoiled, trying to tug free of his grip. He smiled, retaining his hold. The room tilted and her vision telescoped. The background drone of the polite introductions dwindled to an insectile buzzing, leaving her alone in a darkening circle with him.

Abruptly, he released her hand. She snatched it away, burying it like a bruised thing in her skirts.

"Addie," he said, "how enchanting to see you again."

She took an involuntary step backward, colliding into Jack. He caught her shoulders, gently steadying them before releasing her, and at once her sense of isolation faded. Behind her, his chest felt solid, unexpectedly hard, a warm wall against which she could stand.

She was not alone. She was in a room full of people, two of whom were dear to her. This was her home now, hers, not Charles's . . . not anymore. Paul Sherville was here at her sufferance.

"Major," she acknowledged him, finally finding her voice.

His eyes narrowed. "I am delighted to see you have come out of mourning early, Addie. Charles would not have wanted you to pine."

She could not believe the sheer audacity of the man!

"My sister has been kind enough to end her public mourning prematurely as a great favor to me," Ted said.

"Ah, yes! So I see." Sherville cast a long, appraising look over her before turning and looking around. "You've quite refashioned the place, haven't you, Addie? Had electric lighting installed, I see." He gestured to the new wrought-iron heaters. "And central heating. New paint, new windows. And you've turned the entire floor into your brother's studio. Such munificence! Why, the place bears hardly any resemblance to the house to which Charles brought his blushing bride."

She stared at him, transfixed by his brazenness.

"But then I suppose," he paused, looking at her in mock concern, "it would be pointless to try to maintain the place as a shrine. Besides, I'm absolutely certain you have memories of dear Charles that no amount of paint or plaster can ever erase or cover. Ever."

He was baiting her, the same way he'd baited her when Charles was alive, the same innuendo and suggestion, the cruel gibe couched in casual words. How Charles had laughed.

"No. But thank God she *can* cover up his more hideous decorating blunders. I only got a glimpse of some of what had been here and it positively made me shudder. One can only stand so much oxblood," Jack said from behind her.

Sherville, unexpectedly thwarted in his game, scowled at this interruption. He turned his full attention on Jack. A new frisson of trepidation shivered through her. Sherville would make crow's bait of Jack.

Whatever Sherville saw, it was something unexpected. He was staring hard at Jack, like a man who was trying to see through a London fog to a street post.

"Have we had the pleasure?" he asked, frowning.

"If we've had any pleasure, I certainly don't remember it," Jack said, stepping around Addie and languidly fanning his face with his fingertips.

Ted caught back the beginnings of a laugh and Miss Drouhin covered a smile with her hand. The officers in the door sputtered.

"But then again," Jack continued saucily, "mayhap it wasn't that pleasurable?"

"Jack—" Addie hissed.

She heard Sherville's teeth click together as his huge hands curled into fists at his side. Jack mustn't make this man an enemy. Sherville would not react like Corporal Veitch. No, he would bide his time, wait until Jack was unprepared and alone, before striking.

She could see Sherville's rage in the set of his jaw, the dull brick-red suffusing his bronzed cheeks. She had to stop this.

"Major Sherville!" Her voice cracked with urgency. From the corner of her eye she saw Ted move forward, his haste revealing the limp he always so carefully masked. "Major Sherville."

"What?" Sherville snarled, glowering down at her.

Time seemed to slow. She was aware of each person in the room, each nuance. She heard the younger officers' concerned murmurs, saw Miss Drouhin catching Ted's arm as he limped past her. And all the while Jack stood in that absurd, nonchalant pose. Smiling.

"Mr. Cameron is a guest in my house," she heard herself say.

"Well, your guest, Mrs. Hoodless, is about to be taught a few lessons in decency."

"Again?" Ted said. "Really, Jack, we will have to see about getting you lessons in deportment. You seem to have a knack for upsetting people."

Both Jack and Sherville ignored Ted.

"And you are going to give them to me?" Jack's dark brows rose. Only the nearly imperceptible quiver in his hand betrayed that he might recognize the danger into which he had stepped; she had to admire that. Otherwise, no one would guess he felt any trepidation at all. "La! How ambitious of you, Major."

"You—"

"No!" Addie cried out. "You will not give anyone any lessons in my home, Major! Mr. Cameron is my guest and I find him witty and amusing and—"

"Why, thank you, Addie," Jack cut in pleasantly.

"For once, just shut up, Jack," Ted said.

Jack lifted his brows but shrugged apologetically.

She was breathing too fast. Her pulse was pounding in her temples. But it had worked. She had drawn Sherville's attention away from Jack.

He was staring at her as though she had just sprouted wings. His cruel nature had never been more apparent. He looked like he wanted to strike her.

"My." He leaned forward, pitching his voice so only she could hear him. "You sounded quite fierce there for a minute, Addie. Quite unlike Charles's timid little bride. She would never have raised her voice to me. I wonder what has inspired this transformation?"

Then he straightened, tugging at his uniform jacket. "Your wish is, of course," he said loudly, glancing at the others, "my command.

"Forgive my overly zealous attempt to defend your finer feelings. I only sought to serve the memory of your husband, my dear friend. In his memory, I promise to take every care of you . . . just as he would have done."

The junior officers relaxed. For a minute it must have seemed as though their pedagogue was about to tumble from his pedestal by committing the grave social transgression of bringing scandal to the home of a grieving officer's widow. This was more like it.

It was, indeed, a pretty sort of apology, if one didn't recognize the threat it hid.

"Might I prevail upon you gentlemen to await me in the park?" Miss Drouhin suddenly asked. Having let go of Ted's arm, she'd moved to the doorway and stood now, her yellow dress the bright center of an encircling group of uniformed men, a tiny buttercup in a field of red poppies.

"I rather fancy a ride later this afternoon," she continued, her easy tone implying that she had seen nothing untoward. "Something spirited. None of your soft English hacks. Might one of you kind gentlemen arrange it? Perhaps you, Major Sherville?"

He tilted his head in gracious acquiescence. "Of course, Miss Drouhin."

"A spirited horse it shall be, Miss Drouhin," another man chimed in.

"Jolly good, Miss Drouhin."

"Phyfe." Sherville turned to Ted. "I find I rather fancy the notion of my own visage glaring down at me from above the drawing room mantel. I shall make arrangements for an interview," he said.

"What a coup for you, Ted!" Jack crowed.

Ted shot Jack a lethal glance before returning his gaze to Sherville. "I hesitate to be indelicate, Major, but since we are all friends here . . .

I am terrifically overpaid for my work and what with Army pay and all, do you think you can . . . I mean . . ." His apologetic shrug lacked sincerity.

Sherville's face flooded with color.

A young lieutenant snorted. "Sherville can afford a dozen of your dabs, fellow! Found Ali Baba's mine in Arabi or so the rumors say. What of it, Major? Find the thieves' cavern, did you?"

Another young officer shook his head vigorously. "That's not it. I heard he saved some heathen prince's life and was rewarded with the bastard's weight in gold and gems."

"What's the truth of it then?" a third asked.

"What did you do, Sherville," one of them asked, "save some heathen prince or other?"

Sherville pursed his lips smugly. "I wouldn't want to bore the ladies with the tale."

"How modest," Ted murmured dryly.

Miss Drouhin tossed her head, her pale curls bobbing like newly minted guineas. "Please, Major. You'll tell me, won't you? I would purely love to hear a story of manly courage and stoutheartedness." Her long-lashed eyes fluttered in Ted's direction.

"I shall attempt to entertain you on our ride, Miss Drouhin." Without asking her permission, Sherville regained Addie's hand but this time she did not give him the pleasure of trying to pull away.

"I am sure we will meet again, ma'am. I look forward to it more than I can possibly say." He bowed low at the waist. The other men had moved into the hallway with Miss Drouhin, making plans to meet later. Jack had retreated a few feet away and was lounging against a table, but Addie sensed that for all his vagueness, he was attending every word Sherville uttered.

"I must say, my dear," Sherville said, "I am impressed with the extent of your renovations here. Very impressed. Charles must have left you quite substantial means to provide for yourself. Just

be careful you don't overdraw on the income from his . . . invest-
ments." He pronounced each word carefully, giving them odd
added emphasis.

Addie frowned in bewilderment.

Charles hadn't left her anything but gambling debts. She'd
paid them off with moneys from her own inheritance. Her present
comfortable circumstances were solely the result of the inheritance
left her by her grandfather.

"Is that really any of your concern, Sherville?" Ted said.

"Oh, yes. As Charles's friend, I am obliged to make his widow
my concern. His death quite ties us together."

And without waiting for an answer, he left, Jack's blue eyes
marking his exit.

13

Addie repositioned the pot of vermilion paint, her expression thoughtful. Jack had left a quarter hour earlier with Zephrina Drouhin. The petite American girl had prevailed upon him to escort her to the park. Not that he'd been too hard to convince.

Through the entire sitting, he'd put himself out to entertain Miss Drouhin. And heavens, Miss Drouhin had certainly been charmed by his droll wit. Judging by the frequency of her giggles, one would have thought Jack was Mr. Wilde himself.

Paul Sherville hadn't been nearly as amused.

The confrontation with her husband's boon companion had left Addie drained until slowly a fragile sense of astonished gratification had replaced her numbness. She'd actually faced the specter of her husband in the guise of Paul Sherville and she had done so without backing down or running away.

It had been years since she had felt so . . . *effectual.* For months, she had been telling herself that Charles's old cronies no longer had any power over her but today, for the first time, she not only knew they could not hurt her, she believed it.

She could ignore Paul Sherville. She could ignore his jeers and barbed asides and veiled threats. If he proved too much a nuisance, she would publically snub him and damn the scandal. For Charles's parents' sake, she had bowed to society's dictates and worn these hypocritical widow's weeds. No more. She would accept the consequences of her behavior and bear them gladly.

Jack Cameron, on the other hand, would have to beware the next time he met Paul Sherville—or any of Sherville's friends. Jack had made Paul look like a fool and Paul would make sure Jack paid for that entertainment. Paul always made sure people paid. Nothing, and no one, protected Jack from him. His only hope was to avoid Sherville.

Addie frowned.

Jack had come to mean a great deal to her. From the day they'd met, she'd felt an affinity with him, had enjoyed his company, and felt herself relax in his undemanding presence. But lately she'd realized she felt more for him than friendship.

Jack Cameron was physically attractive to her. She wanted to finish what she'd begun in the studio earlier that day. She wanted Jack to kiss her. Truly wanted him to do so, not merely decided she would test her ability to respond to a man's touch. She would not fool herself in this: curiosity did not motivate her. Desire did.

The thought surprised her. She had not felt like this in years. Not since those first days of her marriage when she'd anticipated her husband's arrival with a healthy, pleasurable curiosity. Pleasure had not been a key ingredient in Charles's lovemaking, but neither had pain. Indeed, Charles had set about the business of consummation with prosaic industry. While two nights of marriage had been dissatisfying, they had not been terrifying.

And afterward, thank God, he had seemed to consider the withholding of his marital attentions to be a form of punishment. He'd never appreciated that emotional castration—the form of hurt Charles had specialized in—had been a more than adequate deterrent to sexual interest.

So, while the mysteries of the marriage bed were no mysteries, the mysteries of passion were. Now, unbelievably, this pale dandy had reawakened her desire.

Jack. The sensations he awoke in her were nearly painful in their incipient stirrings. Like being numbed by the cold and then sitting too close to the fire—

"Addie, do stop disarranging my paints," Ted said.

She came round with a start, her cheeks growing hot. "Sorry."

"You're flushed, Addie," Ted said, studying her with concern. "Don't worry. I'll make certain Miss Drouhin leaves her hounds at the door from now on."

Dear Ted. He had been prepared to aid Jack, in spite of his physical impairment.

"Thank you."

"It will be my pleasure. Such hulking creatures tend to block the light, anyway."

"I mean thank you for endeavoring to aid Jack."

"'Aid Jack'?" Ted repeated uncertainly.

"Yes." Addie answered his bewilderment with her own. "When Major Sherville looked about to assault him."

The confusion evaporated from Ted's expression. "I see." He sounded amused. "I hate to admit this, Ad, but rescuing your tame cabinetmaker was the furthest thing from my intentions. It was you I was concerned about. I didn't want you to witness anything unpleasant. I feared things might become, well, to be frank, a trifle grisly."

Addie scowled, disappointed and angry. "You mean that if I had not been there you would have simply stood by and let Paul Sherville batter Jack?"

"Probably not," Ted allowed. "Regardless of her self-professed taste for brutality, I would still be loath for Miss Drouhin to witness any fisticuffs in my studio. Bad for business. Besides, she'd enjoy it far too much."

"I refuse to believe you would not aid Jack should the need arise."

"Did I say that?" Ted asked blandly. "How perfidious of me."

"Oh!" Addie sputtered. "I thought you liked Jack."

"He's an enigma, our Scottish friend. I admit I like a good puzzle."

Addie continued as though Ted hadn't spoken. "He is not so different from you, Ted. He is as absurd and mild-mannered and as imperturbable."

The smile that had been hovering around Ted's mouth faded. "Tell me, Addie, what would you do were you to discover that Jack was capable of great passion, say, even of rage?"

"Jack? In a rage?" Addie chuckled. "I seriously doubt whether Jack has ever even been in a snit."

"Yes, Addie," Ted said, "but what if you discovered that there was a point he could be pushed past, albeit with much concentrated effort, where he would be capable of . . . violence?"

She couldn't really give his question the consideration he obviously wanted her to; it was too patently absurd.

"I should have to swear off men entirely, I suppose," she replied glibly. "Become a papist and take the veil. I rather like the thought of me in one of those fetching little habits, drifting through the cloisters—"

"Really, Addie," Ted broke in. "I am serious."

For some reason Ted's insistence distressed her. She did not like conjecturing about some hypothetical potential of brutality in Jack's character.

"As serious as you are about Miss Drouhin?" she asked, seeking to change the subject.

Her impulsive question met its mark. "Miss Drouhin?"

"Yes. Miss Zephrina Drouhin. The American heiress that

was perched on that chair fifteen minutes ago. You know, blonde, petite . . . inclined to giggle." She couldn't refrain from adding the last, even though she knew it to be catty. But the way she had commandeered Jack still rankled.

"I seem to recall her, yes."

"Seeing how her face is even now staring at you from that canvas, I'm glad."

"Serious about her? I don't know what you mean and why ever are you interested in her anyway?"

"I'm just interested, is all. I'm a scientifically minded sort of woman. All manner of combustibles intrigue me. And the atmosphere in here when you two share the same air is decidedly incendiary."

Ted did not respond.

"Come on, Teddy. You and I have never stood on ceremony. What is it with that girl? I swear, I have never seen a female make such a concentrated effort to annoy someone as Miss Drouhin does you."

"A right little bitch, isn't she?" Ted asked, giving up trying to evade her questions.

Addie tried to call up a severe expression of reprimand. She failed. "Well," she conceded, "yes. Why does she act like that?"

"The truth?"

"The truth."

"I believe Miss Drouhin fancies herself in love with me."

Addie stared, open mouthed, at her older brother. "Oh, my."

"Really, Addie, for the sake of family pride and my own finer feelings, you should at least try to feign a certain understanding of the poor girl's fascination." Ted let slip a short laugh. "It isn't as if she's particularly happy about it."

She gave an apologetic smile. Ted was undeniably handsome but she took his good looks for granted.

"Why isn't she happy about it?"

Ted leaned against the worktable, clearly amused. "Miss Drouhin considers herself a 'real tough American.' A forthright, energetic, and 'bald-faced'—her term, believe me—'gal.' She has told me she plans to acquire a similarly naked-faced husband."

"Yes?"

"Unfortunately Daddy Drouhin has different ideas. Seems the only thing in the world Daddy ever really wanted was a coronet. All of his hard work, all his prospecting, the years he and Zephrina's mother roamed and searched and picked their way from mining town to mining town and finally to that spectacular silver strike in the American west, means nothing if he can't see his blood mixed with European aristocracy."

"Oh my heavens," Addie breathed. She could feel the laughter welling up. "Tell me you're not serious."

Ted's eyes twinkled. "'Tis true. So, being a dutiful, if more than slightly resentful, daughter, Zephrina agreed to spend two Seasons in London. That's all Daddy Drouhin asked of his beloved daughter. Just to give our marquis and earls and dukes the same chance she'd give a cowpuncher."

Addie laughed outright this time. "What conceit!"

"Indeed. But such honesty! She's already told her father she can find nothing admirable about any of England's 'scrawny, lily-white idlers.' In fact, she has told me the only men who bear even a remote resemblance to the 'real' men of her American west are our soldiers. Ergo her entourage."

"She's a fool," Addie said.

"Have pity, Addie. Here she is, an avowed despiser of our effete aristocrats and she finds herself attracted to the quintessential example of what must, in her vocabulary, be exhausted European degeneracy."

"If she is so attracted to you, why the constant derision?"

"She's punishing me for being unworthy of her healthy affections."

"A fool," Addie reiterated. "And I should refuse to continue her portrait if I were you."

"Oh, she makes herself a great deal more unhappy than she makes me. Besides, I can use the money and the publicity."

She knew her sibling too well. There was more to it than that. She just wasn't sure what.

"And how do you feel about her? Are you attracted to her?" Addie asked casually.

"I should say so," he replied without hesitation. "In a purely . . . noncerebral way. What man wouldn't be?"

The sudden blatant reminder of Ted's sexuality brought Addie up short. She'd known about his past mistresses. It had been an open secret that his previous model had captured more than his aesthetic attention. But he had never openly discussed anything about that facet of his life with her. His easy tone represented a new phase in their relationship, one in which he was offering her an unprecedented glimpse into the masculine psyche.

And into Jack.

"Do you think . . . Jack finds Miss Drouhin, ah, attractive?"

The corner of Ted's mouth quirked. "I wouldn't say that Jack finds Miss Drouhin all that attractive, no."

"But you just said that any red-blooded man would."

Ted's answer was a noncommittal shrug.

Frustrated, Addie wandered about the room, squinting at a canvas here, adjusting the velvet covering of a painting there. "Ted?" she said slowly, without turning around. She could feel herself blushing.

"Yes?"

"Do you think—Do you think that Jack is . . . well, is interested in females?"

"Jack? Oh, yes. I think Jack likes women very much," he answered blandly.

Addie frowned in consternation. He wasn't going to let this be easy. "I mean . . . do you think he is interested in females in a . . . 'noncerebral way'?"

"Oh!" The taken-aback sound was a little too prompt and Addie had the lowering suspicion that her older brother was laughing at her, but her cheeks were so enflamed with heat now, she did not dare turn to face him and open herself to more of his teasing.

"Well, now. Let me see. I would have to ponder that!"

Addie tried to hold back a frustrated growl.

"Hm," he murmured, his face screwed up in hyperbolized concentration. "Hm. Is Jack Cameron interested in females in an intimate sense? Hm."

She waited, breathless, his answer meaning more to her than she would have thought possible. "Yes?" she finally blurted out. "Is he?"

"I really don't know, Addie," he finally said in an infuriatingly light voice. "Why don't you find out?"

14

I was just a trifle late for the dinner party," Addie said, then, meeting Jack's incredulous gaze, amended, "Well, for me it was a trifle late."

Jack arched his brows. "What, pray tell, is very late for you?"

"After dessert," Addie replied and Jack laughed. She tucked her arm companionably through his and felt him stiffen slightly before relaxing and allowing her to lead the way to the far end of the Merritts' walled garden.

Inside the townhouse Lady Merritt's distinctive whoop of victory could be heard.

"She and Gerald must have recouped some of the points they lost," Addie said.

"She doesn't like losing," Jack replied.

"That's why she insisted Gerald be her partner against Ted and Mrs. Morrison. Ted is, if possible, an even worse whist player than I."

"Ah. I see. I was wondering why she all but shoved us out the door in the middle of the night."

"Middle?" Addie asked. "Jack, it's barely eight o'clock. Don't try to tell me you're now keeping monastic hours."

"Oh, I assure you, I am quite worthy of a monk's cowl," he said, his voice deepening with odd emphasis. "And while it isn't, perhaps, the middle of the night, it's cold and dark."

Addie looked up at the heavens, surprised by his querulous tone. Above, the sky had turned indigo, spangled over with a million stars. The moon, nearly full, spread a thin veil of milky illumination over the garden. She did not feel in the least bit cold, as the shawl she'd slipped about her shoulders kept her more than adequately warm.

"And that paltry excuse for sending us out here," Jack sniffed, "'November is when the garden is most interesting.' Fustian. She simply wanted us gone. I see evidence of nothing here but her gardener's lack of industry," he said. "Those trees want pruning."

As usual of late whenever they chanced to be alone together, Jack's posing became at once more exaggerated and more obviously a mask. He kept peering around through a quizzing glass, his gaze here and there, everywhere but on her.

They reached the end of the garden, the brick wall covered with holly. A small marble bench stood close against it and without waiting for his invitation, Addie sat down.

He stood by, carefully inspecting the holly, the wall, the bare pear tree, everything but her.

"Jack," she said. "Do sit down or I will suspect that you don't have a proper appreciation of my company. It is lovely, isn't it?"

"Lovely."

"I agree with Lady Merritt, though we might not share the same reasons. Nothing is as fantastical as a winter garden in moonlight."

"I would have supposed you'd preferred autumn with its riot of colors."

She shook her head emphatically and seeing his quizzical glance, continued, "Oh, autumn is very nice with its rich palette. But what the moonlight robs of color, it returns in subtlety and texture." She touched the dark, glossy leaves of the overhanging holly. "There is something about a graphite landscape, the feathered silver on the lawn, the impenetrable blackness of deep shadow, that is mysterious and evocative. Color can too easily hide the essential nature of a thing, its basic structure, its form."

She cocked her head, regarding him closely. "Like you, Jack," she murmured. "What does all that color conceal about you?"

He speared her with a sharp glance, so rapidly come and gone that if she hadn't been studying his face she would have missed it, before a lazy smile spread over his lips. "La, Addie. I am afraid that without my 'color,' as you so quaintly put it, I am merely a sketchbook scribble."

"I doubt that."

"And I appreciate your doubt. Really, I do."

He'd done it again, diverted her questioning. "Please, don't stand there towering over me, Jack," she said, hearing the frustration in her voice. "Be seated."

He lowered himself to balance on the edge of the marble slab. "What can I do for you?"

His head snapped around. "Ma'am?"

"Please. I have asked you so many times to use my given name. It's not that difficult to pronounce. I'm certain I've heard you say it once or twice. It's a friendly sort of gesture and one you seem reluctant to adopt. Each time I think we are friends, you . . ."

"I what?"

"You draw away from me," she said, embarrassed but determined to speak.

"I am sure you are mistaken." He looked at her, a darkness far deeper than the night in his eyes. "I feel quite . . . friendly."

His reassurance frustrated more than reassured her, but she

did not see what more she could say so she returned instead to the subject at hand.

"Very well," she said. "How can I help? Who would you like to meet? I have some rather exalted family connections, but no more lofty than your own."

"My own?"

"Lord and Lady Merritt. They are received by the 'best' people. I'm afraid my usefulness to you would be better served in a different capacity."

"How so?"

"Well, not to put too fine a point on it, while the Merritts are received by the best, I am received by the worst."

He feigned shock, drawing away, his hand to his chest. "In what manner 'worst'?"

She shrugged, enjoying herself. "Oh, artists and their ilk are invariably 'worst.' It is part of their mystique. Even if they don't engage in reprehensible and degenerate behavior—which I hesitate to confide, most of them do not—they would still claim to. They have their reputations to consider."

He laughed and she rocked back on the bench, catching her knee in her interlaced fingers, enjoying herself immensely. "So, whom among them would you like to know?"

The smile stayed on his lips, but the pleasure died from it, leaving it a hollow approximation of enjoyment. She struggled to understand what had happened.

"Oh, I don't think you need bother introducing me to any particular persons," he said. "I am content to fraternize with the artists in your brother's studio."

"Artists don't frequent my brother's studio. And certainly not members of Mr. Morris's lot. They are far too political for my brother. He's an artist, not a revolutionary." She narrowed her eyes on Jack. "In fact, as one of his acolytes, why aren't you more political?"

Jack lifted his head. "My father was a soldier, Addie. He might not approve of what I am doing now"—he spoke this with a strained sort of guilt—"in fact, I know he would not, but I heartily approved of what he was and who he was, and that was a soldier who served his country. I would not dishonor his memory by preaching anarchy."

"A soldier." She'd almost forgotten.

"Yes."

Poor Jack. Pity welled up inside of her. No doubt Jack had failed his father's expectations. "It must have been a difficult relationship," she said sympathetically, "he being a soldier and you being of an artistic nature."

"Not at all."

She glanced at him in surprise.

"He was a fine parent. An exceptional and loving father."

A tingle of apprehension pricked the edges of Addie's consciousness. She shook it off. "Well, be that as it may, you'll find no other artists in Ted's atelier. Except Gerry."

Jack plucked a dried, brown leaf from the ground and began methodically shredding the papery tissue between the tougher veins. "Perhaps," he said, his attention focused on his hands, "this Season, I should be content to watch your brother's work and meet what society comes through his doors—and Lady Merritt's."

Addie frowned. "Society, as far as my brother's Season is concerned, will apparently be limited to Miss Zephrina Drouhin and her"—she bit off the word she had been about to use—"officers."

"Officers can have excellent connections. Only witness my father," he said, grinning.

She smiled at his foolishness. There, he'd done it again. He'd teased her out of her dark musings, made her look beyond herself. He clearly cared for her in some manner, even if it was no more than a fraternal affection. The problem was, she didn't want another brother.

She shifted irritably on the bench. Her shawl caught on the holly vines and was dragged from her shoulder. She shivered in the sudden cold.

At once, Jack shrugged out of his coat and carefully set it about her shoulders. "See? I told you it was cold."

She closed her eyes. She could smell him on the cloth, the tang of his sandalwood soap mixed with the heady male scent that was so uniquely his own. She pulled the jacket closed, relishing the feeling of his captured heat enveloping her body.

He lifted the soft velvet collar up around her neck. The backs of his fingers grazed her throat. Electricity danced beneath his touch.

Drowsily, her lids drifted open. His face was inches from hers, the blue of his eyes cobalt in the moonlit garden, his fair hair gleaming like platinum. His hands stilled then as, slowly, his fingertips skated with exquisite delicacy along the line of her throat, tracing her jawline and tilting her unresisting chin.

She could see the quiver of his nostrils as he took in her own scent, see his black pupils dilate, his lips open a feather's thickness, feel the warm exhalation of his breath on her own suddenly swollen-feeling lips.

She leaned toward him and their lips met. It was sweet. So sweet. A glissade of firm warmth as his lips touched and clung to hers. His hands slipped beneath her heavy coil of hair to cup the back of her head. His thumbs bracketed her jaw, levering her head gently up to his.

Soft. Tender. She kissed him back, pressing her mouth more firmly to his. Her hands slid between them and crept up his chest. Beneath his shirt, his body was hot and tense and hard, his heart beating thickly beneath her palm. His kiss deepened and sighed with pleasure.

At once, his hands dropped and he backed away from her. "Jesus!" The word, though whispered, exploded from him.

"Jack? Jack, what is it? What have I done?"

"You?" He threw his head back. His teeth ground together. "Rather ask me what I have done. No. I beg you, don't. You have done nothing."

"But, why—"

He leapt to his feet and loomed above her, tall and ramrod straight. He took a deep breath and held out his hand. Uncertainly she took it and he pulled her roughly to her feet. "We should go back."

"Jack, I don't understand. Was I too—"

"No!" With an obvious effort he repeated more quietly. "No. Addie, nothing you did was anything but natural and honest and . . . lovely. It is not you, Addie. It is me."

And with those words, he turned and left her alone in the garden.

15

"For God's sake, man, hold your position!" Jack screamed above the deafening roar of firearms and mortar. He could barely see through the swirling smoke and showers of dirt that coated his plaid and his face. Muddy sweat trickled down his forehead and cheeks. The pungent scent of powder mixed with the metallic tang of blood.

High above, a flat bright disc of sun blazed. It shimmered across the battle-woven shroud of sand and dust and acrid smoke, the small vortex of hell the soldiers had created on the hilltop.

A bullet struck a nearby boulder and splintered shards of rock, which hissed past his ear, scoring his cheek. Another bullet sliced through his kilt, filleting the fabric open across his thigh. Another struck his claymore.

A mortar erupted behind him, sending a soldier vaulting head over heels down the side of the hill. Like broken tin soldiers, men lay strewn and bleeding in the short, saw-bladed grass, even more vulnerable in death than they had been in life.

More men—his men—scrambled over the ground, looking desperately for some cover, some leadership, while valiantly trying to defend an indefensible expanse of bare earth.

They should have entrenched. They ought to have dug in. Four times he'd sent word to the commander; four times he'd been denied. Now the Boers had made the summit of Majuba Hill, Colley's "inaccessible position." Expert marksmen picked off his scuttling troops like rabbits on an open heath.

He fired his rifle. Futile. Waste of ammunition. The Boers had crept up the mountainside like lizards. Now they clung just below the rim, hidden and deadly.

Jack bit down on his anger, frustration balling his jaw as he swung his rifle about. What the bloody hell had happened to Colley's men?

"Regroup!" he shouted again above the cacophony of yells and rifle blasts.

"They've hit the sergeant!" yelled Connor, the young piper ahead of him. And then, suddenly, "The colors are down! The colors!"

The lad jumped up from his half crouch. His eyes were fixed on the regimental flag lying beside the outstretched hand of the dead color sergeant. Jack could see the boy's down-covered jaw set.

"Forget the bloody colors!" Jack yelled.

"The colors are down!" Connor called out, pride and determination warring for precedence on a face more appropriate to the schoolroom than a battlefield.

Then it began. Inevitable. Hideously constant.

The boy ran. There was nothing Jack could do to stop the young fool's brave dash for the colors. He'd tried. God, he'd tried. A thousand times, in a thousand different dreams, he'd tried to change the outcome of the lad's mad race.

The too-familiar scream tore from Jack's throat, reverberating in the suddenly empty drum of time and dream.

For the thousandth time, the bullet grazed his forearm. For the thousandth time, the small bird alit on a thornbush and cocked its head before darting away.

"Connor!"

For the thousandth time, the boy sprinted forward.

"No!"

For the thousandth time, an odd, slanting shaft of light struck the gun barrel emerging with liquid slowness from a huddle of rocks thirty feet away. Salty sweat blinded Jack's left eye and, for the thousandth time, he blinked. It would be another dream-elongated eternity before he realized it wasn't sweat but blood.

"No-oo-oo!" *His voice echoed eerily.*

The boy was almost to his goal. Exultantly, he bent forward, his hand stretched out to snatch the flag up on a dead run. You could see it. Read it. The lad was already tasting the glory of his feat. It was there in his eyes, in the dawning smile on his—

"NO!"

The single report of the blast preceded the inconsequential little puff of white blooming from the barrel. A look of startled incredulity bloomed across the piper's face as the impact tripped him and he cartwheeled forward, crumbling, falling . . . dead.

"No."

And now, for the thousandth time, Jack would crawl to the boy's side and—

Abruptly, terrifyingly, the sharp green grass beneath his palm withered. The cerulean sky above him bleached to the palest blue and his knees burned against white-hot sand. With a gasp, he struggled to his feet.

He was in the desert, far away from the familiar, hated African landscape of moments before.

"Captain!"

Before him stood a row of Highland soldiers in full dress regalia, shimmering in the waves of heat rising off the pale, golden sands. He recognized each one of them. They were, all of them, dead.

"What orders, Captain?" *It was the young piper from Majuba Hill.*

"Orders?" *Jack echoed numbly.*

"Aye, Captain." A redheaded corporal swept his hand toward the silent troop. "Lead us. We await only your command."

"I . . . I haven't any orders."

"Excuse the presumption, Captain, but ye do, indeed."

"What are they?" Jack asked. A thread of despair, as if he knew the answer, began uncoiling deep in his chest.

"Lead us home, Captain. Take us on the High Road. The path promised us, the ones who die in battle on foreign ground."

The word was meaningless, an indecipherable phrase he parroted like an idiot. "What is home?"

"Here, with us, Captain," the young piper answered kindly. "Dinna worry, sir. We dinna worry. We know you will do—"

"Jack?"

From somewhere behind him, her voice reached out and touched his heart like the tip of a white-hot blade. Somehow he'd pulled Addie into the dream and she was frightened.

He tried to turn around but the fierce need of these dead soldiers held him rooted, pinned facing forward, forcing him to take this last command. He fought their silent entreaty, fought until he shook, trembling and sweating.

"Jack?" More than fear in her voice now. She needed him.

Somehow he managed to pivot toward her voice even though the weight of the dead company's petition bent his back like an overstrained bow. Their voices called his name as a single distant demand, a cry he could not heed.

Because he saw her.

She stood in clear, cool moonlight, her mahogany hair dancing in a crisp, clean wind. A gentle light refracted in her amber eyes.

"Jack." She held out her hand. "Come home."

And all at once that word had sense and meaning and significance. He only needed to take a few steps across shifting sand and touch her to be there. With her. Eagerly, he stretched out his hand.

Blood covered it.

He gasped, staring down at himself. He was naked. All his clothing was stripped from his body. Naked except for the pall of sticky blood that covered him from neck to foot. Whether it was from his own wounds or another's, he couldn't tell. He only knew he'd been baptized in the stuff.

At the same time, the voices calling him had risen in pitch and volume, becoming a howling wind, a hot blast of reproach scouring his naked flesh.

He heard her gasp and looked up. She was staring at him in horror, recoiling. The breeze that had tossed her hair had become a furnace's roar, her dark tresses lashing her pale face. The hand once held out in welcome now fended off the very sight of him.

"No!"

He squinted into the wind, blinded by the pelting sand. She was being swallowed up by the storm, lost in the roar of the dead company's fury and need.

"Addie!" He bolted upright in his bed.

It was pitch-black. And cold. The soft ticking of the mantel clock mocked the heavy pounding of his heart. His breathing was hoarse, the fine cotton bedsheets sweat-soaked and clinging. He sucked air deep into his lungs and dug his knuckles into his eye sockets.

Majuba Hill. El Teb. Afghan. For years he'd relived the ambushes, conversed with dead companions, led irreversible charges, and fought against unconquerable foes. The dreams were his nightly companions. Familiar demons.

But Addie had never been there before.

Unmindful of the December chill, he got up and paced to the window. There, he braced an arm above his head, leaning his heated forehead against the cold, frosted glass. He stared with unseeing eyes out into the tranquil, star-filled night.

He knew what had authored the change in his nightmare.

Paul Sherville had returned from Arabi a wealthy man. And he'd been a friend of Charles Hoodless.

It was exactly the sort of information he'd begun this deception to acquire.

He closed his eyes. He had no honor left. He'd taken advantage of his last living relatives to ferret out other people's secrets—their little failures, addictions, and misfortunes. He used a grieving butler to pry into people's private lives. He manipulated Gerald Norton, whose only crime was to offer him friendship. Yet, none of these was the worst of his sins.

He'd known from the beginning the damage Hoodless had done to Addie. But he'd not realized the extent of it. Now he knew better. It didn't matter.

He'd considered time and again telling her the truth, but he was in too deep. It was too late. She would despise him for his deception. Even if she could somehow be convinced to let him continue his masquerade, her loathing would expose him. She hated soldiers and that was all he had ever been.

Yes, what he was doing was monstrous. God! So why was he doing it? He knew that, too. He owed it to the men who had died because of their commanding officer's greed. It was a debt he could not ignore. He couldn't stop. He couldn't quit.

But from here out he had to do so with the least possible harm to Addie. She felt more than casual affection for him. It was there in her beautiful eyes, the spontaneous smile of welcome when they met, the eagerness with which she had responded to his kiss. He had to stop that affection from growing. He had to kill it.

"Addie." He wasn't even aware he'd said her name until it dissolved in the air, leaving the room as silent as though it had never been uttered.

16

"Sir! Sir?" Wheatcroft panted from behind Jack.

Jack turned and waited for the older man to reach the landing. Having awoken once again with a feverish need for action, he'd given himself the task of carrying Lady Merritt's heavy crates of Japanese artifacts down from the fourth-story attic.

"Yes?"

"Ah." Wheatcroft put his hands on his hips and bent forward at the waist, puffing a moment before continuing, "Lady Merritt insists you let the footman do this."

"Bloody hell. How did she know what I was doing? Don't answer. Just tell her I've stopped. Tell Her Ladyship I'm lolling beneath a potted palm, sniffing lilies and reading poetry. Tell her any bloody thing she wants to hear. Oh, you needn't look shocked, Wheatcroft. I think I've more than adequately demonstrated my capacity for deceit."

Wheatcroft's expression reflected bewilderment, and Jack's irritation faded. Wheatcroft was not to blame for this infernal coil.

"Sir, Lady Merritt asks that you join her in the morning room. She is making a guest list for Mr. Phyfe's reception."

Wearily, Jack ran a hand across his face. It was to his advantage to be in that particular conversation. He had to make sure Sherville attended. "Aye, then," he murmured. "Tell her I'll be down directly." He started to climb the stairs.

"Ahem."

"What is it now, Wheatcroft?"

"I think you'd best arrange a fitting with Lord Merritt's tailor as soon as convenient, sir."

"What? Have I busted out the seams on these pants, too?" Jack twisted at the waist, looking down at the velvet knee breeches.

Wheatcroft nodded.

"I have had just about enough of this accursed masquerade!" Jack erupted. "I'll be damned if I spend one farthing on another yard of velvet!"

"If I might be so bold as to make a suggestion?"

"What?"

"If you would just refrain from indulging in these daily athletics, you might find it unnecessary to supplement Master Evan's wardrobe." Jack's eyes narrowed. Wheatcroft hurried on. "You have increased in size. Substantially. You no longer look as fashionably wan as you did a few weeks ago."

Jack struggled to recover his temper. He closed his eyes. "You're right," he finally said. "And now, most especially now, I can't afford to appear anything other than a posturing fool."

"Especially now, sir?"

"Last week Paul Sherville came close to recognizing me."

"Sherville was one of the names Colonel Halvers sent you."

"Yes. He was in Egypt at the same time as I. I don't remember him, though he obviously thought I looked familiar. Thankfully," he paused and gestured to the overlong, gleaming strands of hair curling on his shirt collar, "what with all this, and being clean-shaven, I believe he thinks himself mistaken.

"He has all the requisites of our traitor, Wheatcroft. He was in the right places at the right times. He had access to telegrams and strategy sessions and . . . he has returned from his foreign post unaccountably wealthy."

"What of the others on the list? Hopper, Neyron, Lobb, and Hoodless?" asked Wheatcroft.

Jack shook his head. "Lobb acted as secretary to Wolsey. If he were involved, the general would have had to be, too. I wouldn't believe that for a second."

Wheatcroft nodded.

"Neyron," Jack went on, "is the Marquis of Stanton's heir. I doubt he would risk that fortune on something so dangerously acquired and so relatively small. Hopper . . . Hopper could be our man. But his reputation is spotless, both with the enlisted men and his fellow officers."

"And Charles?"

"What of him?"

"Well, sir," Wheatcroft said uneasily, "he was a Royal Dragoon. His name reckons prominently amongst the dispatches Colonel Halvers had copied and sent to you. He was in Alexandria—"

"No," Jack snapped. "No, Wheatcroft. Hoodless was a captain. He would hardly have the opportunity to misdirect dispatches and alter orders. We are looking for a major, at the least."

"If you say so," Wheatcroft said doubtfully before asking, "What can I do to help you, sir?"

"Talk to Sherville's servants. Find out what clubs he belongs to, where he spends his nights, what his vices and weaknesses are."

"Yes, sir." Wheatcroft inclined his head. "Anything else, sir?"

"No, just inform Lady Merritt that I shall join her in ten minutes. Don't worry, Wheatcroft. I'll squeeze into the last pair of Evan's trousers before I go down. And, Wheatcroft?"

"Sir?"

"If you would kindly make the necessary arrangements with Lord Merritt's tailor? Can't show up at Ted Phyfe's fête exposing my smallclothes." He paused. "I imagine Mrs. Hoodless's in-laws will be present as well as her immediate family?"

"Doubtful, sir. The Hoodlesses are rather retiring. Besides, they haven't the—" He stopped, obviously embarrassed.

"The what?"

"The wherewithal necessary to move in society."

Jack frowned. "And the Phyfes?"

Wheatcroft relaxed slightly. "They haven't the interest."

He knew he hadn't the right to ask, to discuss her, but he could not help himself. "They are eccentric?"

A wry smile flickered across Wheatcroft's normally phlegmatic mien. "Extremely."

"I see. Thank you, Wheatcroft."

Without waiting for dismissal, Wheatcroft retraced his steps down the stairs, leaving Jack standing on the landing. He'd wasted enough time. He had a duty to perform.

It didn't matter that he understood exactly what he risked by performing that duty. He risked Addie's heart.

What would happen when she discovered she'd been duped again? How long would it take for her faith in men, in herself, in love, to be restored this time? A year? Five years? Never?

17

It was well past midnight when Jack left the Merritt townhouse. Wheatcroft, in his nightshirt and cap, held the servants' back door for him as he slipped wordlessly from the mansion. He made his way down dark back alleys that twined amongst the expensive row houses and headed for the river. A fine mist had risen from the banks, beading moisture on his cape's shoulders and slicking the cobbled streets.

The growl of a cat and the staggered clomp of an exhausted hack were the only sounds that followed him down the narrow lane to The Gold Braid, the military club Wheatcroft had discovered Paul Sherville frequented.

At the doorway, a half crown convinced the bored attendant of Jack's membership. He shrugged his cloak into the man's waiting hands and took off his hat, raking back his hair.

He queried the attendant and followed his directions to the gaming room. His entrance into the crowded, smoke-filled room produced a pause in the conversation. Jack could understand why. Though the black trousers and velvet cutaway jacket with satin lapels he wore had been the least outré of Evan's clothing, he hardly looked like one of the regulars.

True to its name, The Gold Braid was popular with military men. A full three-quarters of the men in the room sported double-breasted dress jackets, polished brass buttons, and gold braid appliqué glinting in the gaslight.

Jack stood out like a crow amongst a flock of cardinals. A few older men, their grizzled muttonchops bristling with indignation at his foppish appearance, sneered openly in his direction. Jack met their gaze directly with a clipped nod. After a few brief seconds of scrutinizing him, most of those assembled turned back to the more interesting proceedings at the gaming tables.

Hours of smoking cheroots and cigars had built a bluish haze in the room. Empty mugs and glasses stood in wavering lines on tables scattered around the perimeter, a comical testimony to the military rigor of inebriated hands.

Good, thought Jack, taking note of the piles of coin and bills lying on the gaming tables, empty bottles beside them. It was late enough in the evening so that victory and liquor should have loosened tongues and pockets. If he played this right, he might learn something useful.

He went to the bar and hitched his boot onto the brass foot rail, setting his hat down and taking a seat. He glanced over at the craggy-featured balding major beside him. The man continued contemplating his nearly empty shot glass.

Jack motioned for the thin, middle-aged bartender to draw him an ale. After wordlessly complying, the man clomped a heavy glass mug down in front of him. Jack slid a half crown across the sticky countertop. "Keep the change."

Lifting the mug to his lips, Jack downed half its contents before turning and casually surveying the crowd.

"Busy for past midnight," he said conversationally.

"It's when we gets most of our trade. We just gets a-poppin' after midnight." The bartender, eager to foster Jack's unexpected generosity, grinned. "Haven't seen you here before, Cap."

"Cap?" How had he known?

"Just an expression. We gets so many of the military lads in and the faces change so often, I just picks meself a nice, respectful rank and calls all the blokes by it." He leaned forward and jerked his head in the direction of a sullen-looking boy with a subaltern's braid on his uniform. "That's Lieutenant Holmes to his regiment but in here he's a captain. No harm done, what?"

"None at all."

"So, Cap, what brings a bloke like you in here?" His gaze lightly raked over Jack's velvet clothing.

Jack smiled thinly. "I'm looking for a fellow. We shared a mutual friend. I was told I might find him here."

The bartender began wiping up the counter. "Yeah? And who might you be looking for?"

"Paul Sherville."

The swirling motion of the bartender's rag slowed. "Might want to talk to that lost pup down there then. Fair idolizes Sherville, he does." His expression became skeptical. "What friend might you and Paul Sherville share?"

"Charles Hoodless."

"Charles Hoodless is dead." The youngster the bartender had identified as Lieutenant Holmes had twisted round and leaned an elbow against the bar. "It might be interesting to hear how a dead man makes friends."

"Now, Mr. Holmes," murmured the bartender soothingly, obviously worried that the young man would chase off a generous patron.

"That is *Lieutenant* Holmes." The lad turned his attention back to Jack. "Maybe you're a table-rapper and that's how you know Charles Hoodless. You look like one." He snorted with amusement.

Jack laced his fingers around his mug, studying Holmes. The lad was drunk. His eyes were glassy and unfocused and he held himself too stiffly, in the way of a man just barely maintaining his balance. His tone was the aggressive one of the habitual drunk, overly loud and petulant.

"Charles Hoodless's family and mine are from the same county. We were at school together," he said. "He wrote a letter to me some time back."

"Must have been sometime back," Holmes sneered. "He's been dead a year."

"It was," Jack said easily. "I have been out of the country studying for nearly that length of time. I am only newly returned to England. Amongst the letters awaiting me was one from Charles. In it he mentioned a Major Paul Sherville. Having just recently learned of poor Charles's death, I thought Major Sherville and I might lift a glass in his memory."

The young man made a scoffing sound. "Can't see Hoodless chumming about with the likes of you." There was no mistaking the derisive curl to Holmes's lip. "He was a soldier, not a—"

"—artist," Jack supplied smoothly. "I was much more vigorous as a lad." He slid his mug over to the bartender, motioning for it to be refilled. "Take care of my young friend here and any other comrades of Charles Hoodless who might be present," he added in a voice pitched to carry.

The words had a magical effect. The belligerence drained from the younger man's expression, leaving it simply sullen. He held out his shot glass for the bartender to fill. Several men who'd been watching from the nearer gaming tables abandoned their posts and gathered at the bar.

"Young Holmes isn't putting on like he was a chum of Charles, is he?" asked the bald, battle-scarred veteran Jack had noticed earlier. He leaned over the bar and grabbed the bottle of scotch from the other side. "Doubt whether he ever even saw the man."

"Didn't say I did, Ingrams!" said Holmes. "But I sure as hell know Paul Sherville! And that's who this bloke is looking for."

A man with a thick, dark mustache gave a short bark of laughter. "Oh, you won't find Sherville down here anymore," he told Jack. "We're a bit too common for his tastes nowadays. Not that his presence is missed."

"Potter has the right of it," another man said, jerking his head in the mustachioed man's direction. "Sherville plays for higher stakes these days."

Jack took a sip of ale before asking in a bored voice, "Why's that?"

"Ah." Potter plunked his empty mug down in front of the whiskey bottle the bartender had left in front of Jack and glanced questioningly at him. Jack tipped two fingers of whiskey into Potter's mug. He took a deep draught before continuing. "Major Sherville came back from North Africa with a little nest egg he'd managed to hatch."

"Nest egg?"

The bald veteran, Ingrams, grinned. "A tidy sum, a bit of ready, don't you know. He came back with some money and has since parlayed it into real wealth, canny beggar that he is."

"How incredibly vulgar," Holmes muttered. "Talking about a man's personal assets."

"Ye mean his wealth?" Potter asked, grinning unrepentantly. "Aye, that's us at The Gold Braid, vulgar and poor. But then . . . we work for our commissions."

Holmes flushed hotly.

"Nest egg?" Jack asked, trying to steer the conversation back to Sherville. "And how would one achieve that in North Africa? I thought all they had there was sand and camels."

Ingrams shrugged. "Rumor says Sherville plucked a ruby the size of a pigeon's egg off a statue."

"I heard he took a jeweled dagger off a dead prince," Potter said.

"No," Holmes broke in with the smug expression of a man who knows more than the company he keeps. "Sherville and Hoodless found some sort of heathen stash."

Potter snorted. "Hoodless and Sherville, you say? Not bloody likely. They had a falling-out in North Africa, just before Hoodless was killed, God rest his black heart." Potter slanted a look in Jack's direction. "Sorry, old man. Speaking ill of the dead and all, but certainly you must know what type of man Charles Hoodless was."

Jack willed himself to a noncommittal expression. He knew. His investigations always seemed to skirt back to Charles Hoodless. Piece by piece he had learned just "what type of man Charles Hoodless was" and each new bit of knowledge nearly choked him with rage. Because of Addie. Addie, whom he mustn't think of, couldn't think of, because to do so hurt worse than any physical pain he'd ever endured.

Potter had turned back to the young lieutenant and was regarding him sardonically. "But seeing how you are so chummy with Sherville, I'd have thought you'd know that, Holmes."

Holmes straightened, gripping the side of the bar to keep his balance. He glared at Potter. "I did know that, Potter. I know a lot of things." He smiled mysteriously. "For example, I know that whatever Sherville and Hoodless found in Africa, they did so together."

Ingrams leaned close to Jack and muttered, "And how the hell would this pup know that, eh? He weren't never in North Africa."

Jack didn't reply; his thoughts were careening wildly.

Holmes swung on Ingrams, his face suffused with color. "You think you're so much better than me, all of you, just because you've seen more action than I!"

"More action?" asked Ingrams, his brows climbing in mock astonishment. "Make that any action!"

The little group around the bar burst into appreciative laughter. Apparently young Holmes's hubris made him a regular target amongst this lot.

"To blazes with you, Ingrams! Paul Sherville has seen more action than the entire sorry lot of you put together!"

"Oh, yes. Paul Sherville loves 'seeing action.' As did Charles. And if there weren't any about, they made sure they found some . . . or created it."

"What the hell is that supposed to mean?" Holmes demanded.

"Nothing. Just that the number of wounded amongst Sherville's command far exceeded those in any other company."

"Because he doesn't run away from trouble."

"Careful, boy," Potter advised softly into the shot glass he had lifted to his lips.

Ingrams, however, seemed inclined to charity. After a second's hesitation he guffawed lightly and clapped Holmes on the back. "You'd do well to pick a better figure to model your career after than Paul Sherville or Charles Hoodless, son."

The boy swept the older man's hand from his shoulder. "Why?" he demanded. "Because they have fashioned something more from their careers than a bunch of tired old war stories?"

At this insult, Potter started forward, but Ingrams stopped him.

"No," Ingrams said mildly. "Because Sherville and Hoodless fashioned their careers on brutality and exploitation."

Holmes stood stock-still, quivering with rage. One of the other men gathered around the bar barked out a short, clipped, "Hear, hear," and several others nodded solemnly.

"Sherville shall hear of this!" Holmes backed away, slamming his mug on the counter and, with a last sputtering oath, stomped from the room. With Holmes gone and no more free rounds being offered, the men drifted away.

"He'll be running to Sherville's side, John," Potter cautioned.

"Ah, well," Ingrams said. "I shan't fret overmuch. I doubt Sherville will even allow Holmes into his new club's anteroom. It wouldn't do to acknowledge a little would-be pissant like Holmes."

Potter nodded and headed back to the gaming table. Jack's gut twisted and he forced himself to ignore the hot burn of acid in his throat. He did not want to think what he was thinking, suspect what he was suspecting. The idea of the scandal Addie would have to live through if, indeed, her dead husband had been involved in the slave trade was incomprehensible. She would never escape the ignominy.

Paul Sherville and Charles Hoodless. Always, whatever avenue he explored, the two were linked.

He took a deep breath, light-headed and ill. All of his career he had tried his damnedest to do right by his men, his rank, and his queen. He'd never put personal concerns above duty. Not once.

He placed his palm flat on the counter, pushing himself upright. The tremor in his left hand had grown into a shake. His legs felt oddly boneless. He could leave now. He hadn't heard any real evidence of Hoodless's involvement. If he left, he wouldn't have to.

Damned be duty and to hell with debt if it hurt Addie—

"I'd say Arabi," Ingrams murmured softly.

"Excuse me?" Jack's head snapped up so quickly his vision swam. For a few minutes he'd been so absorbed in trying to see his way clear of this hellish dilemma, he'd forgotten where he was.

"Your skin." Ingrams nodded at Jack's hands, clenched tightly about the mug of beer until the knuckles showed ivory beneath the saffron-tinted skin. "I'd say you last served under an Arab sky. Fellows always get that yellowish color, even after the tan fades. Never does quite fade, though, does it?"

"Served?" Jack tried to sound casual.

Ingrams turned and narrowly studied Jack. "Cameron, isn't it?" Jack simply lifted an eyebrow.

Ingrams continued studying him thoughtfully. Finally, he seemed to come to a decision. "I might be mistaken," he said slowly. "You look something like a man I once met. Fine man. Valiant." He tested the word to see if it fit. Apparently, it did. He nodded. "Yes, a very valiant man. Knew the meaning of words like *honor* and *duty*."

How burdensome that word had become, how inexplicable, how nebulous its meaning. He didn't doubt that Ingrams would find him a worthy sort of chap. Addie, however . . . yes, Addie might have another term for Jack Cameron. Traitor? Hypocrite? "Sounds a tiresome sort of chap," Jack finally said when he realized Ingrams was awaiting a reply.

"An uncomfortable sort of chap, perhaps," he said.

"You appear to find Paul Sherville an uncomfortable chap, too."

Ingrams's expression went flat with dislike. "Paul Sherville is an opportunist."

"You know him well?"

Ingrams shrugged. "Not really. He's with the Black Dragoons. I'm with the 60th Rifles." Once more he flashed a piercing glance on Jack. The 60th Rifles had also seen action at Majuba Hill, the scene of Jack's nightmares.

Jack ignored the question in Ingrams's gaze. "Your young friend Holmes seems quite taken with him."

"He does, doesn't he? Poor little bugger. Sherville is the type of man who demands constant attention. Surrounded by a little coterie of fawners. Holmes was one of them."

"Was Charles Hoodless?"

"Hoodless?" Ingrams snorted. "Acting the sycophant to any man? Surely as his 'old, boyhood chum,' you know better than that," he said. "Hoodless wouldn't have kowtowed to God. No. Those two were cut from the same cloth. They were bound by their . . . appetites, not by affection."

"I'm not sure I understand."

"Suffice to say, Hoodless and Sherville loved having native commands."

"Are you suggesting that Sherville and Hoodless used military authority to extort money from their native commands?"

Ingrams laughed. "Good God, no! I haven't any idea of where either man got his money. But I can assure you the natives hadn't a raw penny to give anyone. Nor would Hoodless, at least, have wanted it. No . . . the price he extracted from his command was paid in the coin of suffering."

What sort of husband would a man like that have been?

Jack clenched his teeth, incapable of concentrating on what role—if any—Sherville had had in the illegal slave trade out of North Africa. Every piece of damning information about Hoodless's character turned Jack's thoughts away from the task at hand.

He shook his head, forcing himself to attend what Ingrams was saying.

"Simple abuse of power is ugly, but abuse of power over those helpless to protect themselves is appalling." Ingrams looked up from his glass. "But you weren't asking about Charles Hoodless. Why should you? You knew him. You were asking after Paul Sherville."

Jack nodded a jerky assent, the picture Ingrams's unspoken words had conjured paralyzing his tongue. Small wonder the sight of a uniform made Addie tense.

Ingrams went on. "As Potter said, Sherville isn't about here much anymore. He's acquired expensive taste since his return from North Africa."

"Ah, yes. 'The jeweled dagger.'"

Ingrams snorted. "There is no jeweled dagger."

"No extortion, no jeweled dagger. What could account for his wealth, then?"

"My, you artistic fellows are an inquiring lot, aren't you?" Ingrams downed the dregs from his mug and pushed himself away from the counter. "It wouldn't be gentlemanly to speculate now, would it?"

Jack forced a casual smile.

"But I will say that whatever wealth Paul Sherville discovered in exotic climes, Charles Hoodless found, too. And it seemed to put a strain on that . . . relationship. A great strain."

18

Jack stopped on his way through the door to Lady Merritt's morning room, trying to erase the fatigue from his face. He had spent the morning trying to make sense out of a shell-shocked veteran's rambling account of a failed offensive against local slavers in North Africa. It hadn't taken Jack five minutes to realize the poor bastard would be useless in providing any pertinent information about the traitor Jack hunted, but he hadn't been able to abandon him, staying for the better part of the day at his side, keeping vigil. It had worn on him, on his conscience. He needed to do more to discover who was possibly responsible for this man's fate—and any number of others' fates as well.

"Jack? Is that you?"

Taking a short breath, he relaxed his features into a pleasant mien and plucked a lily from the vase on the hallway table before entering, twirling it between his forefinger and thumb. "Dear lady! I have heeded your call and present myself ready to do your bidding. Now, how might I assist you?"

"It's Addie."

She wouldn't have noticed the way his fatuous smile slipped. "And what can there be about dear Mrs. Hoodless that causes a line to mar your snowy brow?"

Lady Merritt picked up a sheaf of paper from her desk.

"Addie's mourning is officially over and she is now free to attend the reception I have planned for her brother."

"And how is this vexing?"

"It's a question of delicacy, not decorum. I do not know whether I should include her dear, departed husband's fellow officers in the guest list." Lady Merritt tapped a finger against the list of names in her hand.

"I am very fond of Addie. Very fond. Her family and mine have known each other for generations. Our properties adjoin, as you know. Addie quite doted on Evan when he was a lad." Her voice dropped and she gazed inwardly a second at some remembered charm, and for a small space Jack could see the tender pride and real affection she had for her son . . . and Addie.

She cleared her throat, casting a furtive glance at him, as though she suspected she'd been tricked into a sentimental mood. "She encouraged the most unruly behavior in him."

"Really?" Jack asked. He didn't want to hear anything about Addie. He needed to find proof that her dead husband was a slaver. He needed to ruin her life.

"She was quite an energetic girl. But she—how shall I say?— seems to have grown fragile these past few years. Not at all the rambunctious, wayward little harridan she used to be. One would never expect that imp of Satan would have developed into such a retiring young lady."

"Mrs. Hoodless seems quite animated to me," Jack said, aware his tone was stiff.

Lady Merritt patted his hand. "With you she is. With her brother and his friends, she is quite recognizable as the little dickens who ran through my rose beds beheading them with her brother's toy sword."

She smoothed her skirts. "But in society she is so restrained, so subdued. Particularly, I have noted, in the company of Her Majesty's officers."

Jack stared stonily at her.

"I think"—she lowered her voice solemnly—"they are an acutely painful reminder of her loss."

Could she be that unperceptive?

"I don't think I should invite any military persons."

Of course you shouldn't, Jack wanted to shout. Instead, he raised his brows. "Really? Do you think that wise . . . what with Teddy's clientele being so predominantly that sort of fellow?" He felt bile rise in his throat, but not enough to choke him. Not that much. He was still well capable of this. Damned be his soul. "I understand your tender concern for the lady, but, after all, this reception is to promote Ted."

Such a smooth voice, such a perfect imitation of compassion; just a soupçon of distress, a hint of confusion. Satan could be no better a dissembler. "I am certain Mrs. Hoodless would not want you to risk even one bit of Ted's future success on her account."

Lady Merritt absently tapped the end of her pen against her lips, not yet convinced. She might be a narrow-minded, silly, spoiled, and unobservant woman, but she had heart.

Jack's earlier frustration with her fled. He could like her. He could like her for putting Addie ahead of her brother's—and her own—success. It was a noble sentiment.

One he couldn't allow.

"Besides," he went on, "don't you think that—for her own good, you understand—she ought to look the past squarely in the face?"

Lady Merritt spent a thoughtful moment staring at the list of names in front of her before sighing. "I expect you're right, Jack. Someone as young and lovely as Addie should not spend the rest of her life pining. She must eventually reconcile herself to her loss. She cannot do that by hiding."

"No, indeed."

"Exactly," she said, pleased with the outcome of their talk. "Now, we'd best hurry so as not to keep the others waiting. Didn't I tell you? We are expected for lunch." She tugged sharply at the embroidered bell pull. "I'll have the footman fetch our coats."

Then, almost shyly, she added, "Thank you for your help, Jack. I was quite at a loss, but I suspected that you, being as close to Addie as you are, would know what to do."

Somehow, he contrived a smile.

Though Jack had fled from her the other night, the way he had kissed had suggested much to Addie. There had been desire in his kiss: restrained, unwilling, but there. The thought made her smile with pleasure and anticipation because in a few minutes, they would meet and he would take her arm as they strolled along the park. He would look at her and she would once more experience that complete accord she always had when she was with him.

She hurried along the sidewalk, past the window displays and the street vendors, her head tucked down as she made her way toward Regent's Park. At the street crossing, she waited for a carriage to rumble past, exhilarated by the cold, by the occasional snowflake melting against her warm eyelids, the silky brush of her sable collar against her chin, the winter sun dazzling off a patch of black ice near the curb.

She felt young and girlish and beyond dazzling herself as she succumbed to temptation, impulsively sketching a pirouette in the center of the sidewalk before catching the morose eye of a portly street sweeper.

"Here now, young lady! Goin' ta fall, you carry on like that. It be slippery out," he cautioned.

She crossed the street and flipped him a shilling. "For your care," she said gaily. He snatched it from the air and pocketed it deftly, tipping his hat before turning away, mumbling something about the "daft aristos."

She was laughing as she turned the corner leading to the park and she saw them waiting for her in front of the Fleece Hotel: Ted, Gerald, Lady Merritt, and . . . Jack.

And as oft happens when you see someone from a distance that you are used to seeing close by, she realized he was not nearly as thin as she'd supposed, or as languid. Her pace slowed, perplexed but not worried. His golden beauty seemed a shock after nearly four days without seeing him.

She appreciated anew the elegant lines of his brow, how mobile his long mouth was, how clear the brilliance of his eyes, and how aggressive the broad-bridged slope of his nose. And his form! He looked altogether unlike the quaking young man who'd straggled onto Lady Merritt's terrace two months before. Lithe, tensile. His back was straight, his shoulders suspiciously broad. She smiled at the vanity that prompted Jack to have his jacket shoulders padded. And there was an attitude of intense self-possession, almost boldness in the way he held himself, in the flash of his strong, white teeth.

London had changed Jack.

Her heart trip-hammered, matching the pace her feet set as she started forward. The possibilities that Ted had seeded in her mind, having taken root, were flowering.

Why don't you find out if Jack is attracted to you? Ted had suggested. She'd wanted to know more. God knows, she longed to discover if Jack found her as appealing as she found him.

"Ah, Addie!" Gerald hailed her. Alerted to her approach, the rest of the company turned to welcome her. Except for Jack, who had found something interesting to peer at in the restaurant's window. He was squinting through an eyeglass, yet another new affectation, his attention apparently riveted.

Lady Merritt graciously offered her cheek and Addie pressed her own against it. Ted took hold of her hand and drew her near him, next to Jack. And finally, with what seemed like reluctance, Jack dropped the eyeglass and offered her a quick, absent greeting before moving past her.

Her pleasure faded. It was almost as though he didn't want to talk to her, to look at her. His eyes once again passed over her face and went on to study something on the other side of the street.

She forced herself not to react to imagined slights. What had she expected him to do? Drop to his knees at her feet?

Chiding herself for acting so childishly, she forced her worry away and allowed her brother to usher her into the hotel. The others followed close behind, exclaiming delightedly over the opulence of the front lobby.

Begging their pardon, Ted left them clustered near the door and went to arrange seating at the hotel's popular French-styled restaurant. Gerald gallantly disentangled Lady Merritt from her enormous cloak while Jack stared at a painting on the wall.

"I say, Jack, do the gentleman bit, what?" Gerald prompted from behind Lady Merritt's broad form, pointing at Addie.

With a jerk, Jack came forward, a tight smile on his lips. "Mrs. Hoodless, may I offer my assistance?"

"Of course you can, Jack," Lady Merritt snapped irritably. "What ever has come over you?"

"Mrs. Hoodless?" Jack asked tonelessly.

Numbly, Addie presented him her back. Standing as woodenly

correct and silent as Wheatcroft, he took her coat from her shoulders. His formality made her clumsy and she needed two attempts before she managed to shrug free of the garment. Her cheeks were afire by the time she'd managed to disinter herself.

She wheeled around and found herself looking directly into Jack's eyes. They were at once vivid and blank, shuttered and intent. It was like looking at the surface of a vast, intractable ocean, knowing that currents churned away far beneath the smooth surface.

He swallowed and hauled his gaze above her head. For just an instant it seemed as though his fingers tightened on her shoulders, and then he had snatched her coat free and flung it to an eager attendant.

"Jack?"

He pretended he didn't hear the question in her voice. He smiled at her or, rather, smiled at a space somewhere above her.

"What a fetching piece of millinery," he drawled. "Where ever did you find something so utterly . . . original? Who'd have thought to perch that bird thingy amongst those, oh, my dear, those aren't oranges?"

The others, who'd started moving toward the restaurant entrance, paused. Lady Merritt, who'd commandeered Gerald's escort, muttered something under her breath.

Addie waited. Jack hadn't offered his arm. He was too busy staring at her hat, studying it with as critical an air as if he were examining one of Ted's paintings.

"Are they oranges or are they tangerines?" he asked seriously, his eyes never leaving the top of her head.

"I don't know," Addie said faintly, feeling embarrassed and confused. It was as though he purposefully sought to make fools of them both, an amusing spectacle for passersby. Certainly one or two of the hotel's guests had paused within hearing distance and were trying hard to appear not to be listening. The faint derisive smiles they didn't bother to hide gave them away.

"What say you, Gerry?" Jack called preemptively. "Tangerines or oranges or some other citrus fruit?"

Gerald, taking the request for his attention as seriously as if Jack had asked him to judge an atelier show, gently pulled free of Lady Merritt's grip and lumbered over. He lifted an eyeglass and intently studied her hat.

Ted beckoned them from the doorway of the restaurant. Lady Merritt stood, abandoned by her escort, open-mouthed and befuddled.

"What are you going on about, Jack?" she asked in exasperation. "Leave Addie's headgear alone."

"Tangerine, I should say," Gerald declared. "Too much red to be an orange. Unless one were talking about those Tahitian oranges. You know the ones. Like that Gauguin fellow painted."

Some woman behind Addie tittered. Addie's ears burned.

"Ah, yes," said Jack. "I believe you are correct. I am more relieved than I can say. Oranges in November. Too, too *jeune fille.*" He gave a moue of distaste. "I commend you on your taste, Addie. Tangerines are much the better choice for November chapeaus."

And now, now, with heat unaccountably stinging the backs of her eyes, now, while the sun outside slid like a dirty pickpocket behind a dingy gray cloud, now, having traded the bracing wind for air heavy with the smell of mutton, now he looked at her.

"Why, Addie," he said softly, that hateful smile still playing on his lips. "There's no need to look so stricken, m'dear. You have been exonerated of any crimes of fashion. 'Crimes of fashion,' not 'passion,' do ya see? Jolly clever of me, what?"

A muffled giggle drifted from behind them.

"I am ecstatic," she said with forced lightness. "I lay awake last night, fretting over whether or not my hat would meet with your approval."

"Did you, indeed?" He cocked his brow and his eyes, beautiful eyes, skittered over her face like pebbles thrown on an icy pond.

"Well, there really is no need for you to spend any wakeful hours on so trivial a thing—"

"Trivial?" Gerald asked. "I say, I don't think we can call—"

"From now on," Jack continued in that false, bright voice, his words running over Gerald's as though he were afraid if they went unspoken they might lodge in his throat. "From now on, I insist you send your hats over to my rooms for prior approval. I shall try them on myself before returning them to you."

His teeth bared in semblance of a smile. "That will solve all your problems, but should Wheatcroft catch me, it may well be the beginning of mine! But for you, Madame, anything."

The others laughed. Even Ted snorted with amusement at Jack's idiocy. Anger replaced her hurt.

"How munificent of you!"

"Not at all. Can't have a lovely lady like yourself losing sleep. Scant slumber might not affect those silly young debs but mature ladies need to protect those rejuvenating hours."

Her chin jerked up. Gerald's mild gaze finally sharpened with the impression that something was wrong. Stunned and hurt, Addie brushed by Jack, moving too quickly, hoping her tears would not cause her to careen into something.

She swept past Ted, blindly following the hovering maitre d', who dashed ahead to pull out a chair at a large round table near the front window. She did not wait for assistance, taking her seat as the others hustled forward in varying states of bewilderment.

Lady Merritt took the seat opposite her, Gerald on her side. Ted sat to Addie's left across from Gerald. There was only one vacant chair left: the one directly on her right hand.

Humiliation burned her cheeks as Jack hesitated a moment before taking it. She kept her gaze outside the window. Her hands lay clutched on her lap.

Jack sank down silently, his wit apparently spent.

A full ten minutes passed, the polite drone and flow of conversation eddying around and about her. She didn't say a word, remembering one of the lessons Charles had taught her: you can't bait someone who doesn't speak.

But slowly she became aware that if she was quiet, Jack was more so. His attention, true, seemed to follow with almost unnatural avidity the conversation going on at the table. His gaze leapt to and from the faces of those who spoke, like a drowning man leaps at any rope tossed his way. His laughter was a shade too prompt to be spontaneous. The characteristic trembling of his left hand, clenched about the stem of the crystal goblet, translated itself into minute shivers over the liquid surface of water . . .

Something was not right.

This was not Jack. In fact, there was nothing about this brittle, feverish-eyed man next to her that was familiar, that felt . . . honest. There was some reason for his facile unkindness. She was sure of it.

And with each observation of Jack's discomfiture, the certainty that should she open her mouth she would be belittled did not seem so dread. Each barb he'd uttered, she realized with sudden inspiration, had hurt Jack as much as it hurt her. Even now he looked ill, strained.

The idea bewildered her. Try as she might she could think of no reason why Jack hurt them both with his behavior.

"I have heard that the new play at the Lyceum is wonderful," she said, testing her idea. Watching him carefully, she continued. "I should so like to see it."

Jack opened his mouth. He took a deep breath, like an athlete might before endeavoring a particularly strenuous feat. His mouth clamped shut. The muscles balled at the corner of his jaw.

"I haven't been to a play in a long time." She knew she was opening herself up for more of the mockery he'd practiced on her earlier but she was as curious now as she had been hurt then.

Jack's lips flattened a second before relaxing. He shook his head, so slightly she was certain she was the only one who noticed. In negation or ruefulness, she could not tell.

"Then see it you shall, Addie," Ted said.

"Capital notion," Gerald said. "Why don't we make a party of it?"

"I don't know," injected Lady Merritt. "Is it an artistically edifying play or one of those light, satirical pieces of nastiness that are currently all the rage?"

"Well, I'd rather see wit than this Ibsen fellow's stark realist pretensions," Jack put in.

"Really, Jack?" Addie said sweetly. "I would never have expected you to object to pretensions."

He met her gaze, a small self-deprecating curl to his lip. "As you say, Madame."

The rest of the diners tittered.

"She has you there, Jack," Gerald said.

"In all ways," Jack murmured suavely. He sniffed as if suddenly recalling himself and brushed at a few tiny bread crumbs adhering to his jacket's plum-colored plush. "I like my pretensions to be pretty. Why seek the bald face of reality? The hag is all too available as it is."

Gerald laughed appreciatively as Jack patted his mouth with the napkin. "Besides," he continued, "lately I find myself as interested in the process of genius as in the end product. Which leads me to a matter I have been wanting to broach, Ted."

Ted turned a slightly suspicious eye on Jack. "Yes?"

"Yes. I am not at all sure I haven't misspent my talent."

"You don't say."

"Indeed. I do. Say that I am unsure, that is. A dratted spot, to find oneself waffling at this point in one's life."

"I can imagine," Ted murmured. "I always thought you a trifle old to be an apprentice."

"Oh, I'm well beyond the apprentice stage." He looked at the others. "I suppose I should just ignore these sudden misgivings and return to my little Scottish workshop. But the thing is, don't you know, I would always wonder if I'd made a mistake. In giving the world an adept craftsman, have I robbed the world of an artistic genius?"

Ted choked and Lady Merritt, who'd been nodding approvingly, thumped him sharply on the back.

"Excuse me," Ted sputtered. "Water went down the wrong way."

"Of course," Jack said kindly. "Anyhow, Ted old man, the thing is, would you object to me hanging about your garret in a more concerted fashion, takin' notes, lookin' over the terrain, witnessing firsthand the dos and don'ts of the trade?"

"'Dos and don'ts of the trade'?" Addie echoed, nonplussed.

"Ted knows what I want, don't you, old fellow?"

"Yes. I suspect I do. All right, Jack," he said. "Spend as much time 'hanging about' the studio as you'd like. I'll put you to work as repayment for my instruction and I promise, I'll put your talents to good use."

"Thank you," Jack said. "I shall contrive not to get in the way when you have your sittings."

"Can't be done," Ted said. "When Miss Drouhin sits, the world sits at her feet."

"Oh, surely not the world," Lady Merritt snorted.

"A good third of it, I should say," Ted avowed. "What with all of them standing moony-eyed about my studio, I swear I haven't any idea how England manages to win any of these foreign skirmishes that the newspapers report." Ted's bland gaze slid to Jack. "What say you, Jack? Can England maintain her presence in the Sudan, what with the bulk of her troops parked in my apartments?"

Jack returned Ted's gaze. Addie had the distinct impression that a small skirmish of an entirely different sort was going on.

"I couldn't say."

"Of course, he can't say," a mocking voice boomed from behind Addie.

Paul Sherville. She would know his voice anywhere. She felt him close in to stand directly behind her and knew how a rabbit must feel when the shadow of the hawk overtakes it.

"Couldn't help but attend. I have exceptional hearing. This artist fellow—excuse me, I've quite forgotten your name?"

"Cameron, John Cameron," Jack said without standing.

"Ah, yes. Cameron. That's right. Well, a fellow who's spent his adulthood whittling, or splattering, or scribbling is hardly in a position to judge Her Majesty's readiness to meet a foreign insurrection, is he?"

"I should hope not, Major," Lady Merritt said, clearly put out by Sherville's rudeness. "An artist's milieu is beauty. A soldier's milieu is . . . is . . ."

"Lice?" Ted asked innocently.

"Khaki?" Gerald suggested.

A chirrup of laughter escaped Addie. She buried her mouth in her napkin.

"Very droll," Sherville said. "Just see how the young—" He paused and when he spoke again, his voice had sharpened. "Ah, Mrs. Hoodless. I didn't recognize you out of black. Has it been so long since Charles left us?"

She felt herself grow cold.

"And for us to meet again so soon," he went on. "How delightful! Only more delightful is the knowledge that now that your mourning is officially over we shall doubtless meet again, and again . . . and again. I do so look forward to renewing our acquaintance."

She couldn't look at him. She felt exposed, vulnerable. She swallowed hard and closed her eyes.

"Nothing could make me forgo that pleasure," he was saying, "not even—"

"Death?" Jack asked.

Her eyes shot open. Every person at the table was staring in astonishment at Jack. Calmly, he refolded his napkin and placed it aside.

"Excuse me?" Paul Sherville asked, his expression apoplectic.

"I said 'death,'" Jack repeated calmly. "You know . . . 'the soldier's milieu.' Wouldn't it be death? Been sitting here, trying to guess the answer. Thought I'd done rather a nice job of it, too. Must say, no one seems appreciative."

Everyone relaxed. Behind her she felt Paul Sherville step away from her chair. "Yes. Quite so. Death," he said. "I won't keep you any longer. Delighted, as usual, Lady Merritt, Mrs. Hoodless, gentlemen . . . Cameron."

She heard the hushed click of his boot heels on the parquet flooring fade away. She glanced at Jack.

He wasn't looking at her but he seemed to feel her scrutiny. He smiled, sadly. "I couldn't let him. Forgive me."

She could barely hear his words. For the rest of the meal she wondered what he needed forgiveness for . . . and from whom.

19

Paul Sherville strode past the footman into his newly purchased townhouse and snatched up the riding crop he'd left lying on the hall table. He thumped it against his thigh as he stalked to the library, barking out orders for scotch to be brought immediately.

Captain John Frances Cameron.

He'd thought there was something familiar about the whip-cord lean figure when they'd been introduced in that artist's lair. But before he could pursue the sense of recognition, he'd allowed himself to be distracted by the man's offensive overtures. He saw now that it had all been a clever diversion, a ruse to keep him from looking too closely at him. And it had worked.

Still, he couldn't judge himself too harshly. One of the only times he'd seen Cameron, the man had weighed a full stone more than he did now. The Captain Cameron he'd glimpsed in the Sudan had been a vigorous, ramrod-straight officer tanned the very color of the beastly dune he'd been straddling, his expression keen, hawk-like.

He'd been bearded then too, a full bronze-colored beard. But his eyes were the same. Yes. He should have recognized Cameron from those damned arctic-colored eyes of his.

With a snarl, Sherville slashed the riding crop at the papers on his desk, sending them flying, and flung himself down into an expensive leather tufted armchair.

It was damned lucky that baby-faced lieutenant had been at The Gold Braid Club the evening before. Even luckier that he'd received Holmes this afternoon at his club. He'd nearly had the doorman send the upstart off with a flea in his ear.

As soon as he'd been told that Cameron was asking after him, he'd pieced together the enigma of Jack Cameron. He'd given Holmes instructions to report to him should Cameron go nosing about again.

Sherville's scowl deepened as a light rap on the door broke his concentration. "Come in, damn you!"

The butler entered, balancing a crystal decanter and a cut-glass tumbler on a silver tray. He deposited the tray on the black lacquered table by Sherville's side.

"Shall I pour, sir?"

"I can pour my own liquor."

With the wooden impassiveness he was paid far too well to maintain, the butler started picking up the papers from the thick Turkish rug.

"Leave it, you fool. Do you think I want to watch your scrawny ass crawling about? Get out!"

With a murmured apology, the butler backed out of the room. Sherville snatched up the decanter, splashing scotch into a glass.

He needed to think. He was a realist—a practical, hard-nosed man. Those qualities had been responsible for lifting him—the youngest son of an impoverished minister—to this address, to this sumptuously furnished library and this luxuriously fashioned life. He must use those qualities now to protect these things he treasured. No one was going to take from him what he'd worked so hard to acquire.

He tossed half the whiskey down and stared moodily into the remainder of the amber liquid. He needed to decide who constituted the greater threat: Jack Cameron or Addie Hoodless.

He knew Jack Cameron by reputation. He was said to be fierce and fiercely loyal, as dauntless a soldier as he was astute a tactician; his allegiance to the Crown was above reproach. So what the hell was he doing playing "Precious Pet" to Charles Hoodless's widow?

There was only one conclusion he could come to: Jack Cameron was working for the government. Whether he reported to the Admiralty, the War Office, or the Colonial Office was unimportant; he was acting as a government agent.

Sherville gulped down the rest of the liquor, wiping the back of his hand across his mouth. It only made sense.

If he, himself, had taken note of Addie Hoodless's sudden wealth it only stood to reason that Whitehall would have done likewise. All those costly refurbishments: the electric lighting, the centralized heating, the furnishings and draperies. Not to mention the other things he'd seen: the new carriage, the servants, her modest but expensive wardrobe.

Where did her wealth come from? The money Charles had accrued was not nearly enough to account for his widow's lifestyle. No, Addie Hoodless had a new source of income.

But the ultimate giveaway was not the new trappings of wealth; it was her new demeanor.

Addie Hoodless had always put him in mind of a feral fox he had trapped as a lad, cowed, exotic, its very fearfulness exciting. The woman he'd seen today had laughed at him, the bitch! And a few days before, she had looked him straight in the eye and told him—him!—how he was to act. She had all but had him thrown out of her brother's studio!

Surging to his feet, Sherville flung the glass into the marble mantelpiece. The crystal exploded, shattering into a thousand shimmering splinters. With an effort, Sherville composed himself.

The only possible explanation for Addie Hoodless's sudden self-confidence was that she had discovered Charles's hidden cache of "interesting material." She had taken a note from Charles's book and become a blackmailer.

For two years before his death, his old school chum had soaked him for close to three thousand pounds. Luckily, his lucrative sideline had enabled him to sustain the burden. But he'd be damned if he would pay Charles's hot-eyed little bitch a sou! Why she hadn't yet started bleeding him was a minor mystery, but one he had no intention of waiting to discover the answer to. No, the real question was what he was going to do.

Judging by her willingness to antagonize him, he had to believe that she held that damn photograph. He had to get it before Cameron found it. He stalked back to the decanter and poured himself another drink.

Addie wasn't stupid. It would be a mistake to underestimate her. But unlike Charles, Addie had no foreign safe in which to tuck "treasures." That meant that it must be either at her country estate or . . . or here, at the Hoodless townhouse, where she was having everything remodeled.

Yes, he thought, a slight crook to his lips, that was it. She was making an Ali Baba's cave in her own damn house.

20

During the leisurely hours of lunch, a merry mood replaced the earlier, strained one. The diners finished their meal and settled back in their chairs.

"What now?" Ted asked.

"Coffee at Earl's Court?" suggested Gerald.

The others groaned. "No more food," begged Addie.

"What we need is some fresh air!" Gerald said.

"Heavens, Gerry, it's nearly five o'clock. It will be dusk soon," protested Lady Merritt.

"It already is dusk," Ted said. He nodded out the window. The long, purple-tinted shadows of the trees lining the avenue had crept across the street. "Within a quarter hour it will be far too dark for riding or to see anything."

"There are other types of encounters one might experience in the dark besides visual ones," Jack murmured for Addie's ears alone. "And I can guarantee, they are quite exciting."

She tried to pretend she didn't hear him, but he could see she had by the way her eyes sparkled and the slight twitch his words produced at the corners of her full, soft lips.

He straightened away from her abruptly, surprised by himself. He hadn't meant to say anything intimate to her.

He had no self-restraint where she was concerned. None at all. He acted on impulse, his heart constantly sabotaging the judicious plotting of his mind.

"—ice skating?" Gerald Norton was saying.

"Oh, yes!" Addie said excitedly. "But where?"

"They rent skates at St. James Park," Gerald said.

"We can take the London Underground to the west end of the Strand and from there it's only a short walk to the park," Ted said.

"I've never been on the Underground," Addie said, her tip-tilted eyes gleaming from between the thicket of her black curling lashes. "It sounds exhilarating."

"I'm not at all sure that being hauled about like so much cattle in a subterranean oxcart can be termed exhilarating," Lady Merritt said doubtfully. "All this gamboling about is more befitting the dignity of the lower classes."

"Inspiration comes from many sources, Lady Merritt," Ted said. "A hay meadow, a stanza of chamber music, the perfume of an infant's breath, the flush on a woman's cheek."

Lady Merritt turned bright pink.

"Indeed. Nothin' prettier than a handsome woman in the full bloom of her femininity," Gerald put in gallantly.

Lady Merritt's blush deepened. "Well," she said coyly, "I suppose I might come along and watch."

"Splendid!" Ted said, rising.

The others followed suit and left the warm confines of the Fleece for the chill dusk. Overhead the sky was quickly darkening.

Gerald, having offered and had his arm accepted by Lady Merritt, set the pace. Ted, securing Addie's hand in the crook of his arm, strolled after.

Jack stood watching them go until Addie turned. Her eyes met his with a mixture of entreaty and subtle challenge. With no further thought, he fell into step behind them.

He hadn't meant to go. He'd meant to quit their numbers and pursue his own inquiries before stationing himself in Ted's studio. He needed the names of the men who'd served under Paul Sherville and, he thought grimly, Charles Hoodless, so he could question them.

Instead, following at Addie's heels, he hoarded the pleasure of watching her eyes gleam with excitement as she led the descent into the Underground station. Her gasp of delighted trepidation when the tram erupted from the black tunnel was delicious. He nearly fell over himself, catching her arms and pulling her safely back on the noisy, crowded platform.

Her breath was ragged, her breasts stirring with agitation against his chest. Even through the layers of wool and linen, he could feel their weight, the heavy beat of her pulse . . . or was it his?

He looked into the sweet honey of her eyes and felt her hair slip like cold silk over the backs of his hands. He hadn't even realized he'd lifted his hands to cup her head and tilt her unresisting face up to meet his—

He shook his head and released her, stepping back. She gave him a slow, knowing smile and a silvery chime of merriment.

He was a fool, but he could no more leave this fascinating, joyous creature than he could quit breathing. Because Addie was flirting with him. There was no other word for it.

His pitiful attempt to distance himself from her had been absurd, with no more hope of success than the sun has of climbing into the night sky. He simply was not strong enough to knowingly purchase her hatred. With the first shimmer of tears in her eyes, he'd given up.

He could only love her. Aye. *Love.* Impossible, desperate, doomed, and incontrovertible.

Since dinner, for the first time in their relationship, Addie seemed to realize her power over him. It was delightful, charming, being the focus of Addie's new-sprung playfulness, the recipient of her coquetry.

It was also frustrating beyond belief.

Every movement, designed to entice, enthralled. Every warm look ignited insatiable fires; every teasing comment tested his restraint. The bow of her underlip, the sidelong glance beneath the wicked fringe of her lashes, the erotic jostle of her breast beneath the soft fleece of her cashmere gown, were beyond tempting.

For so long he'd tamped down the sexual response she drew from him, content with her mind, her spirit. But now, it seemed, her body wanted to join in the game. And she was making the rules up as she went. And he? He panted after her, scrambling for the favors she was so generously bestowing.

Their ride on the Underground was short and fifteen minutes later the group climbed to the top of the stairs and strolled toward the Strand, past Lipton's tearooms and Harrods. The sun had completely abandoned the sky and London's thick, featureless mantle of fog was creeping over the city, leaving her a place strangely out of time, existing in a perpetual twilight created from sulfur and coal and mist.

The gas streetlights ringing the park glowed with a smoky orange light, tiny snowflakes swirling about their globes, dusting the air and gathering on the shoulders of street vendors hawking roasted nuts and hot chocolate at the park-side curbs. High above the streets thousands of chimney pots sported plumes of pale smoke.

Gerald led the way to an iron bench and headed off to a little kiosk trimmed with yellow and green satin pennants set against the iron rails of the park gate. He returned a few minutes later holding skates, like braces of partridge, laces dripping from both hands.

Addie tossed up her long skirts with the easy manner of a child, and eagerly Jack leaned forward to help her with her skates, reaching out for a cotton-clad calf. Ted cut him off with a knowing smile and a murmur pitched for his ears alone: "I don't care how timorous a virgin you purport to be, I'll lace my sister's boots."

"Of course," Jack said, forcing a harmless smile to his face. He took a seat at the far end of the bench and attached the rented skates as Ted fit the steel blades to the bottoms of Addie's boots.

As soon as Ted finished, Addie scrambled up from the seat and immediately lost her balance. Her arms windmilled frantically, one skated foot slicing left, the other detouring to the right.

Jack leapt forward just as she pitched into his arms. Her hat skewed over her eyes and long streamers of her dark auburn hair uncoiled down her back. She gasped, one hand braced against his chest.

"Good heavens," she breathed.

"Skated often, have you?" Jack asked, amused.

"Never."

"Why didn't you say something?"

She blew a strand of hair out of her face and peeked up at him. Even that slight movement upset her balance. She flailed some more until Jack recaptured his hold on her. "It didn't look like it would be that hard to do," she admitted.

He laughed. "It isn't." Slowly, he released her and skated backward a few feet. She looked after him admiringly and at his nod of encouragement, wobbled forth, her hands held out from her sides like a tightrope walker.

"Would you care to have a go, Mrs. Hoodless?" he inquired formally, offering his arm.

"Thank you." She shuffle-minced over to clutch his proffered arm before letting out the breath she'd been holding and beaming up at him. "How do you do it?"

He leaned close to her ear. A silky curl tickled his lip as he whispered, "Just close your eyes and glide."

She nodded and her eyelids fluttered shut, her smile still playing on her lips. He wanted to lean over and steal kisses from her soft, pretty mouth. Instead, he slipped his arm around her, tucking her close against his side. She covered the back of his hand with her own. He took her other hand in his, holding it out in front of them.

"Glide," he repeated and pushed off.

She was a lousy skater. She tried—valiantly, determinedly, good-naturedly—but she never quite got the knack of gliding. She shuffled. She stomped. She minced. She tiptoed, but she did not glide.

Around them the others were, with varying degrees of success, sailing about the cleared ice or moving in slow sedate circles. Gerald Norton was a revelation.

On ice, his long, awkward body acquired mythical grace. Turning, wheeling, executing clean, smooth circles, or making little vaults into the air, he flew about the ice with the ease and agility of a premier danseur.

After a while, Addie, pink with exertion and cold, asked Jack to take her to a nearby bench. Unwilling to give up even the slight claim of his hand at her waist, Jack nonetheless complied, easing her down.

She shifted her skirts to make room for him and he sat down next to her. For a minute, she didn't say anything. Her shining eyes followed Gerald's course as he gracefully wove in and out amongst the less talented skaters.

"He is wonderful."

"Yes."

"I'm terrible."

"Yes."

She laughed and turned a mock glare on him. "You needn't be so quick to agree."

"I'm honest by nature." Even as he said the words, he felt himself flush.

"Where did you learn to skate, Jack?"

"The Highlands. All those lochs, don't you know."

"Was it nice?"

"Nice?" Jack echoed.

"Yes," she said, looking at him directly. She was a foot away and he could see the faint promise of laugh lines beginning at the corners of her liquid gold eyes. "It occurs to me that I don't know very much about you, Jack. Every time I ask you something, you change the subject. It hardly seems fair. You know so much about me. I want to rectify that."

"I'm sure you know enough," he said.

"No," she protested. "I don't know anything about your boyhood. All I know is that you came from the Highlands and that you are one of Mr. Morris's protégés."

Jack shrugged uncomfortably. "You know I am Lord Merritt's great-nephew, that I am twenty-nine years old, that my name is John—"

"Yes, yes," she cut in impatiently. "I have a dossier of facts, but you've never spoken much about how you have spent those twenty-nine years. What have you done, Jack?"

God, he wished he knew.

She'd tilted her head to the side. A snowflake caught on the tip of her black lash and she blinked. "There must have been school and family and friends . . ." She glanced up at him shyly. "Lady friends?"

"No," he managed to say.

"No family or no lady friends?" she asked a little too lightly.

"No to both."

"I'm sorry."

"For the lack of family or the lack of female companionship?" he heard himself ask. He couldn't help it; she was so appealingly obvious.

Tentatively, she returned his smile. "Family. Although I must admit, I am curious as to why you haven't . . . that is, why you didn't . . ." She broke off and blushed.

"Why I didn't form an attachment?"

Because I was waiting for you. All my life I've been waiting for you. And now it's too late.

"Yes," she said.

"There wasn't time." Nothing like the truth to hide a lie.

"No time?" she asked incredulously. "I'd think that in the Highlands there would be nothing but time."

"You mean nothing to do? Why, there are the sheep and the mountains and the sheep . . . and the sheep . . . and then there are, of course, sheep—" He let out a little *whoosh* as she gave him a quick jab in the ribs with her elbow.

"I am so sorry," she said smoothly. "My arm slipped. Now, you were telling me of all the things one might do in the Highlands."

"You'd be surprised."

She frowned but then, in an impulsive gesture, reached over and placed her gloved hand on his wrist, gazing up at him earnestly. Of its own volition, his hand flew to cover hers. She looked at their hands entwined and smiled.

"Please, Jack," she said softly. "Tell me something about yourself. Tell me what things fashioned your character."

Jack thought desperately. What bit of honesty could he give her? What had made him thus?

Sometimes he felt he had been formed by the deserts of North Africa and the cold, wind-bitten peaks of the Himalayas. Or had Captain Jack Cameron been born beneath the eardrum-shattering report of muzzle blasts, the acrid bite of smoke in his nostril and the metallic tang of blood in his mouth?

As to what had formed his character, that he knew too well. The men who'd put their faith in him. The boys who'd looked to him for direction. Honorable lads who believed in what they were doing. And his task had been to see that they lived to do it. And he'd done that; he'd been faithful to that.

Was it his fault that another had betrayed their trust? Wasn't it presumptuous to appoint himself their avenger? And wasn't that the most blatant of specious reasoning because he wanted above all things to end this charade?

"Jack?" Addie asked, a note of worry in her voice. "Are you all right?"

"Of course he is," a man said.

Jack wheeled about to see who'd spoken and found himself looking directly into the face of his former commanding officer, Lord Hannibal Mitchell.

"How are you, Jack?" the general asked.

21

Jack had known there was a good chance that eventually someone from his past would recognize him. He was, however, surprised by the overwhelming sense of relief he felt. His only real regret was that he wished he could have told Addie himself, rather than have her discover it like this.

He rose slowly, certain this was what a man standing in the dock awaiting a verdict must feel: trepidation but also gratitude that he no longer need anticipate his sentence. "Sir."

"You're looking well, Cameron." Lord Mitchell inclined his head but his gaze moved to Addie. As soon as she had realized that the old man towering over her wore Her Majesty's uniform, her smile had faded. She had never looked more like her brother. No emotion, not one telltale thought, was betrayed on her countenance.

"Mrs. Hoodless." The general snapped smartly forward at the waist. "I don't know if you remember, but we met at a military ball some years ago."

It was impossible to gauge whether Addie did remember; her polite mask remained firmly in place.

"I have never had the opportunity to express in person my condolences over your bereavement," the general continued. "Allow me to do so now."

"Thank you," Addie murmured, her gaze fixed on her lap.

Lord Mitchell bowed once more before returning his attention to Jack. "How are you doing, Cameron?"

"Very well, sir." He took a deep breath and lifted his chin. "My shoulder—"

"Good," broke in Lord Mitchell. "You must come by the offices some day soon and tell me all about it."

"Sir, I am no longer—"

"Really, son, I am well aware of what you are and are not. I have kept apprised of your movements for years."

Son? thought Jack blankly.

"I promise I will not try to draft you into service again. I just wish to spend a few minutes with you, out of respect for your father."

Jack stared. As far as Jack knew, Lord Mitchell had never even met his father. What the hell was going on?

The general smiled as his gaze passed once more over Addie, who was still sitting in a fair approximation of lifelessness. For just an instant, Lord Mitchell's polite expression sharpened as he considered her averted face.

"Promise me you'll visit me at my office at Whitehall, Jack. I insist."

Numbly, Jack nodded. For whatever reason, his masquerade had not only been noticed but was being allowed to continue. Encouraged to continue.

Satisfied, Lord Mitchell clapped him on the shoulder. "Good. Shall we say this Friday at four? Or are you awake by then? Your ilk rather burns the night oil, or so I've been told.

"And don't worry, you've no need to explain the path you've chosen." Lord Mitchell's keen gray eye held Jack's gaze. "Though

I would like to know how it came about. It should prove to be an interesting story. Four o'clock, did we say?"

"Yes," Jack responded slowly. "Four o'clock would be fine, sir."

"I'll see you then." He bowed to Addie again and with a brief "ma'am," took his leave.

"What was that about your shoulder?" Addie asked, regarding him quizzically.

"It was injured sometime before we met."

"How did it happen?"

"I was in the wrong place at the wrong time." She'd never know how wrong. "I was angry and lost in my thoughts. I should have been watching what I was doing. I won't bore you with the details."

"Oh, Jack. I'm sorry."

For the second time in a matter of minutes, he was confounded, this time by her open pity.

"No doubt he'll subject you to a diatribe about how disappointed your father would have been in your chosen profession."

"I doubt it. Lord Mitchell is a soldier, not a knave," he said. She blinked up at him. Apparently his response had been just as unexpected as hers had been for him. "And neither was my father."

"I'm sorry. I was presumptuous. I fear my own experience with . . . with military gentlemen has colored my perceptions. I—" Her gaze faltered. "I have never imagined a soldier in the role of doting father. If he had lived to see the path you have chosen, do you really think he'd approve?"

He could see her very real confusion and her desire for an answer.

What could he say? Would his father approve of the deception he practiced, no matter what the reasons? Would he applaud his constancy to his dead comrades or damn him as a manipulative imposter?

"Jack?" She touched him gently on the back of his hand. Her fingertips felt warm. "I didn't mean to cause you any pain."

"It isn't—"

"I say, Jack!" Gerald hailed him as he skated up. "Who was the military chappie?"

"Lord Mitchell."

"Lord Mitchell?" Gerald pursed his lips, looking impressed. "The general?"

"Yes," Addie said. "Apparently he's an old friend of Jack's father."

"Ah, yes. The 'Scots heathen.' 'The burly, claymore-wielding Highland warrior.' Lord Merritt's demagogue and Lady Merritt's nemesis—"

"And Jack's father," Addie interjected softly.

Gerald blushed. "Oh, dear. I say. I am sorry, old chap. Just that one never expects that you would have sprung from the loins of someone as fierce as your pater is supposed to have been."

Jack smiled. "My father was fierce."

"Lord Mitchell seemed to know you as well as your father, Jack." Addie eyed him questioningly. "Did he really try to convince you to enter the military at one time?" From her tone it was obvious she considered the very idea preposterous. Her next words proved it. "He must be a terrible judge of men. How could he think you would ever align yourself with those type of men?"

"'Type of men'? I assure you, Lord Mitchell is everything a gentleman could wish to be, Addie," Jack said mildly.

She frowned. She hadn't expected him to defend the general. "Lord Mitchell has made a career of death. You accused Paul Sherville of it this very afternoon."

"Addie, there is nothing remotely similar between those two men excepting a uniform."

Addie's brows inched together in consternation. She tipped her head back to search his expression. "You don't really believe that."

"I know this." *But you never will believe it, will you?* Still, he had to try. "Addie, few of the soldiers I have met are bloodythirsty brutes."

"Well, most of those in my—" She broke off. "What kind of man is attracted to a career that virtually guarantees that you shall be required to kill people?" she asked hotly.

"Men who believe that the lives and freedoms we enjoy are worth dying to protect."

"No." She stumbled to her feet and slipped. Jack reached out to help her but she batted his hands away. "That is rationalization. Pretty-sounding excuses for barbarity!"

"If I might suggest that such generalization—"

"And I might suggest that you take your head from its ostrich hole," she countered. She kept trying to put her hands on her hips and losing her balance, having to clutch at the back of the bench and glaring at him as though her unsteadiness was his fault.

"Addie," Gerald said suddenly, drawing their attention. His face was florid with distress. Lines furrowed his homely brow. "Please, don't upset yourself this way, m'dear. Jack, can't you see how agitated you are making Addie?"

Addie blinked at Gerald, who looked as though he might start weeping at any minute.

"Oh, my," she said, shuffling over to Gerald and patting his arm. "Don't look like that. Everything is all right, isn't it, Jack?" She stared at him, silently demanding his collaboration.

He realized she was telling the simple truth. She might be stubbornly convinced that her blanket judgment of military men was correct, but she certainly hadn't been afraid to speak her mind. Quite the contrary, she'd all but rung his ears. Despite their heated exchange, she was not the least bit intimidated by him. And that realization, despite everything that had transpired, made him grin like an idiot.

"Well?"

"Huh? Oh, yes. Yes, indeed! Addie's right, Gerald, old man. Right as rain. In every way correct."

"Ass," Addie mouthed, but she was smiling.

"I am too sensitive, I expect," Gerald sighed dramatically. "Or too idealistic. I envision that utopian paradise where all mankind—and womankind—lives in harmony, as friends."

"We're not mad at each other. Are we, Jack?" She shot him a self-assured glance and he wanted to lift her in his arms and hug her until she was breathless; he was that pleased with her self-confidence, her faith in their friendship.

"Certainly," he replied graciously. "Addie can be stubborn and pigheaded whenever she wants. I most certainly am munificent enough to ignore her shortcomings."

"And Jack has my permission to put blinders on whenever the whim takes him."

"Ah," Gerald said, glancing between the smiling pair of them. Seeing no animosity, the worry seeped from his face. "I don't like arguments, meself," he said, adding ingenuously, "I expect it's because I never win 'em, don't you know."

Addie chuckled and Gerald looked gratified.

"Addie," he said, holding out his hand, "allow me to teach you a few rudimentary skills before old Cameron here ruins any chance you have of learning how to skate properly."

"We can't all prance about like grotesques at the penny ballet, Gerry," Jack sniffed.

"Envy is such an unbecoming emotion, don't you think, Addie, dear?" Gerry said with a smug smile at her.

"Very," Addie agreed, grinning. She took Gerald's hand and within an hour he had her cutting a pretty—if wobbly—figure across the darkening ice.

Standing about in the bitter cold, watching a gaggle of capering imbeciles break their limbs on a frozen mud hole," Lady Merritt muttered irritably as she allowed the footman to help her off with her coat. "I shall undoubtedly take ill. Undoubtedly. All that foolishness in the park has me quite chilled. Is there a fire in the library?"

"Yes, milady," the footman answered.

"At least someone considers my health. Even though I must pay them for their consideration." She sniffed.

"Dear madame," Jack began soothingly, "had I known you suffered one moment's discomfort I would have insisted we quit the wretched arena immediately! But you bore our juvenile pleasure so modestly that no one had the slightest clue you were in any way discomforted."

"Yes. Well." Lady Merritt was clearly not pacified. "Larkin, have Cook make up a tray of sandwiches and fruit to be sent up. No. Have her make something hot. Jack, if you would be so kind?" She jerked her head in the direction of the library and Jack leapt forward, pulling the massive oak door open just in time for her to sail in, head high, bosom thrust forward, feet stomping the marble parquetry. Something more than not being the cynosure of her little artistic stable had Lady Merritt in a stew.

He followed her into the room and, seeing that she was awaiting his aid, hurried to her side and eased her down into the huge wingback chair. She settled like a plump Ottoman prince.

"I shall suffer the rheumatism for days thanks to that little entertainment."

"Shall I fetch a medic?"

"No, no, no."

"Some fruit then? Something to stoke the old furnace, what?" He picked up a brownish pippin from the sideboard near the door, grimacing as he realized his faux pas. *Excellent, Jack. She is going to love being called an old furnace.* He began paring off the apple's thin skin.

"I don't need a medic," Lady Merritt said, "I don't need any fruit. I need answers."

The thin coil of apple peel fell to the silver platter beneath, making a hushed thump in the suddenly silent room. "Answers?" he asked. "To what questions?"

"You are a fraud, Jack Cameron," Lady Merritt said darkly.

He waited. Years in the military, dealing with senior officers— both superior and inferior—had taught him never to presuppose another's information. It was always best to see the lay of the land before giving ground. He sliced the peeled apple into thin wedges before turning and bringing his offering to Lady Merritt's side.

"Well. Have you nothing to say? I have just called you a faker, a fraud!"

"Yes, so I heard."

"Well?" Lady Merritt prompted impatiently.

"May I ask how you have come to this conclusion?"

"I have eyes, sir. I may be a few years your senior, but I can still see what is clearly placed before me. You are a wolf in sheep's clothing, Jack Cameron. And you have quite duped my darling Addie."

He regarded her stonily. "Yes."

"Aha!" She thumped her fist triumphantly on the padded brocade arm of her chair. "You are even so bold as to admit it. You have slipped beneath Addie's guard. You have duped us. All of us thinking you had your gaze fixed on a higher plane when all the while your intentions have been as base as . . . as base as . . ." She cast about looking for an adequate comparison before her eyes gleamed triumphantly. "As base as Lord Merritt's."

For the second time that day, Jack was at a complete loss. "Ma'am?"

"'Ma'am' me, will you, you Lothario!"

"Lothario?" It occurred to him that Lady Merritt might have suffered some sort of mental event.

She flung herself back in her wingback, her eyes narrowing. "Addie told me about that young American girl Teddy is painting. The Drouhin girl."

"What could Addie possibly have told you about her? And how on earth—"

"All this feigned bewilderment is quite useless. You don't even do it very well. You are way overacting the role."

The irony wasn't lost on Jack, but he could not find it amusing. "Please. What did Addie tell you?"

"She said you had quite captivated the Drouhin girl, charmed her to within an inch of her little American boots."

"Addie said this?"

"Yes. And that is when I began to have my suspicions about you, Jack Cameron. Because there is no doubt in my mind that dear Addie is feeling quite put out about the Drouhin chit. And it is all on your account."

He could not subdue the spark of unworthy pleasure that leapt into flame at her assertion. "And this is why you see me as a Lothario, because Addie thinks I have spent too much time making a young foreigner feel welcome in our country?"

"Dissembler!" Lady Merritt cried dramatically. "It isn't only that. You have been keeping low company. You have been seen!"

This was unanticipated. He wouldn't have expected anyone in Lady Merritt's circle to frequent the diverse haunts in which he'd spent the last several nights searching for men who might have served under Paul Sherville. Or Charles Hoodless. "By whom, Lady Merritt?"

"Larkin, the footman. His brother is employed at one of the establishments you visited last night. I was informed this morning. And really, look at you, boy! You have grown positively haggard these past few days. Indulging in sin and depravity, I'll warrant!"

Jack shrugged ingenuously. "Boys will be boys."

She sent him a chill look. "Yes. Which is why I didn't take you to task for your subterfuge earlier. I attributed it to a temporary lapse in your artistic focus. But now, after seeing how you behave with poor Addie, I must assume the worst. I demand you confess your intentions!"

"I have no intentions," Jack said. It was easy to adopt insouciance where nameless women were concerned but he would not have Lady Merritt running tales to Addie.

"Well, I should hope not!"

"Ma'am—"

"No. I will have my say. You are toying with Addie's affections. Do you think it isn't obvious? You . . . you." She stumbled to an uncharacteristic halt before she began again, her tone low, scandalized, "My God, man! The way you looked at her tonight, when you held her, when you thought no one else noticed . . . it was rapacious. Your gaze alone compromises her!"

He had no answer for that; she was undoubtedly right.

"I won't have her hurt. She has suffered enough."

"I would never—" He stopped short of the promise, because he would. He must.

"She is just now beginning to enjoy life again. I never thought to see her like this. She took Charles's death so hard." Lady Merritt gave him a hard look. "I warned her about you. I did and you needn't go all hard and rigid. It is a fait accompli, for what little good it has done."

"When?"

Lady Merritt lifted her chin. "This evening, as we walked back to that horrible noisy underground train. I felt it my duty. I told her where you had been seen. I told her about the way you looked at her."

Frustration and apprehension filled him.

"Unfortunately, the willfulness she was known for as an adolescent has made an untimely reappearance. She refused to take my warning seriously. She laughed! She's changed these last weeks. Which is why I must appeal to you, Jack," she finished sententiously.

"You are appealing to my finer feelings?" Jack almost laughed then. It was absurd. Clearly, given what he was doing, he had none. "You are asking that I . . . what? Ignore her? Snub her?"

"No. She is clearly infatuated with you, Jack. If you have any decency, you will not lead the poor girl on."

Decency? The word had become alien to him.

"I know what you artists are. Incapable of committing to anyone or anything but your muse. It wouldn't be fair to suggest to Addie otherwise. Promise me you won't hurt her."

"I would be loathe to hurt Addie, Lady Merritt." *But, the devil take me, I cannot promise I will not hurt her.*

"Good. Because if you did I would have to reconsider my plan to introduce you to society and I should hate to do that. Merritt hasn't seen you yet!"

His eyebrows rose. This was insensitive even for Lady Merritt. She seemed to realize her gaffe. "I mean, Merritt would never forgive me if I were to set his last living relative adrift, alone and without friends, in the dark, soulless city."

Balderdash. He hadn't fulfilled his role yet. He had not been used to embarrass Lord Merritt yet. Fate had cast him in so many roles and the only one he wanted—that of Addie's lover—was denied him by the others.

He had to keep his eye on the prize now, more than ever before. His best chance of discovering the traitor would be over in a short while. He could not afford to indulge some fantasy regarding Addie Hoodless.

"I am not completely friendless, Lady Merritt. You needn't worry that your Christian charity might be questioned on that account."

"Oh, really, Jack." He had never heard her try a conciliatory tone before. "You wouldn't rob me of your delightful company just because I love dear Addie and am concerned for her, would you? Besides, I had a letter from Evan. He and his father will be home soon."

His gaze sharpened. "When?"

Lady Merritt shrugged and tittered. "Oh, a week or so. Perhaps in time for the reception I am giving Ted. Please, let us forget the unpleasant words between us."

Desperately Jack raked his mind for some direction. A week? Lord Merritt knew Jack had been a soldier, was a soldier. He'd arranged for Jack's transportation from Alexandria, for his installation at Gate Hall. With Lord Merritt's arrival, this masquerade would be finished once and for all.

One week.

Lady Merritt smiled winsomely. "I can hardly wait for Merritt to see you. Let us be friends."

"Of course, dear lady. I can't tell you how very much I, too, look forward to his return."

23

Over there, Cameron," Ted said. "On top. No. More to the side. Hm. Try moving it back. Now forward. To the opposite corner." He squinted as Jack lugged the massive piece of plaster from one end of the platform to the other. Finally, he sighed. "Sorry, old man," Ted said. He didn't sound particularly sincere. "I guess that won't work after all. You can take it away."

Jack muttered several oaths before complying. He returned the column to the corner he'd toted it from and bent over, hands on his thighs, panting slightly.

Ted shook his head. "It's not rest time yet, Jack." He motioned him over. With a dark look, Jack came.

Ted turned to her. "It just wasn't quite the flavor I'm aiming for, don't you know. I want an element of mystery, Addie."

Addie nodded mechanically, distracted by Jack's proximity and by the disturbing realization that his jacket had not exaggerated his figure, but had disguised it. He was lean but very well formed. No, beautifully formed. Beneath his sweat-dampened shirt, hard ridges and muscular planes revealed themselves with each movement.

She wondered suddenly if his trousers—trousers she'd assumed were stuffed with augmentations—encased muscle rather than horsehair. Could his limbs be as long and strong as the tight modeling of his trousers suggested? She gulped.

Surely when they'd met this past autumn the fit of his attire had suggested reedy shanks at best.

"Addie?" She jerked around guiltily to find her brother was smiling at her in an odiously knowing manner.

"You look quite befuddled, m'dear," Ted said. "Is something bothering you about Jack's attire? It's rather hot in here to insist he wear a coat, but if his lack of apparel offends you I can have him—"

"Of course not!" Addie broke in, trying not to sound flustered. "I was thinking of something else. What was it you said?"

"Well, if you're certain Jack's masculine posturing isn't offending your matronly dignity?"

Jack, who'd been standing silently, made a sound in his throat.

"Don't be an ass!" Addie clapped her hand over her mouth as the three prospective clients stopped chattering to stare at her in chill reproach.

Then, making offended noises, noses held collectively high, they filed from the studio, the last member of the party pausing to give them a quelling look. "We may be back."

"Oh, Ted," Addie said, "I am sorry!"

"As well you should be, hoyden!"

Seeing the gleam of amusement in her brother's eye and realizing he didn't give a fig for the prospective clients, she dropped her hand. "I take that back. Now what did you say to me?"

"I was simply asking your opinion. What do you think would add an exotic aspect to the painting? It is to be an Odalisque, after all. I need to instill a more eastern quality to it."

Other than a peacock fan her father had once had in his studio, she had no experience with the Middle East. "I'm sorry, Ted, but any suggestion I made would only be supposition."

"Ah, yes. We do want it to be authentic." His gaze slewed toward Jack. "What about you? Know anything about the Middle East, Cameron?"

"No."

"Really? Nothing at all?"

"No."

"Use your imagination. What do you think a harem woman would wear?"

"I couldn't say and, like Addie, I would hate to mislead you by putting forth an opinion." Jack's voice was growing strained. Addie listened, puzzled. He should be used to Ted's twitting by now.

"I see," Ted said. "You don't want to mislead me. Or Addie?"

"Of course not." There was a sudden bleakness in Jack's tone that set Addie's heartbeat stuttering with inexplicable trepidation.

What was happening? Something was eating away at Jack like a gangrenous limb. Every day since their skating party, he had grown more uncommunicative, more distant, gathering whatever wounded him to himself as though it gave him some perverse pleasure.

"Ted, stop hounding Jack," she said sharply.

Ted regarded her for a second before saying, so softly she had to lean forward to catch his words, "I applaud your rediscovered ability to speak up in another's defense, Addie. I've missed it. But could you defend yourself—if it should be necessary?"

"Don't speak nonsense. Charles is d—" She broke off, realizing how much she had nearly revealed. "I don't intend to ever be in a situation where it will be necessary."

"Life does not take into account our intentions," Ted said quietly, his gaze holding hers.

"What would you like me to do next, Ted?" Jack broke in roughly.

"There are some large brass urns and a divan stored above the servants' quarters. I believe there are also some marble slabs. They might inspire the proper mood. If you would be so kind?"

"Ted, you can't use Jack like this. First, the Sultan debacle, then making him build a dais you never use, and now this!" Addie protested.

"I disagree. I can use Jack any way Jack allows himself to be used," Ted said. "As long as he doesn't protest, why should you? At least I am quite upfront about 'using' him, as you so vulgarly phrase it. After all, he asked me. I didn't ask him."

"He's quite right, Addie. Everything worth having has its price," Jack said. "Including this."

"But, Ted—"

At that moment a commotion in the outer hallway interrupted Addie. The unmistakable American twang of Zephrina Drouhin could be heard, laughingly rejoined by male English accents as, with her customary élan, she made her entrance.

"See? We can take a peek at the portrait after all. I told you he would be here." She waved the two military officers trailing behind her forward. "He always is. Quite a slave to his . . . craft? Profession?" She lifted her hands toward Ted in a pretty study of confusion. "What do you call what you do?"

Ted didn't bother rising to her bait. He regarded her blandly. "Unchaperoned again, Miss Drouhin? How fortunate my sister is here—once more—to see that your reputation remains . . . spotless? Untarnished? Passable? What do you call it?"

Zephrina's full, pouty lips thinned discernibly. "Not at all, Mr. Phyfe. I have brought my maid along. She is waiting below stairs. A treasure she is, too. It is so hard to find a maid able to maintain the judicious and discreet distance that allows one's escorts to whisper"—she paused and smiled naughtily—"pleasantries."

Her unique American vivacity was refreshing and Addie found herself wishing circumstances were such that she felt warmer toward the young woman. Indeed, she remembered what it had been like to be vivacious and eager and self-confident. In sudden sympathy with the spirited young girl, Addie returned her smile, until she noted the way Zephrina's inquisitive gaze had lit on Jack.

"Mr. Cameron! Why, look at you. I did not realize anyone amongst the upper classes knew the meaning of honest labor." She bestowed a radiant smile on her two escorts. "With the notable exception of my military companions, that is."

The two officers huffed and snorted, at a loss for words. Zephrina probably had that effect on most men, Addie thought wryly. Even Jack seemed momentarily befuddled by the petite vision standing a few feet from him, sizing him up as though he were one of her American quarter horses.

"Who'd have guessed you looked like this under all that lace and velvet?" She tossed her head back and laughed. "My, my. Appearances can be deceiving."

Addie felt dislike replace her earlier empathy for Zephrina. Jack came out of his slack-jawed trance. "Unspeakably vulgar of me to be seen in my present *dishabille*," he drawled.

"Not at all. You're quite a Michelangelo statue come to life, all strapping and masculine, and therefore in every way appropriate for an artist's studio."

Addie felt her own smile freeze. The woman was incorrigible, and the disparaging look she darted at Ted was enough to make Addie want to slap her face.

"You, Miss Drouhin, are very fast," Jack said.

"I know." She dimpled. "And you, Mr. Cameron, are intriguing. Even Major Sherville is intrigued. He was very upset with you, you know. After that amusing little scene you enacted last week.

Very upset. He spent inordinate amounts of time assuring me that whatever your proclivities, his are completely natural."

"Good Lord!" Ted said, his suave demeanor finally disturbed. "Whether you have no care for your own reputation, Miss Drouhin, kindly remember that my sister is not accustomed to your audacity."

Zephrina turned to Addie, her gaze traveling with telling blandness over her clothing, making Addie aware of how she must compare to the American girl's brilliant femininity. From her subdued navy-blue taffeta skirt with its prudent little bustle to the narrow band of ribbon fastening the discreet collar of her tan shirtwaist, Addie was drab and dowdy.

As Charles's wife she'd chosen her dull wardrobe purposefully, desperately trying not to call attention to herself. And since coming out of mourning, she had not spent much time with a modiste. Miss Drouhin's elegant laces and ribbons, ruffles and bows, could not be a more striking contrast to her homely ensemble.

Jack was studying the tiny American avidly, his usual urbane manner having deserted him. He looked intent, focused, making Addie keenly aware of why her brother had all but laughed at her for asking whether or not Jack was "interested" in women.

Without a doubt he was interested in Zephrina Drouhin.

A prick of some unfamiliar feeling made Addie shift restlessly. For years she had breathed a sigh of relief whenever a man—any man but her brother and a very few of his friends—gave up trying to engage her in a conversation and left her alone. Now Jack's attention had been captivated by this lovely young woman and she felt . . . jealous.

"So sorry, Mrs. Hoodless," Zephrina murmured and there was no mistaking her embarrassment. "I didn't mean to offend you, ma'am."

She couldn't do anything about her wardrobe yet, but this bit of a thing wasn't going to make her feel gauche or matronly!

"Offended, Miss Drouhin?" she asked. "I assure you, any of Paul Sherville's proclivities, whether natural or otherwise, only inspire boredom."

Zephrina blinked in surprise. Addie continued smiling.

"Now, Addie," Jack said, his gaze still riveted on Zephrina. He was going to fall over if he leaned any farther toward her. "Mr. Sherville is obviously a good friend of Miss Drouhin's."

"Yes." Zephrina glanced toward Ted, who'd turned his back and was wiping brushes. "A very good friend."

Jack sighed. "I wish I hadn't gotten off on the wrong foot with him."

Addie stared at him in amazement.

"La! You certainly did that!"

Jack shrugged. "He seems an interesting chap. Been all about the world and all. How thrilling to be so well traveled. I wish I were."

"Indeed, he has known many exotic places," Zephrina said. "He's been to North Africa and Egypt and India."

"Fascinating. I would love to hear his stories. I have quite a passion for the Middle East, don't you know. But I don't suppose I'll get the chance now."

"I should say not," Zephrina allowed. "Too bad, too. He does spin a wonderful tale!"

"Perhaps . . . Perhaps you might be— No, no. I couldn't ask it." Jack broke off, shaking his head. He could not have found a better way to pique the bold little American heiress's interest and Addie suspected he knew it.

"Please," Zephrina purred. "What were you going to ask?"

"I was going to ask if you would do me the honor of taking a carriage ride with me tomorrow, perhaps relate a few of Sherville's choicer tales or tell me about your American frontier. If there is anything I am as passionate about as the Middle East, it is the American frontier."

Addie felt the blood drain from her cheeks with Jack's proposal. It was against all rules of etiquette to make a proposal to a single person in front of a group the invitation excluded. As it had excluded her.

"That's odd, Jack," Ted said. "In all the time you have spent with my sister and myself, I have never heard you mention the American west before. Addie, has Jack ever mentioned this 'passion' to you?"

"No."

Jack regarded Ted with an odd fire in his eyes and a harsh, bitter quality to his smile. No, not a smile, a sneer. "It just goes to prove how little we know each other, doesn't it?" His words cut like a knife. "I would never have mentioned any passion I have to Addie. It would be fruitless."

"Yes. Mrs. Hoodless has never lived in the American west," Zephrina said. All three of them turned to stare at Addie, as though her presence had been forgotten.

"Precisely." Jack managed a smile.

"Well, I'd be delighted to satisfy your curiosity, Mr. Cameron. In fact, this afternoon I haven't any engagements—"

"But, Miss Drouhin," protested one of her escorts, "you are promised at Lady Curtis's musicale."

"You shall simply have to tender my regrets. I couldn't stand to be cloistered in some stuffy drawing room on so glorious a day. I am unused to all this indoor living. You wouldn't want me to pine away, would you?" She fluttered her eyelashes and both men shook their heads. "Then you'll carry my regrets?"

"But we could all—" one of the duo started to say.

"No, no. I would never dream of robbing Lady Curtis of your company just because I am feeling homesick. I would never forgive myself."

The officers fell into an unhappy silence. Zephrina turned back to Jack. "It's settled then."

"Splendid."

"Shall we say two o'clock? Most unfashionable, I know."

"You, Miss Drouhin, are the sort of young lady who sets fashion," Jack said admiringly.

"You've outdone yourself, Cameron," Ted said in disgust. "You're positively unctuous."

"Ted," Addie said, "didn't you have something you wanted Jack to move? I believe you mentioned slabs of marble. Lots of slabs of marble."

"Yes. Many, many slabs." He tapped Jack, still smiling in that nauseatingly moony manner at Zephrina, on the shoulder.

"Come along, Jackie, me lad. You've work to do if you're to play this afternoon. And, believe me, you'll want to allow time to bathe afterward."

24

Though they tried to hide it, the shopgirls and models at Mssr. Drexhall's store regarded Addie's plain gown and severe hairstyle with much the same pitying expression as had Zephrina Drouhin.

Addie took a deep breath. "Scintillation," she announced in answer to the head modiste's query.

The master couturier—Mssr. Drexhall, who'd been lolling indolently in a brocade armchair—turned at this.

"What was that?"

"Madame asked what I would like my new wardrobe to inspire and I told her."

Her words had an unexpected effect. Mssr. Drexhall, well aware of his reputation as London's most exclusive couturier, narrowed his eyes. Clearly, he was reassessing the drab woman who'd entered demanding a new ball gown by week's end and an entire wardrobe soon thereafter, price being no object.

Money alone was not enough to spur the interest of an artist of Mssr. Drexhall's reputation. He'd studied for years under Worth.

And while he wasn't about to turn away a small fortune, he obviously was having trouble working up enthusiasm for the project of outfitting a woman just coming out of mourning.

"Scintillating," he murmured, rising from his chair and approaching. He took her hand and lifted her arm, his gaze traveling with detached consideration over her figure. He walked around her, stepped back, and cupped his elbow in one hand, drumming his fingers against his prominent chin with the other. His satin, tasseled cap slipped back on his round head, exposing a balding dome.

"You are sure you do not mean, say, 'attractive'? 'Very pleasing'?"

"Quite sure. I did not pick the word out of a dictionary. I know what I mean. I know what I want."

She wanted Jack Cameron. She wanted him to look at her like he had the tiny American. Intent. Rapt.

Artistic fervor replaced the suspicion that had darkened the master's features. "Yes," he said as if to himself. "Yes. Scintillating I can do."

Addie relaxed.

"But—" He held up a warning finger, causing her to hold her breath. "But, you must put yourself entirely in my hands. Entirely. I will brook no interference from you. None."

"Monsieur, I—"

"No. I will show these foolish Americans who leapfrog over themselves to buy Worth's facsimiles. I will show society the genius I am capable of when given a free hand. And a free hand I must have. I can promise you a gown that will burn the eyes of any man, but you must trust me implicitly. Do you agree?"

Did she? "Yes."

Rather than looking pleased, a huge scowl deepened the lines on Mssr. Drexhall's swarthy face. He flopped down in a chair, steepling his fingers in front of his lips and glowering at her fully five minutes before barking, "Louis XIV's embroidered jacket. The drake-green silk. Now! The silver paillettes, too!"

The attendants broke like partridges from a covey, scattering about the workroom on their various urgent missions.

"Now, Madame, I warn you. You will suffer for my art."

And she did. She spent the rest of the morning being pulled, twisted, and stuck with pins. But she did so with grim resolve. Jack Cameron would see her as a woman. Not a widow, not a friend, not a sympathetic sister but a woman. A scintillating, irresistible woman.

By the time she had finished her fitting and returned to her townhouse, her head had begun to ache, but it did not overshadow her satisfaction. Even the realization that the dratted new furnace had once again gone defective and was pumping ungodly heat into the rooms couldn't dampen her delight. She mopped away the sweat beading on her forehead. It was swelteringly hot.

"Greer!" she called for the housekeeper. No answer.

What little staff she employed had apparently found "errands" to get them out of the oppressively hot townhouse. Either that or they were off looking for someone to fix it. Since the system had been installed she hadn't seen anything of Foster's Domestic Heating Services besides their outrageous bill.

She cursed, barely noticing she was doing so. As the youngest child in the loose society of a house peopled by lax-mannered artists, bohemians, and rambunctious older brothers, she'd been exposed to an extensive vocabulary of epitaphs.

She'd been doing a lot of cursing lately. Ever since Jack had disappeared from the studio with Miss Zephrina Drouhin two days ago. Since then the timorous affection she had been nursing for Jack had disappeared, shredded by the realization that she was in love with Jack Cameron.

Not like, not fond. There was nothing tentative or sedate about the feelings Jack had roused in her slumbering heart. She loved him; his wit, his kindness, his genial nature. But it was more than companionable accord that fevered her dreams and wrecked her peace of mind.

Their one kiss had pricked her with frustrated longing. She wondered what it would be like to have his mouth open over hers, to feel his chest naked against her, to have those strong, clever hands caress her . . . not worshipfully, not reverently, but masterfully, passionately, ardently.

She supposed that she at least owed the American girl thanks for that. She might have gone on for months, perhaps even years, subsisting on milquetoast emotions if it had not been for Zephrina Drouhin. With her abrupt awakening from her self-imposed numbness, she had come to another certainty: if she wanted Jack Cameron, she had damn well better do something about it.

She raked the damp, curling tendrils back from her forehead. She was accustomed to being the center of Jack's gentle attentions. But there hadn't been anything gentle about the expression he bent on the pretty girl.

Her scowl deepened and she pulled out the hairpins that had vexed her all morning. Her hair tumbled free. She wanted Jack to look at her like that, not like she was some fragile, purposeless curio he was afraid to touch.

A sudden loud bang and clatter ringing from the floorboards, followed by a sinister hiss from the radiators, interrupted her thoughts. The dratted things sounded like they were about to explode. She'd best see if Ted could wrestle the beast into behaving.

She climbed the stairs to his studio. Inside, it was not quite as hot as below stairs. She looked up and saw that the skylights had been propped open with empty paint cans, allowing a single eddy of cool air in.

"Ted?" she called. No answer. She looked around. There was no sign of her brother. He was probably waiting out the sauna experience in a nearby pub.

She angled her head sideways to look at Ted's most recently finished painting where it stood propped on an easel. Another officer in the Black Dragoons. Her gaze went stony with distaste.

Ted was so much better than that. So much better than a mere society portraitist. He had a real gift for composition, for the juxtaposition of texture and color.

She wandered over to the far end of the studio where Ted worked on his noncommissioned paintings. For months now he'd been working on an outsized Odalisque. Carefully, she peeled back the velvet drapery that hung over it. She stepped back and sighed with pleasure when she saw the progress he'd made.

The harem woman reclined in the classic Odalisque position, supine on sumptuous red velvet pillows. Her ankles were crossed discreetly, the brass glint of her ankle bracelets a stunning contrast to the satiny sheen of her pampered flesh. Ted had chosen not to do his harem girl as a traditional nude, but instead had clothed her in harem garb. The effect was more erotic than mere skin would have been.

About her torso she wore open an abbreviated red satin vest, heavy with thick gold embroidery and encrusted with thousands of winking glass pearls. Between her partially covered breasts, a shadowed valley was a mauve-stained mystery. The sheerest of gossamer silk harem pants revealed rather than concealed her long legs. A girdle of hammered gold and ruby red stones lay against the naked jut of her hipbone.

In an outfit like that any woman would be scintillating.

A twinkle caught her eye and she stepped behind the painting to the dais upon which the model posed. A low-slung divan stood squarely in the middle, covered with pillows and draperies. The harem costume lay in an untidy pile on top of the plush cushions.

Curious, Addie reached out and picked it up. She smiled. Though fashioned of nothing more than paste and glass, cheap wire and stained satin, Ted had made it look opulent and expensive in the painting. Just as he'd transformed the model, whom Addie knew had a Cockney accent and a missing front tooth, into a sultry harem girl.

She was about to leave when she caught sight of herself reflected in one of the windows. She stared at her image until a sudden, cheeky grin was reflected back at her.

Why not? Wasn't scintillation to be her new byword? An innocent bit of role-playing would put her in the proper frame of mind. Besides, no one was about and since Ted was gone, no one was expected. The studio's entrance was locked. She'd seen that on her way up the stairs. And if her servants returned, well, they weren't allowed to come up to the studio even when Ted was here.

Why not, indeed?

Her grin broadening, she kicked off her slippers. Reaching behind her, she undid the buttons on the back of her dress, dropping it to the ground. Then she untied her single petticoat and unlaced the modest corset she wore, kicking those, too, free. With a tiny thrill of delicious wickedness, she peeled off her combinations and stockings and finally stood stark naked in the studio.

She stepped into a pool of sunlight coming from the overhead skylights. The warm air bathed her exposed skin and dazzled her eyes and she shivered in delight. She had never stood naked in sunlight. It was wanton. It was wonderful.

For long minutes she just stood, relishing the unaccustomed sensations, gazing at her image in the window with surprised pleasure, reacquainting herself with the look of her body, the size of her breasts, the length of her legs. It had been so long since she'd taken any conscious delight in her femininity.

Then, like a schoolgirl playing dress-up from the attic trunks, she slipped into the harem pants and linked the metal girdle low on her hip. She undid the last of the pins striving unsuccessfully to confine her hair and shook the thick waves out, luxuriating in the silky feel of it spilling over her naked shoulders, down her back and breasts. Almost regretfully she slid her arms into the short jacket. The model was much better endowed than she, and the jacket gaped loosely, barely covering her.

She turned and regarded her image once more.

A smoky-hued seductress stared back at her. Her long tip-tilted eyes seemed mysterious. Her cheekbones appeared exotically high and the rich red brocade of her jacket accented the deep plum color of her full lips. Her hair looked almost black in the window reflection, coiling sinuously around her neck and shoulders.

She looked knowing and enticing and confident.

She stretched her arms above her head, enjoying the pretense. With what she hoped was a come-hither toss of her hair, she mounted the dais, the sensation of her unbound breasts jostling as she moved an odd and unexpectedly erotic one.

She sank to her knees on the warm, dense velvet pile of cushions and with a purr of pleasure, lay down, sliding against the soft fabric. She closed her eyes and rolled onto her back, a harem woman well versed in pleasure and pleasuring: bold, haughty, absolute in her sexual confidence.

She arched her back, ready to receive her lover's caress, his body's adulation, to offer the perfection of her throat to his lips, her breasts to his mouth and—

—heard a man's strangled oath.

Her eyes snapped open.

Jack Cameron stood in the doorway balancing a heavy rolled-up carpet on his shoulders. His unbuttoned white shirt hung open and her breath caught in her throat as she saw for the first time how truly well formed he was. His chest was lean and sleekly muscled, a fine matting of reddish gold hair traversing its hard planes. His belly was flat, corrugated, and glistening with sweat.

Beneath the strain of supporting the carpet, his arms quivered. He didn't seem to notice. His blue eyes gleamed with indigo darkness.

"What the hell are you doing?" The words came out in a harsh roar. He heaved the carpet from his shoulders and dropped it, then strode across the room to where she lay. He looked about wildly. Spying the velvet cloth that had draped the Odalisque, he snatched it up, hurling it at her. "Mother of mercy, cover up."

For an instant she recoiled from his vehemence. But only for an instant. The Odalisque she played at being recognized that Jack was much more shaken than she.

And just as aroused.

There was no mistaking his body's response to her; his trousers had been fashioned too closely. He saw where her eyes traveled and growled. Grabbing her unceremoniously by the wrist, he pulled her upright as effortlessly as if she had been a doll. Where had she ever gotten the notion that Jack Cameron was frail? He was incredibly strong.

She stumbled on a cushion and he snatched her from falling, pulling her against him. With the abrupt movement her jacket slipped from her shoulders, crushing her naked breast to his sweat-gleamed body, her nipple abraded by the fine hairs on his chest. He thrust her away as though scorched, holding her at arm's length, his hands on her upper arms shaking.

"What sort of madness is this?" he demanded, looming over her. His tone was fierce, angry.

She should be frightened. Angry men always frightened her. But she wasn't that meek creature anymore. She was the harem favorite, used to dealing with men . . . and their passions.

She touched his chest with the very tip of her forefinger then, very slowly, very deliberately, traced the course of a single rivulet of sweat, following the hard contour of his pectoral over his flat copper-colored nipple down to where the golden hairs darkened in a thick line low on his belly. He flinched back, a sound—half oath, half moan—torn from between his gritted teeth.

He gave her a little shake. "What are you doing? What is this?" And now bewilderment replaced anger, and something more . . . despair? She smiled, a slow liquid smile, rife with promise. He had nothing to despair of.

"Jack," she whispered. "Kiss me."

He reacted as though she'd asked him to cut out his heart. He froze, his tightening grasp on her arms the only indication he had heard her. For a long minute, he stared at her, motionless except for the rapid rise and fall of his chest.

"Addie," he finally said, "what has happened? What is this supposed to be?"

She remembered his gentleness, his profound kindness, his controlled ardor.

"This is who I was supposed to be," she said. Jack, of all the people in the world, would understand. "I was supposed to find joy in the physical act of love. My parents did. My brothers . . . All my family have been earthy, passionate people. It was my legacy. Before Charles, before my marriage, before . . ."

She felt her jacket slip further down and dipped her arm, allowing it to fall off completely, baring her breasts. His gaze touched them and he closed his eyes.

The enormous effort it cost him to stand quiescent was clear. His control was compelling, but so was her need.

"I want you to kiss me. Please. I want to feel a man's hands on me. I want to discover if the pleasure a man's touch once promised is ever kept."

He groaned and his hands clenched even more tightly about her arms. "Someday a man will keep those promises."

"Someday? Jack, years have gone by already. Years that should have been mine."

"Addie, it won't be long." He sounded so miserable. "You have only to crook your little finger and any man with an ounce of red blood in his veins will come running."

Their gazes locked. Slowly, she pushed him away, and then she lifted her hand, extended her forefinger, and crooked it.

"Oh, God."

"It isn't some 'man' I want. It's you. I want your hands on me, Jack. Your mouth—"

Whatever she was about to say was lost. He crushed her to him, his mouth open, seeking.

She had expected lust. She had played the wanton expressly to experience carnal pleasures. This was more. So much more. There was desperation in the hungry motion of his mouth slanting across hers, desperation and a need as deep as her own.

She had never been kissed like this. Her head swam, her whole being focusing on his body, his mouth. She was overwhelmed with sensual impressions: his scent, sweat-sweet and sharp detergent tanged; his touch, the callused pads of his fingers stroking across the full swell of her breasts, moving tantalizingly close to her nipples; his mouth, sweet heated moisture. Light-headed, she pulled back, needing to breathe.

Immediately, he stepped away. No. She speared her hands beneath his open shirt, thrilling to the silky-hard slide of muscle bunching beneath her palms as she pulled him to her. Masculine skin, heated and smooth, like burnished metal in the sun.

"Addie, not me. Not like this. Not now," he begged.

"Make love to me, Jack. Keep the promise," she whispered. "Only you can keep the promise."

In answer he winnowed his fingers through her hair, his fingertips skating with breathtaking deliberation. The tremor in his left hand translated into a breath-stealing shiver as his fingertips passed over her temples, her cheeks, until they found the point of her chin and tilted her face upward. Gently, tenderly, he coaxed her mouth open. With stunning artistry, he tongued the plush inner lining of her lower lip.

He angled his head to deepen his kiss. Her hands crept up to his neck, and she clung to him, urging him closer. Effortlessly he scooped her up and laid her gently onto the deep, down-filled cushions, sinking down on his knees beside her. Their eyes met. He wanted her. She could see it. He swallowed painfully and would have drawn away then, but she held fast, making him brace himself above her on his forearms.

"Addie—"

"Shh. I'm not a virgin, Jack. I'm not holding my maidenhead like a sweetmeat to offer my groom on my wedding night."

"I don't want to take advantage of—"

"Ah," she broke in, finally smiling. "But I do."

"My God, Addie. I won't be responsible for any more hurt to you—" His tone was desperate, beleaguered, lost. He had no smile to answer hers.

"Jack. I don't know what you've gauged about my marriage." She stopped. She didn't want to say his name. He had no place here, with them, now, but she knew that if she didn't clear this between them, it wouldn't be right for Jack. "But Charles's cruelties did not extend to the bedroom."

"You don't have to tell me this, Addie."

"Yes. I do. We . . . did not live as man and wife except for those few days after we wed." She felt herself blushing with embarrassment and he caressed her cheek.

"Jack, I want this. I'm falling in—"

He dropped his head and kissed her hard and swift, cutting off her declaration. She could feel his heart beating against her breast. She scooted deeper into the pillows, refusing to let go, pulling him with her.

His leg pressed intimately against the juncture of her thighs and she could feel his arousal, solid and potent. An aching congestion began between her legs and she squirmed. It only exacerbated the sensation. She wanted him. She wanted him to kiss her, to touch her, and to sate this seemingly insatiable need to feel him, all of him, his body, tongue, and hands.

"I'm not what you think I am, Addie," he said. "Jack Cameron doesn't exist. He's a fabrication."

His words inspired a sudden chill, momentarily distracting her. She wouldn't allow herself to be distracted. After years of living in a dry and barren place, she had suddenly found this oasis burgeoning with pleasure and promise and ardor. She wouldn't let him dispel the magic, wouldn't let him call her back to that sterile little world. Mirage or no, she wanted to stay here. And she would.

She strained upward, her mouth seeking his. For a second he resisted her, trying to speak. She took advantage of the access he provided, slipping the tip of her tongue along the opening seam of his lips. He moaned.

Her hands roamed low on his ribs, tugged at the waistband of his trousers. Finding no satisfaction there, they deliberately prowled along the hard shaft delineated beneath the tight fabric. He reared back, and she was reminded of her first impression of him, demon-angel.

His blue eyes blazed in his pale face and he rose on his knees astride her and, catching her roaming hands in one of his, pulled them above her head, holding her effortlessly.

"Pleasure," he rasped. "Your pleasure. Yes. I'll keep the promise, Addie. My own way."

Slowly he released her hands and then she forgot everything else in the ecstasy of his touch. His hands kneaded her breasts, cupping the mounds reverently yet erotically, his thumbs working her nipples to engorgement. She twisted feverishly and he dipped his head to one breast, taking the full coral tip into his mouth and suckling gently.

Lightning shot along her nerve endings. She arched her back, offering him more, silently begging him to feast on her. His fingers joined the erotic play, stroking her flanks and skimming along her hips. They dipped beneath the ill-fitting garment, finding the exquisitely sensitive flesh of her inner thigh.

Too light, too gossamer. The pleasure between her legs swelled, a hot itch desperate for relief. Her hips bucked to greet his too-leisurely touch. The heel of his hand rode her mons, pressing hard, rocking against her as his finger slid along the moist cleft, unfolding her like the petals of a flower. Deliberately, he fingered the pulsing, oversensitized nub between forefinger and thumb, initiating an excruciatingly languid, rhythmic massage.

She gasped, bowing up from the soft pillows, her heels driven deep into the warm velvet. Fractured light chased across the backs of her eyelids as she spun out of control, into a vortex of pure sensual pleasure. The rhythm changed and he tugged faster, suckled more deeply on her swollen breasts, caressed more solidly her arms and thighs and throat as she panted, every muscle tensed and straining, striving for an end to the torturous stimulation.

"Let it go," he whispered. "Let go!"

She twisted, panting, but he stayed with her, wouldn't let her rest, compelled her and pushed her, lashed her with tongue and hand and voice and—

With a hoarse cry she found the release. Wave upon wave of distilled pleasure coursed and eddied and washed along her nerve endings, holding her at the peak of the experience for one timeless moment until, with a gasp, she collapsed, limp and spent.

Slowly she became aware that he had withdrawn his hand from between her legs and that his mouth was no longer on her. She was being petted and stroked with the gentlest of caresses. Her eyes fluttered open. Jack was braced over her, a tender expression on his tragic angel face.

He had given her everything, returned her pleasure in her womanliness, kept all the long-delayed promises. Why he had not even—

With a start, she bolted upright, nearly knocking him in the chin with her head. "You didn't make love to me!"

A sardonic smile curved his beautiful lips. "I beg to differ."

"I mean"—she was blushing again, a hot wave creeping up her neck. "I mean you didn't—there can't have been any joy—I mean what I just felt, you must want to feel that, too!"

He grinned.

"Don't you feel it like that?"

"I don't know," he said. "What exactly did it feel like?"

She had the distinct feeling she was being teased. His tone was far too quizzical but the thick ridge of flesh still pressed against her thigh belied his casual tone. She loved being teased by him.

"Jack." She reached up and feathered her fingers through his hair. "Make love to me. With all of your body."

The smile died on his face, replaced by a look of desperate yearning. "Addie, I can't."

"I won't get pregnant. I've just had my—I won't." She tried to pull him close for her kiss. "And I won't force you to any commitment. I promise. I want to share this pleasure with you. Please."

"Don't." He grasped her wrists tightly, pulling them down and away from him. Then, taking a deep breath, he smiled and gently replaced her hands in her lap. He knelt back on his heels, breaking away from her as he rose to his feet.

"If I stay here, seeing you like this, all flushed and rosy and sated, I will make love to you. I haven't the strength to resist."

"I don't understand! Would that be such a sin?" she asked despairingly.

"Oh, yes," he said. "I think so."

25

Jack's hands were still shaking by the time he reached the Merritts' townhouse after having fled the entreaty in Addie's eyes. Thankfully, the early winter winds had somewhat cooled his body's fire if not his longing. A good thing, too, he thought helplessly, because just the thought of Addie as he'd had her—or nearly had her, his mind mocked—swelled him painfully.

Unable to face any interrogation by Lady Merritt, he entered the house through the servants' door at the rear and found his way to his room. Only then did he shed his overcoat to discover that his shirt still hung open to the waist. The sight brought a swift visceral memory of her hands smoothing over his back, stroking his chest, the taste of her nipple, the buck of her hip seeking jointure as he rubbed and fondled the sleek, heated fold of her clitoris. It had been part heaven, all hell, nearly burning him to a cinder with desire. He'd taken a masochistic sort of pleasure in sipping the cries of fulfillment from her lip, lapping the thin, glistening shroud of passion from her throat and breasts, matching the rocking, inborn cadence of her hips with his fingers. Because though he could not deny her request to be pleasured, he would not allow himself to know her fully. Not when she thought he was something else, someone he could never be, the chimera he had tried to tell her he was.

Not knowing the grief he might visit on her, the ruin he could bring Ted's career, the shame he could heap on her family.

God! He pounded his fist against the wall. This had to end. He could not go on like this any longer. Before the week was out, come hell or high water, Addie must know the truth.

The decision eased the tension that coiled tighter each day since the charade had begun. Even though he knew the end of this could only bring him her damnation—and rightly so—the relief he felt was nearly palpable.

Wearily, he shrugged out of his shirt and pulled on a fresh one. He was supposed to meet Lord Mitchell in half an hour.

Though he longed to ignore the summons, he could not. He wanted to know why his former commander had supported his masquerade. Besides, going to Whitehall would give him some direction in a series of days that had grown ever more blurred and ill-defined.

Twenty minutes later he was ushered into Lord Mitchell's oak-paneled office, to stand before the huge ebony desk that belonged to Whitehall's newest "paper general."

He was surprised to see Colonel Halvers there, also. Out of friendship, Halvers had sent him the names and copies of the documents pertinent to Jack's investigation. He had never asked Jack why he wanted the information and Jack had never told him. He met Jack's questioning glance with a small shake of negation.

The general glanced up from a sheaf of paper he held angled in such a way that Jack could not help but note the famous signature scrawled at the bottom: Gladstone. "Well, Cameron, so you didn't die," Lord Mitchell finally said.

"No, sir."

"Who'd have believed it, eh?" He leaned back in the burgundy leather chair and motioned Jack to take a seat across from him. With a curt bow, he did so, removing his gloves and placing them on the desk before him.

"And now it appears you have become an artist." Lord Mitchell's bushy brows climbed into peaked ridges above his piercing black eyes. "An interesting change of career."

"Life takes us in odd directions, sir."

"Very odd," the older man mused. "For instance, the War Office finds itself embroiled in a situation that demands the most delicate treatment."

He looked up, gauging Jack's reaction. "Here we were casting about, trying to find someone who is in a position to do something—and having no damn luck at all, I might add. Then, one day, a trusted officer mentions that he has seen a former captain of the Gordon Highlanders who not only is in a position to do his country a great service, but against all odds, seems to have begun to do so under his own auspices."

The Gold Braid, Jack thought, that fellow . . . Ingrams.

"Would you not call that fortuitous, Cameron?"

"I might, sir."

"Might?"

"It would depend on whether or not the former captain did, indeed, have the same goal in mind as the War Office."

The general peered intently at Jack a minute before saying, "Let's cut to the chase, shall we, Jack? We need you. This goes no further than this door, Cameron."

Jack felt his face suffuse with indignation. He had never betrayed his honor as an officer and a gentleman. He had sacrificed much to pursue his private inquiries and meet the demands of duty. Mitchell must know that. His remark did not even warrant a reply.

He shot a hard glance toward Halvers but the man studiously avoided his gaze. The general cleared his throat.

"Well, damn it, man. You needn't look so offended. It is not my career I am concerned with. It is the Old Man's."

Jack's eyes widened with surprise. "Sir?"

"The Khartoum debacle has Her Majesty spitting nails," Lord Mitchell said. "She blames Gladstone entirely. And the popular press is having a field day calling for the Old Man's head. If only the rescue expedition had been a day earlier . . . or a week later," he mused with cold-blooded logic, "but to have the damned troops show up a single goddamn twenty-four hours too late to save Gordon's neck . . . !"

"It was a tragedy," Halvers said.

"Tragedy my ass!" erupted the general. "Gordon had countless opportunities to leave Khartoum! He could have taken a packet on the Nile a half dozen times. And you know why he chose to remain there, sending his missives on the same boats that could have just as easily carried his hide to safety?"

The general did not wait for an answer.

"He was trying to force our hand! He wanted to provoke an incident so that Britain would be obliged to launch a rescue operation and, once in Khartoum, reestablish a military presence in the Sudan. Well, he got his wish . . . at the cost of his head!"

He settled back, his anger appeased by the reminder that "China" Gordon had paid the ultimate price for his stubbornness.

"The Old Man knew he was being manipulated by Gordon. Didn't like it. Would have left Gordon there to rot if the populace hadn't raised such a hue and cry. And then Her Majesty got into the act and demanded we rescue him. But we waited too long and now the Old Man is seen as either a heartless ogre or a blundering old fool. He can't afford any more bad press. Not while he is making another bid for the Prime Minister's seat. It would mean the end of his career."

"I don't understand what that has to do with me, sir," Jack said.

His ire spent, the general leaned back in his chair. "Never did agree with that North African policy," he murmured. "Now, what it has to do with you, Jack, is this. Gordon scripted myriad letters to the War Office during the siege. Most of them are just rambling nonsense. The man was obviously over the edge of reason. But in between the ravings were some things that we cannot ignore."

He leaned forward and braced his forearms on the desk. "Several of his letters suggest that amongst the Black Dragoons was an officer who used his position and influence to allow the native slavers to operate without interference.

"Do you have any idea of the repercussions should these assertions prove to be true? If it should come out that one of the men—no, not just a man, a member of the premier regiment in the nation—used his position to manipulate troop movements so that slave trades could run freely between Africa and the Middle East, it would be a political nightmare!

"Right now the citizenry is crying out to punish the Mahdi responsible for lopping off Gordon's head. All very good and well, but it could just as easily turn into a cry for withdrawal from North Africa and then Arabi and from there, God knows where it will stop!"

"And that would be disastrous?"

"You aren't a fool, Cameron. Britain needs those protectorates. They feed the wealth that flows through this kingdom."

"Slavery notwithstanding," Jack said grimly.

"Exactly."

Both men gazed coolly into each other's eyes. Neither gave an inch of ground.

Finally Jack said, "Again, sir, I must ask how this involves me."

"We have been working hard to expose the suspected traitor. But while we have compiled a dossier of information, we have no rock-solid proof. You are in a position to possibly secure the evidence we need."

"I doubt that, sir," Jack said. "Paul Sherville won't let me near him. Thinks I'm the most contemptible catamite." He'd made a serious blunder in antagonizing Paul Sherville. One he could ill afford. Somehow he had to reinstate himself with the man.

"Paul Sherville?" Mitchell scowled. "What are you talking about? We're discussing Charles Hoodless."

Jack stiffened even though he'd suspected as much. If these men knew Hoodless was their traitor for a fact, there was nothing he could do to avert Addie's social ruin. Nothing he could do except to warn Ted and persuade her brother to take her out of the country.

Mitchell's words sounded a death knell of all his dreams. Every secret unvoiced hope he'd harbored against all reason was shattered, blasted away in the space of seconds. Addie would never forgive him. It didn't matter, not really, because he'd never be able to forgive himself his hand in her downfall.

"We have little doubt Hoodless is the fellow we seek." He heard Mitchell's voice as from a distance.

"Hoodless is dead," Jack said, desperate for some way to salvage Addie's future.

"Exactly. Dead. But justice must still be served."

"Why do you think it is Hoodless?" he asked bleakly.

"Small details, but numerous. He was one of the few officers in Alexandria at a time we know a number of slavers off-loaded their human cargo. He delivered dispatches to his commanding officers on more than one occasion."

"So was Paul Sherville—"

"Charles Hoodless fits every circumstance we can track this traitor to," Lord Mitchell insisted.

It should have been funny, Jack thought. Somewhere, some twisted, malevolent deity was probably laughing his celestial ass off because here Jack was prepared to fight tooth and nail for the reputation of a man he knew to be a sadist and a misanthrope, the abuser of the only woman he'd ever loved. But that was exactly what he was going to do.

"Yes. It fits all the circumstances rather nicely, doesn't it? One must admit it is convenient to have one's primary suspect rotting in his grave. I wonder if you would be so keen to name him if he were alive and could be brought to stand trial."

The general stopped shuffling his papers.

"That would necessitate a court-martial, wouldn't it?" Jack continued grimly. "But if the traitor is dead, why, then no one needs to know about it. Justice will have been served and your potential political disaster averted, wouldn't it? I can see how you wouldn't know anything of Paul Sherville."

Lord Mitchell went tellingly still even as Halvers shifted uneasily on his feet. Jack waited, knowing his words were an outrage, wounding and galling to a man with Lord Mitchell's stature and sense of honor. But they needed to be said.

"Damn your impudence." Lord Mitchell's hand balled into a fist atop his desk. "Yes! It would be convenient if Charles Hoodless were the traitor. But I have never bowed to convenience, not in thirty years. You have no right to question my integrity."

"I would never question your integrity, sir. I am questioning your impartiality."

"Then I suggest you question your own while you're at it!" the general shot back.

Jack's head snapped back as if he'd been hit. Of course, Mitchell would have seen. The only one who'd come late to the realization of where Jack's interest lay was Addie herself. Even Ted's snickers had begun long ago.

"Find out who the traitor is, look wherever your inquiries take you. I want the truth. But look to Mrs. Hoodless first."

"Excuse me?"

"She undoubtedly has letters, notations. She may have books, bills of lading, receipts. She must have some records of where her money comes from . . . somewhere amongst her dead husband's belongings there must be some piece of concrete evidence."

"Why don't you simply ask for her cooperation?" Jack asked stiffly.

"Think, man," Lord Mitchell said in disgust. "If Mrs. Hoodless knows or even suspects what we think her husband did, how forthcoming do you think she will be in providing information that could result in turning her and her in-laws into pariahs?"

"It would never come out. You as much as said so."

"Not officially, but you know this sort of thing would eventually find its way out. The rumor mill is often more damaging to reputations than the courts."

Damn the man, he could be right.

"Do you think she would willingly court social ruin by helping us?"

"Yes," Jack said, though in truth he was not certain she would easily let Ted and her parents-in-law suffer for Hoodless's crimes. "She is an honorable woman."

"Your faith—or infatuation—notwithstanding, I will not risk it. No. There is only one thing to do. You must find the evidence for us."

Jack rose, his upright bearing testament to a decade of tutoring under men such as Lord Mitchell.

"I am sorry, General," he said. "But no."

"What did you say?"

"No, I will not spy on Addie Hoodless. I will not pry into her belongings, nor will I steal from her."

The general flushed a deep, angry red, his silvery hair a stark contrast. "You used to be a damn good officer, Cameron. Your men loved you. Yes, not only respected but loved you. Is this how you repay their regard? By allowing some sentiment for a widow to interfere with your duty to your dead comrades and your country? Why did you fight, Cameron, if not for God and country?"

"I did not say I would not hunt down the traitor, sir. I said I would not spy on Mrs. Hoodless nor riffle through her effects like a sneak thief. I *will* find out the name of the traitor. I swear it."

"And this is the best way to do so, man! And if you don't find anything, why, then, you will have cleared Hoodless from the list of suspects," Mitchell insisted. "Besides, I am not asking you to do anything that you yourself haven't already embarked on, and you know it. Why else have you played at being the simpering fop, if not to discover the traitor?"

Jack lifted his chin. "I was trying to find atonement."

"And right you were, lad!" the general said. "Honor demands you seek out this criminal, regardless of the personal cost."

With measured deliberation, Jack reclaimed his gloves from atop the desk. "Thank you, Lord Mitchell. You've clarified what I must do, something that has been obscure to me for months."

"Good! It's about time you came around."

"You mistake my meaning."

"Which is?"

"I will not risk a woman and her family's reputations, their prospects, or their happiness, for vengeance. I owe my life to those men who fought for our country and its values, and that I would gladly pay at any time. But I do not owe them my soul. And I dishonor their memory by thinking they would ask that of me. As for God . . . He extracts his own price."

"What the hell do you mean, Cameron?"

He inclined his head respectfully. This man had done great things, would do great things. He was a noble man and fearless defender of the nation. He was not, however, God.

"I mean, no. I will find another way." And he walked out of the dark-paneled room into the pale winter sunlight.

26

By the time Jack left the Whitehall offices, the streets were emptying. A light drizzle mixed with snow had begun and the few dray horses left on the streets slipped and stumbled as they made their way back to the congested stables that sheltered them.

Jack paced the ice-glazed pavement, oblivious to the deserted landscape. His former commander's words replayed in his mind. The general would have fallen like a wolf on the bits of information he'd garnered from Zephrina Drouhin, seeing it as further testimony damning Charles Hoodless. Until he had incontrovertible proof of Hoodless's involvement, he would not risk telling Lord Mitchell. The general would look no further.

Jack had spent two days with the American girl only to discover that she hadn't known much. She was more interested in disparaging her portraitist than discussing Paul Sherville.

Those few things he had ultimately learned, however, had been telling. Paul Sherville had boasted to Zephrina of his "North African gold mine." He'd only spoken once about Hoodless after having imbibed "rather too deeply." Sherville had said that

Hoodless had "gathered information like a banker gathers coins, and parlayed it into even more money," a bit of verbiage that would have shored up Lord Mitchell's conviction that Charles Hoodless was their traitor.

A year ago, Jack would have gone directly to Lord Mitchell with that information, discounting any other considerations as secondary and willing to let the higher-ups make of it what they would. But a year had changed him.

A year ago he would have laughed at anyone who suggested that he would count amongst his friends a lame, taciturn portraitist or a giant, effete, ice-skating illustrator. And a year ago he hadn't been in love with Addie Hoodless.

The thought of Addie brought a small, intense flicker of pleasure and pain. Tomorrow, he would tell her who he was, *what* he was. He could go to her tomorrow morning—he released a brief sound of irritation as he recalled Addie's laughing comment about spending the entire day being "transformed" by some dressmaker or other for the ball. He would have to tell her later. At the ball.

He entered the townhouse and handed his hat to the waiting footman.

"Mr. Phyfe is here to see you, sir. He has been waiting some hours. I suggested he might return tomorrow but he insisted on staying," the footman said, helping Jack out of his coat. "He is in the drawing room."

"And Lady Merritt?"

"Her Ladyship retired some while ago, sir. She was not feeling well."

"Bring us whiskey, please."

He found Ted sitting in a club chair in front of the fireplace enjoying a merrily sputtering blaze and idly twirling the silver handle of his walking cane between his clever fingers. Seeing Jack, he set the cane aside and stood up.

"Been out and about in this weather, Cameron? You'll take your death."

Jack regarded his visitor suspiciously, motioning for him to retake his seat. "To what do I owe this pleasure so late at night?"

"I'd wait until this interview has ended before you call it a pleasure, Cameron."

"Oh?" Jack sprawled in the club chair opposite Ted's, stretching his legs out. "This sounds ominous. What? You want me to don that ridiculous turban and pose for you again?"

"No. I think you've done quite enough masquerading, wouldn't you agree?"

An alarm sounded in Jack's mind. "Perhaps."

"I find I have had enough of this, Cameron," Ted said. "Especially now, today, after coming home to the studio and seeing—the props for the Odalisque are in disarray. Addie is floating about the house, her hair down on her shoulders, humming."

Jack waited in chill silence. He wasn't going to discuss what had occurred between Addie and him with anyone. Least of all her brother.

"She's taken with you, Cameron. I'd say she was half in love with you. Maybe more."

The silence stretched between the two of them. The patter of sleet against the windowpanes and the hiss of green wood the only sounds.

"What?" Ted finally said, an unpleasant smile twisting his lips. "For months now, you have impressed us all with your ready wit. Has your cleverness suddenly deserted you? I have just told you that my sister is more than a little in love with you. Doesn't this mean anything to you, Cameron?" Ted tilted his head, staring at Jack as though he were some perplexing and contemptible specimen.

"Yes."

"May I ask what?"

"No."

Ted settled back in his chair. "That creates something of a problem."

"This doesn't concern you, Ted. It is between Addie and myself."

"Oh, I beg to differ. It does." The muscles in Ted's jaw worked even though his tone remained neutral. "I love Addie, you see, and I have had . . . just . . . about . . . enough of seeing her hurt!" The last words exploded from him.

Jack's own frustration and grief boiled up in response, goaded by Ted's. "And I don't want her hurt!"

With an obvious effort, Ted regained his vigilant self-control. "Then you'll be giving me some explanations," he said in a clipped voice. "Who are you?"

"I am Lord Merritt's great-nephew. I am a devotee of the arts—"

"You are no more an artist," Ted cut in with hushed, strained tones, "or craftsman than Gerry's Burmese cat. You aren't even a dilettante. For some reason you have sought to insinuate yourself with Addie—or is it me? Or Gerald?—and I have allowed it."

Jack eyed Ted warily.

"Do you want to know why I have allowed it—aside from the fact that your burlesque performance has been more entertaining than a night in the East End?" Ted didn't wait for an answer. "Because of Addie. Because you afforded her an opportunity to champion someone."

"My, how munificent of you."

"Don't play so hard at being feckless. Your eyes give you away, Cameron. They have from the start."

Jack ignored the remark. A discreet tap at the door presaged the entry of the footman with liquor and glasses. Jack took the tray from him at the door, motioning for him to leave, and returned to fill a glass and lift it in Ted's direction.

"Drink, Ted?" he asked.

"Answer me. Who are you?"

Jack sloshed some seltzer into the glass, his back to Ted.

"Damn you, man! Addie deserves better than this!"

"Don't you think I know that?" Jack pounded the decanter down and gripped the edge of the table with both hands.

"Can you at least assure me that whatever it is you play at, you won't hurt Addie?"

"Hurt Addie?" Jack echoed, hopeless and raging. "Good God, I would pay in blood to be able to give such an assurance."

"Don't evade the question, Cameron!"

"What can I tell you? That I would not willingly hurt Addie? I wouldn't. That I may have already done so?"

"Damn you!" shouted Ted. "How dare you toy with her heart? Have you no feeling?"

It was too much. Jack surged one step forward before catching himself back and impaling Ted with a hot-eyed glare. "Yes and yes and yes! Do you want to hear my feelings? Do you want to hear that I love her with every worthy fiber left in me, every bit of emotion that can be wrung from my heart, everything I am? Will that be enough for you?"

Slowly, Ted sank back in his chair.

"Do you think that my loving her automatically protects her from my hurting her?" Jack asked helplessly. "Then you are a fool!"

Ted's gaze grew hooded as he studied Jack's combative stance and clenched teeth.

"Addie knows you're a fake," he finally said in a much more moderate tone. "Oh, she might not consciously choose to acknowledge it, but she knows. She was raised in a house full of artists. She cut her teeth on Rossetti's discarded paintbrushes. John Ruskin would have been her godfather—had he believed in God.

"I have often thought that was part of the appeal Hoodless held for Addie," Ted said. "She was drawn to the regularity, the discipline and conformity he represented and her upbringing so extravagantly lacked." He returned his attention to Jack. "How could she not see what you are, or, more to the point, what you aren't? You out-Gerry poor Gerry with your outrageous pretensions and affectations. And all that cologne . . . Lord, you've given me a headache on more than one occasion with that pretty stench you soak yourself in."

"If you've suspected for so long, why didn't you say anything?"

The smile faded from Ted's lips. "I told you. Because you made Addie forget that monstrosity she'd married."

Jack made a strangled sound.

"I watched that bastard turn my spontaneous, laughing, vibrant little sister into a fearful, still-faced caricature of herself."

Impotent rage boiled through Jack's veins. "Why didn't you do something, man?"

"I tried!" Ted countered angrily, his gaze flickering to his leg, reminding Jack that Hoodless had run him down with his carriage, crippling him. "I just wasn't successful. And later, after my . . . accident"—he made a sharp dismissive motion toward his leg—"Addie would not hear a word about seeking a separation. She never confided in me after that but I suspect Hoodless threatened the rest of us if she did so. At any rate, she insisted things were better and then she simply withdrew from him, from her family, from society . . . from life.

"And then Hoodless was killed in North Africa, and I thanked God, certain that she'd reclaim herself. But a year passed and she was still solitary, joyless." He raised his gaze, looking Jack directly in the eye. "And then you came along and she . . . she began to rediscover herself. You made her take risks on your behalf she might never have taken for her own sake. You made her feel things. That's why I let it go on."

"You shouldn't have," Jack said.

"Shouldn't I?" Ted asked. "I don't know. You're not going to tell me what you're doing here, are you, Cameron?"

"No. Not before I speak with Addie. I intend to do so tomorrow night at the masquerade ball Lady Merritt is holding in your honor."

Ted studied him for a few minutes more before hoisting himself heavily from the club chair. "Then I should trust you?"

"No."

Ted snorted. "Such an honest charlatan. How novel. Well, Jack, since you won't tell me your motives for this charade, I shall simply have to wait. Don't bother seeing me out."

He made his way across the room and paused at the doorway. "Of course, if things don't end well, I shall kill you."

Paul Sherville pulled back from the carriage window as Hoodless's gimpy brother-in-law vacated the Merritt townhouse. Phyfe paused to open his umbrella, a smile of unmistakable satisfaction on his face, then limped down the steps and disappeared into a cab.

Paul did not know what to make of that smile. Phyfe had actively disliked Hoodless—Charles had on more than one occasion laughed at his brother-in-law's ineffectual attempts to induce Addie to seek a divorce. Perhaps Phyfe smiled because Hoodless was on the cusp of being revealed as the blackmailing bastard he was . . .

Sherville thumped the leather seat with his fist and bit at the knuckles of the other as panic capered through his veins. No! That wasn't it. Phyfe was far too fond of his shivering, timorous little sister to find pleasure in her imminent social ruin.

Far more likely Phyfe had been visiting Cameron with the purpose of finding out how much the former captain knew about Addie's little foray into the dangerous—if lucrative—game of extortion.

That had to be it! And judging by the Nan-boy's smirk, Cameron had yet to procure any evidence. Which meant—Sherville's eyes widened—that the photograph was still in Addie's care, in the Hoodless townhouse.

He rapped his fist against the carriage roof and called for the driver to take him to his new club, a far more exclusive establishment on the Thames than The Gold Braid.

He'd already seen to it that Addie's country house had been thoroughly searched. Thoroughly. It hadn't been hard. With all her money, one would think she'd at least keep an adequate staff at the East Sussex manor, more fool she.

The search had proven fruitless. Not a thing, not a scrap of Hoodless's personal belongings was there. Well, now at least he knew where to find the photograph, and tomorrow night, while Addie danced at Lady Merritt's masquerade ball, the two men he'd made such good use of in Alexandria would retrieve it.

27

Addie dashed up the outside steps to the Merritt townhouse's front door where the doorman bowed her into the front hall-way and she handed a waiting attendant her cloak.

She was late. Again. She thought she'd allowed the newly hired lady's maid plenty of time to dress her hair. How was she to know it would take nearly an hour to tuck, coil, crimp, and tug her tresses into a fashionable arrangement?

She took three deep breaths. Jack would be here. How would things have changed? He had shown her what her body was capable of feeling with a reverence and ardor she'd never dreamt possible. Now, she was not afraid of how he would act, but how she would.

She suspected she would wear her heart on her sleeve for all society to see. Well, she didn't really give a fig! She loved Jack. What of it?

At the entrance to the ballroom, she stopped and touched the slick, tinted salve that the maid had brushed on her lips. From there, her fingers traced an incredulous path across the gossamer-thin dusting of powder on her cheeks. Paint. She'd actually painted her face. And there was no second-guessing herself on the reason why; she'd wanted to look enticing. To Jack.

She felt another rush of the pleasurable anticipation she'd experienced every time she'd thought of him. She did not doubt he cared for her profoundly and passionately—and whatever his reasons for denying them a complete union, she knew it was only a matter of time before he did. She meant to hasten that moment.

And she would, she thought delightedly, her gaze traveling over her new ball gown. In this dress she could have affected the capitulation of a monk!

The thickly embroidered front panels of poor Louis XIV's lavender-colored satin jacket had been remade into the close-fitting bodice of her dress. There hadn't been a great deal of cloth left after Mssr. Drexhall had taken shears to the priceless antique, but there hadn't been a necessity for much. The sleeveless bodice barely covered the crests of her breast, pushing up her fulsome endowments and nipping in tightly at the waist.

Sinuously curving drake-green silk inserts began beneath her arms at the side seams of the bodice and flowed in provocative lines beneath her bosom, twining together where they met. The same drake-green satin bow decorated an extravagantly draped bustle. The underskirt was palest lavender silk moiré studded with tiny silver beads.

It was exotic, quixotic, and undeniably sensual. She stepped into the crowded ballroom feeling confident, utterly feminine, and knowing she'd never spent money so well in her life—

"Ah, Mrs. Hoodless!"

Paul Sherville was at her side, his gaze greedily devouring her. "And who are you masquerading as, dear lady?" he mocked. "It is a masquerade ball, if you recall."

Her nascent self-confidence teetered in the face of his leering derision. But just for a moment. In the next, she saw him for what he was: a weak, malicious man, so ineffectual in his own mind that he needed to taunt others to convince himself of his own superiority. How pitiful he was! As, she thought with sudden acuity, had been Charles.

"Why, Major Sherville, I didn't feel the need to masquerade as anyone. I am quite happy with who I am. But let me see, whom might you be portraying tonight in all that black cloth? Wait." She paused and let her gaze travel insolently over him before snapping her fingers lightly. "I have it. The Marquis de Sade!"

In answer, he stepped forward, closing the distance between them so that he towered over her. "You are feeling very brave tonight, Mrs. Hoodless. But I would have a care. One can think oneself invulnerable . . . until one isn't."

She had no idea what he meant. He really was ridiculous with his theatrical pronouncements and his threatening mien.

"Major Sherville, the only thing that shall disappear is you. When I turn my back," and, suiting action to word, she moved easily past him, walking sedately into the throng.

Several times on her way to greet her hostess, she was hailed by former acquaintances, both people she'd known as a young girl and people she'd met through her brother. For the first time in years, she found herself looking about her with a sense of pleasure at seeing familiar faces rather than trepidation at encountering one of Charles's cronies.

And when she was finally, as she knew she would be, greeted by one of Charles's casual military acquaintances, she was gratified by how easily she responded to his polite conversational gambits and, with a touch of surprise, discovered he was not a monster but simply a tongue-tied young man in a red coat.

But she was not yet so confident in her newly rediscovered self-assurance that she was entirely comfortable with him. And she could not deny her relief when he bowed politely after escorting her across the room to where Lady Merritt held court and Addie found herself pushed to the front of the queue to greet their hostess. As she caught sight of Lady Merritt, her mouth twitched.

A huge construction of peacock feathers and life-sized gilded snakes rose a full two feet up from the top of Lady Merritt's head. What appeared to be the remnants of a Persian carpet were suspended from her shoulders, flanking an enormous—and highly polished—sheet of metal. With a start, Addie realized it was a breastplate. Beneath this she wore a skirt so stiff with Oriental elements it could easily have stood by itself.

"Ah, Addie, m'dear. Queen Zenobia gives you greetings!" Lady Merritt held out her heavily beringed fingers.

"Queen Zenobia?"

"Yes, you silly chit!" Lady Merritt's gracious greeting eroded into peevishness. "That is the problem with our society, the horrendous deficiency in young people's education. How can you fail to recognize one of history's most flamboyant queens?"

"To be sure," Addie managed to say. "Queen Zenobia. Of course. Have you seen Jack?"

"No, I haven't. He had Wheatcroft playing valet to him for quite a long time. I can hardly wait to see what he is impersonating." Her gaze traveled in perplexity over Addie's gown. "Who are you tonight, m'dear? I can't quite put my finger on it. Helen of Troy? Guinevere?"

"Addie Phyfe."

Lady Merritt's smile was fond. Taking Addie's hands, she pulled her close for a quick embrace, the sharper points of the breastplate digging into Addie's skin.

"Your hair is stunning," Lady Merritt said sotto voce. "And that dress! Your brother's hand, no doubt."

"Her brother had nothing to do with it," Ted said from beside her. "Though I warrant I know who did."

Addie turned to her brother. He was outfitted in severe black, his dark red locks brushed forward on his high forehead. Byron, he had informed her earlier this evening, also limped. "Oh, I doubt that, Ted."

"I was referring not to the actual dressmaker," Ted said, "but to the person who inspired it."

Lady Merritt impatiently flapped a hand in Ted's direction as Addie blushed. "Ted, why must you always be so oblique? Can you not simply say a thing?"

"It's much more amusing this way."

"Ted lives to be amused by the foibles of us mere mortals," Addie said, her gaze passing over her reprobate brother. "But I have a notion that he shall shortly find himself much more involved in secular entertainments."

"How kind of you to invite me to your party, Lady Merritt!" Zephrina Drouhin trilled charmingly in her unmistakable accent. As usual, her appearance was foreshadowed by the phalanx of red-coated army officers who invariably escorted her. They opened ranks to allow her to waft forward in a cloud of white-netted tulle, feathers, and seed pearls.

She curtsied prettily to her hostess and turned to Addie, a momentary frown marring her lovely features before recognition dawned in her wide blue eyes. "Mrs. Hoodless! How delightful to meet you again."

"The pleasure is mine, Miss Drouhin," Addie said sincerely, watching her brother with a twinge of malicious amusement. She had decided that the infatuation Ted had claimed Zephrina had for him was not all one-sided. It did her heart well to see her pre-eminently self-controlled brother put off his stride by this petite, disdainful little wretch.

Sure enough, Ted's animation disappeared behind a bland mask of indifference as he bowed formally in his client's direction. No one could be that cool. "Miss Drouhin."

Zephrina arched a thin brow. "Good evening, Mr. Phyfe. Gentlemen"—she turned to her little coterie—"Mr. Phyfe is the artist who is painting my portrait. He is a strict disciplinarian. 'Tis he who makes me decline all your vastly intriguing propositions to sit for hours posing for him in his studio." Scowls were immediately directed in Ted's direction.

"Pray, Miss Drouhin, do not allow my painting to interfere with any—even seemingly incidental—aspect of your social life. Please," Ted said, seemingly all graciousness.

Addie held up her hand to hide her smile but did so too late; Zephrina knew she'd been bested. She snapped her fan open, frowning fiercely behind the long white ostrich plumes.

"I suppose you will want to begin my sittings all over again now that you have seen me in my swan guise." She sighed heavily as her escorts all murmured hearty concurrence.

"Good heavens, is that what that is?" Ted asked. "I'd thought you were emulating a disemboweled pillow. You know: insubstantial, lightweight, delightfully inconsequential?"

Addie couldn't stand there any longer. If she did, she risked breaking out into laughter. She turned her chuckle into a cough and, avoiding Zephrina's suspicious glare, made her apologies, saying she needed a refreshment.

Only when she was well away did she peek over her shoulder. Ted's reputation for blandness in the face of anything was undeniably being threatened. His countenance was darkening perceptibly. Zephrina's was already red. They were squared off, facing each other, smiling determinedly through clenched teeth, those around them obviously forgotten in their concentration on each other.

Addie laughed again. Ted had apparently found Waterloo. Now it only needed time to determine who was to play Wellington and which unfortunate would be cast in the role of Napoleon.

"If you are laughing at my kilt, I am afraid I shall have to challenge you to a duel. We Scots take our plaids seriously," a deep voice drawled.

She looked around, her heart racing, to find herself face to face with Jack. She returned his smile eagerly, like a young woman on spying her beau after a prolonged absence.

A flicker of puzzlement crossed his features.

"Ah! The dress. It is new," he murmured. He barely afforded her new sumptuous gown a glance before his gaze returned to her face. "You are so beautiful, Addie."

He'd barely noticed her gown, hadn't commented on her hair, her jewels. He thought *she* was beautiful.

A sudden shift in the crowd jostled them apart, allowing Addie to see Jack wholly. Her eyes widened. True to his word, Jack was dressed in a plaid—a Scottish plaid regimental uniform.

The red jacket he wore open over a pristine white cambric shirt served as a foil for his extraordinary good looks. The elegant fall of the lace jabot and cuffs only emphasized the blatant masculinity she'd somehow never noticed earlier on in their friendship. Over one broad shoulder was draped the plaid, a dark blue and green with a yellow stripe that matched the pattern of his kilt. A sporran hung from his waist, and in his stockings the hilt of a ruby encrusted *sgian-dubh* glittered.

He looked uncannily at home in the garb, more poised than she'd ever seen him before. His stance seemed broader, his posture straighter. His calves were muscular, a deep scar crossing one knee. Only his hand, balled into a fist near his hip—where Addie knew officers wore their swords—seemed awkward, as though he was used to resting that strong hand on something other than his hip.

The implication was subtly unsettling, and she moved back. Then she remembered his father had been a Gordon Highlander.

"Raid the attic trunks, did we, Jack?" she asked. The archness she strove for sounded more like an entreaty.

"Not at all," Jack said. "These are my clothes."

"Of course they are," she agreed quickly. "As are mine. How silly of me to think anything that fit so superbly could be rummaged from a trunk. But I wouldn't let any of these officer chaps know you had a dress uniform made up as a costume. They believe their regimental dress is nigh-on sacred."

He was silent a moment before finally saying, "Your concern is duly noted, Addie. But I doubt that anyone would take exception to my wearing this—"

"As you will," she cut in quickly, uncertain why she'd interrupted him. All she knew was that she didn't want to talk about Jack's regimental uniform. She'd thought herself nearly over her discomfort about military types. Apparently she wasn't. Not quite yet. "But we could stand here chatting about costumes all evening and, as you know, fashion is hardly one of my chief interests."

She recognized a lilting tune issuing from the ballroom and turned eagerly toward the sound. "The dancing has started?"

"Yes. But, Addie—"

"I haven't danced in five years."

A crooked smile lifted the corners of his beautifully molded lips and he bowed. "Mrs. Hoodless, would you consent to joining me in this dance?"

She dimpled. "Are you not afraid I am as competent in dance slippers as I am in skates?"

"Not at all," he said smoothly. "Should the need arise, I can always carry you."

His tone was light but his gaze was hot. The tactile memory of his strong arms lifting her effortlessly, his body, hard and warm, pressed against her, flooded her thoughts. He held out his forearm.

"Shall we?"

She placed her gloved hand on his forearm, stunned by the electricity that shivered through her at such casual contact, even through so many layers of cloth.

He clearly felt the attraction, too, for he kept his gaze riveted ahead, escorting her wordlessly through the churning crowd. The lights from the electric sconces, shimmering off his golden hair, touched the scar at his temple. At the ballroom, he took her hand and turned her to face him.

And then they were dancing, swirling in graceful rhythm through a clutch of Cleopatras and Harlequins, Little Bo Peeps and Bonapartes. Jack never looked away from her. His attention was focused entirely on her.

The intensity of his regard made her heart pound madly, out of tempo with the music. She cast about for something to say. Something that would allow her to catch her breath and buy time for the blood to retreat from her overheated cheeks.

"Mr. Wilde is here tonight," she said.

"Yes?" he murmured.

"Have you ever met him?"

"No."

"He's quite a nice man. Very witty."

"Oh."

"But he does rather like to tweak society's cheek. Have you seen what he is dressed as?"

"No."

"A sunflower."

He took a misstep. "You are teasing."

She grinned. "No. He really is. A big yellow and green sunflower with huge, floppy petals ringing his neck."

Jack threw back his head and laughed. It was a booming sound, relaxed and genuine.

"I would have thought you would seek his acquaintance. Ted says many of your *bons mots* have been pilfered from Mr. Wilde's plays." She peeked at him from beneath the fringe of her lashes.

"Ted is right." There was no apology in his voice. He smiled. "But the very best *bons mots* were mine."

"Of course," she said, responding to his good humor. "Still, I am surprised you haven't sought him out. I can arrange an introduction."

"That isn't necessary. I'm sure he's excellent company. But there is only one person in this room I want to talk to and be with and that is you."

His voice had grown husky, the flavor of his Scottish accent pronounced. She could not answer the silent demand in his voice with words. Instead, she moved a shade closer to him to bask in his heat, to pretend that the arms so carefully holding her had forgotten restraint and were crushing her against him. With a sigh of pleasure, she let her eyes close and drifted, the music and the sense of being in his embrace working an intoxicating magic on her.

They executed a quick turn and the couple behind them bumped against Jack's back. He caught her close and she opened her eyes, surprised by a strained, hungry expression on Jack's face.

"We have to leave," he said tightly, doing nothing to reinvent the proper distance between them.

"But, Jack—"

"I cannot do this any longer. Addie, you have to come with me. Now." The tension was palpable in the lean body pressed close to her.

She nodded. He let loose the breath he'd been holding and, taking her hand, led her off the dance floor.

"We must thank Lady Merritt before we go, Jack," she said.

"What? Yes. Yes, of course." He craned his neck, looking around for their hostess. He shouldered his way through the crowd, drawing her gently after him to Lady Merritt's side.

Her ladyship smiled vaguely past them, her gaze traveling restlessly over the crowd, searching for someone until, with a start, her gaze swung back to them. She stared in horror at Jack's garb.

"Jack? How could you?" she demanded in a fierce whisper.

"Could I what, ma'am?"

"Wear . . . that!"

"It was all I had to wear, ma'am."

Darting quick, displeased looks about her, Lady Merritt leaned forward. "No, no. You don't understand. *Merritt has returned.* He is to be here. Tonight! He sent a message. Though why he should feel this urgent need to see me after all these years . . ." She trailed off, her cheeks turning a brilliant crimson.

Beside Addie, she saw Jack tense. "My felicitations on your imminent reunion. But what has my great-uncle's arrival to do with my wardrobe?"

"Don't be willfully obtuse, Jack." Lady Merritt's brows lowered ominously. "You should be dressed differently. As something else entirely. Like a . . . a lily."

"I beg your pardon?"

"You should be dressed in the mode of Mr. Wilde. It's what I expected. If Merritt sees you dressed as some Highland savage, he'll assume— It will rob us of the element of surprise! Damn. He'll be here at any moment."

"I'm sorry to have disappointed you and that my appearance has proved inconvenient. So you'll be happy to know that Addie and I are leaving. Now," Jack said roughly.

"You are?" Lady Merritt's heavily rouged cheeks fell and she drummed her fingers impatiently against her steel breastplate. "Yes. Yes. I suppose that's best. We'll just have to wait until later. Well, Jack, be quick about it! Begone! And wear velvet knee breeches tomorrow."

With no need for further encouragement, Jack ushered Addie away. Each moment the urgency that drove him seemed to grow.

At the front door he barked out an order for her cloak to be fetched and a cab to be called. He waited impatiently, her hand still held tightly in his, only relinquishing his hold to wrap her tenderly in the thick, velvet folds of the cloak before leading her to the waiting carriage.

In the dark interior of the cab, he settled her on the overstuffed leather seats. His face was turned and she indulged herself by studying his fallen-angel profile: the firm cut of his lip, the strong line of jaw and throat, the high slant of cheekbone, and the intriguing bump on his formidable nose. He caught her looking, turning suddenly so that their eyes locked. Without volition she swayed forward, wanting to test the texture of his lips. His jaw snapped shut and his throat worked. With a strangled sound, he dropped into the seat opposite her.

Without hesitation, Addie crossed the short span of the carriage and settled in next to him, snuggling close. Their breath, in the chill, dim interior of the hansom, mingled like phantom spirits. He groaned. She smiled. What chance did his noble intentions stand? She was, after all, the woman he loved.

28

It was going to take far too long to reach Addie's townhouse, but then five minutes would have been too long. He couldn't speak here, now. It wouldn't be fair to confess his duplicity where she could not send him away. And regardless of all his hopes, that was exactly what he expected her to do.

But the warmth and weight of her body nestled intimately against him; the cool silken texture of her hair on his cheek was undoing his best intentions.

It was more than a physical craving: He wanted all of her. Forever. The self-confidence that had been growing in her for months had burst into full bloom tonight. Open and warm, brave and canny, exuberant and more than a shade mischievous, she was absolutely irresistible.

He'd watched her deal with Paul Sherville, hovering in case he'd spied any sign of distress. There had been none. She had been poised and disdainful.

Her new-sprung certainty was playing havoc with his heart and soul. She had the manner of a woman who knew she was loved. Her eyes glowed, her laughter was infectious, and when her hand sought his, it was without hesitation, eroding his principles.

His fingertips betrayed his honor, turning her hand over and tracing patterns on her palm. She laid her head on his shoulder, rubbing her cheek against the wool fabric covering his chest.

"Am I shameless?"

"Aye. Shameless."

"And you are a fake!" she chuckled.

His body, already strung tight, went rigid. She didn't seem to notice, because she went on in her husky, mellow voice. "You play at being one of John Ruskin's followers, and I have heard you rather vigorously defend women's suffrage, yet you resist the concept of"—here her head dipped lower on his chest—"free love."

"There is no such thing as free love, Addie," he muttered, brushing his lips against her temple. "Good God, it is anything but free."

She angled her head to look up at him, her hand creeping up to his neck. "Semantics," she whispered. "I am just trying to reassure you. I want you to make love to me. That is what you want, too."

His laugh was tinged with desperation. "Oh, yes. I want. God knows. But you—"

"You have always respected my intelligence, my right to make my own choices. Will you gainsay me now?"

"Lord, Addie. Just a few miles more, a quarter of an hour, and I'll stand—or fall—before any choice you make."

"A quarter of an hour? At my home?" She smiled, delighted, and tugged his head down toward hers. When he resisted, she frowned. "Won't you kiss me, Jack?"

A kiss. Perhaps the last kiss he would have from her?

In answer, he wrapped his arms around her, pulling her onto his lap. The cashmere blanket bundled around their legs as he crushed her against him, finding her mouth. She opened her lips for him, sweetly, hungrily.

Her lips were heated and her cheeks were chilled and he kissed her as though he would never stop kissing her: warm, deep, wet kisses. He held her face between both hands as he kissed her and she wriggled on his lap, twining her arms about him, sighing softly into his mouth, touching him, stroking him.

He didn't know how long he would have kissed her thus. Time seemed to slip by in a sensual rush, longing and gratification hopelessly commingled. But the cabby was suddenly pounding on the top of the carriage and from the sound of it, had been doing so for some minutes.

Gently, Jack lifted her from his lap, taking a second to brush a loose strand of mahogany-colored hair from her eyes before opening the door. He leapt out and tossed the grumbling man a half crown, then turned.

Addie stood at the doorway, her eyes languid and content, her skin rosy beneath the lantern's light. He lifted his hands and she came to him with such grace, such trust, it nearly broke his heart. He clasped her narrow waist and lifted her to the ground, holding her against him for too brief a second.

"We're home," Addie said happily.

"Yes." The dread and hopelessness that only her touch had kept at bay returned in full force. With leaden feet, he escorted her to the front door.

"I don't have a footman, just Partridge, and he's waiting for Ted at the Merritts'," Addie said in answer to his silent query. "I told the housekeeper to take the night off. The parlor maid is gone, visiting her sister."

"What a democratic employer you are."

"It's de rigueur in artistic spheres to cosset one's servants." She hesitated. "But then, of course, you know that." Ted was right; at some level, Addie knew he was a fraud. She just refused to acknowledge his duplicity.

He took a deep breath, unlocking the door and pushing it open. He followed her in, the click of the closing door echoing in the silent, dark hallway.

"Won't you please wait for me in the sitting room?" she asked, the sweet touch of formality in her voice the only thing betraying any uneasiness. She slipped her cloak from her shoulders and tossed it onto a table. "There is some brandy, upstairs in Ted's studio. I'll be down directly."

He nodded, watching what little light there was catch and release the shimmering embroidery on her gown as she hurried up the stairs.

No battle he'd ever been about to join had ever caused him so much anxiety. He steeled himself, heading into the room she'd indicated and looking around. Addie's hand was evident everywhere.

The sitting room was done up in burnished bronze and pale peony pink, bare of all accouterments save those that were comfortable and pleasing to the eye. There was a deep bronze and shell-pink striped divan set between two armchairs. A single parquetted table held an enormous glass bowl stuffed with huge pink hothouse tulips.

He picked up the book that lay open on one simple mahogany end table. Émile Zola.

Such literature, he thought with renewed despair, could only confirm Addie's lessons about male brutality. And now he would teach her another lesson, this one about male duplicity. He set the book down, raking his hand through his hair.

He stalked back across the room, heading for the hallway and the confrontation he knew would end in his permanent banishment. Why wait here? Why not save himself some steps?

He had just entered the hallway when he heard her scream.

29

Jack vaulted up the stairs as Addie's scream was abruptly choked off. At the top, he snatched the *sgian-dubh* from its sheath and sprinted toward the open door to Ted's studio.

And stopped.

Two men were in the room: One, short and stocky with slack lips and beetling brows, held Addie, a beefy arm wrapped around her throat, his dirty paw covering her mouth. Above the gag of his hand, Addie's eyes were wide with terror. The other man was younger, wiry, with pomaded hair and quivering with rabid intensity. Jack spared him no more than a glance.

"Any move, gov, and I snap 'er pretty neck," the man holding Addie said. "Now, puts down the sticker and we'll all make nice."

"Let her go."

"Not bloody likely. We'll just get what we come for and maybe a few mementos of Her Ladyship here and then we'll see about leaving. Now, put down the knife before someone gets hurt!" For emphasis, he yanked his arm tighter around Addie's neck. Tears sprang to her eyes as she stared at Jack in mute appeal.

"Stop!" Jack barked, dropping the blade and kicking it a few feet in front of him. "It's dropped. Now let her go!"

"Pick it up, Joey," the heavy man ordered. The skinny younger man darted forward and scooped up the blade. Smirking, he feinted the deadly blade at Jack's belly, laughing as the razor-sharp steel slashed through his plaid.

Jack ignored him, his attention riveted on the man holding Addie.

"There's no one else in the house," he said, trying to sound conciliatory. "She could scream bloody murder and no one would hear. There's no reason to hold your hand over her mouth. Let her breathe."

"Maybe I likes the feeling of her kissing me palm." The heavy man snickered.

"You said no one would get hurt."

"Well now, I ain't never been known for me truthful ways. And it appears Joey has taken a dislike to you, gov," the beefy man said. Joey nodded in menacing agreement and proceeded to flicker the dirk closer and closer to Jack's throat. "Seems you might get hurt."

Addie's muffled cry cut him more sharply than any blade could have done.

"Tha's right," mumbled Joey. "Bad hurt. I don't like namby-pamby boys. Specially ones what wears skirts."

"That ain't no skirt, Joey. That be a kilt. Scots regiments wear 'em. You know that!"

"I say it's a skirt, Hal! And lookit 'is hair! Ain't it pretty?" Joey moved closer and flicked Jack's hair back with the blade, scoring his cheek in the process. "Any man wears a skirt like that doesn't have the right to call himself a man." An evil grin slowly spread across his vulpine face. "If he is a man. Maybe we oughta have a look?"

"Ow!" With an oath, Hal snatched his hand away from Addie's mouth.

She took advantage of her sudden freedom, dropping heavily to her knees. In that instant, Jack seized Joey's forearm and yanked it savagely behind him, hearing it break with an audible crack. Joey howled in agony and Jack snatched the blade from him, wheeling about in time to see the beefy man raise one huge hand to strike Addie.

"Bitch." His fist swung down toward her unprotected head.

"No!" Jack's bellow reverberated through the room as the dirk flew from his nerveless hand, impaling itself in the meat of the man's shoulder.

Jack followed the blade's trajectory, launching himself across the room and hitting the man low in the gut. Together they fell, crashing into the floorboards.

Jack twisted, pulling Hal beneath him and straddling his thick chest. He thrust his knee into Hal's throat to hold him down so he could pummel the face of the animal who'd threatened Addie—something crashed into his injured shoulder and lights of pain rocketed across his vision.

He fell sideways, half off Hal, dazed. Joey held the broken leg of a chair in his good hand, waving the makeshift cudgel threateningly. Until he saw Jack's eyes. He backed away.

Hal took advantage of the brief distraction, knocking Jack the rest of the way off of him, kicking him in the gut before climbing to his feet, the blade still buried in his filthy shirt.

"Knocker it, Joey!" Hal shouted, clawing the blade free. It fell, staining the carpet with blood.

The scrawny youth was already gone, leaving his mate to bolt after him.

Jack lurched heavily onto all fours, his head lolling forward, gasping for air. Addie could have been hurt. She might have—

A hand touched him. With a roar, he surged to his feet, seizing the wrist on his shoulder and dragging his assailant around—

He held Addie's wrist in a death grip. She crouched at his feet, her elegant coiffure tumbled down her back, the strap of her gown fallen from one shoulder. She stared up at him, amber eyes stark in her pale face.

"Addie!" He fell to his knees beside her, lifting her upper arms, trying to read her expression. "Are you hurt?" He gave her a little shake. "Are you hurt?"

"You fought him," she whispered incredulously. "You threw that blade like an expert. Oh, God! You are an expert, aren't you?"

"Addie—"

"Answer me." She didn't wait but continued speaking in a low, bleak voice. "You aren't an artist or a craftsman or even a dilettante. That uniform. It isn't a costume; it's yours. You're a soldier."

"Addie, I tried to tell you."

"You're a soldier. Like Charles." She twisted free of his grip, sinking to the floor, crumpling beneath the weight of her emotions like an orchid in a deluge. "You lied to me. To all of us."

"Please!" The word was torn from his mouth, echoing in his heart, his soul. "For God's sake, Addie, listen to me. Please."

"Please?" A sudden thought occurred to her and she slowly straightened, horror replacing the pitiable desolation in her eyes. "Did you know Charles?"

"Addie, you have to let me explain," he begged.

"Did he get drunk some night and tell you about what he did to me? About how much I hated him and what he did? Did he tell you about the inheritance I would come into? Was that the inspiration for your charade?" Her voice had risen.

"No, Addie. I never met Hoodless. I knew nothing about you before I came to my uncle's house. This has nothing to do with your inheritance."

"Oh, God. Jack, how could you?" The anger broke for a second, revealing the anguish beneath it.

"I felt I had no choice."

"No choice?" Her expression had taken on a dazed quality. "No choice," she repeated forlornly. With each passing moment, she was being lost to him.

"I am a captain in the Gordon Highlanders. Was a captain," he amended. "I was injured and sent to Gate Hall's dowager house to convalesce. But just before I was injured, I received information about a traitor in the Black Dragoons. I had to try and find him, and I knew making queries as an officer would put the traitor on his guard.

"Then I overheard Lady Merritt talking about your brother having received the commissions to paint the Black Dragoons officers and I formed a plan. In the relaxed atmosphere of your brother's studio, as an inconsequential artist hanging about the fringes, I would be invisible and thus privy to the confidences men exchange in unguarded moments. I thought in that way I might discover some clue as to the traitor's identity. So I could avenge the men he betrayed.

"It was my duty, Addie. My obligation to those men who died or were hurt because of this officer's treachery. As God as my witness, Addie, I did not mean for you to be involved!"

A burble of hysterical laughter struggled free from her throat. She bit it back, staring about her wildly.

"I love you, Addie. You have to believe that. I know this is appalling. That you feel betrayed—"

"Yes!"

"Listen to me, Addie! I never meant to hurt you—"

"Too late!"

It was true. All he could think to do was reassure her about tonight's threat. "I know you don't think you can forgive me now, Addie, but at least let me assure you that you have nothing to fear from those men. I will never let anything hurt you again. I'll do whatever is necessary, everything in my power to protect you. I'd give my life—"

"No!" The passionate denial erupted from her lips. She stared down at him, panting and wild-eyed. "Take it back! I don't want your death or your blood!" she cried. "Take it back!"

But he couldn't.

"How can I? Anything, anyone who threatens you, Addie, is not safe from me."

"And me? Am I safe from you? What happens when you decide my own judgment threatens me?" she asked hoarsely. "Maybe it begins with a horse you decide isn't safe for me to ride, or a carriage that you deem sprung too high. You'd keep me from those? Because they 'threaten' me!"

It wasn't what he meant. But she was relating a history she'd never spoken of before.

"I'm not Charles."

She ignored him. "Sooner or later, I take what you consider one too many drinks, or a brother's behavior 'taints' my reputation, or you say a pet dog bared his teeth. And drink is banned, the brother eschewed, the dog destroyed. And then what is left? Nothing but the endless waiting. To see what next you might take from me."

"Addie—"

"I don't want your protection."

"Addie. I love you." He had only one other weapon to use in the battle for her heart, one thing more. He used it now. "And you love me."

She did not deny it. She simply closed her eyes while a single tear raced down her white cheek.

"Addie, you love me."

Her eyes snapped open and she stared at him. "I loved him, too."

He took her words like a physical blow, lifting his head to face her scorn full on.

She met his gaze, quivering, implacable. "Stupid heart," she said bitterly. "Twice deceived. Ignorant, callow organ. But I won't be ruled again by its destructive blindness. No. Twice deceived but not twice destroyed."

"I am not Charles. I will—"

"You will go!" she said. "If you have any portion of the affection for me you claim, you'll leave. Now!"

"Addie, I can't. Those men may come back!"

"Go," she sobbed, covering her face with her hands, her shoulders shaking. "Oh, Jack," and now she was begging him, "please go."

He longed to gather her to him and cradle her in his arms and convince her of his love, but he could not force her.

And so, weary and despairing, he left.

＊

Four hours later, Ted climbed out of the carriage and started up the steps. Jack, abandoning his post in the deep shadows of the alleyway, called out.

"Cameron, what are you doing out here?"

"Two men. Thieves, I think. They were in the house when we arrived."

"Is Addie all right?" he demanded urgently.

"She wasn't injured."

"Where is she?"

"Inside. I think . . . she's asleep. Her light went out an hour ago."

Ted peered through the mist at him. "Good God, man. Were you hurt? You look awful!"

"I'm fine. I just didn't want to take the chance that they might return. I'm not sure . . . Something one of them said. They might be more than simple cracksmen."

"Why the hell didn't you stay inside?"

"Couldn't. She wouldn't . . . I have to go. I might be able to find out who . . . if . . ." He knew he was barely coherent, but he'd had four hours to stand in the bleakness of a London midnight, each minute an isolated instance of loss, an interminable reminder that he had forfeited an irreplaceable love.

Only his resolve to find out who threatened Addie offered any solace. "I have to go."

———◆———

"Addie!" She heard her brother call from the hall.

"Go away."

"Addie, let me in or I shall sit out here until morning." Ted pounded on the door.

He would, too, Addie knew. So, she rose, heedless of her gorgeous gown, wrinkled and ruined, her disheveled hair, her tear-streaked face, and opened the door. Ted took one look at her ruined appearance and gathered her into his arms. "Did Cameron do this?"

"Do what?" Addie asked bewildered. "Oh. No. No. I just . . . I didn't change."

Ted took her shoulders gently in his hands. "Tell me."

And because he was her big brother and loved her and had always stood by her, had even been crippled for her, she did. "He's a soldier, Ted. Jack is a soldier."

Ted heaved a sigh and, slipping an arm around her shoulders, led her to a love seat by the foot of her bed. He settled her there before kneeling down in front of her, taking her cold hands and chafing them in his. "Aye. I suspected as much."

"You did?" she asked, stung by this second betrayal. "Why didn't you say something?"

"I suspected, just as you did."

She shook her head. "I did not."

"You are a perceptive woman, Addie. That Jack Cameron is in no manner an artist could not be more apparent. And really,

Addie, where else could a man get scars such as Cameron bears? Palette knives?" His gentle mockery brokered no answering smile because she had none to give. But he was right. It all seemed so obvious now.

"You chose to delude yourself. Who was I to question that?" And then he added, more quietly, "You have fallen in love with him, haven't you?"

She looked away.

"Haven't you?"

She gave up. "Can you believe anyone could be so self-destructive?"

"Addie," Ted said. "You didn't deserve what Charles did to you."

"Didn't I?" She looked up at him. Her eyes were clouded with self-doubt. "Doesn't anyone who loves foolishly deserve what happens to them? If I'd been smarter, or less willful, less romantic, I would have seen what Charles was. I would have known. I should have known. Everyone told me. God, Ted, even his own parents told me. And now, I've done it again."

"No, Addie."

"You said so yourself. I refused to see what was right before my eyes."

"It's different with Jack."

"How can I know that?" she asked poignantly.

"Your heart—"

"My heart is a fool."

"Addie, one mistake—"

"Two."

"Jack Cameron is not like Charles. I'd stake my life on it."

"But would I bet mine?" she asked, and buried her face against Ted's shirt and wept.

30

"What I want to know is *why* they picked that particular house," Jack said to the grizzled old veteran sitting across from him. His satisfaction at finally having found someone willing to talk about last night's aborted robbery was bittersweet. It was impossible to say how much the man knew and how much he was making up in order to get a free drink.

He'd been chasing down even his most tentative army connections, calling in conscience dues from every man he could think might be persuaded he owed him something. He'd hunted amongst the dockside taverns and the low-rent serving houses, asking questions, loosening suspicious tongues with cheap drink. Finally, finding his way here, to this man.

"Thirsty sorta mornin', ain't it, Cap? Could do with a spot more to drink."

Jack shoved the bottle across the stained and greasy plank table. The soldier grabbed the bottle and emptied it into his cup. "Thanks kindly, sir. Now, why it were that house I don't rightly know, Cap." He furrowed his brow. "But if you've set your sight on finding Hal and Joey, you can ferget it. They're gone. Disappeared like they never was. Probably jumped a steamer if they got wind of yer askin' questions."

He didn't want Hal and Joey. He wanted whoever had sent Hal and Joey. "Why did they choose that house?"

"I wouldn't even be talkin' wid ya like this if you weren't captain to me old mate, Jim Gill. He says hows youse always took care o' the lads. That counts fer somethin'. So, I'll give ya this." The old soldier leaned forward, his rheumy eyes sliding back and forth. "It were set up by some other bloke, a bit of hire work, and it weren't jewels they were sent for."

"What was it then?"

The man flopped back in his seat, fiddling with the empty bottle until Jack motioned the bartender to bring them another.

"Don't know exactly. But Joey was pleased as a whore on leave day. Said some bloke was paying him twenty quid for a spot of starring the glaze and lifting some papers, maybe a photograph? Weren't payin' him much heed when he was jabberin'." The old soldier dried his lips with the back of his sleeve. "Youse wouldn't be carrying a bit of the powder?"

"No. Who was the bloke?"

The man, clearly disappointed there'd be no cocaine to chase his whiskey with, shrugged. "Don't know. Didn't never say. Some toff."

"How would this toff find them in the first place?"

"I tells you, I don't know," the man said querulously. "Hal just says something about it not being the first time he'd taken orders from this bloke. I do recall thinkin' it was funny, the way he said it like that. Orders. Just like he was back in the army."

Jack tossed a crown to the filthy tabletop before leaving. He'd wager everything that he knew who had given those orders. But then, he already had.

———— ❖ ————

Paul Sherville waited fifteen minutes after the butler announced Jack Cameron before going to meet him. He wanted Cameron impatient, angry. An impatient, angry man was much more likely to reveal his strengths and weaknesses.

The ex-corporal whose interesting talents he'd made such good use of in the Sudan had botched this job. Then he'd had the temerity to come whining to him about his pierced shoulder, asking for money. Sherville bounced his heavy knobbed walking stick in his hand. Hal wouldn't be bothering him again. He and Joey were well out to sea by now, with no return in sight.

He paused outside the library to study Jack from the shadows. He was mildly surprised by the man's appearance. He'd expected to find Cameron tricked out in his adopted satin and frills. Instead, he wore an ordinary coat and trousers, only the absence of a neckpiece and the crumpled collar noteworthy. That and his face.

Gone was the supercilious expression. His face looked haunted and strained, lines bracketing his mouth and deeply scoring his lean cheeks. He looked . . . dangerous. Apparently he'd abandoned his guise.

For a second, Sherville wondered if perhaps he should just refuse to see Cameron. No. He'd outsmarted half the commanders in the Middle East. No mere captain could prove a worthy adversary.

"My, Jackie," he said, sauntering into the room. "What's happened to your velvet breeches? Did you wear out the knees?"

He'd thought to provoke Cameron and was nonplussed when he turned casually. Sherville took an involuntary step back from the devilish lights gleaming in Cameron's cursed cold eyes.

"Let's cut to the chase, shall we?" Cameron suggested softly.

"Why, whatever do you mean?" Sherville asked, striving to regain his aplomb.

"I know you were the officer who aided the slavers in North Africa."

"Have you gone mad? What are you talking about?" Sherville asked, pleased at the outrage in his voice.

"I suspect you somehow manipulated troop movements to account for the twenty-four-hour delay in Gordon's rescue. Perhaps you were in contact with the Mahdi. You must have realized Gordon had found you out."

Cameron didn't have any proof. If he had, he'd be at Whitehall now, telling his masters. He was bluffing.

Sherville clapped politely. "Have you given up the—now just what was it you were supposed to have been? Oh, yes. A woodworker. Have you given up the chisel for the pen, Cameron? Because I vow, this is quite a fascinating piece of fiction you've manufactured."

"I'm not in the mood for games."

"Really? Then maybe you'll tell me exactly what you are doing here, smelling like a dung heap and making offensive accusations? Quite uncivilized, old chap. We aren't in the cesspools of Africa or Afghanistan anymore." He waited eagerly to see how Cameron took the news that his ridiculous charade had been discovered.

Cameron did not blink. "I've come to tell you that you're going to pay for your crimes, Sherville," he said. "And I'm going to make it happen."

And now, for the first time, Sherville felt a real chill of apprehension. He turned away to mask his fear. Nothing, in a career and life that exulted in danger, had ever looked so lethal to him as Cameron's cold smile.

"Get out," he said. He was trying to provoke him into making some admission.

"Not yet."

"I'll have you put out." He could hear the shrillness in his own voice but was powerless to prevent it.

"Please. Try." Again, that flickering, dangerous smile. "I have one more thing to say. One more issue we must discuss. If I find out you hired those men to break into Addie's house last night, I will come back, and I promise, you will not enjoy the visit."

He masked his fear by sneering. "Addie, is it?"

He didn't see Cameron move. One instant he was smirking at the man, the next he was dangling by a viselike grip on his lapel, inches from Cameron's hot, gleaming eyes.

"Yes. Addie. And whether or not you had those men in her house last night, know this: If you ever, ever threaten her again, directly or indirectly, I'll tear your spine out."

Cameron shoved him away. Sherville stumbled and fell into the chair behind him. By the time he looked up, Cameron was gone.

He was afraid and with good reason. But he had to be careful. Cameron would be watching closely, anticipating a hasty, panicked next move on his part. He would be disappointed.

As of yet, Cameron might have no proof.

And by God, he had to make sure he never did.

"The man you are looking for is Sherville," Jack announced as soon as he'd been ushered into the morning room where Colonel Halvers was enjoying his first cup of tea. "He hired two thugs to enter the Hoodless townhouse to steal some papers or photographs that I believe incriminated him."

"Hoodless was *blackmailing* Sherville?"

"I believe so."

"Good God." Halvers set his cup down and leaned forward excitedly. "And you know where these men are?"

"No." The frustration he felt at having been unable to locate Hal and Joey burned him again. "I found a man who overheard the thieves boasting in a dockside tavern prior to the robbery attempt. Unfortunately I haven't been able to find them . . . yet."

"But this man heard them mention Sherville by name?"

Unhappily, Jack gave a single negative shake of his head.

Halvers's mouth tightened in disappointment. "Then you don't know whether they were successful."

"No. But I don't believe they were. We came upon them in the act and they fled."

"Is Mrs. Hoodless all right?"

"She is physically unharmed."

Halvers studied Jack in silence a moment before speaking. "Do you have access to Hoodless's personal belongings?"

"No."

"Can you get access?"

"No," Jack spat out the word, his admiration for Halvers dimming.

Halvers made an impatient movement with his hand. "Then, if you refuse to help us in this matter, I fail to see what you are doing here."

"I want protection for Mrs. Hoodless," Jack said tersely. "If the thieves did not secure whatever they were looking for, Mrs. Hoodless may still be in danger."

"Be reasonable, Cameron. I can't have an armed escort accompany Mrs. Hoodless on the merits of a random robbery— No. You'll let me finish.

"You have nothing on which to base your speculations about the supposedly nefarious purpose of this robbery but the word of a drunk. He couldn't even tell you the name of the man he said hired them. You assume it is Paul Sherville. You may be right but, damn it, you have no proof, only speculation. That alone is not enough to convince the War Office to protect your widow."

"She isn't mine."

"A poor choice of words," Halvers said.

"Colonel, I spoke to Sherville. I would lay my life he is your traitor."

"Damn it, Cameron! You have put him on his guard!"

"No, sir. I have pushed him past his guard. And that is why you must protect Addie Hoodless. He will be nearly frantic to get the evidence he is certain is in the Hoodless house."

Halvers pursed his lips and stared thoughtfully. Jack waited. Finally, Halvers looked up.

"I'll have a man watch her house, but only for a while. And let me say this, if you are correct and this supposed evidence is still at large, I suggest you see if you can search for it before Sherville does. For her safety."

"I would rather ask her to do so herself."

"Ask a woman to hunt for evidence that her husband was at best a blackmailer and at worst a traitor? Essentially ask her to not only secure her own position as a social pariah for the unforeseen future but also her family? This beloved and upcoming society painter? What do you think the chances are of her complying?"

"Excellent," Jack clipped out without hesitation. Yes, it would hurt her. It would torment her to know that she had contributed to the Hoodlesses' disgrace, her brother's downfall, but she would choose justice.

"I wish I were as sanguine. But I'm not. Even if she does agree to search for it, how hard do you think she will look? How thorough do you think she will be? Or even *can* be, knowing what is at stake?"

"The devil take you!" The words erupted from Jack's throat.

"Quite likely."

"You seem to have manipulated me into being your sneak thief very adroitly, Halvers."

"I have merely taken advantage of the situation as it presents itself. In my position, you would do the same."

"Do you sleep well, Colonel?" Jack asked bitterly.

"About as well as you, I expect."

31

Take pity on the man. He's been begging to see you for days," Ted said.

"No," Addie said.

"If nothing else, you owe it to yourself to hear him out."

"I owe it to myself to get on with my life. Nothing Jack Cameron—Captain Cameron—has to say matters to me."

"'Get on with' your life?" Ted asked. "Is that what you call this? Sitting in this damn room?"

"I like this damn room."

He chuckled. "It's a fine room, as long as it doesn't become a prison.

"Listen to me, Addie. I don't like what Cameron did. But you need to hear his reasons for what he did precisely because you do need to get on with your life—whether with or without Jack Cameron. As it is, you'll forever be dodging him, worrying about a chance encounter."

"I just need time. A few more weeks."

"Dear sister," Ted said gently, "don't you see that you're repeating your history? This is exactly what you did after you married Hoodless. You hid away from society and friends and family. It seems to be your standard self-imposed sentence for assuming people aren't what they appear to be: life in limbo."

He was right. She had hidden away from the hurt, gone to ground. And she didn't want to do it again, because much of the past few months, she had felt whole again. She'd approved of herself.

She already missed that.

"Lord, Addie," Ted was saying. "You should see the man. He looks terrible."

"Good!" She could not help saying it. "Good! But I still won't see him."

"Addie, let me say one more thing and after that I promise I won't pester you again."

She nodded mutely.

"You never allowed Hoodless to destroy you. You retreated from the battle but you didn't let him win. Don't let him win now."

"This hasn't anything to do with Charles," she cried softly.

"It has everything to do with Charles. Don't let him achieve in death what he could never do when he was alive."

"And what is that?"

"Make you give up on yourself—on the life you could have— on the love you could have."

"Jack doesn't love me." It didn't matter that Jack had said he did. He'd said a lot of things. Most of them lies. Indeed, right after he had told her how much he loved her, she'd discovered his betrayal.

"Then see him. Make sure," Ted insisted.

The thought of seeing Jack again, however painful, was like a siren call. Perhaps she did need to see him. She needed to see what about him had made her so blind, had made her repeat the old habit of self-destructiveness.

"All right," she said. "But not here. I'll see him at the Merritts'."

⬥

She must hold her head up. She must not let him see how he had hurt her. She must be composed; she must be serene. Taking a deep breath, Addie handed the footman her gloves and coat.

"May I say it is a real pleasure to see you again, Mrs. Hoodless," a dignified voice spoke from above. Addie looked up to see Wheatcroft coming down the stairs. He made a dismissive motion to the footman as he said, "I will show Mrs. Hoodless the way. Lord and Lady Merritt are in the morning room."

"Together?" she asked in surprise as they walked down the Merritts' marble-tiled main hallway.

"Yes, ma'am. Together. I shall inform Captain Cameron of your arrival. He has retired upstairs."

"Oh?" She tried to sound nonchalant. "He is unwell?"

"No, Madame. He is not ill. But as the lunch hour passed, he became convinced you had forgotten your kind acceptance of his invitation and . . . well."

"I see." She was late. He'd assumed she wasn't coming.

"In the meantime, Lord and Lady Merritt will be pleased for your company." He bowed as he pushed the door to the morning room open and retreated, murmuring, "I shall inform the captain of your arrival."

"Thank you, Wheatcroft."

In the morning room, she was confounded by the sight of Lord and Lady Merritt huddled together on a small mint-green divan, their hands entwined. In the light of their long estrangement, the sight of them together was so unexpected that Addie stopped short.

Both the Merritts were dressed soberly—Lady Merritt's dark gray gown and Lord Merritt's somber suit coat more befitting a funeral than a morning at home.

"Lord Merritt?" she asked when neither seemed to notice her entrance. Lord Merritt blinked up at her. She remembered him as a blustering, vigorous man with a booming voice. He was still muscular looking, his shaggy white head sitting squarely on his bulky shoulders. But the aggressive self-confidence had disappeared from his florid features. He looked confused, aggrieved, like a small boy who'd had his favorite slingshot taken away.

"Addie, how kind of you to come. To what do we owe the pleasure?" Lady Merritt asked in a subdued whisper, drawing Addie's attention.

If Lord Merritt's appearance had undergone a dramatic change, Lady Merritt's had doubly done so. Her habitual bulldog expression was absent, replaced by bewilderment. Her powdered cheeks were streaked with gummy rivulets of tears and the hard line of her mouth looked wounded.

"I had to come," Addie said. Lady Merritt nodded and took a deep, shuddering breath. Her husband patted her hand consolingly.

"You've heard about him, then."

"Yes, of course." She hadn't realized the Merritts would take Jack's masquerade so hard. Outrage, she could understand . . . but this . . . grief! And Lord Merritt! She'd have expected him to be at least somewhat mollified by the fact that Jack was not the artist he'd played at being.

"It was not our fault," Lord Merritt said defensively.

"No, of course not. It had nothing to do with you. He told me."

Lady Merritt stared. "He told you?"

Addie frowned. Surely Lady Merritt must have suspected their friendship—even if it had been merely an illusion. "Of course. The night of the party, when he took me home."

Lady Merritt peered at her in perplexity a moment before enlightenment dawned in her eyes. She heaved a dramatic sigh. "Oh. You're talking about Jack."

"Yes. Jack. Who else? His deception, his exploitation of you, your home, your friendship. He gulled us, Lady Merritt, and you must not hold yourself accountable. He was very good—"

"Yes, yes." Lady Merritt sighed again, and leaned her head back against the cushion on the divan, closing her eyes. "Jack has been naughty."

"Naughty?" Addie's tone echoed her astonishment. "He uses you—he uses all of us—and all you can say is 'Jack has been naughty'?"

"Really, Addie. I don't have the emotional energy right now to deal with Jack's transgressions. Lord Merritt and I have a far greater betrayal to deal with." Her lips quivered. Lord Merritt patted her again.

"A greater betrayal than Jack's?"

Lord Merritt squeezed his wife's hand and cleared his throat. "You might as well be told. The rumor mills will be grinding soon enough. Our son, Evan—" His voice cracked and Lady Merritt moaned. He tried again. "Evan has entered a seminary."

"Excuse me?"

"Evan has converted. He is becoming a . . . a . . ."

"A Roman Catholic priest!" wailed Lady Merritt and flung herself in her husband's arms.

"There, there, Harmy." With difficulty, Lord Merritt hefted his wife to her feet. "You'll excuse us, Addie," he said solemnly and proceeded to stagger through the door under the weight of his sobbing wife.

Addie stared after them, amazed.

"It's the only thing I can conceive of that would have effected a reconciliation between them." Jack stepped into the doorway, clad in a dark suit that could not disguise the athletic breadth of his shoulders or the hard, lean length of his legs. Her heart skipped uncomfortably at the sight of his haggard face. He'd cut his hair, she thought, aware of the irrelevance of the observance. It was not so light now, but a soft nut-brown.

"What might do the same for us?"

"Nothing." She lifted her chin. "I have come to tell you that your supplications via my brother have fallen on deaf ears. After today, I will not meet you. I thought it only fair to inform you in person so you might not be taken unawares should we chance to pass in public."

The muscles strained in his jaw. He took a step forward and she countered with a step back. He started to reach out toward her but then dropped his hand, his fist clenched at his side.

"Addie. You must let me explain."

"So Ted tells me and so I am here. Please continue." Her coldness did not alter his expression; it remained one of profound gentleness.

"Will you please sit down?"

"No. You may have instigated this interview, but I have been manipulated by you long enough. Whatever you have to say, say it from there." She kept her gaze on his shoulders. If she looked into his blue eyes she would lose her resolve. She must not make the mistake of believing in him again.

"All right," he said. "All right. I was, as I told you, a captain of the Gordon Highlanders. I was in the regiment for over a decade, Addie. It was my life. As it was my father's life."

"That was not a lie, then."

"No," he finally said, "that was not a lie."

"Go on."

"I was a good soldier. A better officer."

"Good at killing."

"No." The words were instant, sure. "Good at keeping my men from being killed."

She could not question his conviction.

"Soldiers aren't cut from one mold, Addie. Some believe in what they are doing. Some are forced into their careers. Some are idealists. Some are brave; some are craven. A very few enjoy carnage; the vast majority are sickened by it. Some just go through the motions, marking time while they serve. Whatever their reasons, it was my responsibility to see that they did their jobs and stayed alive."

Seeing that she was not going to respond, he went on. "There is a brotherhood amongst soldiers that is born on the battlefield. Men depend on each other and, in turn, on their commanding officers. It is the only way soldiers can expect to live. That mutual trust."

Her determination to cling to her anger faltered. She steeled herself. Words were easy.

"I discovered that one of the officers in the Sudan had betrayed that trust. He made money by working for the very slavers we were there to vanquish. In doing so, he knowingly forfeited his own men's—perhaps my men's—lives."

She could hear the rawness in his words.

"I could not let him get away with it."

She took a deep breath. "What has that to do with me?"

"The only thing I knew about this officer was that he was a member of the Black Dragoons. The man who told me died as he spoke. I couldn't hear all of what he said, but I did hear that he'd seen some sort of evidence, some written proof of the traitor's guilt. Before I could act on this information, I was wounded."

She couldn't keep herself from moving forward, just a step, but a telling one. He acted as though he did not see it. Jack would never use pity to gain an advantage.

"Under instructions from my last surviving relative, Lord Merritt, they shipped me to Gate Hall. There I recuperated under Wheatcroft's tender ministrations. It was a protracted convalescence and by the time I was better, the war was over, the men dispersed, anything I might have found in North Africa was gone." One corner of his beautifully sculpted lips curled in wry memory.

"How long were you at Gate Hall?"

"All spring and into summer. Long months when the only things that kept me from going mad with frustration and anger and boredom were the drive to find this traitor. And you."

"No."

"Yes," he said. "I heard you taking tea on the terrace beneath my window, walking in the garden with Lady Merritt. I would listen to you, for you. I came to know you, the cadence of your footstep, the contentment in your silence. I knew the way you watched the sky by how often you were told to mind your freckles. I knew when you listened to the same bird's song I did, for you would pause while others spoke when a thrush trilled from the meadow. I fell in love with you, Addie, before I ever saw you."

He waited quietly, exposed and acquiescent and so very vulnerable. Everything in her heart longed to believe him. She mustn't listen to that defective instrument again.

"You loved me so much you plotted to deceive me." God help her, she wanted to be convinced.

His sigh was filled with remorse but he went doggedly on. "While I was recovering, I wrote letters to the War Office, to my old mates, to anyone I could think of, asking for information. Slowly, with Wheatcroft's help, I compiled a list of the officers who could have been the traitor. There were only a few who were in a position of enough authority or who were in the right places at the right time. And of those, four were having their portraits painted by your brother."

"I see."

"No. You don't," he said vehemently. "I didn't have any proof. The only way I could think to find some was to get close to those men, in some guise that would not alert the traitor to my purpose.

And when I heard that your brother had been commissioned to paint the very officers I suspected, I saw a way. God help me, I took it. I had to. I knew too well what you thought of soldiers. You would never have allowed me near you—or your brother's studio."

"Why didn't you just tell the military authorities?"

"Tell them what?" he asked bitterly. "That on the merits of a dead native's word I was seeking to dishonor one of Her Majesty's most distinguished officers?"

"So you would have continued deceiving me, using me, if I hadn't found you out," she said.

"No!" He mastered himself with a visible effort. "No. I was going to tell you. That night."

"Why?" she asked, trying to make sense of why he would abandon his plan. And then, suddenly, horribly, it made sense. "Oh God," she said numbly. "It was Charles, wasn't it?"

He stared at her, pity and misery in his eyes. "No. That is, I can't be sure. I don't know." He swallowed visibly, as though trying to choke down something offensive. "I believe Sherville is the culprit but I also believe that Hoodless was involved. I am not sure in what capacity. Either as an accomplice or he knew what Sherville was doing."

"But then why wouldn't . . ." She trailed off as she filled in the blanks Jack had left. "You think he was holding his knowledge of what Paul Sherville was doing over his head."

"I know it is unspeakably vile to make such an accusation without proof, which is why—"

"Which is why you want to look for that proof," she finished. She felt numbed, her head filling with a hundred terrible scenarios: reading the newspapers' reports; her neighbors' sidelong glances; the taint of association that would destroy Ted's career.

"I don't know that there is any," Jack said carefully. "I think the men who were robbing your house were actually sent there to look for something that Hoodless had, or they thought he had."

"There's nothing there," she murmured, still trying to absorb it all. "Nothing."

"Be that as it may, Whitehall will not be satisfied until they have searched for it themselves."

Her head snapped up at that. "Strangers? Going through my things? Can't you do it?"

"I would but"—his beautiful mouth twisted into a smile—"I am not impartial. Part of me would not want to find anything. I wouldn't trust myself to be thorough."

She stared up at him, reading the conflict revealed in his terse expression. "Addie, please. This man, whoever he is, is not only responsible for the deaths of our soldiers but also the misery of untold men and women and children sold into slavery."

Our soldiers. Yes. Yes. Of course. A sense of rightness overcame her earlier panic and fear. How could she do otherwise? Ted would understand. "Very well."

"They will be discreet."

She nodded.

"I hope I am wrong, Addie," he said with sudden savagery. "For your sake, I hope to God they find nothing that implicates Hoodless. I hope this is all happenstance and that I can search for this traitor somewhere else, where it will not affect you or those you love. Please, Addie, you must know me well enough to believe that."

"Know you? How can I make such a claim? How can you ask it? You aren't the man I thought you were."

"I *am* that man." He spoke urgently, willing her to believe him. And she wanted to. God, how she wanted to! "My charade was just window dressing. Beneath the mask, I am the same man."

"I loved an illusion."

For some reason he seemed to take heart at her despairing words. "No. Let me prove it," he pleaded. "Give me a chance."

"A chance."

"Let me court you, Addie. I won't make any demands. You will see that I am a gentle man as well as a gentleman. Test me all you want. I love you, Addie. Let us start again. That's all I ask."

Her head spun. He'd lied and deceived her but he had also revealed why he had done so and his reasons were substantial. And honorable. She hadn't any answers. Nothing but experience to fall back on.

And her experience had been bitter.

"Just give me a chance to prove myself to you."

She could refuse him and she intuited he would never bother her again. Or she could take a chance and discover once and for all if she could trust her suspect heart.

"All right," she heard herself say. "A chance . . . a test."

32

"Why did you join the Highlanders?"

Jack looked up from the tray of silk ribbons the Covent Garden vendor had called him over to examine, as surprised by her question as she was to have asked it.

It had been two weeks since he had told her about Charles. Since then, true to Jack's word, the men from Whitehall had most discreetly searched her house and, true to her predictions, come away empty-handed, a fact that had released both Jack and herself from Charles's specter. And though Addie had no doubt that Jack continued his hunt for the scoundrel who'd betrayed so many, knowing that his investigations need not cast a shadow over her life, she allowed him to court her openly, a courtship that was restrained and gentle and unflagging.

And allowed her to ignore his military record.

Occasionally others would draw from him a story about his tenure, but when they were alone, it was a topic she never broached and he never introduced. Which was ridiculous, she realized. Being a cavalry captain was as much a part of him as . . . as . . . as his brogue.

Now, though surprised, he answered readily enough. "One doesn't join a Scots regiment, Addie. One is born to it."

"Rather like being born with a caul?" she asked.

He met her derision with genuine amusement. "Yes. Now that you mention it, it is rather a mystical thing. A boy has to be given to the regiment from birth."

She smiled at that. He always managed to turn her attempts at brusqueness on end. "Come now."

He placed a hand across his heart. "'Tis true. My father told me that a full company of Highlanders in dress uniform arrived for my baptism, where they gravely presented my mother with an infant-sized kilt, sporran, and badge, and suggested to her—strongly—that I should be dressed in it for the ceremony."

She chuckled. "And what did your mother do?"

"Being a good, honest Englishwoman, she refused to have anything to do with their hocus-pocus."

"Your father must have been gravely disappointed."

"As good an Englishwoman as my mother was, my father was an even more devious Scot. It was only after the service that she discovered my nappy had been pinned with the Gordon Highlanders' badge. My fate, as it were, was sealed."

She burst out laughing and he smiled, his strong white teeth gleaming in his tan face. His good humor was irresistible, drat him. She simply could not provoke his temper. And she wanted to see what form Jack's anger took because each day, she had fallen more in love with him.

They continued strolling through Covent Garden, the rest of their party having drifted some distance ahead, leaving Addie alone with Jack. Not that this was any great surprise. Jack always contrived to be close to her. Not obviously. He would never make her the object of speculation.

She wanted to ask another question, amazed that this was so. But, in truth, those few stories Jack had related of his service riveted her. He never chronicled the details of warfare, as Charles had loved to do, describing the carnage and slaughter. When Jack had spoken of actual battle it had been obliquely and then with great sadness.

No, mostly his tales had opened worlds for her. He'd conversed with pashas and sultans, visited great temples and palaces, feasted in a tent under a desert sky, and traveled on roads built by civilizations that predated Britain by thousands of years. It was fascinating.

"Well, Addie?" Jack asked quietly, cutting into her thoughts.

"Well what?"

"Have I passed muster yet? I love you. I will always love you. Marry me."

She stepped away from him, pretending interest in a street vendor's gaudy bits of jewelry. He had asked before, many times, and each time she'd had to stop herself from crying "yes" and relinquishing her heart once and finally to this—stranger's care.

She studied him from the corner of her eye, as he stood braced, awaiting her reply. In some ways, he actually did look like a stranger.

His natural grace was now apparent. He moved with the casual confidence of men accustomed to command. His stride was open, relaxed. His face, no longer forced to exaggerated expressions, was even more handsome. There was firmness about his mouth as well as sensuality. His eyes were open and clear. He was watching her now, tenderness and longing in his gaze.

"Addie?"

"I really cannot say. If you've grown tired of courting me, by all means quit the game." She should have been pleased by how cavalier she managed to sound.

"This isn't a game. Say you'll marry me."

She faced him, raising one brow. "Are you trying to force me into making a decision prematurely?"

"No. I would never try to force you to do anything. I am not like—"

She swung away before he could utter Charles's name. Each day, her memory of her dead husband grew more vague. His actions, once the source of night terrors and day tremors, now only engendered anger that he had taken so many years from her.

She had gone half the length of the street before Jack caught up to her. His hand on her arm was light but unyielding.

"Addie, forgive me." His gaze devoured her face, awakening a deep thrill in response. "Lord, you are so beautiful," he breathed ardently before abruptly stiffening.

Addie followed his gaze. A small boy stood a few feet away beside a vendor's booth, sucking on a stick of peppermint and watching them with wide-eyed interest.

Jack grabbed her arm and led her behind a gaily colored tent filled with flowers.

"Addie. You must believe me when I say I will never force my will on you."

"How can I be sure of that? Give me one good reason to believe you."

He chuckled. "You would never let me."

She stared at him. Of all the answers he might have given, the promises he might have made, she would never have expected that one. And, she realized breathlessly, it was true. That he not only had seen this but recognized it ahead of her, and admired it, nearly broke her resolve.

Yes, he loved her. She believed that. But was it enough? Would it last? And if it did not, what could she expect afterward? He himself had once said the military's milieu was death. It had been bad enough being abused by Charles, who, she understood now, she had never loved. It would destroy her to be abused by Jack, whom she did.

She could not make that commitment until she was sure. He would just have to endure.

As would she.

33

It seems Evan's new career choice has had unforeseen benefits for Lord and Lady Merritt." Jack glanced meaningfully at where the newly reconciled couple sat with their hands entwined in a public show of unity while they hosted a musicale reception for Ted.

Addie followed his gaze, her mouth curved with impish amusement. Since she had given him leave to prove himself to her, for nearly six weeks now she'd done everything in her power to test him. He never knew whether his overtures would be met with smiles or chill aloofness, a look of welcome she could not mask or a brittle suspicion.

She'd forgotten herself now. Her eyes gleamed as she studied Lord and Lady Merritt. They had taken a position at a small table in the center of the conservatory where the party was being held and were giving a fine impression of regal isolation. Occasionally, Lord Merritt cast a tender glance at his wife, who returned his regard with a brave smile.

"Yes," she returned in a whisper. "I must admit, I am surprised they are hosting such an entertainment . . . what with their"—she tried to quell another smile—"bereavement. But then again, nothing draws people together so well as shared grief."

Jack smiled. "True. And the greater the misery the greater the accord."

"Just think of the possibilities should Evan have become an atheist," Addie suggested. "Why, their solidarity would become so complete that in a few years London would be knee-deep in Merritt heirs and heiresses."

Jack laughed and several of their fellow diners, busy balancing china plates on their knees, paused to see what was so amusing.

"You've a wicked imagination, Addie."

"So I've been told." And then it happened, as it had so often in the past month. The moment of accord passed and studied sophistication replaced her naturally genial expression. Though those brief instants of connection came more and more often lately, still, she pulled back from him.

She had put him through his paces; teased him, ignored him, imperiously commanded him, all with a hard facade of worldly carelessness. And she'd watched, like an abbot with a novitiate, suspicious, untrusting, and always trying so damn hard to give him the impression that she didn't care whether he failed her "tests" or not.

"Jack, I'm thirsty," she said suddenly, ruining the image of a spoiled, willful beauty by accompanying the comment with an apologetic glance.

"May I get you a refreshment?"

"Please. A lemon—no. No. I believe I will have a whiskey."

He schooled his expression to bland acceptance. "I will see what I can do."

He almost laughed when he saw her start of surprise. If Addie thought that courting public censure by drinking a tumbler of whiskey was an adequate test of his self-control, he was certainly willing to comply.

He made his way through the fantastical ornamentation with which the Merritts had decorated the conservatory, turning it into a proper setting for the evening's musical rendering of *The Tempest*. He found a footman who obliged his request for whiskey and was returning to Addie's side when he saw Sherville.

The man posed an uncomfortable conundrum. Despite his continued efforts, Jack hadn't been able to uncover one bit of concrete proof that Sherville was his traitor. He could document many circumstances that were suggestive, and rumors abounded, but he had no evidence. Just as he had no evidence that Charles Hoodless had been blackmailing him.

He marked Sherville's path through the room. Even Wheatcroft's connections to London's close-knit community of servants had failed to produce any information. Sherville's butler was newly hired, as was most of his staff. If the thugs who'd attempted to rob Addie had, in fact, found some material Hoodless had used to blackmail Sherville and delivered it to him, no one in Sherville's household knew anything about it. But then, they wouldn't. Sherville was too careful to make that sort of mistake. If, that is, there was any blackmailing going on in the first place . . .

Damn! There were too many ifs and not enough facts.

Worse, ever since he'd warned Sherville with what would happen if he offended or threatened Addie, the man had seemingly turned over a new leaf, becoming one of Addie's admirers. Jack didn't believe it. And it about killed him to see the bastard dogging Addie's feet, flattering and flirting with her. And for Addie to allow it.

Of course, what else could she do? Sherville was a decorated major in the Royal Dragoons, a member of society, and a client of her brother's, which was why he'd been invited here tonight. Besides, for weeks his demeanor had been above reproach. So much so that even Addie had begun to doubt his culpability.

Sure enough, like a hound that scents a hare, Sherville found his way unerringly to Addie's side, taking Jack's own vacated seat and sidling it closer to hers.

With an effort, Jack fought the snarl from his lips, approaching Addie and Sherville on stiff legs.

"Ah! Our thespian!" Sherville said. "Someday, Cameron, you must tell us what you were *really* doing lurking about Mr. Phyfe's garret like a failed Harlequin."

Lady Merritt had given out some contrivance explaining his charade, which society had more or less accepted. Silently, Jack offered Addie her drink.

"Oh, Jack has quite a penchant for playacting. See? Only now he quite captures the flavor of a disapproving nanny."

Sherville snickered. "I do, indeed. An old, querulous retainer at that. But, Mrs. Hoodless, if ever there was a woman who should not suffer the objections of an overly familiar attendant, it is you. If I might be so bold, you are fair blooming this evening, ma'am."

Addie looked away, blushing, as Jack's hand tightened to a white-knuckled grip on his glass. He'd break the damn thing if he wasn't careful. Her throat, bare of ornamentation, was a pale, slender column begging for the attentions of a man's mouth. Sure enough, unseen by Addie, Sherville's tongue flicked out to quickly wet his lips.

The blood thrummed in Jack's temples.

Sherville continued. "I would never have believed the pretty but meek girl I met at Charles's house would grow into such an exciting and independent woman."

Addie's expression grew chill. "I do not wish to discuss that poor creature."

"Charles?" Sherville's brows rose. "Poor?"

"No," Addie replied brightly. "I was referring to myself. Or rather, to the girl Charles married. A poor-spirited thing, she never had the mettle to stand up for herself, never believed in herself enough to choose her destiny."

"So you, too, believe one can choose one's destiny?" Sherville asked approvingly.

"Oh, yes. I believe so, Major Sherville." Her voice had grown tense, rife with meaning. "If one keeps one's wits about them."

Even though her gaze was locked intently with Paul Sherville's, she was talking to him, Jack realized. About her past. Their future.

"A person may be obliged to pay for their past mistakes but if they are smart, they will only do so once. Only someone craven does so twice. I'm sure you understand, don't you?"

"Yes. I do, indeed." Sherville's answer was uncharacteristically brief, but Jack barely noted him, being fully engaged in the conversation going on behind the words. "Well, I suppose one can only hope the past stays where it belongs, in the past."

"It doesn't, though. Not when the past is clearly visible for anyone to see."

"On the other hand," Jack said, "sight is no guarantee of clarity."

"What the devil does that mean, Cameron?" Sherville snapped, his mood seemingly soured with the conversation.

"Only that there are mirages, Sherville. Surely you, as a veteran of the African deserts, know this. Mirages that appear so real you would swear you could touch them."

Addie's lips trembled ever so slightly. "Then it is even worse because there is no way one can tell if one is about to be deceived."

"Not at all," Jack said. "Even with a mirage, one feels the difference. I merely suggest that in striving for clear-sightedness, one should rely on all of one's senses, both demonstrable and indemonstrable. One must follow intuition as well as intellect."

Addie shook her head. "No, thank you. People who follow their hearts too often end up lost."

"Hear, hear," Sherville said, lifting his cup. Addie ignored him, her dark eyes riveted on Jack's, her chin angled with subtle challenge. They might as well have been alone in the room.

"Do they, Addie?"

"Yes." There was uncertainty in that avowal but more, there was a desire to be repudiated.

"Addie—"

"Seems you've lost that debate, Cameron," Sherville cut in, shattering the moment.

"What has Jack lost?" Ted asked, approaching with Zephrina Drouhin by his side, her pretty eyes bright with curiosity. "What's that all about?"

"Cameron here was just expounding on the human heart. I can't determine whether he means to be droll or not," Sherville said. "I mean, regardless of his bizarre masquerade over the past few months, Cameron is a soldier. Spent most of his life in barracks. What would he know of the more tender emotions?"

"Oh, I don't know, Major," Zephrina said and flitted to Jack's side, where she laid her hand on his sleeve. "I would be willing to take lessons from the captain, should he be offering instruction. I'm sure he has much to teach."

She was such a shameless flirt, arching her brows and posing so prettily. Jack might have even been mildly flattered had her bright eyes not strayed so often to discover Ted's reaction to her coquetry. Poor Zephrina, Ted was not even attending. He had commandeered Addie's abandoned cup and after sniffing the contents in disgust was draining it into a nearby centerpiece. Though she struggled to conceal it, Jack, attuned as he was to the nuances of a hopeful heart, felt his sympathies engaged with the unhappy girl.

Damn Ted's arrogance, anyway. It was high time he felt the sting of emotions he'd so declared himself above.

He covered Zephrina's hand with his own. "I fear you overestimate me," he said, smiling wolfishly down at her.

She chuckled, supremely comfortable with this familiar game, and rapped him playfully with her fan. "Of that, I am unsure. But maybe the question ought to be, do you underestimate me?"

"But give me the opportunity to demonstrate, Miss Drouhin."

"La!" Zephrina's eyes widened in mock scandalization. "Captain Cameron, I declare, I like you far better as a self-assured officer than that pretty piece of repartee you pretended to be. Tell me, why did you act the part of a . . . dilettante?" She darted a taunting glance at Ted.

"A bet, my dear. You are, I am sure, a gambler?"

"Of course! A bet inspired your charade. I should have guessed. And yes, Captain, I have been known to make a few wagers."

"And if you lose, do you pay?"

"Always. And graciously." Her voice lowered to a husky caress.

"Then I shall have to see to it that I lure you into a game I cannot lose."

"Too warm, Cameron." A warning lightly laced Ted's suave voice.

Zephrina shot Ted a haughty glance before tucking her arm through Jack's. "He's correct. It is too warm," she said, deliberately misunderstanding. "Won't you show me the gardens, Captain Cameron? I have heard the Merritts have an evening garden, fashioned only for night-blooming flowers."

"It will be my pleasure, Miss Drouhin."

34

"You'll excuse me, Mrs. Hoodless," Sherville said, bowing in Addie's direction.

She barely took note of his leaving, staring after the spangled netting on Zephrina's gown. "I swear, Ted, if you don't kill that girl, I will," she growled without thinking.

"Shall we flip for the pleasure?" he asked.

"Of all the hoydenish—"

"Here," he broke in, offering her his arm. "Let's find some privacy before you vent your spleen."

"I do not have a spleen," Addie exclaimed, too loudly, and then, noting the interested looks turned on her, took her brother's arm and allowed him to escort her to a pair of chairs set in a secluded corner of the conservatory.

"Green becomes you, Addie m'dear," Ted said as he seated her.

Addie pleated the rosy, silk-shot tissue of her skirt between her fingers, her eyes averted from Ted's. "I don't know what you mean."

"This is your doting big brother, Addie. I know you better than anyone in the world—with one possible exception." He spared a telling look at Jack's broad, ebony-clad back as it disappeared through the glass doors leading outside. "Miss Drouhin has succeeded in creating an even more outrageous persona than the one you have been so busily fashioning this past month."

"I don't know what you mean."

"You are being redundant—as well as transparent. Look at this dress. I blush to think of a model of mine wearing so scandalous a piece of frippery."

Addie raised a challenging brow.

"Well," Ted conceded with a rueful smile, "maybe not blush. But it is outré. How do you keep the thing up? Glue?"

"My womanly charms can withstand the challenge, thank you very much," Addie replied primly.

Ted snorted. "Just don't make overuse of the pepper mill at dinner tonight, my dear, or I may be obliged to use my cane on some poor, overly interested man if you sneeze. Although Jack will have already positioned himself for the defense."

"Why do you say that?"

"Really, dear. Look about. You must realize the sensation you are causing, have caused with your hoydenish behavior. Do you honestly think people still receive you because of your grandfather's title or my talent with a brush?"

"Drat it, Ted, stop being so oblique."

"Jack." Ted's light manner evaporated. "Any snickers, any coarseness, any impertinence aroused by your antics and he is there, making sure it never reaches your ears or goes any further."

"How?" Addie's brows inched together in a scowl. "With threats?"

Ted looked honestly surprised. "Good God, no. He does it by being a gentleman himself. His very bearing and address reminds any titterers that they, too, have pretensions to good breeding. Good manners are a very effective deterrent to coarseness."

"I didn't know."

"No," Ted said. "I don't expect you did. But now you do. And what I want to know is simply this: How long, Addie? How long are you going to demand perfection from this man?"

"You don't understand."

"Yes. I do. It's you who doesn't understand." Ted sounded both frustrated and disappointed in her, and he seldom had been either. Worse, she had the terrible sense that she deserved both. And more.

"Sooner or later you will finally manage to trip him up, provoke him to the point where he loses his temper, perhaps even upbraids you. And you'll richly deserve it. But then what? Having won—what will you have lost?"

Her eyes filled with sudden tears. With a sigh, Ted took hold of both her hands in his. "Addie, Jack isn't perfect. He has a temper and if you search long enough, you'll find it. That doesn't mean he's a bully, or a brute. Or like Charles."

He shook his head remorsefully. "I look at you and I am filled with regret that I didn't kill that bastard. I only wish I had had the opportunity."

"No!" she cried. "No, you mustn't. You would have ended up spending the rest of your life in prison. Charles already took too much from our family. I'll never forgive myself for what he did to you, Ted. To your poor leg. Never." Her hands trembled in his and he clenched them tightly.

"It's all right. What's done is done," he said. "And were I to have it all to do again, I would do it the same." A wry smile curved his perfect lips. "Except, perhaps, I'd have ridden up the drive rather than walked."

"Please, don't make light of it," she begged.

"Listen to me, Addie. The point I want you to understand, the thing you must realize, is that I was going to that house with the express intention of beating the living hell out of Charles."

She dashed the tears from her eyes, studying him in confusion.

"Even though you think me a gentle man, by my own words, you know I am capable of violence. Almost anyone, man or woman, will protect those he loves by whatever means necessary. That is certainly the case with Jack."

She rubbed at her temples. "I don't know. I don't. Oh, Ted, I don't know anything anymore."

"You trust me. Can't you trust Jack?"

"I know you!"

"You know Jack."

"I thought I knew Charles," she countered.

"You did. By the time he died, you knew Charles far too well. Ask yourself this question: Is Jack Cameron anything—anything at all—as you remember Charles?"

"No," she answered, surprising them both with the vehemence of that single word.

Ted smiled.

"Oh, Ted. I'm confused. I need to think. Please."

"Of course. I'll have the carriage brought round at once."

"I . . . I wish . . . I wish I were someone else. Someone who had never known Charles Hoodless. Someone who could love Jack without equivocation."

He squeezed her hand. "Jack doesn't."

Her breath caught at that. No, Jack didn't.

"I'll tell him you've left," he assured her as he stood up. "And then, I've a few things to tell Miss Zephrina Drouhin."

Paul Sherville grabbed his coat from the stiff-lipped butler and ordered a cab be called immediately.

Addie Hoodless had found it. Somewhere, somehow, the little bitch had found that damned photograph.

In the past weeks, when no demands had been forthcoming and Addie Hoodless had made no intimation of its existence, he had all but become convinced the photograph had disappeared and no longer posed a threat. He had relaxed, allowing himself to become complacent. But it had all been a ruse, a cat-and-mouse game the little bitch had been playing.

She declared herself tonight with those thinly veiled taunts about a person being "obliged to pay for their past mistakes," and the "past is clearly visible for anyone to see," all while staring him dead in the eye.

Well, the gypsy-looking bitch wouldn't have her "evidence" long. Tonight, while she teased and tempted all those bloodless fools at the Merritts', he would search her house until he found that photograph. He had hours in which to do so. The men he'd sent to find the photograph had said that Addie did not keep many servants and those she did were wont to flee the house as soon as their mistress's back was turned. It would be hours before her brother's reception ended.

A cab pulled up at the entrance and the butler dogged his heels down the flight of stairs. He flipped the old man a copper, then waited impatiently while the coachman placed the stepping stool. At least thanks to the would-be thieves, he knew where the photograph wasn't. It wasn't in the lower rooms. On that score Hal had been adamant. It must be in Phyfe's studio. Clever puss.

He allowed himself a self-congratulatory moment. She wouldn't expect him to take such expedient action. She didn't know the mettle of the man she was dealing with. But she would. Once he had Charles's blackmail material, she would see who had the upper hand.

His lips spread in a narrow smile of anticipation. God, he could see the attraction of bringing a piece of haughty tail like her to heel. She had been appealing as Charles's fearful little wife, her constant apprehension having its own piquant allure. But this bold and haughty woman she'd become! The thought of breaking her spirit, of bringing her to her knees, made him grow hard with lust.

And with that thought, he climbed into the cab, shouting the Hoodless address up to the coachman.

Wheatcroft clenched the coin Sherville had tossed him in his jacket pocket, his gaze tracking the retreating cab. Major Paul Sherville was the man Captain Cameron suspected was ultimately responsible for his nephew's death.

What possible business could he have at Mrs. Hoodless's home with neither she nor her brother there? For months, he and Captain Cameron had been searching for some proof that would see the bastard in front of a firing squad. But for all their work, there didn't seem to be any solid leads, let alone proof of Sherville's treacherous activity.

Now, Sherville was bound for Addie Hoodless's empty house. Captain Cameron said Sherville had had the Hoodless house robbed by thugs. But though the robbers had been surprised in the act, he didn't know whether they'd found what they'd come for. He'd suspected they had.

But now Paul Sherville was going back. Wheatcroft could not ignore the implication that Sherville had discovered the whereabouts of that elusive piece of evidence Captain Cameron believed existed.

He briefly considered finding Captain Cameron, but, by the time he might find him in the crush of over five hundred guests, Sherville may well be there and gone. It might cost Wheatcroft his place to leave in the midst of the party, but there were some things more important than one's position or pension; family was one of them.

Quickly, he dashed inside, returning a few minutes later in his overcoat, his pocket bulging, and, once outside, hailed another cab.

———◆———

"You can stop now. We're well out of Ted's earshot," Jack said, not unkindly.

Zephrina composed her face into a mask of pretty confusion. "I'm sure I don't understand, Captain Cameron."

It was one thing to play this game when there was an audience, but tedious when there were only the two of them. Poor Zephrina; she wasn't quite as fast as she wanted so desperately to appear. As soon as they'd entered the garden, she'd withdrawn from his side to a completely unexceptional distance. Only her conversation continued to be flirtatious.

"Ted. He isn't here to impress."

"You're mistaken if you think I care a fig for Ted Phyfe," she said. "I have no interest in inanimate reproductions." As if to give credence to her words, she snuggled against him. "I much prefer real men."

Jack sighed. He was so damn tired of games. "Stop it, Zephrina." There was nothing intimate in his use of her first name. He sounded like an aged uncle.

A scowl clouded her face. "You're being mean."

"No. I'm trying to help you. Stop trying so hard to force Ted to conform to your idea of masculinity. I assure you, Ted is quite completely a man."

"Ha," she replied with honest heat. "He is a wax figure. He might as well be posed in Madame Tussaud's gallery."

"Why? Because he doesn't snort and huff and paw the ground when you go through your feline repertoire?"

She started to turn away, but he caught her arm.

"You're a lovely, spoiled brat, Zephrina Drouhin."

"And you are as bloodless as the rest of English males," she shot back. "Playing lapdog to Addie Hoodless!"

"We aren't discussing Mrs. Hoodless."

"I am. What is it about her that has you so captivated? You and all these other men, chasing after her. I'll grant she has a pretty bosom but she hasn't a clue as to how to use her own charms. She gives away her every thought, her every emotion. Even these new gowns she's taken to wearing cannot camouflage her artlessness. It is quite clear she is taken with you. All society knows it. And you—" She broke off, blushing. "A man ought not to look at a woman like that publically. In America, you'd be horsewhipped!"

Jack laughed and Zephrina, startled by the real amusement in his voice, stared up at him. "You're right, Miss Drouhin. She is artless and she is obvious. And I am, too."

Feeling in charity with her, he decided to offer the girl a favor. "Isn't it past time you stopped looking for one of your penny-dreadful bandits to come and carry you off?"

"You mean, to act more like you and Mrs. Hoodless? I—I am not going to wear my heart on my sleeve."

"As far as I can tell, you never wear sleeves." He chuckled as she tried to decide whether she'd been insulted or not. "Your infatuation with Ted is every bit as clear as my love for Mrs. Hoodless. Might not your heart be worth listening to?"

She scoffed, but not altogether successfully. "He's nothing like the men to whom I am attracted, or like the man I will marry."

"But, my dear, he assuredly *is* the man you are attracted to. So, stop punishing him for it. And yourself. Give it a chance."

She regarded him fretfully, looking more like the young girl she really was rather than the racy miss she played hard at being. "Do you really think so?" she asked, sounding a bit lonely and a good deal confused.

He nodded. "Let's go back." Without waiting for her agreement he drew her back along the path and into the conservatory.

Once inside he scanned the room, already tensing in anticipation of seeing Sherville wetting his lips over Addie's cleavage. Sherville was nowhere in sight, but he found Addie on the far side of the room. Her eyes, even from this distance, looked unnaturally bright, as though they held tears.

Their gazes met across the room just as Zephrina, seeking to be overheard above the din of the tuning orchestra, curled a slim hand about his neck and pulled his ear down to her mouth and whispered, "Thank you."

He didn't reply. His gaze met, and for a second still locked on, Addie's. Then she spun, a shimmer of rose-tossed light, and vanished into the entry foyer.

He swore. From where Addie had stood it must have looked as though Zephrina had fondly kissed his cheek. He looked around, spying Gerald Norton's tall, lanky frame bent over a punch bowl. Catching his attention, Jack motioned him over.

"Gerald, Miss Drouhin requires a seat," he muttered and, leaving Gerald beaming happily at the tiny American heiress, went after Addie.

35

Addie let herself into the house. Partridge had apparently taken advantage of her expected late return to take the night off. And the housemaid, who was being paid court to by the neighbor's doorman, was gone, too.

It was just as well. She expected Jack to arrive at any moment. Jack had no more interest in Zephrina than he did in Lady Merritt. When their gazes had met as Zephrina had pulled his head down, his distress that Addie might misinterpret it had been written all over his face. She hadn't misinterpreted anything; not for an instant had she doubted Jack Cameron's love for her. It was honest, clear, and unwavering.

Jack would never try to manipulate her emotions, or cause her to be jealous. He would never play games with her heart or allow her a moment of distress on his behalf. And that is how she knew he would come here, to see her, as soon as possible.

And that is why when he did, she would cease her own senseless games and tell him then that she loved him, with all her heart, with all her soul, and would marry him any time he chose, wherever he chose. Because how could she continue along this stupid course, answering his honesty with falseness, his faithfulness with artifice?

Ted was right. It was self-delusion to think she could choose when and where to bestow her love. It already belonged to Jack.

She'd started up the stairs to her rooms when she noticed that the door at the far end of the hall was unaccountably open. Ted always kept his studio private; he was going to be annoyed that someone had been poking around in it. She went down the hall to shut the door and glanced inside. A dark figure lay crumpled at the top of the steep stairway that led to Ted's attic spaces.

With a cry, she dashed up and dropped to her knees. It wasn't the housemaid met with some accident; it was Wheatcroft. There was no time to wonder what he was doing here. Even in the dim light, she could see the blood flowing freely from the side of his head. She sprang to her feet to go for help—

An arm wrapped around her waist, dragging her back as a hand closed over her mouth. "Scream and I shall slit your throat. Do you understand?"

She nodded. The hand dropped from her mouth and she was spun around to face Paul Sherville.

He grabbed her wrists and yanked her forward. "Where is it?" he demanded, his fingers bruising Addie's skin.

"Where is what?" she asked in terror. He looked deranged, his little eyes burning, his mouth a downward slash in his red face.

"The photograph, you blackmailing little bitch. The one with me and the Mahdi."

"I don't know what you're talking about!"

He let loose with one hand and slapped her hard across the face. She gasped at the impact.

"That's for thinking you could ever take over your husband's filthy trade." He slapped her again and she just stood there, paralyzed by his anger, another man's rage superimposed over the present, crippling her. "That's for thinking I—I!—would ever let a mere woman blackmail me."

Once more he slapped her, almost casually. "That is for sending that butler after me! Fat lot of good it did him."

He yanked her forward until his mouth, pink and wet with spittle, was inches from her. "Tell me where the photograph is. Look at you! Do you think you can hold out against me? You? Now, tell me, you pathetic bitch!"

And finally, with those words, the paralysis fled, leaving only the fury. Fury that he'd broken into her house, that he'd hurt Wheatcroft and left him unconscious in the hall. Fury that he'd laid hands on her. Fury that he'd called up a ghost of that poor girl who'd married a monster and then felt guilty for it. Fury that he saw her as Charles had and that the indictment had nearly come true. And finally, fury that he'd done all of it for nothing. She didn't have any photograph.

"You're a fool, Sherville," she said. "You have pronounced your own guilt with your actions. And for nothing. I don't have any photograph."

"You do," he shouted, grabbing her hair with his free hand and jerking her head back until tears sprang to her eyes. "Did you think you could mock me with your little hints? Your dead husband was a filthy blackmailer and so are you. He bled me for years, growing fat on my money. Mine! But I'm not about to let a silly little whore like you suck a single penny from me. Do you hear me?"

"You've gone mad, Sherville." She gasped in agony when he twisted her head at an unnatural angle.

"Tell me where you've stowed Charles's things."

"They're gone," she managed. "I burnt every one of his personal possessions. Everything."

He stared at her, uncertainly.

"Do you suppose I wanted any reminder of him in my house, my life?" she ground out. "I exorcised him. I burnt every single shred of his correspondence, every bit of evidence of his existence."

He jerked her head again, making her stare into his face. She met his gaze. "You have done this for nothing, Sherville."

"It's gone? All of it?"

"Yes!"

He threw back his head and laughed. "Oh God! How rich! How splendid! You, my enemy's widow, destroyed the only thing that could have linked me to the Sudan and Charles's death."

She went suddenly very still. "You killed him."

He nodded, happy to tell her. "Let us say I arranged his death. You should thank me. I even made him look heroic. As I shall make you look."

Panic fired through her. "You won't get away with it."

"Oh, yes. I think I will. The butler, you see. He has made a little sideline of thieving from his master's guests while they are being entertained at the Merritt home. Too bad you surprised him while he was robbing your house. Even more unfortunate that while I arrived in time to kill the blackguard, I wasn't in time to save you," he said as his hands wrapped around her throat.

The world dissolved into swirling, red-shot darkness, the pain exploding in her lungs, and her anger surged that he might win, that this loathsome, vile man might cut short the life she had just begun to live again, and it fueled her efforts.

So she fought. She fought hard and long, but in the end she could not fight long or hard enough. She kicked and thrashed, dimly aware of the sound of rending cloth, the horrible gurgle in her own throat, the pressure of cruel fingers tightening around her neck.

"Let her go!"

Abruptly he released her. She slumped to the ground, gasping, and scrambled backward, falling against the easel as chaos erupted around her.

A table smashed into the wall. Tubes of paint and glass jars crashed and shattered, skittering across the floor. A chair splintered into pieces at her feet. Frantically, she crawled to the wall and only then looked back.

Jack and Sherville were locked in a mortal combat, Sherville's fingers digging deep into the flesh of Jack's neck, Jack's face dark with blood and rage. As she watched, he swung both hands up, palms flat, and smashed them over Sherville's ears.

Sherville howled in pain, his grip loosening. Jack jerked free and Sherville struck viciously at Jack's face. Jack dodged the blows, his fist pounding into Sherville's belly. Sherville collapsed around the deadly impact, the air bursting from his lungs as Jack delivered a huge strike to Sherville's jaw.

Sherville fell to his knees, groaning, but Jack grabbed a handful of Sherville's hair, jerking his head up, and rained blow upon blow on it with the other fist. Sherville threw up his arms, trying to protect himself from the beating, whimpering.

"Damn you, you filthy coward. Stand up. Fight! You can threaten Addie easily enough!" Jack shouted, panting. He grabbed Sherville's shirt and hauled him to his feet. Open-palmed, he struck Sherville's face. Blood exploded from Sherville's nose and mouth.

Like a dog shaking a rat, a growl issuing deep from within his chest, Jack yanked him upright again, landing a blow to Sherville's unprotected ribs. And now Sherville had stopped moving and hung limply from Jack's grip. He drew his fist back again.

Dear God, he was going to kill him. He could be placed on trial for murder.

Addie struggled to her feet and stumbled forward to clutch at

Jack's arm. "No!" she sobbed, her words barely intelligible over the harsh sound of Jack's breathing. She pushed herself between the two men, flinging her arms around Jack's neck. "No!"

Released from Jack's implacable hold, Sherville fell senseless to the ground. Addie buried her face against Jack's chest. His heart raced madly, his chest heaved.

"My God. Addie."

She lifted her head. He was staring at her, his big body trembling within her embrace. "My God," he whispered, "what have I done?"

With shaking fingers he touched her cheek and flinched back as though burnt, staring at his hand. She looked at what had so horrified him. His fingertips were bright with blood. He must have marked her with Sherville's blood where he'd touched her cheek. She drooped against him once more, laying her forehead on his heaving chest.

Behind her, Sherville groaned. She turned to watch him grope his way to his knees. Jack grasped her shoulders and set her behind him. "Addie, where is that bloody telephone you had installed?"

"In the downstairs hallway."

"Listen to me. You have to put a call through to Colonel Halvers. Tell him that Jack Cameron has taken Paul Sherville into custody—"

"For what?" Paul Sherville said, his voice rattling in his throat. He staggered to his feet, hissing with pain as he tried to find his balance. He gave them an ugly smile, exposing a chipped tooth coated with blood. "For what?" he repeated again and laughed, the horrid sound breaking off into a choking cough.

Jack eyed him coldly, carefully keeping Addie behind him. "For treason."

"Oh, 'treason.'" Sherville nodded mockingly. "And what proof do you have of my supposed treason?"

"Your actions tonight have more than proved your—"

"My what?" sneered Sherville. "My yen for a blowsy widow? Excuse me, m'dear"—he bowed mockingly toward Addie—"but your charms were so well displayed and so obviously offered. If I mistook the situation, I beg your pardon. I may have become a bit presumptuous."

Sherville laughed again. "Go ahead. Call Halvers. Even should he believe you, what do you think the military establishment will do? A scandal of this proportion while Gladstone is seeking reelection? And you with nothing more than an embittered widow's testimony? Ha! At worst, I may have to take half pay for a few months."

"You won't get away with this. The men you betrayed—"

"Men," Sherville sneered. "What men? The enlisted rank and file? You make me sick with your plebeian sympathies, Cameron. So, a few men died that their betters might prosper. They'd have died anyway."

"You're a monster," Addie gasped. "You're worse than Charles."

Sherville's eyes narrowed on her. "Am I, now? You should understand, even if he doesn't. You have the blood of kings in your veins. The masses," he spat, "what good are they if not for cannon fodder? The London slums breed them for that very purpose. They are nothing—"

The air cracked with a sudden sharp sound.

Sherville's shirt bloomed crimson. He gaped at his chest, a second of simple incredulity washing over his features. Then, he dropped dead on the floor.

Jack grabbed Addie, flinging his arms around her and wheeling about.

Standing in the door was Wheatcroft, his nephew's service pistol still smoking in his hand.

"No, sir," he said to Sherville's corpse. "*You* are nothing."

"I can't just let him go," Halvers said.

"Yes. You can. You will," Jack said. "You wanted this handled discreetly, no taint to be reflected on Whitehall or Mr. Gladstone. Now you have your opportunity."

"But he shot an unarmed man—"

"The execution of a traitor responsible for the deaths of God knows how many men."

"That all sounds very well, but we can't have men taking justice into their own hands."

"It was the only way justice was going to be served. There is no proof."

Halvers paced the studio, raking his hand through his thick hair. Sherville's body had been removed. Wheatcroft was being held downstairs in the kitchen. Ted, having been called from the Merritts', had arrived to take a white-faced Addie away.

The thought of her stricken face still turned Jack's stomach with anguish. Later. He would think about that later. Right now he had to save Wheatcroft's life.

"I don't know, Cameron. What story could we possibly give out?"

"Anything you like. No one present is going to contradict you." Jack shrugged. "Say that Sherville was shot by unknown assailants on his way to viewing his portrait. Ted Phyfe will undoubtedly substantiate that he intended to meet Sherville here for that purpose. And," he added grimly, "there has already been one reported break-in in this house."

"And Mrs. Hoodless?" Halvers asked. "What is her role to be? Are you willing to place her at the center of this?"

"No," Jack bit out. "Mrs. Hoodless was not even here. She was in the house proper, quite separate from the studio, having had her purse returned to her by the Merritts' dutiful butler, who saw that she had left it behind and hurried over with it lest she become anxious at its loss."

Halvers considered Jack a moment. "It might work."

"You have no choice."

"All right, Cameron. You win," Halvers said.

With the image of Addie's bloodstained face and torn dress burning in his mind's eye, Jack looked up. There was no victory in his gaze. Nothing but desolation.

"Do I?"

36

I'll see if the cap'n is receiving visitors, mum," the little, fresh-scrubbed maid said, her eyes wide with curiosity. She bobbed a quick curtsey and scurried off, leaving Addie to wander around the small, untidy sitting room of Jack's newly rented apartments.

Jack did not own much. There were several boxes of books, a few good pieces of furniture, and a rather exceptional Persian rug, but none of the stuff and nonsense most people carted after themselves.

She angled her head and read the titles on the spines of an open box of books. They represented several languages, including, she noted, Hindi. She picked up a slim volume. It was Edward FitzGerald's translation of the Persian poet Omar Khayyam. Curiously, Addie leafed through the book. Her eyes widened. In several poems, Jack had scribbled notes in the margins, refuting Mr. FitzGerald's word choice and substituting his own.

Some while later, Addie closed the book with an admiring sigh and set it down and glanced at the mantel clock. Twenty minutes had passed. Either the maid had gotten lost, or Jack—her heart thudded dully—did not want to see her and the maid was too cowardly to come tell Addie.

Well, he had to see her. She had not seen him since he had whisked her away from the scene of Sherville's death, bundling her into a carriage and sending her off with Ted. After that there had been a few days when Ted—and the doctor he'd engaged—had insisted she lay abed.

She had expected to hear from Jack but each day passed without a word. Finally, yesterday, she'd sent a note to the Merritts, asking to see him. When he didn't respond, she'd swallowed her pride and driven to the townhouse. Without any hint of the tragedy they'd shared reflected in his dignified mien, Wheatcroft had informed her that Lord and Lady Merritt were going abroad and were closing the townhouse. Jack had taken apartments elsewhere.

She hadn't hesitated to secure his new address from Wheatcroft. She loved Jack. And the thought of the proud and hopeless expression he'd faced her with five days ago haunted her. She had been unfair. Worse, unwise.

She strode purposefully up the staircase to the first-floor rooms. They were empty. Taking a deep breath, she mounted the stairway again, making her way to the second floor and the bedchambers.

Quietly she opened the first door she came to and entered a small room with a four-poster bed occupying one end, and a writing table, chair, and settee on the other. Jack stood on the far side, backlit by a tall window, his fist braced above him, staring out at the wintry street below.

"Jack," she said, shutting the door behind her.

He swung around and when he saw her he could not contain the joy that leapt to his face, the eagerness in his expression. And then, as spontaneously as it had appeared, the pleasure fled from his features, leaving only resignation in its stead.

"Addie." He inclined his head and smiled politely. "I was just about to come down."

"Were you?" She went to him, on gaining his side tilting her head and looking up at him.

His gaze traveled hungrily over her face. "You are . . . you are recovering?"

"Yes," she hurried to assure him. "I am fine."

"There have been no ill effects? Gerry assured me you were healing well, but there are other forms wounds take."

"Gerry?"

One corner of his mouth lifted with dark wryness. "I expected any queries I made of Ted would be answered with an imprecation that I go to the devil."

"Whyever for?" she asked, honestly mystified.

"My investigations put you in danger. I confronted Sherville earlier, setting him on edge."

"No. Charles put me in danger. Is that why you haven't called on me?" When he didn't answer, she tried another tack. "And you? He struck you violently. Are you all right?"

"Of course. You forget. I am an old hand at bloodletting."

The sound of his voice was bitter.

"I haven't forgotten," she said softly.

For a moment he stared at her and then, shaking himself from his absorption, cleared his throat. "We should go down." He took her elbow to guide her to the door and the less intimate regions below stairs. She shook off his hand, unwilling to leave yet. Misreading her evasive movement as a reluctance to be touched, he dropped her arm, stricken.

She cast about, looking for some way to begin. "Wheatcroft . . . everything will go well for him, won't it?"

"Ah." He nodded. "Wheatcroft. Yes. Everything has been handled satisfactorily."

"Good," she murmured. "And what shall you do now? Go back to your regiment?"

"No," he replied. "The wound I told you about renders me unfit for active duty. Can't aim a gun anymore. Apparently there was some nerve damage to my hand. My grip will never be strong and there are tremors when I get tired."

"Yes. I noticed."

"You did?" he asked, surprised.

"Of course." She smiled ruefully. "Vain creature that I am, I had imagined that I caused your hand to tremble."

"Oh, God, Addie—" Hunger, so intense that it took her breath away, suffused his features, eclipsing all other emotions. Hunger and restraint. He'd always held himself in check for her. Always molded his will to her well-being.

She knew her course now. She reached out, no shyness slowing her movements, and spread her hands flat against his chest. His heart pounded beneath her palms. His heat spread through her fingertips, sent delicious tremors along her arms.

"What will you do?" she repeated quietly.

He covered her hands with his own, pressing them tightly to his chest, unconscious of his actions. "I don't know. Halvers wants me to work at Whitehall. It's all I know, Addie. The military. It's what I am."

"That's not what I meant. What will you do now?"

He closed his eyes and when he spoke, she had to lean closer to hear his words. "What do you want me to do?"

"Love me."

His mouth turned in a beautiful smile. "I do. I could not possibly love you more than I already do, Addie." He stood firm, his eyes still shut, his hands still pressing hers to his chest.

She exhaled in relief.

His eyes opened and he shook his head, his mouth tender and remorseful. He'd misread her sigh. "How can I ask you to believe me? I promised you would not see any brutality from me, never again witness a violent act from me, and then not only do I cause you to be attacked but I smear your cheek with another man's blood."

"You were protecting me."

"I was out of control. If you had not intervened, I would have killed him. I've never killed a man with my bare hands, Addie, but I was going to kill Sherville."

His anguished gaze had grown remote. She could feel the distance he was building between them with each word.

"Jack," she said urgently. "You *did* stop. You didn't kill Sherville."

He continued studying her face, as though committing each of her features to memory.

"Listen to me," she insisted, frightened. "When I thought you might kill Sherville, I was terrified." His small hiss of pain made her flinch. She hurried to explain. "But not of you. *For* you! I placed myself between you and Sherville with no fear for myself, no doubts. My only thought was that you mustn't stand trial for Sherville's death."

She moved her hand higher on his chest, willing him to believe her.

"I couldn't let that happen because I could not let you be taken from me. In that instance, I saw my life as it would be without you, without love, retreating once more into that barren, chill place I'd lived in for so long. I love you, Jack."

He bowed his head. "Thank you."

Her hand closed in a fist, braced in frustration against his broad chest. "Don't thank me. *Marry me.*"

He stared at her, stunned. "You don't mean that."

"I do." She bracketed his lean cheeks with her hands, trying to make him understand. "I married Charles because he was a soldier and soldiers are responsible and dutiful, everything my famous and infamous family is not." He started to say something but she had to finish. "Please, let me go on.

"And when I discovered that Charles was none of these things, and worse, the antithesis of those values I assumed all soldiers held sacred, I felt betrayed. Betrayed not only by Charles, but by myself. How could I have misread his character so absolutely? Even after his death, I was afraid, afraid my heart was blind, indiscriminate, and untrustworthy."

"Addie, please. I know I failed—"

"You did not. You never failed me," she said fiercely. "You made me finally realize that my heart was never unsound; Charles was."

He frowned. Gently, he cupped her shoulders. "What happened with Charles was not your fault."

"I know that now. But it is my fault that I judged all soldiers by Charles's example. That was unfair of me."

"It was understandable."

She touched his cheek. "It was unfair," she insisted. "And I might have gone on, suspicious and mistrustful, afraid to live . . . to love . . . had not another soldier appeared in my life. One who perfectly embodied all those attributes I sought in Charles: honor, bravery, loyalty, and compassion. My God, Jack. How I love you."

She pulled his head down to hers. Tenderly, she pressed her mouth to his. His hands closed tighter about her shoulders but aside from that single, involuntary movement, he was still. She wrapped her arms around his neck, relishing the heat of his hard male body seeping through her thin dimity bodice. She followed the seam of his firm lips with her tongue. Hungrily, his mouth opened beneath hers. And still, he made no move to tighten his light embrace. Disappointed, she drew back, searching his face for a reason. He stared back, hot-eyed and hungry, his breathing ragged, his heart pounding.

"Yes. Please," he said. "Marry me. I swear you will never know one minute of fear at my hands."

She understood then and understanding made her smile. "Do you think I don't know?" she asked. "Do you think I didn't recognize how you have always subjugated your desires to what you thought were mine? I did. I do. It's been driving me mad."

His breathing stopped and his dark brows dipped in consternation.

"Your self-control has caused me to question my desirability on more than one occasion," she told him.

"Jesus," he groaned.

"Don't you want me, Jack?"

"Yes." He laughed, a choked sound. "Yes."

"Won't you make love to me?"

In answer he bent and caught her behind the knees and swung her up high on his chest. She gasped as he strode to the bed but he did not stop. Nor did he pause as he lay her there or followed her down or kissed her mouth, her throat, her shoulders.

His passion was breathtaking, irrefutable, and concentrated. He peeled his coat off, stripped the shirt from his torso. His chest glistened with a feverish sheen, the muscles of his body rippling with animal elegance as he bent over her, braced himself above her on trembling arms, and hungrily nipped the point of her jaw. She arched into his caress, offering her neck, bowing her body.

Like a starving man, he feasted on her throat. Open mouthed he breathed in her fragrance, licked the sweet-salty taste of her aroused skin, smoothed his hands over her shoulders, found the heartbeat in her wrists and kissed those, too.

She twisted beneath him, her fingers playing over his back until finding ruined flesh. Her eyes, half lidded with passion, widened. He groaned at this intrusive reminder of what he was but she only played her fingers again across the ugly scar, her gaze full of love and ferocity.

"My soldier. My love," she whispered, and those words, more than anything she had said or allowed, freed him of his last restraint.

He delved his tongue deep into the warm, slick interior of her mouth. Between them, her hands worked frantically to free herself of her suddenly hated clothing. And then he felt her soft breasts' warm bounty cushion against his chest. He groaned.

He rolled onto his back, dragging her atop of him. Panting, she straddled him. Her bodice was open and her hair spilled in glorious waves about her bare breasts where pink and puckered nipples rose and fell with each agitated breath. Her skirts were rucked up about her waist, and her slender calves lay against his thighs. Her lips, swollen and voluptuous, parted. Between her thick black lashes her eyes were sensual pools of amber heat, lambent and erotic.

"I love you, Jack," she said. And then added in a shaken voice, "I want you, Jack."

He had never thought she could look like this, filled with love and a longing that matched his own. He could stand no more. He stroked her gently, down her slender flanks, over the column of her thighs and up. She panted, watching him, uncertain what to do.

He found the slick center between her legs. With one hand on her hip, holding her against the possession of his other, he played with her. Her eyelids fluttered shut and her head fell back as she moaned, her hips seeking the instinctive rhythm of lovemaking.

And then, suddenly, her eyes flew open. "No," she said in a low, hoarse voice. "No."

She lifted herself to her knees, away from his touch, and scooted back to sit on his thighs. Her hair streamed over her face and her fingers, made awkward by passion, pulled clumsily at his trousers' front closure. There was a second of intense pleasure and frustration and then his trousers opened.

He sprang, thick and turgid, free of the cloth. Her hand closed about him, swift and clumsy. He gasped. She looked up, meeting his gaze. Her hand moved once and he groaned with pleasure. Triumph washed over her features. She pumped her fist once more about him. His hips jerked away from the bed and he groaned once more.

Her honey-gold gaze transfixed him. She looked feral and erotic, bold and demanding, so sensual the image of her alone was enough to make him spill his seed. She moved her hand again and he grabbed her wrist.

"I am just a man, Addie," he gasped. "Don't push this beyond what I can control."

She could not free herself from his gentle constraint, so she bent her head and touched him with her lips. He flung his head back, grinding his teeth together and fighting for dominion over his body. He needed to wait, to master his responses, to temper his ardor so that he could give pleasure to his beloved. He wouldn't last another minute at this rate.

She looked up. "Lose control, Jack," she said softly, urgently. "Always, you have given me sovereignty. Let me prove myself to you now. I want your passion, Jack, as well as your love. I am not afraid of anything about you, anything you are, any aspect of your love or ardor." She laughed softly. "Indeed, if I cannot have all your passion, I will be bereft. Let me show you."

He squeezed his eyes shut, quivering with want and doubt.

"Lose control, Jack."

He groaned and his hands slipped down to her hips, pulling her roughly against him. She splayed her palms flat on his rippling belly and took him into her, the hard throbbing length of him. He shuddered and surged upward, labored and straining, his chest gleaming with moisture, heaving with each ragged inhalation.

He felt it, the swirling, irresistible passion of her intimate embrace. A sweet near-violence of desire flowing from her, spurring him beyond mere physical want. She met his passion, she wanted him. *Him.* He trembled, suspended between desire and fulfillment, and just as he found his ultimate release, he pulled her mouth to his, drinking in her cry of completion and giving back his own.

EPILOGUE

I can't believe she is marrying you." Ted brushed a fleck of lint from his otherwise immaculate morning coat. "Marrying some paper-pushing bureaucrat in the War Office when she could devote her life to Art. How did Whitehall talk you into accepting that post anyway?"

"They convinced me my talents for investigation could avert miscarriages of justice." He was still surprised he'd accepted, but Halvers and Mitchell had been persuasive.

"If she has the sense that God gave her, she'll not show. We've never had a Scotsman in the family. It's beyond lowering."

"She'll come."

"Yes." Ted sighed. "I expect she will. Poor besotted creature."

Jack chuckled and turned from his post by the front window of the drawing room. The wedding guests, Lord and Lady Merritt, Gerald Norton, and a few other intimate friends from both the artistic and military communities were milling about, eyeing each other warily as they waited for the ceremony to begin. All they wanted was a bride to start the proceedings.

"Speaking of besotted creatures, where is Miss Drouhin?" Jack asked, his gaze straying once more to the street below.

"Doubtless playing a pipe while some poor officer dances to her tune," Ted replied casually. He shrugged at Jack's sharp glance. "It was too much of a challenge even to my talents to try and capture what was essentially a child."

Jack's brows rose.

"Yes. I told her we would resume sitting when—and if—she finally reached adulthood."

"Ouch."

Ted smiled, his usual suave curve of lips, but Jack saw the shadow in his eyes. "We'll see," he murmured. He looked out over the other guests, his gaze picking out the portly bishop.

"I must say, you showed remarkable restraint in not inviting Evan to officiate."

Jack laughed. "We're not Catholic. Besides, he hasn't taken his final vows, or we might have."

Ted studied his soon-to-be brother-in-law approvingly. "By God, I believe you would have. And I know my sister well enough to bet she'd have hand-penned the invitation. If ever there was an imp of Satan, it is Addie." He frowned in mock consternation. "Tell me, Cameron, have you given this step the consideration it deserves?"

But Jack was not attending. He was leaning forward on the windowsill, his eyes alight with pleasure and love.

The street below was choked with morning traffic, making it impossible for the Merritts' carriage to pull up directly in front of the townhouse. It had stopped a half block up the street. Suddenly, the door was flung wide.

Addie scrambled from the interior, a vision in ivory satin and lace, her long, flowing veil tossed cavalierly over one shoulder, her face flushed and beautiful.

She dragged the enormous train of her gown clear of the carriage and looked up toward the window at which he was standing. Their gazes met. A smile of perfect beatitude spread across her lovely face. Her honey-amber eyes glowed with joy. Picking her skirts up high in both hands, she dashed forward, pushing through the throng of street vendors and nannies and businessmen crowding the walkway, heedless of the stares she provoked. She made the front steps and disappeared from sight.

Below, he heard a door bang open, the sound of slippered feet dashing across tiles and up the stairs. He turned just as she entered. His eyes found hers and locked with promise and elation. The party started to close about her but she wriggled through the well-wishers, her gaze riveted on him alone, and ran down the aisle. Ran to his side. *His bride.*

"Am I late?" she asked breathlessly.

"No. No," he said in joyful wonderment. "You're just in time."

AUTHOR'S NOTE

There is no British regiment called the Black Dragoons. It is a fiction created for this work simply because I couldn't bring myself to populate any real regiment with the likes of Charles Hoodless and Paul Sherville. Likewise, though the relief of Khartoum did in fact arrive but a day late to save General Gordon and indeed, Gladstone and Gordon had very different views on Great Britain's role in Egypt, the suggestion that the relief effort was subverted is entirely a fabrication.

ABOUT THE AUTHOR

Photo © 2010 Heidi Ehalt

New York Times and *USA Today* bestselling author Connie Brockway has received starred reviews from both *Publishers Weekly* and the *Library Journal,* which named *My Seduction* as one of 2004's top ten romances.

An eight-time finalist for the Romance Writers of America's prestigious RITA award, Connie has twice been its recipient, for *My Dearest Enemy* and *The Bridal Season.* In 2006 Connie wrote her first women's contemporary, *Hot Dish,* which won critical raves. Connie's historical romance *The Other Guy's Bride* was the launch book for Montlake Romance.

Today Brockway lives in Minnesota with her husband, who is a family physician, and two spoiled mutts.